Ank Chakra

(Indian Culture And Basic Numbers)

Dr. Chandrapal Sharma
Formerly Reader and Head
Department of Hindi
Rana (PG) College, Pilkhuwa (Hapur)

DIAMOND BOOKS
www.diamondbook.in

Publisher : **Diamond Pocket Books (P) Ltd.**
X-30, Okhla Industrial Area, Phase-II
New Delhi-110020
Phone : 011-40712200
E-mail : sales@dpb.in
Website : www.diamondbook.in

Ank Chakra : Indian Culture And Basic Numbers
Author – Dr. Chandrapal Sharma
Translated by: Sadhana Arun Kumar Bhatt

Acknowledgement

Every creative author has the desire that the words of his pen should reach out to maximum patrons. With the title of 'Do Shabd' (two words), I have given a clue of this text to large group of readers. The text has received so much abundant love from its readers that the first edition published in 2017 is reaching out to the readers with its second edition in 2018. Actually, the hard work of Diamond Books is worthy of compliments and congratulations.

The title through which I wish to put forth my thoughts, its main character is dear sister, Sadhana Arun Bhatt. I have been writing since last fifty years. Almost twelve (12) books and around two hundred fifty (250) articles have been published, but my extended reach was limited and restricted to only readers in Hindi. It is the tireless effort of Sadhanaji's success that very soon, I shall be able to reach out to the readers of English. This is a classical scriptural book, so its vocabulary is contained with traditional philosophy. To translate it was an arduous task, but Sadhanaji has fulfilled this task with great patience, heed and studiously. She has done this work with incredible labor, and expressing mere thanks is very subtle statement. With the depth of my heart, I praise Sadhanaji's 'Sadhana', convey her compliments and congratulations.

In this work of pure dedication, my daughter, Dr. Neerja Arun's penchant and co-operation also have been very creditable and commendable.

– Dr. Chandrapal Sharma

Author's Note

Almost 25 years before, in the journal of college, one of my articles was published. As a result of hearing words of appreciation from colleagues and faculty members, one article multiplied to 11 articles which were published in 'Yugvarta' Delhi in 1994 and were forwarded to their customers, newspapers - Yugvarta used to give Rs. 20/- as honorarium, but if any article got its space in more than 20 newspapers then Rs. 10/- were given in the form of encouragement. The writer of these lines has got the encouragement amount of Rs. 10/- many times. The intention was that these articles got the readership of large number of readers. They were published all over India in many journals. Some other journals published these articles with the courtesy and affability of 'Yugvarta', 'Hindu Chetna' published 11 articles in 11 months by demanding from the writer. I was satisfied because

'आपरितोषाद् विदुषां न साधुमन्ये प्रयोग विज्ञानम्'।

Because of urge and encouragement of some friends, some material was collected and in the year 1998 one book of almost 100 pages was published. After retiring in 2000, the only thing remaining is self-study. The book got sold quickly. So in the year 2006, another book of 176 pages was published, which also got lot of love and response from readers. So, again in the year 2012 one more book was published comprising of 253 pages, which was also immediately sold self-study continued, new material were found. So the present book is before you.

It is humble request to the intellectual readers that my age is increasing and a person has limitations of his potential. This subject demands expansion, So the learned readers and scholars should take the pledge to carry this burden and keeping the limitations of the book in mind, work ahead, so that the untouched and unexplored context of Indian culture are brought forth. I have received many blessing of many scholars for this book. Well-known authority of Hindi and scholar, Prof. Naamvar Singh is respected and revered for me. His words are like blessings to me. Famous Sanskrit scholar, Padmashri Dr. Ramakant Shukla and well-known authority on Ved vidya Dr. Ganeshdatt Sharma, Vice-president, Sanskrit Academy. Government of Delhi are like my younger brothers. With their words and suggestions, there has been increase of dignity of this text.

I will always be obliged to these two scholars. It was not possible to publish this book without the efforts of dear Dr. Jeetram Bhatt and Dr. Kumar Vishwas (my youngest son). Both are entitled for my blessings.

– Dr. Chandrapal Sharma
Sahyog, Sarvodaya Nagar,
Pilkhuwa-245304
Mob.-09411054501, 08171969096

Preface

The knowledge of numbers is as ancient as the creation. One Brahma then Nature and Man, These two then Satva, Raja, Tam these three qualities and this way the creation is said to be of 25 elements. Shaddarshan, numbers of measurements and astrology, grammar, ayurved, literature etc, the presence of numbers is clearly seen in these disciplines. In Vedas through the medium of numbers many examples are found for publishing special scopes. In the 24th and 25th mantras of 18th chapter of Shukla Yajurved with help of easy and difficult numbers, havan is performed by paired and unpaired stom. This is the mantra :

'एका च मे तिस्रश्च मे तिस्रश्च मे पञ्च च मे पञ्च च मे सप्त च मे सप्त च मे नव च मे नव च मे एकादश च मे एकादश च मे त्रयोदश च मे त्रयोदश च मे पञ्चदश च मे पञ्चदश च मे सप्तदश च मे सप्तदश च मे नवदश च मे नवदश च मे एकविंशतिश्च मे एकविंशतिश्च मे त्रयोविंशतिश्च मे त्रयोविंशतिश्च मे पञ्चविंशतिश्च मे पञ्चविंशतिश्च मे सप्तविंशतिश्च मे सप्तविंशतिश्च मे नवविंशतिश्च मे नवविंशतिश्च मे एकत्रिंशच्च मे एकत्रिंशच्च मे त्रयस्त्रिंशच्च मे यज्ञेन कल्पन्ताम्॥

-(शुक्ल यजुर्वेद 18/24)

Here, Shatpath Brahmin, have the ordination or statute of the havan of mantras through unpaired stomas. These numbers are 9/3/3/2 according to the shruti of adhayaujstoman juhoti first shruti is taken, second left out-third is taken and similarly leaving paired shrutis, the mantras of unpaired numbers is used. For the exponence of Adratishayit everywhere it is repeated. With the hom or offering of unpaired stom all the passions are acquired as is said in Shatpath Brahmin

'एतद्वै देवाः कामानाप्त्वायुग्भिः स्तोमैः स्वर्गं लोकमायंस्तथैवैतद् यजमानः सर्वान् कामानाप्तवायुग्भिः स्तोमैः स्वर्गं लोकमेति।'

-(शतपथ 9/3/3/2)

'तद्वै त्रयस्त्रिंशदिति। अन्तो वै त्रयस्त्रिंशोऽयुजां स्तोमानामन्तत एव तद्देवाः स्वर्गं लोकमायंस्तथैवैतद्यजमानोऽन्तत एव स्वर्गं लोकमेति।'

-(शतपथ 9/3/3/3)।

There is special configuration of special mantras by the assigned rites and stom paired rule of Tandayadi (Shaptapth 9/3/3/2). They are of two types- ayuj (dainty) and yugm (paired). In ayuj stom 33 is the last, after that it is not there. Life the numbers of gods are 33. In the same way, by the hom or offering of 33 stom a host can fulfill all his wishes and attain heaven. So it is clear that in the spoken mantra it is not only the objective of count of only difficult numbers but it is the statute law of havan by the stom inherent with difficult numbers. In the next mantra cue has been given for havan with paired stom.

चतस्रश्च मेऽष्टौ च मेऽष्टौ च मे द्वादश च मे द्वादश च मे षोडश च मे षोडश च मे विंशतिश्च मे विंशतिश्च मे चतुर्विंशतिश्च मे चतुर्विंशतिश्च मऽष्टाविंशतिश्च मेऽष्टाविंशतिश्च मे द्वात्रिंशच्च मे द्वात्रिंशच्च मे षट्त्रिंशच्च मे षट्त्रिंशच्च मे चत्वारिंशच्च मे चत्वारिंशच्च मे चतुश्चत्वारिंशच्च में चतुश्चत्वारिंशच्च मे यज्ञेन कल्पन्ताम्।।

-(शुक्ल यजुर्वेद 18/25)

In Upanishads, in the mantras of Dwasuparna Sayuja, Sakhya numeric words have been used with a purpose, so that is easy to facilitate and reason and explain by the scholars. In Puran, the number of every feast and chapter is given which has a special genre. At some places, with the medium of numbers, intensive, deep and serious philosophical thoughts are expressed. For example, the 27the shloka of second chapter of 10th skand from Srimad Bhagvat can be taken

एकायनोऽसौ द्विफलस्त्रिमूलश्चतूरसः पञ्चविधः षडात्मा।
सप्तत्वगष्टविटपो नवाक्षो दशच्छदी द्विखगो ह्यादिवृक्षः।।

-(श्रीमद्भागवत 10/2/27)

Here, while praising god, Vasudev says this world is an eternal tree, the foundation of its genesis is only you. The refuge of this tree is nature. It has two fruits happiness and sorrow. It has three mool (roots), Satva, raj and tam. There are four rasas (flavors), Dharma (Religion), Arth (Economy), Kam (Passion) and Moksh (Salvation). To know them there are five things- ears, skin, eyes, taste and nose. These have six nature- to arise, to stay, to grow, to change, to deteriorate and to be destroyed – **'अस्ति जायते वध 'ते परिणमते अपक्षीयते नश्यति'** These have seven skin or bark- rasa, blood, flesh, fat, bones, bone-marrow and shukra, these are the seven metals. This has eight branches-Panch Mahabhoot (earth, water, heat, wing and sky), mind, intelligence and ego. In this, nine gates are the guards-mouth, eyes, ears, nose etc. It has ten leaves-Pran, Apan, Vyan, Udan, Saman, Nag, Kurm, Krikal, Devdatt and Dhananjay. On this worldly tree two birds reside-living and god.

In Pali Tripitak, in Suttapitak of the 11 nipat of Anguttarnikay, very interesting and important information has been given. Most of the information related to Buddhist religion has been given from ekak to ekadasak nipats. (Refer-History of Pali literature-Dr. Bharat Sing Upadhyay, third edition pages 205-220). These are divided in four bid varga or nipat in Itivuttak. First in ekak nipat preaching related to number one are enunciated. In duk, tik and chatukk, nipats Buddha's teachings have been respectively given in the form of prose and poetry two, three and four texts. **(पा. सा. दृ. पृष्ठ 256)**

All India Radio, Delhi had broadcast a series of talks in Hindi. The talkers had enlightened the special features of numbers. This written was invited to present the special features of number eight for which be compiled materials form 'Hindi Shabd Sagar' and 'Hindi Vishwa Kosh' and by decorated it for presentation. My younger brother, Dr. Vishnukant Shukla, published a lyrical essay in Sanskrit language entitled 'Panech me', in which the writer presented interesting and enlightening material. Some years before he also informed me that at present he is engrossed in his efforts to publish a pamphlet based on number nine.

Eminent writer of Hindi and faculty professor Dr. Chandrapal Sharma, through his own prospect has concentrated only on basic number (0-10) has assimilated, through very interesting and simple language, extracted the epitome of Indian culture in his book entitled 'Bharatiya Sanskriti aur Mool ank'. This book of Dr. Sharma was published in 1998. Prior to this most of the articles were already published in 'Yugvarta' and 'Hindu Chetna' in 1994 and have received appreciation from readers. In 2006 and 2012 the changed and revised edition of the book was published and now in 2016, its rectified changed and edited version is for publication. The attraction of this book is by itself successful.

There is a saying in Sanskrit **'एकसम्बन्धिज्ञानमपरसम्बन्धिज्ञानस्य स्मारकं भवति'** That means with the knowledge of one thing, one remembers many things related with it. Dr. Sharma has started his book with the first number 'Ek', with this reasoning. In every society and culture, some words and numbers are such, that by the mere utterance of that word or number many incidents, personalities, procedures or approaches or principles are recollected. Such numbers or words, cherish the detailed long history of any religious, social, cultural and political life of any caste or nation. The numbers from one (1) to ten (10) are the basis of all following numbers thereafter. So according to this viewpoint, these ten are the basic numbers. The main purpose of this text is to tell where Indian psyche is attracted when these basic numbers are mentioned or uttered. These numbers have amazing ability to create awareness about the various regional knowledge of India. (In Bharatiya Sanskriti aru Mool Ank- page 17), the writer has clarified his purpose in his text. After this, he has presented the filtrate of Indian culture in the most attractive visage with interesting and knowledgeable material. In number 1 (one) the writer has discussed about one Almighty, which can be accepted as the propitiatory or inaugural ceremony of the writer. It is also said in the Padmavat Jayasi text.– **'सुमरो आदि एक करतारू'** The writer had fully tried to prove his statements by quoting examples from the glory of Gita, Ramcharitmanas, Kathopnishad Ved, Kabir, Nirukt, Principles of Vidur etc. Readers have also been made available with the memorable Subhashit (inspirational quotes) and Sukti (beautiful verse), by whose rote and deep thought the reader will have increase in understanding common sense and knowledge. By the elaborate presentation Vedic literature to the inspirational quotes (Subhasit) of the contemporary. Dr. Sharma has presented beauty without limits in his writings of intellectual praise. In the context of his number 2 (Two), he mentions two types of sadhana of speech, two types of living beings two types of cleanliness, two types of persons who retire to Brahmalok, two types of thoughts in the mind and two types uncleanliness. He has presented all this material of Shruti-Smirit Puran and examples of other texts. Similarly in three (3), Three gods, three tama, three sins, three achaman (sip of water before yagna or puja) three homes of humans, three Vedas, three padas of Gayatri mantra, three major vaastu, he has elaborately discussed the colloquial and textual knowledge. In the same way, in the context of other numbers also he has presented valuable knowledge.

At the end of every chapter, the writer, in the form of summary and conclusion, has presented interesting deep and thoughtful material in the most wonderful way:–

"अतः एकाकी में उस एक परमात्मा से प्रार्थना करता हुआ कामना करता हूँ कि एकता के लिए भारतीयों को सद्बुद्धि प्रदान करे और हमें यह अनुभव करने का सामर्थ्य प्रदान करे कि 'हम सब एक हैं'।"

In Bharatiya Sanskriti aur Mool Ank, at the end on 2 (Two), the writer cautions giving a message about riding two boats at a time. At the end of 3 (Three), he meditates on Triyambak, Lord Shiva. At the end of 4 (Four), he desires the benevolence of four armed Saraswati. At the end of 5 (Five), he prays to God Panchanan for the shade of five trees. At the end of 6 (Six), he wishes that every Indian should remain immersed in six holy karmas. At the end of sapta (7), he wishes that our country should be the best, a classic in seven worlds. At the end of eight (8), asks to bestow intelligence form the eight-eared Brahma, to participate in eight daily routine services of Shri Nath ji and to gain enough knowledge to study the eight chapters of Panini. At the end of nine (9), after the worship of nine goddesses ardently. Wishes for the welfare of the world, accepting the nine types of bhakti or devotion. At the end of ten (10), the writer remembers the ten-headed victorious Ram and wishes that for future ten generations, there should be hundred fold welfare.

The writer has also written a chapter on zero. India has introduced zero to the other countries. Zero denotes both emptiness and completeness or fullness. The writer has enunciated the importance of zero by the invocation of the mantra "पूर्णमदः पूर्णमिदं,- In the end the writer wishes to extricate the living from the zero titles and to merge them with the zero honor. That is his ambition and that the worshippers of Indian culture will definitely, gain the summit of knowledge, if not the treasure of knowledge through this medium.

I understand that Dr. Sharma has used the word the tip or summit of knowledge due to his humility. Actually, for the perception of complexion of knowledge of Indian culture, this text is available with all desirable thing and a wish granting tree. In this text the long standing deep study and thought of Dr. Sharma are inherent, as well as his teaching attributes and his personality are also expressed, which presents the most difficult subjects in simple and interesting manner and have the ability to make them comprehensible to common people. In the text, the Indian literature's best quotes have also been presented in the form of relevant examples. The personality of the reader will gain importance through its memory and retention, contemplation and expedient usage Sharma ji deserves all our greeting and accolades for his ardent wish for the well-being and welfare of India and the world, at the end of all the chapters.

If the contextual examples encountered in this text are given in the next edition, then the utility and value will increase.

I, convey my heartfelt abundant greetings and congratulations to my dear elder brother Dr. Chandrapal Sharma ji for this dedication to goddess Saraswati.

—Ramakant Shukla
R-6, Vani Vihar
New Delhi-59

Forewords by:

1. Professor Namvar Singh
2. Dr. Ganeshdatt Sharma
3. Dr. Urmila Kishore
4. Dr. Ramgopal Sharma
5. Smt. Sadhan Arun Bhalla

To work on the book of 'Mool Ankomen Sanskriti ke Swar', by his interesting and amazing style, by the medium of numbers from shoonya-zero to 10-ten through praised worthy examples has prepared this moralistic book. Dr. Chandrapal Sharma has accomplished this work by incorporating important facts and points from numerous Hindi and Sanskrit texts. He has written this compilation by his own style of delivery by taking he ideas and opinions of Chanakya, Vidur, Mammat, Manusmriti, Shukraneeti, Upanishads and Purans along with Tulsi, Jayasi, Prasad, Pant poets and many other scholars.

The writing of such books is significant and meaningful. This book is an amazing gift by the writer to the society.

In this book, through the medium of numbers, various aspects and standards of civilization, culture and spiritualism have been shown.

My very best wishes to writer Dr. Chandrapal Sharma.

–Prof. Namvar Singh

The meaning of 'ank' is sign. The word 'ank' is numerical. The numbers from 1 to 10 numeric are the numerical signs. Actually the word numbers is **'सम्यक् ख्यानं यद्वा सम्यकज्ञानम्'** On the basis of this interpretation, actually neutral or meditative knowledge is the denomination, and it is the neutral knowledge of Indian Shaddarshan and in that context, the twenty five basic elements of object (pind) and brahmand (universe), through Sankhyan or Maharshi Kapil who created the confederation and humbly wrote Sankhya Darshan. It became famous due to the numbers.

If seen from the elemental point of view, then every numeric or number from 0 and after that from 1 to 10, gives us the knowledge of some eternal truth and facts learned writer and compilation expert Dr. Chandrapal Sharma has brought forth in concrete form this fact in this book.

This creation is an evident proof that 'Its wise writer Dr. Chandrapal Sharma has presented this book for the welfare of people after doing medium and neutral churning of Vedic and contemporary all texts of Sanskrit and Hindi literatures of Vedant period.

कोटिशः वर्धापनानि to Dr. Sharma for this conspicuous excellent contribution.

– Dr. Ganeshdatt Sharma

A very well-known writer of Hindi, Dr. Chandrapal Sharma's book "Bharatiya Sanskriti aur Mool Ankoke Swar" is an invaluable gem of his deep study and thinking extracted. After turning from the ocean of knowledge. It clearly reflects his intensive study of the subject matter, his contemplation and his ardent labor. The importance of the text is in its depth. To attain this purpose the writer must have had to do so much study and also must have had to rummage through so many literary books. This is extremely considerable and also commendable.

The writer must have collected so much abundant material after deeply studying the glory and greatness of numbers from Ved, Puran and various texts. A reader does not get tired of reading enough about numbers, which are more than two hundred fifty pages, but finds out invaluable pearls by ducking in the vast sea of knowledge.

The book is sententious, revealing and worth as a collection.

– Dr. Urmila Kishore
A-5/20, Ganga Satellite, Vanvadi,
Pune-40 (Maharashtra)

Dr. Chandrapal Sharma has opened a startup and exposed many fulgent and lustrous facets of Indian culture in the context of global culture through his deep study related to the numbers. His entire study spans over from the study of Vedas to modern literature. The Vast and intense sea of knowledge is floating in this study.

What relation each number has in India culture and through this knowledge, how far the attitude of human knowledge has progressed, this can be understood through this text, in interesting style and visage,

The text is written by compiling and accumulating nectar like cultural knowledge from various dematoglyphics, Puranas etc. This creative text, in the tradition of perpetual and eternal text is considered with high respect and is worth collecting as a treasure.

Dr. Chandrapal Sharma is definitely to be complimented and congratulated for the enunciation and investigation simple the vast Indian cultures secrets of human welfare and well-being on the basis of numbers.

–Dr. Ramgopal Sharma
'Dinesh'
C-7/1, Garima Vihar, Sector-35,
Noida-201307 (U.P.),

At the very beginning, my pranam to Dr. Chandrapal Sharmaji, who gave me this work of enlightenment for translation and has bestowed faith in myself to accomplish this work.

It was through and through a work full of joy, revelation and emancipation. I cannot express in words. This joyful journey of translating this invaluable creative work. Truly, my knowledge has increased manifold and has touched my personality.

Dr. Sharmaji, lots of good wishes and compliments to you. I pray to the Almighty you may sojourn many more creative journeys in future also.

With Regards

– **Smt. Sadhan Arun Bhalla**
M-31/260, Vidyanagar Hats,
Opp. Himmatlal Park, On 132, Ring Road,
Ahmedabad-380015 (Gujarat)
Phone-26749523

Contents

of property of a householder, Three who are deprived of the rights of wealth, Three scarce matter, Persons of three colors, Three types of glory, Three types of lights, Three monkeys of Gandhi ji, Three types of departures, Three goddesses, Three places, Three destroyed when three say the truth out of fear, Three types of evidence or proof, Three purposes of three qualities, There renounceable, Three desired, Three gems (Buddhist), Three things of Bhamashah, Three reasons for a renunciate (sanyasi) to go to a king, Three castes, Three eras, Three requests, Three qualities of one who has controlled his senses and gained victory over them, Three types of worship, Three nights, Three spots of Ramkatha, Stories of three communities, Confluence of three cultures, Three heroes of a story, Three tasks of Ram, Three conditions or states of truth, Three potential people, Three types of fathers, Three types of people, Memorable retention of three sages, Three sages, Three types of fire, Three time-periods, Three karan, Three parts of day, Three coaches, Three gems (Jain), Three follies on stupidity, Three faults, Three balms, Triphala (three ingredients), Three base of concoction, Three mites, Three letters, Three ceremonies after birth, Three salts, Three hones, Three types of services, Three qualities of a person, Three tasks to be performed during the three parts of the day, Three depths of a woman, Three notes of music, Three qualities of literature, Three lovers who keep their lover's trust, Three should not be abandoned in crisis, Three qualities have immortality, Three notes of victory, Three divine bows, Three inspirations, Three things for subjects calamity, Arjun does not have the memory of three things, Three types of japa, Three cannot shake their empty palms, Three increase when they remain, Three types of rates of men, Three sins equivalent to murder of Brahmin, Threee distinctions of an eye witness, Three righteousness of Kshatriya towards a Brahmin, Three parts of wealth, Difficult to enunciate three, Three put to an end when asked for, Three conditions of bet for stable friendship, Three benefits of imparting knowledge, Three distinctions of knowledge, Three distinctions of Ayurved treatment, Three divisions of body, Three types of advice, Three symbols, Three qualities, Three streams or channels, Three types of pilgrimages, Three from whom praise received is annulled, Three states of the body after death, Three curses of giving honor to the non-deserving and no to the deserving persons, Three original colors, Three ways to accept anything, Three damages to be paid by a Brahmin who deserves punishment, Three types of yagna, Three tapa, Three donations, Thee reasons for creation of nature, Three heroism prowess, Three

human life, Four types of diseases, Four painful or distressful, Immediate influence of four, Four karmas that give fearlessness, Four bad qualities, Four forbidden karma, Four karmas of students, Four renounceable for a king, Four great crimes, Four ungratified, Four verbal iniquities, Four specialties of speech, Four bases of beauty, Four types of sons, Four develop due to obeisance, Four means to receive wealth, Four types of bravery, Four places of kumbh, Four peeths, Four holy cities, Four stages of life, Four holy months, Four armed forces, Four feet, Four pricking and hurting relations, Four fit for disrespect, Four grief of Buddhist religion, Four who are not indifferent, Four types of women, Four types of performances or acting, Four types of actors, Four equals, Foolish and scholar are equal due to four, Four wretched persons of Mahabharat, Four respectable of Arjun, Four horses of Krishna, Four forms of gods in Dwapar era, Four in times of crisis, Four forms of worship, Four means of desired intense meditation, Four sins devoid of atonement, Four places without masters, Four bases of restraint or abstinence, Four glorified due to four, Four who create catastrophe, Four enemies, Four ways to follow non- violence, Four supreme rascals, Four bases of birth, Four attainments after worship of a Brahmin, Four body parts having reddish luster, Four intensives of liberation, Four days of leisure, Four personified actual with four, Four worries, Four useless tasks, Four conditions of good austere person, Four dhams of Uttaranchal, Four renounceable in four eras, Four mean to procure money or wealth, Respectable due to four reasons, Four orators and listeners of Ramcharitmanas, Four pleasures of a king on his subjects, Four duties of a king, Four who are not fit for scandalous behavior, Four occasions for gaining immortality, Four types of karma, Four Brahmins, Four rungs or steps of knowledge, Four ways to test gold, Four types of external cleanliness, Four types of edible food, Four characteristics of persons desirous of attaining salvation, Four means, Four qualities, Four qualities of a sage, Four reasons for protection of Draupadi, Four rare, Four parts of yagna, Four threads, Four types of friends, Four famous weaponry, Four that make you burn, Four blemishes of four ashrams, Four ways to ultimate journey, Four guards at the gates of enlightenment, Four faults of speech, Four types of intentions, Four ways of purification of the mind, Four distinctions of sights, Four worth killing, Four types of strengths, Four sons of Guru Govind Singh, Four words with 'G', Four means of enlightenment, Four during fasting, Four tasks of four castes, Four during types of valiant persons, Four distinctions of texts, Save from four, Four

Shoonya (Zero)

The literal meaning of zero is solitary/secluded place, Sky, Vishnu, Heaven, Formless, Empty, Endless, Devoid, Aimless, Without Answer, Dot etc. With numbers the relation of zero, for the first time, starts after nine but after the fractional theory has become prevalent, zero is used before fraction of ten is also zero. The theory of fraction was already known in India in 200 B.C. Actually, the symbol of zero is infinite. Therefore, to express the infinity of numbers zero is required. Zero is the basic point of mathematics. This is the most powerful, when attached to any number, its value increased ten-fold. The exclusivity of zero is that, when added to zero, it remains as zero. When it is subtracted from zero, then also remains as zero only. Also, when multiplied or divided, then also remains as zero.

Actually, zero is totally complete in itself, whose exclusivity and uniqueness is mentioned in Brihadaranyak Upnishad as below

पूर्णमदः पूर्णमिदं पूर्णात् पूर्णमुदच्यते।
पूर्णस्य पूर्णमादाय पूर्णमेवावशिष्यते।।

To the medieval Buddhist thinkers and philosophers, Shunyavad (Theory of Zero) is the name of a Principle. According to this, Truth, Untruth, Good Behavior, Bad Behavior these four and apart from this, not explicit trait has been accepted.

This trait or element is nothing but zero. In Sanskrit and especially in Astrology the word 'KH' is used for zero. 'KH' is also a symbol for sky which is actually only zero. In the 40th chapter of Yajurved, in the last mantra 'Om Kham Brahma' is pronounced, which means that the Almighty or Brahma is also 'Kh', that is like the sky and also omnipotent and omnivalent. Therefore, this word 'Kh' is also in the true sense the form of Brahma.

Zero is the discovery of Indian rishis. The number world, has been given first by India. The first experiment of zero is found in the book of Acharya Pingal 200 B.C. After that Jinbhadra Bhaskar and Aryabhatt like mathematician had used then in their manuscripts. Zero is the smallest of small drop or dot and biggest of big sky. In the words of Kathopnishad- **अणोरणीयान् महतो महीयान्**. The main meaning of zero is useful, Formless, the other form of Vishnu. It is the symbol of the perfectness of Brahma. The magnanimous form of zero is the Formless Brahma. Its form in specific state is the sky. This zero is the entire universe and it embraces the whole world of stars in itself. Everything emerges from it and in the end it merges in it. Every unit is the image of zero. All moving particles also move in resemblance to that image whether it is the path of planets or the particles of dust or the wheel of a vehicle, all are in the shape of a zero. Lord Vishnu is himself is a synonym of zero and his abode is also zero (Heaven). The symbol of Formless Brahma cannot be other than zero. Therefore, zero is formless, omnipresent, most powerful Parbrahma. Zero is in incomplete and also it is complete zero and completeness are the synonym of Vishnu.

Mathematics has an important place in all the faculties of science and knowledge. Zero is the biggest invention of mathematics. There is no option for it in the world of creation. The discovery of numbers were first done in India and from here these numbers went to Arabian countries. These numbers were called 'Hindsa', and so they were given recognition as taken from India. Like the numbers, the experiment of zero in mathematics was also done in India, that is to multiply any number ten times by adding zero to it was known to India during the 4th century. Before this, the accounting was $9 + 1 = 10$. A zero put before the number 1, and then becoming 10, the concept of mathematics and accounting both were changed. Today, the biggest of accounting is possible because of zero. Although there is no actual value of zero, but it has the potential and ability to give 10 times the value to any number. The value of any number is not possible without zero.

Fifty years from now, in an illiterate society, the highest number was twenty which was called Bisi. As a writer, I am aware of such people, who would say 100 rupees as 5 Bisi. This count was also the same, like for example today people don't count beyond crore but instead write or say as 3000 crore or 3 lakh crore. They adhere to the European Million (10 lakhs), and go with it. The counts of kharab, Neel, Padam, Shankh are not propagated. It is a matter of doubt, that Indians who are educated in the western education system, may be aware of counts above crore, like Arab, Kharab, Neel, Padam, Shankh or may not be aware. 20 was the greatest number in illiterate society, its limitations are seen even now. For example, while building a house, kadi-bamboo and plates of stones were shown as per the rate of 20, which is called 'kaudi'.

The discovery of zero is surprising. How far is it appropriate to call zero as an appendage is like the flow of water in a river or like it makes no difference to the sea when clouds take the water from it, the same way, if something comes and adds to zero or leaves zero after subtraction, the situation remains as it was before. Zero is prevalent in everything. If any number is subtracted from that very number, the remainder is zero. That means it is not possible to subtract or diminish zero. So by adding, subtracting, multiplying or dividing zero is unaffected, that means zero is dominating, but the attitude of zero, like the good, is benevolent. Those who tackle the good on the left, those are the impartial good ones. The places of worship are on the right side, that is the ritual even today. Zero also, when on the right side, or in a friendly state makes the friend attached with it 10 times, but when it comes on the left side does not increase the value nor does it harm in any way.

When zero makes 1 into 10, then it is evident that zero is great. Your greatness is beyond measure and space. At one point, you call yourself devoid, and at the other point you make 10 times the biggest of the big numbers. May be, because of you, the Indian culture is tenfold. Clearly, when you become a companion those 10 counts have become ten-fold. Zero, you are limitless, that is why the sky expresses its image of depth and wideness through you. Sky is not just like zero in its image, also it is a void, which is also the main meaning of zero.

In the language of mathematics zero, is a state of void, the result is that, in mathematics, in four different elements, addition, subtraction, multiplication and division, zero is not in a position to make any difference. This is an aspect of contemplation. There is another aspect as well and that is, zero is the only one that remains unaffected by any addition, subtraction, multiplication and division that zero remains as zero.

In philosophical language it is said as-

पूर्णमदः पूर्णमिदं पूर्णात्पूर्णमुदच्यते।
पूर्णस्य पूर्णमादाय पूर्णमेवावशिष्यते।।

When complete is taken out of complete, it is complete. Zero is that complete.

Basically in zero, there is the essence of void. Whether it is void of intelligence, void of knowledge, or void of feelings and emotions. The world is full of void of intelligence and void of knowledge. To fill up the void experiments are being done for knowledge and science. All educational institutions are busy in this endeavor. The void of senses may make us unhappy for a short while but void of emotions destroy the whole life. That without concept or meaning is also void. Even though, the womb of zero may become elliptical and different, but its inside soul is filled with emptiness. Surprisingly, it is filled and that with emptiness. In fact, emptiness is a feeling a religion which cannot be understood by the persons who are void of true knowledge.

In this fort of the body, there are nine doors and one secret 10th door also, this is in the form of zero that is why it is called as 'Shunyapadavi'. Bathed by this shunyapadavi, blindfolded by Brahma, these Hath yogis, in the quench of their thirst by Amrit (nectar/elixir) remain as sudhaks with sadhana all through their lives. In Buddhist religion, the entire philosophy is based on Emptiness. They may not believe in Buddha as God or the Vedas, but they have not been able to ignore emptiness. They see the entire world in the form of emptiness. The theory of Void/Emptiness is actually a cult. Only the atheist have faith in Emptiness. According to shoonyavad, there is no soul nor there is particles in elements as such. According to their theology, there is nothing known, nothing to be known, and there is no knowledge, all are zero. In this soulless cult, the world is a complete zero, and their philosophy is the Voidism. Even the atheist cult has faith in zero, that is the prominence and greatness of zero. Even while neglecting Brahma and life and the world, they acknowledge the importance of zero.

In the language of Philosophy, the position of void/emptiness is unique. Emptiness/void seems dark sometimes, and at other times a solitary place. If voidism is the other name of the Almighty then Shoonya is the void of creation or proliferation. An empty or void body, it is unaware of its knowledge of karma is a fool and gullible, then a void heart is lost in aimless thoughts. One who is Shoonya vikram (empty victory) is clean of his heart and knows no malice or doubts. The path of all divine souls is through the Shoonya path (void path), the sky. If after everything is done, only a fraction of void remains, then only a void remains. Acharya Chanakya had full faith in the wide spectrum of void. Thus, he writes:

अविद्यं जीवनं शून्यं दिक् शून्या चेदबान्धवा।
पुत्रहीनं गृहं शून्यं सर्वशून्या दरिद्रता॥

Life without knowledge is void. Without friends, direction is void. Without a son, a home is void and in poverty void is everywhere, all around.

Zero, your greatness is supreme, that you are omnipresent. In the absence and emptiness of one, everything is a void, a zero. As said by the great poet, Rahim, it is true-'Without water all is void'. The very state of emptiness is the name of zero. The work of zero is to take care of all big and small. For the householder, it is a slumbering phase, on the other hand, sanyas is complete and boundariless.

Eminent Hindi poet, Bihari Lal, had sought the greatness of zero/void in the field of shringar (love). In colloquial language zero is said to be a 'bindi' (dot). The same image of zero like 'bindi', adorns the forehead of a woman. Now, the 'bindi' that adorns the forehead has established a right of its own, otherwise to put 'bindi' on the forehead was the first right of a woman after marriage. Unmarried young girls had no relation to cosmetics. So when any young woman, after being married, adorn a 'bindi' on her forehead her beauty would be enhanced. Narrating that special incident Bihari Lal writes

कहत सबै वैंदी दिए, आँक दस गुनो होत।
तिय लिलार वैंदी दिए, अनगिन बढ़त उदोत॥

After extracting the void titles from life, and a desire to joyfully submit to the void, conclude the greatness of zero/void with an ardent hope that the worshipers of Indian culture, through this manuscript/book, if not knowledge, but at least of essence of knowledge will surely be achieved.

❑

1 (One)

In every society and culture, there are some words and numbers, whose very pronunciation reminds of the incident, persons, traditions and principles of that particular word or number. Such numbers or words are preserved in the religious, social, cultural or political long history of any civilization or nation. Numbers from 1 to 10 are the basis of all remaining numbers. From this point of view, these 10 numbers are basic numbers while pronouncing these basic numbers, the Indian mind moves to various places. This is the main objective of this book. These numbers have tremendous potential and ability to represent and introduce to various regional knowledge and details.

In numbers, the first introduction is with number 1 (one). The literal meaning of 1 is extraordinary, beautiful, alone or unknown etc. Actually, this whole definition is of that of the self-created Almighty, who is the main reason of his nature creation.

Therefore, the very utterance, reminds us of that Almighty God. That almighty is the foundation of this world. In the foundation of this world, a Great Power is present. All puritanal souls or gods are the various forms of it, of that Supreme Formless and Boundless has three images- Brahma, Vishnu and Mahesh that Almighty being one is known in the images of three gods. The godly and truth element of that image is the Vishnu, the materialistic element as Brahma and the dark element as Shiva. These satva (truth), rajas (material) and tamas (darkness) are the unseen qualities. That Almighty is ever Joyful and Truthful. Its three fold existence is the truth, Mind is knowledge and Joy is above all pleasures and sorrows. In the words of Goswami Tulsidas

व्यापक एक ब्रह्म अविनासी। सत चेतन घन आनंद रासी।।

The worshipper of Lord Krishna proves his greatness by the medium of 1

एकं शास्त्रं देवकीपुत्रगीतम एको देवो देवकीपुत्र एवं।
एको मन्त्रस्तस्य नामानि यानी कर्माप्येकं तस्यं देवस्य सेवा।।

There is only one theory, that is the only theory sung by the son of Devaki, Krishna, is the 'Geeta'. The son of Devaki is the only god, his name is the only holy chant and his service is the only karma. At another quote also, it is said,

सर्वशास्त्रमयी गीता सर्वदेवभयो हरिः।
सर्वतीर्थमयी गंगा सर्ववेदमयो मनुः।।

All theories are included in 'Geeta', Lord Vishnu is in all forms of incarnations of god, all pilgrimages are complete in one Ganga, the Religious Scripture of Manu is complete with Vedas. It is a root. In 'Kathopanishad', the king of Religion, Dharmaraj tells Nachiketa the image of the Almighty:–

अशब्दमस्पर्शमरूपमव्ययं तथारसं नित्यमगंधवच्च यत्।
अनाद्यनन्तं महतः परं ध्रुवं निचाय्य तन्मृत्युमुखात्प्रमुच्यते।।

Almighty is wordless, imageless, essence less and dour less, He is not destroyable, always new, everlasting, boundless, free from frivolity and always true element. By knowing that Almighty, a man becomes free from the clutches of death. That Almighty alone takes the form of different gods. Or we may say that all gods, are the different forms of Him. That Almighty is fire, sun, air/wind, moon, venus, Brahma, Indra, king of animals, Varun, Rudra, Shiva etc. takes different forms to do different tasks, this is mentioned in the mantras of vedas. In Srimad Bhagvat Gita, Lord Krishna tells Arjuna, whichever god is worshipped, that comes to me. This essence of Gita, was expressed by Swami Vivekanand in the 'All Religion Conference' in Chicago-

आकाशात् पतितं तोयं, यथा गच्छति सागरम्।
सर्वदेवनमस्कारः, केशवं प्रति गच्छति।।

That Brahma when spoken as one word it is known as Om. 'Om' is only one word. Brahma is the result of that proposition. Omkar is the image of Brahma that is Pranav or love. Pranav is the root and basis of all. This form of love has been analysed by many rishis, saints and philosophers, but in the end the state of all is the same, failure. In the pronouncement of Pranav, the balance of speech and its high and low notes is true knowledge. Analyzing and discussing the form of Brahma in the epic Mahabharat, Maharshi Ugrashrava quotes it as the most ancient reason. All knowing and Timeless are one word and Ever Truth. He is the supreme creator of this moving universe, Ancient man is simple and pure, benevolent and godly. That Brahma is fantastic, Without-thought, Unexpressed, Utterly-tiny, Image with a reason and is unspoken. Rishis have sought the help of many synonyms to describe this Almighty. Maharishi Angira while describing the form of Almighty says that-Fire is his forehead, Sun and Moon his eyes, directions are ears, Ved is his speech, Air is his breath and universe is his heart. The world has originated from its feet, he is the soul of all that is living.

अनिर्मूर्धा चक्षुषी चनद्रसूर्यौ दिशः श्रोत्रे वाग्विवृताश्च वेदाः।
वायुः प्राणो हृदयं विश्वमस्य पद्भयां हृयेष सर्वभूतांतरात्मा।।

The actual form of Almighty's worshipper, Goswami Tulsidas, describes the formless Brahma, thus-

बिनु पंगुं चलै सुनै बिनु काना। कर बिनु करई करम विधिा नाना।।
आनन रहित सकल रस भोगी। बिनु बानी वक्ता बड़ जोगी।।

In the context of philosophy and its expression, it is said that in the beginning of creation, the Supreme element, which is also called truth, was alone. Sometimes its desire was-'To be many in different manifestation' or 'To be present in different purposes'. I am alone become many and that was the beginning of creation. This supreme Brahma is the mother of Advaitism. Taking this as the basis, one god theory came into existence. The widening and multiplication of that element is creation of life. This one horizon and infinity is expressed and described in the same way. That Kabir who had never touched ink, paper and pen, in his opinion that element is present everywhere, all around-

जल में कुंभ, कुंभ में जल है, बाहर भीतर पानी।
फूटा कुंभ, जल जलहिं समाना, यह तत कहौ गियानी।।

Philosophers have said this in different ways. Vedanta has said as- **'ब्रह्म सत्यं जगन्मिथ्या जीवो ब्रह्मैव नापरः'** or **'अहं ब्रह्मास्मि, तत्त्वमसि, सर्वं खल्विदं ब्रह्म'**, 'Brahma is truth, World is untruth, Life is not possible without Brahma' or 'I am Brahma, I am element, Everywhere there is only Brahma', this has thus been proved. Brahma is truth, World is untruth, there is no difference between life and Brahma, I am also Brahma, you are also Brahma, this whole world is Brahma. Such statements explain the width and depth of Brahma. The difference between life and Brahma is seen in the form and context of Maya. With the Almighty, there is a special power since time immemorial which is called as Maya or Ignorance. That which is neither truth nor untruth, that is inexplicable. With the relation of Maya the connotation of Brahma is God and with the relation of ignorance it is called living object.

In the beginning, middle and end of creation, it is the supreme dominance of that Brahma. Prior to the creation, he was breathing through his own power, air/wind. That 1 (one) has been defined in the scriptures as- **'एकं सदविप्रा बहुधा वदन्ति'**. Basic dominance of power is only one, that is mentioned as vipra in many forms. The creation of this universe, its nurture and control is done by the only one controller which is resting in the Almighty. Even though its name may be different. Only one Supreme Power in various task forms is described in three images, which is called Brahma, Vishnu, Mahesh. This is the reason that in the scriptures the three gods emanate from one another.

परस्परस्माज्जायन्ते ब्रह्माविष्णुमहेश्वराः।

World's most ancient scripture is Veda, that was also one. Its division in three Vedas and four Vedas was later.

एकस्य वेदस्याज्ञानाद् वेदास्ते बहवः कृताः।

Veda is one means knowledge is one. A person according to his ability, divides it and restricts it to his own convenience that also proposes the existence of only one Almighty. Reverend

Shankaracharya has proved the principle of Vedanta on this basis. In Yajurveda's Mantra, it is proved that whatever is there in this universe, that all is covered by the Almighty.

ईशावास्यमिदं सर्वं यत्किंच जगत्यां जगत्।
तेन त्यक्तेनभुञ्जीथा मा गृधः कस्यस्विद्धनम्॥

Whatever is static and wide moving universe in it is god, that means, in all that one god is existing and that is to be understood. That is to be relished and used with the feeling of surrender. One should be away from lust. This treasure belongs to nobody. It is said as **'एकमेवाद्वितीयम्'** one within two or one as second as an option for description. That one supreme element is pronounced as Ved Hiranyagarbha. Rigveda says

हिरण्यगर्भः समवर्तताग्रे भूतस्य जातः पतिरेक आसीतु।
स दाधार पृथ्वीं द्यामुतेमां कस्मै देवाय हविषा विधेम॥

(Hiranyagarbha was first born, who was the ruler/king of all. He held this world and the heaven. We worship that joyful image). Shwetashwatar Upanishad has described that one man, as thus-

सहस्रशीर्षा पुरुषः सहस्राक्षः सहस्रपात्।
स भूमिं विश्वतो वृत्वा अत्यतिष्ठद्दशांगुलम्॥

(That man has thousand heads, thousand eyes and thousands legs. He surrounds the entire universe and is standing on ten toes that means, he is widespread in ten directions).

That one Almighty has three legs, Morning, Afternoon and Evening. Four Vedas are his horns, sunrise and sunset are two heads, Gayatri and other holy couplets are the seven hands, that who is bound by mantra, Brahmin and imagination

'चत्वारि श्रृंगां त्रंयो अस्य पादा द्वे शीर्षे सप्त हस्तासो अस्य' This means that four directions are four horns, three phases and three universes are the three legs, earth and heaven or two heads, the five elements-earth, water, fire, wind and sky, importance and ego are seven hands. That one Almighty is omnipresent, inspiration of all hearts, punitive giver of evil and sinful people and is one who is himself unborn-

कविर्मनीषी परिभूः स्वयंभूः।

That Supreme Brahma is the form of a word. The meaning of that word and complete knowledge means complete introduction of that Supreme Image and right type of thought, meditation, relinquishes desires of this earth and fulfils the desires of the other world. That means one who is known to him and who meditates on him, he has no leftover desires- **एकश्शब्दः सम्यक् ज्ञातः सुष्ठु प्रयुक्तः स्वर्गे मर्त्ये कामधुक् भवति।** The form of that Supreme Soul is the smallest and the biggest- **'अणोरणीयान् महतो महीयान्'** Its part image is Hanuman the server of Lord Rama, the incarnation of Vishnu, sometimes he becomes as a mountain and sometimes as small as a mole. Hanuman is a living being and Brahma is existing in Brahma.

After hearing, one recollects the shloka of the principle of Vidur:–

'एकः स्वादु न भुंजीत एकश्चार्थान्न चिन्तयेत्।
एको न गच्छेदध्वानं नैकः सुप्तेषु जागृयात्।।'

Do not relish tasty food alone, do not thing alone. Do not go on a travel alone, and do not be awake when all are asleep. This main shloka has a deep hidden meaning of loneliness which will irritate you. If a man wants his welfare, peace, fulfilment and joy in one's life, then he has to take support for each-

एको धर्मः परं श्रेयः क्षेमका शान्तिरुत्तमा।
विद्यैका परमा तृप्तिरहिंसका सुखावहा।।

(One religion only gives blessings, forgiveness is the only giver of peace, knowledge is the only giver of satisfaction and non-violence is the only giver of happiness). Number one (1) is the symbol of sun. Just as the sun is the source of all energies, in the same way there are many due to one. Many are also one. The base of all is one.

One is the sign of the extraordinary. By pronouncing one, it is natural to remember the extraordinary of different fields. Like in brilliance sun is extraordinary, the same way in speed it is wind, Yama in anger, Earth in forgiveness, Sky in depth and width,

Brahmin in human beings, Kamdev in beauty, Kuber as in wealth, Ved in all scriptures Indra in gods, Vishnu in kings, Marich in deer, moon in satellite, mind in the senses, Shiva in rudra, fire in vasu, Sumeru in mountains, Kashi in pilgrimages/holy places, Six words in mantras, Guru/teacher as protector, Brahaspati as Pandit, Skand as the commandant, Sea as water bodies, Period of truth in periods, Padamrag in gems, Kush in grass, Cow ghee in havans, Gandiv in Gayatri in lyrics, Gold in metals, Bhrigu in rishis, Himalaya in estate, Peepal in trees, Narad in devrishi, Manu in rajrishi, Kamdhenu in cows, Garud in birds, Elixir in medicines, Bali in brahmin disciples, Arjun among valiant, Chitrarath among singers, Kapil among the achievers, Uchchay-shrava among horses, Erawat among elephants, Crocodile among reptiles, Ganga among rivers, Self-knowledge/realization among knowledge, Magh among months, Vajra among weapons, Vasuki among snakes, Narsimha among demons, Lion among animals, Parshuram among warriors, Spring among seasons, Vasudev among householder, Ushna among poets, Parvati among women, Vishwakarma among sculptors, Daksha among the kings, Pushkar among islands, Maya among tangles, Sanyas among ashrams are all extraordinary. In their own fields they have extra ordinary tales, which is not possible to describe in this small book. In the 10th chapter of Gita, Krishna elaborately describes these all different tales of different field to Arjun. All these are the super ones in their own fields. In their category no one can compare them.

Among these extra ordinary people, animals, birds are known to even common people in India. For example the anger of Yama is known to all and all are scared of him. Kamdev and his consort Rati's beauty and their story of love is on the minds and hearts of people. Kamdhenu has become the synonym of extraordinary. Its child Nandini also became the controversy and struggle between Vasishtha and Vishwamitra. Kuber is the god of wealth who adorns himself with an earring-kundal. Even though He is the god of wealth, Kuber has no exclusive status among all gods. Being defeated by the king of demons, Ravana, he had to surrender Lanka and Pushpak aircraft. In the famous scripture of Kalidas, Yaksha was the servant of Kuber. Kuber's new home Alkapuri was one at the top of all places. By the blessings of Lord Rama after the victory of Lanka, the Pushpak aircraft was again given to Kuber. In modern period, the business community remembers Kuber by writing **'श्री कुबेराय नमः'.**

May be Sumeru mountain is not visible in physical way, but it is known to all that it is of gold and the conference of gods is conducted on Sumeru mountain only. Kashi is a unique city among all seven cities, it hangs on the trishul (trident) of Lord Shiva. The day temperature, from sunrise to 12.00 noon and from noon to sunset remains the same throughout, it is believed so by the pandits, death in Kashi gives salvation, this is the city of Lord Vishwanath, by diverting to the road to Kashi, with the desire of heaven, devotional people get scratches on their body, such beliefs still prevail among thousands of Indians. This is also a universally known belief that close to Kashi, if somebody dies in Maghar, he goes to Hell, but Saint Kabir took birth in Kashi and lived there all his life, but decided to die in Maghar, so that this blind superstition can be ended-

क्या कासी क्या ऊसर मगहर, राम हृदय बस मोरा।
जो कासी तन तजै कबीरा, राम कौन निहारा।।

Due to the intelligence of the guru of gods, Brahaspati, the problems of gods finds solutions. His son Kach had gone to learn the knowledge of medicine from Shukracharya. Warrior god, Kartikeya, was solely born to protect all gods. Kamdev sacrificed himself for its need and success. During the test of three gods great rishi Bhrighu, stumped with his foot on the chest of sleeping Vishnu which was permanently borne by Lord Vishnu. In the words of Kalidas, great Himalayas are the great godly souls, and is the only giver of food, water and medicines for India. Without it India would be a desert, it is an accepted fact. Narad due to his migratory attitude and nature, concern for the welfare of people and playing on the veena, is known to all. Due to the curse of Kapil, 60 thousand sons of Sagar were burnt to death, as a result of which the holy Ganga came to this earth. From its very birth Ganga is the centre of faith and trust of thousands and crores of devotees. Even staunch scientific believers also wish the immersion of their ashes in Ganga. Poet Senapati, while describing the glory of Ganga, promise by the name of Rama and calls it beautiful:–

राम जू की आन कोई तीरथ न आन देख्यौ।
गंगा के समान होतो वेद तो बतावतौ॥

Great rishi Dadhichi's bones made Indra's weapon very sharp. The son of the demon, Hiranya Kashyap, was Prahlad who was famous for his devotion. Because of him, till today we celebrate Holi Utsav. Garud is the carrier of Lord Vishnu and the king of birds. The Parshu of Parshuram spread lot of fear and terror around its example is seen in Valmiki Ramayan when king Dasharath sees Parshuram while returning to Ayodhya with sons and daughters-in-law. Seeing Parshuram, Vashistha, other rishis, sons except Dashrath, all others became unconscious. King Dashrath joined his hands and pleaded for the life of his sons.

मम सर्वविनाशाय सम्प्राप्तस्त्वं महामुने।
न चैकस्मिन् हते रामे सर्वे जीवामहे वयम्॥

O! Great rishi, why have you come to destroy me? If you kill Rama, because of Shiv Dhanush (Bow of Shiva) so by the death of Rama alone, all will relinquish their lives. The couplets of Gayatri are great and indescribable; this is the Mother of Vedas, great mantra, this mantra is pounced first by the gods. Old beliefs are still embedded deep in the Indian society. Kurma Puran says to the extent that this single mantra has the weightage of all the four vedas. Basant is the king of seasons, Kam (Love) is his friend. When Mahadev had been evoked with the feeling of attraction for Parvati, Kamdev was with him. In this season where there is the dominance of greenery and fragrance and where men-women, animals-birds, creepers and trees and plants all are seen influenced by the emotions of love. This also evokes love in the hearts of old and unattached also, Vasudev is the incarnation of sixteen skills of love of Vishnu. Those who do not believe in incarnation theory, accept the fact that in this smart world, nobody else has been born. His friend Arjun is not only extraordinary among Pandavas but he is the best archer of his period. While staying on this earth, we commit so many crimes against it, but even so it keeps filling us with food and prosperity the scientist of 21st century have not been able to measure the width and depth of the sky. Indra is the king of gods. He is very shrewd to save his title and is expert in doing so. In Vedas, there are many mantras in praise of him. There Indra is parallel to god, Vishnu is his younger brother, so he is Upendra. Indra in the Puranas are also involved in many immoral and illegal activities. The Manusmriti of king of rishis Manu is well known till today. Bali, the devotee of Brahmin, gave three acres of land in charity to Woman ignoring his guru Shukracharya's warning. In short, it can be said that those who have been described as extraordinary they are unparalleled, they are the only like themselves.

When pronouncing one, one such sinner is remembered whose sins are irrevocable. There are many kinds of sins in this world. Murderer of Brahmins, drunkard, thief and one who breaks promises, these sins of the sinners can be expunged and forgiven through their penance, but the sin of ungrateful and disloyal person is beyond the possibility of forgiveness **'कृतघ्नस्य नास्ति निष्कृतिः'**. One writer has found an ungrateful person not fit to have his progeny. **'कृतघ्नो नार्हति प्रजाम्'** One who is ungrateful bears the sin of killing a Brahmin **'ब्रह्महत्या फलं तस्य यैः कृतं नावबुध्यते'**. Mostly it is said that the right answer is only one or truth is one, but many a times this one is also seen as an exception. For example, one adding to one becomes two for material, but one and one enemy become zero. Both fight and get destroyed. One and one two friends make eleven like Ram-Hanuman, Krishna-Arjun, Chanakya-Chandragupta etc. Husband-wife or lovers are two in bodies but still they are one.

In the tradition of creation, there are some who take care of their entire responsibility alone. After one, there is no other number like the three gods- Brahma, Vishnu, Mahesh. They do their work alone. In their individual fields there are no options. With one's name Lord Ekling is remembered in a natural way. As such, the whole Hindu community worships Lord Ekling, but he is the supreme God of the rulers of Mewar. The ruler of Mewar is also Elking ji. All kingdom courts were operated in his name and with his seal.

Maharana or Rana were only rulers for name sake, and were only the chief diwan of Eklingji. Among the pilgrimages of Rajasthan, Eklingji is an important pilgrimage. Here Lord Shiva is in the form of panchmukhi (five faces).

Everybody desires for a son but son should be have good qualities that is also natural. Therefore compared to hundred foolish sons, it is best to have one good son- **'वरमेको गुणी पुत्रो न च मूर्खशतान्यपि'**। Ekdanta Ganesh, is the first to be worshipped among all gods. Sitting solitary in a place, the parents of Ganesh, Shiva and Parvati were guarded by him. Parshuram came with the idea of their darshan, Ganesh took to a fight with Parshuram and lost one of his teeth. Therefore Ganesh's another name is also Ekdant. Among the ten disciples of Adi Shankaracharya, one who is revered most is Ekdandi sanyasi. This sanyasi is called Hansa. In the Matsya incarnation period of Lord Vishnu, during the tumultuous period Manu had taken one horn from a fish to fasten his boat. To divert the mind from other outside attraction, sadhaks with a pin pointed one aim influence all with their Sadhna and penance. One circle Bhuvanbhaskar, with only one wheeled chariot, encircle the whole universe (although this is not acceptable to astronomers). Followers of one single path achieve double success. **'एक पंथ दो काज'**. This saying is not just connoted. This expresses total commitment and universality. The saying of gopis is its true witness.

चलो री सखी उस देश को, जहाँ कृष्ण को राज।
नीर भरैं दर्शन करें, एक पंथ दो काज॥

One lonely maiden's lovelorn sorrow melts the hearts of all who see her and all are well aware of the demerits of autocracy. Therefore, in solitude, I pray to that Almighty, and desire that for the unity, he provides good thoughts and good will and give us the ability to experience the thought that 'We Are All One'.

❐

2 (Two)

In all religions of the world there is a belief that at the beginning of creation Almighty was one. Creation is the result of desire of the Almighty. Somewhere he said 'Be it' and creation was there somewhere he said that 'One light should be there' and the form of creation came into being. According to Indian religious belief, Almighty was alone prior to this creation and used to feel joy within himself. He thought I am lonely, let me be many- **'सोऽकामयत। बहुस्यां प्रजायेति'** This desire of the Almighty, brought about the existence of two. On number one Almighty is there and on another that is number two His power, nature or illusion is there. Man and nature are the first couple. Almighty and nature are the root of creation.

Almighty is the Man and this man has two differences immortal and mortal, that which is destroyable gets degenerated is the material mortal and one that does not degenerate is immortal. Soul is immortal and universe/nature is mortal. The name of nature itself is ignorance or Maya. When nature unites with the Almighty then it is called Maya and when it unites with the life and living, then it is called ignorance, nativity. Maya is the power of illusion of Brahma. Because of this illusion, world seems to be peal. Creation is the reflection illusion of the Almighty. Just as the reflection in a mirror looks live and true but it does not have any existence that is the position of nature. As the nature of dreams is not acceptable to a common person similarly, the knowledgeable people do not have faith in the existence of this material world.

For pure ascetic life, it is essential to have the control and dedication of speech. This sadhana is of two types-to ensure one's speech always pure and true and to be popular one has to practice self-speech, self-realization. **'सत्यं ब्रूयात् प्रियं ब्रूयात् न ब्रूयात् सत्यमप्रियम्'**. These are in consonance with self-talk sadhana. To make the speech of others according to our convenience or requirement, these efforts or are called as other sadhna. While looking at the world our viewpoint is also of two types. Some we see as friends and others as enemies, with hatred, but Veda believes :- **'मित्रस्य चक्षुषा समीक्षामहे'** We should see with friendship. By seeing this way our desire is hidden, that which shows us the difference between Shiva and non-shiva auspicious and inauspicious gentle and wild. Good feelings are naturally for the dear ones and friends and bad feelings for enemies, but in Indian culture, the feeling of good will and welfare for all, stays strong. **'संसार के कल्याण की है, कामना उस राम से।'** We are the worshippers of that culture where we pray for everyone's happiness and welfare-

'सर्वे भवन्तु सुखिनः सर्वे सन्तु निरामयः।
सर्वे भ्रदाणि पश्यन्तु मा कश्चिद् दुःखभाग् भवेत्॥'

When two comes there is the likelihood of differences. After 'I' comes 'You'. 'I' is the first person or the best person and 'You' is medium. By their creation is another being or man. With two as the number Man and Nature, life and illusion or life and world became two from one. We have already discussed, Almighty and nature. Life is under the control of Maya. This Maya, according to one's desire, frolics with the worldly lives and makes them dance to its tunes. Saint Surdas prays to the Almighty **'अब मैं नाच्यौ बहुत गुपाल'**. Now, please scold your Hariya cow, the Maya's image, that it does not make me dance. Saint Kabir is well aware of its three fold qualities that which tightly binds all big or small with the qualities of satva (truth), raja (material) and tama (darkness). Gun or quality is also called as a rope. For strength, this gun is bound three fold into one strong rope. The noose of Maya is also three-fold and very strong. Therefore, Kabir has called this as the greatest cheater **'माया महाठगनि हम जानी'**. Goswami Tulsidas has called it another or dvait. **'मैं अरु मोर तोर तें माया'।**

In this world, there are two types of living beings 1. One with godly qualities 2. Second with monstrous qualities. First quality leads you towards heaven and second towards pain and hell. These habits being inborn changes the influence of the tradition or cult that is why being born in the highest family traditions, demons like Ravana and Kumbhkarna are born and being the son of Hiranyakashyapa Prahlad turns out to be the top most devoted. In Kathopanishad there is the mention of two paths-shreya and preya. By satisfying the curiosity of Nachiketa, Dharmaraj said that shreya and preya are two different paths. One who aquires shreya, he is blessed, but one who adopts preya, gets deprived of a great benefit. The path of shreya leads towards god and the path of preya takes towards worldly sensual pleasures, Karma is also of two types- 1. One that encourages and 2. Second that warns. By doing the first one, one gets benevolence, whereas by doing the second, one gets cursed as sinner truth, non-violence, generosity, forgiveness, compassion etc. emotions or feeling are related to the first group. Robbery, Loot, Jealousy, Untruth, Debate, Sadism feelings are related to the second group.

Cleanliness (purity) are of two types- external (outside) and internal. **'शौचं तु द्विविधं प्रोक्तं बाह्यमाभ्यन्तरं तथा'** Cleanliness of the body is external. Cleanliness of feelings that means to purgate the feelings like- jealousy, anger, hatred, greed, lust, attraction, ego, enmity, despise etc. is internal cleanliness. This worldly disease can be destroyed by two medications; to study good literature and to be in the company of good persons. Dhata and Vidhata are not the synonum of Brahma but both are the sons of Brahma, Lakshmi is their sister, and parents are both gods. **'मातरं पितरं चैव साक्षात् प्रत्यक्षदेवताम्।'** The two wives of Yagyavalkya are well-known in the world of religion. Two men are not honored due to their indifferent services-householder without work and sanyasi involved in worldly and mterial tasks:-

द्वावेव न विराजेते विपरीतेन कर्मणा।
गृहस्थश्च निरारम्भः कार्यवांश्चैव भिक्षुकः।।

–विदुरनीति-1-62

To believe anything there are two bases- 1. To be with scientific background and 2. Not to be against nature. Adi Shankaracharya opinion states that if anything is stated in Vedas also, then he begs to differ the same. The path to progress are also of two types-human or material and supernatural. All this hectic schedule is for these two types of progress. Human or material progress is for worldly pleasures like wealth and name and fame. For supernatural progress tapa, meditation, fast etc. is taken as the sole support. In this field also, there are two types of people one is seen as medium or middle path person and the other is seen as the extremist path person. Persons who adopt the path of middle, take core of both material and supernatural equally and try to improve both of them. Extremists, either live the worldly life with the attitude of 'Eat, drink and be Merry' and follow that principle or they relinquish and surrender everything like Gautam and Mahavir and do only supernatural meditation. This sadhana also has two phases- 1. Material or worldly meditation or Karma Yoga and 2. Soulful meditation that is knowledge Yoga. While living in this world, materialistic come to us in the first place. On the basis of religious meditation, progress for the supernatural comes through soulful meditation.

Religion also has two categories based on the differences of the materialistic and the supernatural. This can be called as a dedicated service. Thus, the fact is that the service done is religion. These are the two faces of progress- **'यतोऽभ्युदयनिः श्रेयस सिद्धि स धर्मः।'** This means that by which there is worldly progress and welfare is achieved that is religion or in other words those that give worldly pleasures are the persons with the Karma are also those who are religious. Those who are planning for salvation, persons devoted to service is also super natural service or religion.

Religion also has two differences of importance when a person is combined with the good qualities of truth, non-violence, kindness, goodness towards others, sympathy etc. acts for the benefit of all, then he is seen to be following the common religion. When he is supposed to perform his tasks and render his services in accordance with, caste, age, ashram or position in society, then some special tasks have to be done, that is called special religion or service like the service of brahmin, the service of sanyasi, the service of king, service of a son or a wife. In some scriptures, both these are considered common services. Services that come in the second group are those that are done by giving up the self-centeredness of near and dear ones and attaining immense happiness by doing so like Prahlad, Vibhishan etc. services. Some learned men have stated a third group as Apaddharma. Here religion is equivalent to service. Service is supposed to be according to religious texts.

Vyas tells us of two characteristics of ancient religion. 1. Kindness towards all living and, 2. Charity. According to him ancient religion is to follow it with mind, heart and service.

अद्रोहः सर्वभूतेषु कर्मणा मनसा गिरा।
अनुग्रहश्च दानं च सतां धर्मः सनातनः।।

Goswami Tulsidas has restricted religion and non-religion all the more **परहित सरिस धर्म नहिं भाई। परपीड़ा सम नहिं अधमाई।।** In a home where there is no mother and wife is ill-tongued, in these two situations, it is good for a person to go to the woods.

यस्य गृहे मातानास्ति भार्या चाप्रियवादिनी।
अरण्यं तेन गन्तव्यं यथारण्यं गृहं वनम्।।

The mind is of two types- pure and impure **'मनो हि द्विविधं प्रोक्तं शुद्धं चाशुद्धमेव च।'**. Pure mind is constantly into the thoughts of god, tapa, meditation and hearing good things. Impure mind is filled with worldly desires and lusts. The attitude of the mind is also of two types-. Full of quarrels or quarrelsome, 2. Without quarrels or peaceful. This is called good and bad attitude. Those attitudes which are guided and controlled by jealousy, anger, enmity, ego, benefit, lust and illusion are the ones which bring about unhappiness and troubles. Generous feelings are- kindness, good gesture, non-violence are the attitudes which are far from unhappiness. In this world, man is inclined towards two types of great achievements. First to acquire, those pleasures in the future, he makes plans second, he tries to avoid the ensuing sorrows and unhappiness in future. For this also the efforts made are of two types. 1. Security of that which is achieved or got, 2. Trial for the effort of the desired achievement. This is Yog-Kshem. Efforts also are two-good and bad.

The mental state of human being are of two types-1. Puragami and 2. Pratigami. One who follows and does his work with mind and heart is Purogami. He moves ahead in the path of progress. Pratigami person is the one who does his work without thinking and carelessly. Such a person gets diverted and lost from his path, and goes towards regression. Two, do not expect any purity by any other like 1. Fire and 2. Water. They are always pure. After external impurity also they become pure themselves. Fire burns out any impurity and turns it into ash, which is a symbol of sanctity. Water, even though impure and polluted, gradually settles and sends all impurities and pollution at the bottom of it because the very nature of water is purity and coolness as symbol. However, you boil water, it gradually cools down. Dirt or heat are external factors, cleanliness and coolness are internal factors. On this fact, water coming from the depth of earth, water of well, waterfall coming out gushing from the heart of rocks, rain water from the sky, water in the clouds and water flowing in the rivers, all are considered pure and without pollution and dirt and are even so.

Two types of persons reach the Heaven. One who has done yagna and meditation, who is a sacred soul and whose work has brought about benevolence to the world? According to the ancient scriptures, one who is sanctified and sincere in his work and discharges his duties with complete honesty and commitment, that is itself yagna and meditation. Others are those yogi and learned, who have not collected or treasured their karma or in other words have not done their duties with the desire of lust. The karma (duties) of such persons gets submerged in the lust and they reach Heaven. For the achievement of the Holy Land, where good work is to be essentially and constantly done also mental and physical two types of cleanliness or Shuchita is also of special importance in life. The cleanliness of the body with water, mud or soap, externally. This is body cleanliness, Shuchita. For the joy of the mind and its liveliness external cleanliness is essential. After bathing, wearing clean clothes, sitting in clean environment, it is possible for the mind in the best of tasks. Mental cleanliness is when one gives up jealousy, anger, greed, attraction, despise etc. evil thoughts and nourishing good and welfare thoughts for all. Cleanliness of the mind is mental cleanliness. Both these cleanliness have a close relation. The uncleanliness of one, makes the other also like it. If the persons with good looks are not clean, then it is natural to be surprised. Such persons are said to be golden pots full of poison-

'मन मलीन तन सुंदर कैसे। विष रस भरा कनक घट जैसे।।'

Great poet Kalidas is sure that those who are beautiful in looks are not otherwise in their qualities. When Dushyant marries Shakuntala scarify with nature as witness and returns to his capital then one of the friends of Shakuntala starts having doubts that the king, after returning to his palace, will forget our friend then another friends reply validates, this fact- 'न तादृशा आकृतिविशेषा गुणविरोधि नो भवन्ति'। Gods and rishis have sombre and pleasant countenance and demons and monsters have fearful and horrible countenance, must be the basis of that saying.

Mind also has two types of work. It is pleasant towards some and unpleasant towards some and unpleasant towards some. To do these two tasks, he chooses oath of unity or option as the basis. 'संकल्पविकल्पातत्मकं मनः।' It is the nature of mind to imagine, \to give oath or to choose option. This mind is connected with two syntax- 'Sam (With) and Vi (Without). By aligning with them, two situation occur. By aligning with 'Sam', communication, able, totality Samadhi (deep thought) tuning etc. occur, but by aligning with 'Vi', debate, useless, excited, lethargy, disease etc. occur. Therefore the mind should be made to align with 'Sam' otherwise by debate and rebellion, disease and stress will be welcomed. Mind and speech is also a couple in the words of scriptures it is said to be the relation between mother and son-their relationship is so close, just like if the calf is under control the cow will not go elsewhere and if the cow is tied with a strong rope to the pole, then the calf has to come to the cow, the same way, if mind is under control then speech cannot be impure and if the speech does not utter wrong or false then the mind has to stay under the control of speech. The calf makes the cow to be able to produce milk in its teats. Mind makes the speech, a fountain and source.

In life, there are two types of uncleanliness which keep on coming and to be free of them, there are principles. These are known by the names of sutak and patak. When a child is born in a family it is sutak and during the time of death it is patak. Till a havan is done, till then this uncleanliness remains. It is forbidden to even during to even drink water from the unclean homes of sutak and patak. To desire for wealth and prosperity is a natural act, there are two means for its acquirement-good path and bad path. Wealth acquired through ones hard work and pure means gives happiness and stability. This is called the wealth acquired through good path. Wealth acquired through robbery, loot, kidnapping, bribery etc. are earned through low means gives sorrow and is short-lived wealth amassed through illegal means has a life span of ten years.

'अन्यायोपार्जितं वित्तं दशवर्षाणि तिष्ठति।
प्राप्ते चैकादशे वर्षे समूलमेव विनश्यति॥
अन्याय अर्जित संपदा, दस वर्ष तक ही ठहरती।
दस वर्ष के उपरान्त तो, सर्वस्व लेकर बैठती॥'

Friendship is of two types-attached with lust and detached from lust. The friendship between Ram and Sugreev was attached. Both needed the friendship of each other. The friendship between Krishna and Sudama is detached. Sudama does not take Krishna as his friend with some desire. Due to the pressure from his wife, he goes to Dwarka with an embarrassed and shy mind, he does not have any greed or ambition. The welcome and co-operation given by Krishna to Sudama is the best example of detached feeling of friendship. Karma and knowledge are also two. 1. Worldy task and worldly knowledge. 2. Soulful karma or soulful knowledge. By worldly knowledge and karma, one can acquire wealth and prosperity and by soulful knowledge and karma, one can acquire salvation or to get the nectar of peace and tranquility. Brahmachari are also of two types-One who is a student that stays in gurus ashram with austerity and simplicity. 2. The householder who stays away from intercourse with his wife during pregnancy and period of menses. First Brahamachari is the main and the second is the unimportant one. In Indian Upnishads a guru has two main qualities-1. Who is a learned man of Vedas and 2. Who has total faith in Brahma.

With relation to property, there are two types of fears-1. Doubt of the one that is got, 2. Hindrance in the path of one that is not got. There is the fear of losing wealth, property, position, reputation by all. Besides, there is also the apparent fear that terrorizes us for the hindrances that come in its way. By fearing these two types of paths, some persons give up the path of activity and become the traveler of a retired life. These two categories are the two paths for a person. Goswami Tulsidas considers two attraction for the ones on active paths-one is gold and the other is woman. In the absence of these two, one has to go to retirement. He writes-

नारी मुई घर संपत्ति नासी। मूंड मुडाय भए संन्यासी।।

Knowledge is also of two types-Para and Apara. The luminary of Ved-Angira in his discourse expresses its form in this way-Rigved, Yajurved, Samved, Atharvaved, education, arts, grammar, poems and astrology-these are Apara and in the knowledge where one has the enlightenment of Indestructible Brahma, it is Para. Para knowledge is self-knowledge by which human beings get free from the bondage of life and death. He attains salvation.

'सा विद्या या विमुक्तये' अथवा 'ये नाहं नामृता स्याम् तेनाहं किं कुर्याम्।'

These types of statements, express the desire for this type of knowledge. In the Upanishads, there is the detailed description of Para, Knowledge of Brahma or Self-knowledge. Through Apara knowledge man tries to attain the ability to procure materialistic comforts in this world. This knowledge is also of the best category. The progress and development of the world is on the basis of this knowledge. This knowledge alone inspires towards Para knowledge.

In the context of two among the group of gods, the doctors of gods, Ashwini Kumars are reminded naturally. These two twins were born from father Ashwaroop Vivaswan and his wife Sangna. Both these two brothers are known by the name of Ashwini kumar. As such their names are Nasatya and Dasra. Dhanvantri and Shushrut, teachers and experts of Ayurved, are their disciples. Pandus wife Madri gave birth to Nakul and Sahadev with the help of Ashwini kumars. With two, we recollect the two incarnations of Vishnu-Anshavtar (part in carnation) and Poonavatar (compete incarnation). The field of work of Anshavatar is single faceted. The result of their works remain incomplete. Lord Parshuram is the Anshavatar of Vishnu. He destroyed the lustful and evil Kshatriyas, but there remained the persons of extreme evil elements like Bali and Ravana. To complete the incomplete work of Anshavatar Parshuram, Poonavatar Ram was born as an incarnation. Poonavatar Aishwarya (Prosperity) and Madhurya (Sweetness), both are complete with power whereas among Anshavatars these exclusiveness is not seen. Among the ten avatars of Vishnu only Ram and Krishna are Poornavatars.

While counting and dividing the period of a month, there are two fort nights-Dark fortnight and Light fortnight. In Northern India, the month begins from dark fortnight and in South India it begins from light fortnight. In northern India, the date of dark night or Amavasya is 30. In this context, the calendar of South India is more accurate and appropriate fifteen days of a month, that is after full moon, Pratipada to Amavasya, the period is Krishna-Paksh (Dark fortnight). When the moon gradually grows then it is Shukla-Paksh (Light fortnight) and when the full moon gradually decreases and completely become dark this is called Krishna-Paksh (Dark fortnight). The earth is also divided in two parts-an imaginary line of division, on one side is Uttarayan (movement towards north) and Dakshinayan (movement towards South), so named Uttarayan is called the days of the gods and Dakshinayan is called the night. India is situated in Uttarayan, so Uttarayan is considered auspicious in our country. Post winter (Shishir), spring and summer are the seasons of Uttarayan rains, autum and pre winter are the seasons of Dakshinayan. Therefore, during the period of Dakshinayan mostly auspicious occasions are exempted. Period is related to the sun. Therefore, when sun is towards the north, then the movement of sun is called Uttarayan. Seasonal changes are dependent on the position of the sun in north or south. It is the desire of Indians that during their death, the sun's movement should be in Uttarayan. The son of Ganga, Bhishma, had taken oath on the bed of arrows for the sun's movement to Uttarayan.

Because of two Dvait theory was established, Soul and Brahma or Brahma and living is based on this theory. The propagator of the Dvait theory is Madhvacharya. He believes in the difference of life and god. Considering Brahma as truth, they do not consider life and world as untruth. In the beginning, Madhvacharya had taken his tutelage in the path of Shankara, but later on he deviated from this path, differed from one soul theory (Ekatmavad) and Advaitwad and established Dvaitvad (two soul theory). Two kinds of people are considered glorious in this world. 1. Who does not speak harsh language and 2. Who does not give hospitality to ill mannerly persons? Two types of persons remain very happy and joyful- 1. One who forgives even being strong and capable, 2. One who takes interest in charity even though he is poor-

'द्वाविमौ पुरुषो राजन् स्वर्गस्योपरि तिष्ठतः।
प्रभुश्च क्षमया युक्तो दरिद्रश्च प्रदानवान्॥

—विदुननीति-1-63

Wealth is used in improper way in two ways. 1. By giving charity to undeserving, 2. Denying to give charity to the deserving, wealth given such is not used in a proper way-

न्यायागतस्य द्रव्यस्य बोद्धव्यौ द्वावतिक्रमौ।
अपात्रे प्रतिपत्तिश्च मात्रे चाप्रतिपादनम्॥

—वही-1-16

Two persons are destroyed by the earth-1. King who does not oppose an enemy, 2. Brahmin who does not serve in a foreign land.

द्वाविमौ ग्रसते भूमिः सर्पो बिलेशयानिव।
राजानं चाविरोद्धारं ब्राह्मणं चाप्रवासिनम्॥

—वही-1-58

Two should be tied to stones around the neck and drowned-1. Wealthy man who does not give in charity, 2. Poor man who does not work hard-

द्वावम्भसि निवेष्टव्यो गले बद्ध्वा दृढ़ा शिलाम्।
धनवन्तमदातारं दरिद्रं चातपस्विनम्॥

—वही-1-65

Two types of persons reach heaven after penetrating the sun's galaxy-1. Sanyasi who is a yogi, 2. Courageous and valiant soldier who faces death fighting in the war field.

द्वाविमौ पुरुषव्याघ्र सूर्यमण्डलभेदिनौ।
परिव्राड् योगयुक्तश्च रणे चाभिमुखो हतः॥

—वही-1-66

The wife of rishi Kashyap, Vanita's two sons are exclusive and extra ordinary in their own fields. Garud became the carrier of Lord Vishnu, who is the extraordinary one in speed. Second son Arun is the charioteer of sun, who being invalid also drives the chariot that has one wheel and seven horses. The savior of Veda Kumaril Bhatt mentioned two reasons for getting burnt in the fire of snow-1. To prove disloyalty to his Buddhist guru, Dharmakirti of be the reason for the destruction of his progeny, 2. According to prior evaluation, the proposition of god's existence. God is existing in Shruti and is prosperous by the world. Therefore to find the meaning of god is a sin. Analysts believe in Veda, not in God.

A woman makes two families holy. The father's and husband's family is holy because of the holiness of women. King Janaka expresses his satisfaction by saying **'पुत्री पवित्र किए कुल दोउ'**. When Draupadi goes to Kunti to seek her permission to go to the forest, Kunti says **'साध्वीगुणसंम्पन्ना भूषितं ते कुलद्वयम्।'** You are enriched with the good qualities of a sati, you have glorified the positions of husband and father. Inspiration is of two types- 1. Outer and 2. Internal-Outer inspiration can be seen with the eyes or heard with the ears that means its facilitators are the senses whereas internal inspiration evolves in the mind or soul. State of the body has two differences-outer state and inner state. As per outer state the five senses and five works of the senses is included whereas in internal state the mind, intelligence, ego and feelings are counted. Outer state works under the influence of inner state.

The sighting of the moon is always enchanting but the sighting of the moon on the second day is not only enchanting, but also believed to be auspicious. Seeing the second day moon of Shukla Paksh, even today the village folks greet each other by saying 'Dooj ki Ram Ram'. The Yama dwitiya moon is important and famous in Puran. On this day sisters pray for the well-being of their brothers Whether it is winter or summer, the time of noon gives heat. The land that produces two harvests, Rabi and Kharif is considered good. In Yoga scriptures, there is the vital importance of two nerves Ida and Pingla on the two sides of Sushumna nerve. They are also called Ganga-Yamuna. According to Yoga scriptures the southern breath is named Pingla in which Shiva resides and the northern breath is Ida or Ingla in which the Godess of Power resides. It is the work of the devotee to merge one into another. Ida is situated or the right side of the spine system as is the nerve dominated by the sun. Pingla is called as Ganga and Ida Yamuna. In the centre of the spine is the moon, sun, fire kind of Sushumna nerve. All these three converge at the Mooladhan Chakra.

In India, there are two such holy cities where Lord Shiva has Joyful Dance (Anand Tandav) all the time- Kashi and Alka, Kashi is the land of karma. Devotess do their sadhana here. They reach the highest levels of knowledge.

Since the ancient times to this day, its supremacy is permanent in the field of knowledge. Alka is a city of Lust. Kuber is the ruler here, the god of wealth. This is the city of the successful. Both these two cities have the blessings of Shiva. Kashi is considered the city of Lord Vishwanath. Kashi has a geographical place but Alka is an ancient city. Two things should never be forgotten- 1. One who has been kind and generous to us and 2. The crime committed by us. Two things should be immediately forgotten. 1. The kindness and generosity by us and 2. The ill behavior or bad words by somebody to us. Fools are also of two types- 1 One who gives advice without being asked and 2. One who does not believe in giving even good advice. In this world, in comparison to other living being, human beings have two specialties. Only a man walks with his head high towards the sky and only a man's hair changes color. Venom is of two types. 1. Static Venom that is produced from medicines or edible roots, 2. Jungle Venom is produced from sun's rays, scorpion, mosquitoes and insects.

The worship of god is also by two means-knowledge and devotion or Nirguna and Saguna. Those on the path of knowledge, worship the Nirakar image of god. Worshippers of Saguna consider the sakar or real image of god as the basis of their worship or devotion. But Goswami Tulsidas does not fall in the clutches of this difference, he considers both as the path of salvation from earthly bonds-

ज्ञानहिं भक्तहिं नहिं कछुभेदा। उभय हरहिं भव सम्भव खेदा।।

In worship Nirakar has no image, no dimensions. It cannot be seen with the senses, but the image of Saguna's image is seen, voice can be heard, feel the comfort of his touch. Nirguna and Saguna are both the images of Brahma. Tulsidas says-

अगुन सगुन दुइ ब्रह्म सरूपा। अकथ अगाध अनादि अनूपा।।

This world has two names which defines a person. A person is identified due to these two. One is due to looks or beauty and second due to name and reputation. Ramayan and Mahabharat are the two epics of Indian culture. This is known in the form of ancient literature. For all Indian languages and their literature these two literatures have been the source. In the cult of Guru Nanak, there are two paths of followers-Udasi and Nirmala. Nanak's son Chand had established the path of Udasi and Guru Govind Singh has the credit for the birth of Nirmala path. Pandu who became famous for his five sons, his two queens Kunti and Madri are also the two names known to all.

Yudhishthir, Bheem, Arjun are the sons of Kunti, and Nakul, Sahadev are the sons of Madri. Madri became a sati with Pandu. Therefore, all the five sons were raised by Kunti that is why, all these five are collect Kunti's sons.

Two types of weapons are used in war those that are thrown and hit are called ammunition and those that are operated by hands is called weapons. A couplet with two lines is called doha, although it has four steps of expression. Like the doha, there is also the dohi couplet with two lines. In doha the numbers are 13-11, and in dohi 15-11. Dojiya or a woman who is pregnant with twins is considered as holy as per her desire. To fulfill this desire of Sita Ram went to the woods with Lakshman. Though it was later turned into exemption. Ganesh and Kartikeya are two brothers and sons of Shiva-Parvati. Ganesh has two wives Riddhi and Buddhi and also two sons by the names of Shubh and Labh. Dance having many forms has two main differences-Tandav and Lasya. The dance of man is called Tandav. This dance is related to Lord Shiva dance related to a woman is called Lasya. This is connected with Goddess Parvati. The first play directed by rishi Bharat-Yam-Yami dialogue has Shiva Parvati who both present dance.

In Gita and in Chhandogya Upnishad, the travel to heaven, after death has two distinct paths-1. The learned, by their selfless meditation, go to Brahma land through the route of godly flight, from where he does not have to return. 2. The persons who perform yagna and do charity and with the feeling of goodwill, such devotes reach the Moon Land, through their father's flight where they have the pleasures of their good deeds, and when their karma diminishes, they return. Gita has named these two travels as Shukla Gate and Krishna Gate. Yagna is also of two types- 1. In the ones where only the Vedic mantras are used in the function, they are of the first category. In the second category of yagna ancient and Vedic and Tantrik literature and its various practives is being accepted. By performing these yagnas, results are acquired. Rajsuya Yagna, Ashwamedh Yagna come under the category of the routine Yagnas or temporary Yagnas. Two things make our body weak. 1. One who is poor and desires for valuable thing. One who shows anger even when he is weak and incapable. In Mahabharat two valiant soldiers were away from the war. One Balram and second Rukmi. Balram has sympathy towards the Kauravas, but seeing Krishna on the side of Pandavas, went on a pilgrimage to the place of Prabhas. Because of Rukmi's high boasting, both the parties has declined to take any help from him. Catastrophes are of two types. One is external second internal. These two have two differences- 1. Created by self (Swakrit) and 2. Created by others (Parkrit). The catastrophe which is the reason of our self is Swakrit and the one whose reason is somebodyelse is Parkrit.

Intelligence is of two kinds-Simple and Evil or complicated. The behavior of a king should be simple, but be should have the knowledge of both. A king has two types of strength and power- 1. Prakrit and 2. Aharya. Prakrit is of four types family, lot of wealth, secretary and intelligence. Aharya has eight things-elephants, horses, chariot, infantry, boat, other things, people of the country and animals. Pleasure or happiness is of two types-Physical and Mental. Charity is also of two types-one for the other world and one for this world, charity given to good people is of the first kind and those given to bad people is of the second kind. Two is also related to food. In the Shanti Parva of Mahabharat, Bhishma says-

सायं प्रातर्मनुष्याणामशनं वेदनिर्मितम्।
नान्तरा भोजनं दंष्टमुपवासी तथा भवेत्।।

Food is supposed to be taken by man in morning and evening, according to the texts. There is no rule to have food in between. One who follows the rule of taking food twice, he gets the benefit of fasting. Materials are of two types-dead and living. Living are those which have speed and movement like human-beings, animals, birds, etc. Dead or non-living does not have its own speed or movement like the five earthly elements, iron, mud etc. Those who consider the world to be the (Vishvraksh) or Tree of Poison, also show two elixir for it-1. Devotion towards God and 2. Good company of the devotees. Brahma is also seen in two images-1. Word Brahma that is Veda and 2. The Almighty. Word is created out of letters. Therefore words are also immortal Almighty is within himself and Veda is without life. Karma are of two types-1. With activity and 2. Without activity. First category puts us in the wheel of work and travel and the second gives us freedom from this wheel.

Thoughtfulness has two sides. Self-thought is one's thought, one's deep thinking, one's opinion or experience and expression. To explain some thought through discussion or some other medium is other thought. One has food at someone else's place under two conditions-1. There is mutual love among the two or 2. One who desires to have food is in trouble. Krishna had rejected to have food from Duryodhan on these two basis. This human body has two types of mechanics-1. Self-service and 2. Dependent service-Respiratory system gastric system, heart etc. machines, continuously give service to the body without even resting. These come in first category. Hands, legs and other senses make movement only when they get the orders and advise. That is why their importance is less in the body. If hands, legs, and eyes are removed from the body, then also the body is living, but without the respiratory system and heart, it will be dead. Fruits on the trees are also of two types-1. One that has a flower first which turns into fruit. That is in first category, like mango, guava etc. On the second category of trees fruits are borne without any flower like peepal, banyan and gular etc. All types of produce are divided into two types-1. Natural and 2. Man-made. The produce of the farmer is the gift of nature. Whatever is produced from knowledge and learning is the gift of the society because both are acquired from the society. So the production of this category comes under man-made category.

To hit upon a king or a cow is a sin similar to the killing of foetus in womb. The king is the representative of god and within the body of a cow all gods reside, this is the belief of religious people. So one should not hit upon them. A Kshatriya should always protect two-1. Brahmin and 2. Ved. The result of two is seen immediately-1- The chanting of Brahmin and 2. Ved. The result of two is seen immediately-1. The chanting of Brahmin and 2. The courage of a Kshatriya. The king of Ayodhya Dashrath's four sons have two sons each, Rama has Luv-Kush, Bharat has Tarksh and Pushkar, Lakshman has Chitrangad and Chitraketu, and Shatrughna has Subahu and Shoorsen. In Jainism two types of non-violence is mentioned. On the physical ground which is called violence. Second on the mental ground which is called Anekant or the faith of having trust in the opinion of truth of others, although it may not be seen by us. The thought of this type of thinking is the process of mental non-violence and it is known as Anekantvad. Two things always exist in the lives of human-being-1. Fear of sorrow and 2. Temptation of happiness. God is supposed to have two faces-1. Fire and 2. Brahmin. Knowledge is of two types-1. Natural or god gifted and 2. Temporary or Acquired with effort. The knowledge about animals and birds is of the first type. Natural knowledge does not increase. That goes on and on generations after generations, whearas temporary knowledge goes on growing and expanding. In this world, there are two basis for events or happenings-1. Hard work and 2. Destiny. Hard work is under our control but destiny is under the control of God.

Tulsi says, that in Kaliyug, immoral propaganda and sins are dominant. Everywhere we see lecherous and sinful people. In such a situation, only two are the saviours of mankind:-

कलि पाषंड प्रचार, प्रबल पाप पांवर पतित।
तुलसी उभय अधार, रामनाम सुरसरि सलिल।।

The bad results of two things are to be faced by the entire society-1. Where undeserving people are admired and honored and deserving people are despised and neglected. In such a place catastrophe, death and fear create the terror-

अपूज्या यत्र पूज्यन्ते पूज्यानाम च विमानना।
त्रीणि तत्र प्रवर्तन्ते दुर्भिक्षं मरणं भयम्।।

When two is pronounced many couples come to our memory. At somewhere it is of equal rank and friendly and at others it is enemy like or unequal rank like Ram-Krishna, Ram-Lakshman,

Sita-Ram, Radha-Krishna, Man-Woman, Man-God, Husband-Wife, Father-Son etc. are the duos that are equal rank or friendly category but Truth-Untruth, Sin-Virtue, Ram-Ravana, Benefit-Harm, Lose-Win, Reputation-Disgrace, Happiness-Sorrow, God-Demon, Life-Death, Enemy-Friend, Wealthy-Poor, Victory-Defeat, Honor-Dishonor, Heaven-Hell, Good-Bad, True-Fake, Yogi-Lustful, etc. duo words are of unequal rank or enemy category. Apart from these two categories there are other duo words which are not of equal or unequal status, but when two are mentioned, they immediately come to our memory like Animals-Birds, Insects-Butterfly, Woods-Serenade, East-West, North-South, Ganga-Yamuna, Water-Land, Imagery-Non-imagery, Activity-Retirement, Faith-Devotion etc. In the category of equal and unequal couples, in the absence of one the other automatically disappears. Their inter-relationship is described by the great poet Sumitranandan Pant as such-

'बिना दुख के सब सुख निस्सार, बिना आँसू के जीवन भार।
दीन दुर्बल है रे संसार, इसी से क्षमा दया और प्यार॥

In the light of the importance of two and its positive aspect, some things can be said in its otherwise aspect of negativity. Double faced and mouth person is lecherous and is disliked by all. Dogala is such a bad word which is not possible to tolerate. This expresses a dual and underlying meaning. Dogala is an illegitimate child. Hybrid seeds may become very popular the mixing of blood is shameful. A person is also detested for talking in two different ways.

At some situations two gives a permanent statement like Ram clearly says- **'रामो द्विर्नाभिभाषते'** Ram does not say two things, Yudhshthir does not get loan from two families. Struck by jealousy, Duryodhan tells his father Dhritarashtra- 'O king! Panchal due to relation and Andhak and Vrishni due to friendship, both the families don't give any tax to Yudhishthir-

द्वौ करौ न प्रयच्छेतां कुन्तीपुत्राय भारत।
सम्बन्धिकेन पांचालाः सख्येनान्धकवृष्णयः॥

—महाभारत, सभापर्व 52-49

Arjun has two pledges-1. Not to express pity and 2. Not to run away from war

'अर्जुनस्य प्रतिज्ञे द्वे न दैन्य न पलायनम्'।

When the two are glorified, Shwetashwar Upnishad's mantra cannot be left out where both god and living are friends and are mentioned as sitting on the branch of a tree- **'द्वा सुपर्णा सयुजा सखाया समानं वृक्षं परिषस्वजाते'** On a tree like nature, man and god like two birds are sitting. These two are friends. Among them the living birds has birth, age, connection, feelings like happiness and sorrow, tastes the fruits of it and the other is the god like bird, who does not taste the fruits but remains as witness. The living birds stays on the nature like tree with attraction and also gets deceived, bemoans, but after being free from bondage, sees his other friend, god, and becomes free of sorrows after seeing his magical powers and magnificence. A son born to an unmarried mother is of two types-1. Kanin and 2. Sahodh. One who is born before marriage, is called Kanin, like Karna. One who comes into the womb prior to marriage and is born after marriage is called Sahodh. The mothers of these sons whom they marry, they are believed to be their fathers.

Worldly disease can be destroyed by two medicines-1. Study of good literature and 2. Company of good people. In the end, it will not be inappropriate to say in this short life of two days, those who put their legs on two boats to move, may think themselves to be smart and clever, but in the end they have to crave for even two grains. With these very thoughts, those Indians who have faith in 33 crores gods and goddesses, worship the duo mothers and duo body, Ganesh in the beginning. By accepting the importance and greatness of two, there will not be any limitation of two slices of bread (roti) also there will be milk-jalebi, dry fruits-misri, milk-cream, ghee-milk for all men and women, whether they take it hot or cold. One has to make a choice between heaven and hell.

❒

3 (Three)

In many languages more than one number is the beginning of plural. Due to the strong faith on god, ved and sanskrit, plural starts with the number three, the cultural, traditional and religious language of India. Plural means many. The number of three, maintains its influence of plurality on the Indian minds. When a farmer, who is far off from literacy and has no connection with the worldly knowledge, tries to measure his crop, he says 'Rama hi Rama' on his first counting number. 'God is One'- what can be the best example for this principle? So number one is for Rama. Second number is (5 ser or 5 kg weight) 'Do Aayee Doa' after that he weighs three saying 'Bahute hi Bahute', that means, the farmer also knows that three is for plurality. That is the reason that the Indian community has accepted the belief of 33 crore gods and goddesses, they believe in worshipping, Tridev, as their first and foremost. This Tridev or Trimurti are only Brahma, Vishnu and Mahesh who are believed to be the reason to create, nurture and destroy. This Tridev is the self-existing Almighty's three idols. Lord Vishnu is the image of good qualities and essence and is the reason for content nurturing, the Raj image of Brahma, as the crops, work for the nature and creation and shiva with Rama qualities destroys. As such, there are three gods. These three gods are the images of the Supreme Ancient Power or Almighty in different forms. Other gods being related to them, come under the category of gods. The wives of these three gods became the goddesses. Because of Shiva, his two sons became gods.

When Tridev or Trimurti represent three qualities, then it is natural for the human being of this world to have the three types of behavior. On the basis of Satva, Rajas and Tamas, man and woman are believed to be of three categories- Excellent, Medium and Low.

The quality of Satva becomes the reason for happiness and acquirement of knowledge. Within the Satva quality sham (Control of mind), Dam (Control on senses), Titiksha (Empathy), Right thought, Meditation, Truth, Kindness, Memory, Satisfaction, Dedication, Detachment towards the material, Faith, Chastity, natural abhorrence towards sin, self-realization, Charity, Politeness, Simplicity etc. are included when there is increase in the good qualities within the body and heart and when the senses and intelligence of mind is on the rise, it is to be understood that Satva quality is increasing. When the senses are closely attracted towards the light of knowledge, the real wants to get the light of philosophy, then there is the height of Satva quality. The special qualities of Rajogun are Desire, Effort, Pride, Thirst, Dissatisfaction, Freakiness, Boastful nature, Plead for money and wealth from gods, dual-mind, Lust for material, Excitement due to intoxication, Attachment towards prestige, False Strength, By being in some industry out of compulsion. Rajogun increases when Greed, Attraction, Desire to do intentional work, Lack of peace, thirst for worldly things are seen as the reason. The qualities of Tamogun are Anger, Non-cooperation, Greed, False talks, Violence, False Plea, False Pride, Hard work, Quarrels, Sorrow, Lust, False Anger, Demeaning behavior, sleep, Hope, Fear, Laziness etc. When lethargy towards duty, unnecessary efforts or likeness for sleep increases, then it should be understood that Tamogun is also increasing. One who has Satva qualities goes to Heaven. One who has Rajogun goes to the sexual side of humans. One who has Tamogun takes birth as animal. The work of all these three qualities is in the position of exemplary qualities, that person is for above recognition and reputation and has the same feeling for friend and enemy and is totally detached from all karmas. All these three qualities, when united with faith and dedication, divide into three parts. Those who are with Satvik (good) faith, worship the gods service which is done with the detachment of fruit and with total faith, such Karmayogi come in the category of Satvik. In the fake pride of getting honor and reputation a person with Rajogun, with the faith of materialism and submerged in Rajas duty, worships demons and monsters. Those with the faith of Tamas worship the ghosts and dead souls. Their duties are inspired by foolishness or persuasion and thus become the reason of harm to others. With this work they themselves also succumb to their own sorrows.

In Srimad Bhagwadgita, tapa has three types. Where there is the description of body dedication, speech dedication and mental dedication. In these the importance of body, importance of the speech and above all the minds specially is accepted. The simplicity and holiness of attitude, to follow chastity, worship of god, brahmin, teacher and learned persons and belief in non-violence come under the tapa of the body. In tapa of the speech, the tongue is to be controlled. The tapa of mind is only possible after the inner self is holy. Such ascetic, with peace, and in the shelter of silence and by experiencing joy, is bent on purifying the mind and heart. Fire is the god of three places. On earth, it is in the form of fire, in sky, it is in the form of lightening and in the universe, it is in the form of sun.

Like asceticism sin is also of three types-Mental, Spoken and Physical. One who commits spoken and physical crime, becomes a criminal of society and state and faces the outrage and deprivation of the society. One who commits mental sin, does not undergo any external punishment but remains unhappy from within. In Veda, all the three worlds are described with all its glory-Earth, Sky and Heaven. The god of the earth is fire, that of sky is wind and that of Heaven is the sun. A religion has three branches-Yagna, study and Charity. Devotion and Asceticism is Yagna. Through study one acquires knowledge or study is knowledge.

Charity is karma or to perform karma, it is charity. Three things are the enemy of learning-Lack of service, Hurriedness and self-Praise. One has to render service to the gurus through their blessings alone, education is acquired. Lack of patience is supposed to be hurry or restlessness. In education, there is the prime need of accuracy and seriousness. Those with self-praise base the lack of curiosity, which is a hindrance in the path of education. Strength or power is of three types- Mantra, Treasury and Relationship or Human. Mantra is mind power, treasury is wealth power and in the man power ones family relatives, friends and acquaintances are included. Strength and power has one more division-the power of god the power of mantra and the power of zest.

To begin any religious duty, for the purification of body, Achaman is done three times, in which water is taken in palms and three times recitation is completed, with 'Om Keshvay Namah'

'Om, Narayanay Namah' and 'Om Madhavay Namah'. This Achaman purifies the three impurities of the mouth. There can be three types of impurities in the mouth-Evil or Harsh speech, Bad and Harmful speech and Untrue or False speech. Evil or harsh speech, bad or harmful speech and untrue and false speech are related to happiness, therefore the moth is impure. With Achaman, it is purified. Three things are considered as sins equal to Brahmin's murder-To gain success by telling lies, to nitpick behind back to a king, and to wrongly accuse the gurus or elders. The importance of a flower is due to three reasons- Beauty, Color and Fragrance. In the flowers where these all three qualities are there in measure, they are considered as more important. On the basis of his thoughts, man has three categories- First, those who love wealth, second those who love reputation and wealth and third those who love reputation and honor. They are counted as the worst, medium and excellent categories simultaneously.

अधमा धनमिच्छन्ति, धनं मानं च मध्यमाः।
उत्तमा मानमिच्छन्ति मानो हि महतां धनम्॥

Ved is the speech of god, without a form. Ved is meant to be knowledge. This wealth of knowledge was divided in three parts, it was called as Vedtrayi, Rik, Yaju and Saam are the synonym of Vedtrayi. Later on, Ved had four parts. Every Ved has normally three parts-Sahita, Brahmin and Upnishad. 1. Sahita is the part of mantras related to the worship and praise of gods. 2. Brahmin is the part in which it is mentioned about the mantras which a Brahmin need to know the uses in different Yagnas. 3. Aaranyak are the mantras establishing the elements and their description in the woods by the rishis. Upanishads come under the Aaranyak. Four Vedas have four Upved. Rigveda has Medicine, Yajurved has Archery, Saamved has Music and fine arts and Atharvaved has Wealth or Economics. In some texts the Upved of Atharvaved is mentioned as Architecture. The ancient experts of Ayurved are from Brahma to Sushrut and many more, among whom Ashwini kumar, Dhanvantari, Parashar, Charak etc. names are most prominent. The propagator of Dhanurved is Acharya Vishwamitra. Singing, dance and theatre come under Gondharvaved, who teachers are simultaneously Narad, Mahesh and Bharat. There are 64 skills associated with Arthashastra is considered as the teacher of Architecture who considered Architecture as Upved. In all these three divisions are-karma, worship and knowledge. The entire collection of mantras in Vedas is divided into three parts. Karmakand means, to clear the impurities of the progress of the heart through some means, matras which speak about the different Yagnas, Upasnakand is to concentrate the mind and idol worship to fight back the frivolousness and its mantras and lastly Gyankand-mantras to inculcate knowledge and fight back illusion, Sahita is the mantra part of Ved. Richas are the recitation of mantras during yagna. In Brahmin texts the invocation of yagna and its procedures along with the results and its process etc. are explained in detail. The content of Upnishads is Brahma and the Element of the Soul. In these there is Supernatural thinking, which is principal. The main collection of Ved mantras is called Sahita Brahman explain the uses of these Ved mantras and their elaborate meaning. Upanishads are the summary Vedas or the last part. Therefore, they are also called Vedanta. Upanishad is principal knowledge. Four Vedas are also called four Sahitas. In every sukta of sahita, there is rishi, god, poetry and connection. Rishis have deeply studied the Vedas, so they utter the mantras. The god is for that mantra in whose praise the mantra is written. Being written in poetic form they are also called poems. The purpose for which a mantra is used that is called the connection or viniyog for example, if we take Gayatri mantra, its rishi is Vishwamitra, god is the Sun, poem is Gayatri and its connection is for the purification of the mind. Every Sahita has its own Brahman. Rigved has two Yajurved has two, Saamved has eleven and Atharvaved has one, that means, total there are 16 Brahman texts. Brahman texts also have three parts-Brahman, Aaranya and Upnishad. Those who give up this world and who move towards supernatural instincts through the study of Aaranyak texts, this is for those who live in the jungles for it. Everty Sahita has its own Aaranyak and Upanishad. Upanishads are about 108 or may be more in number. But 11 Upanishads are more famous. Their names are-Ish, Ken, Kath, Prashna, Mundak, Mandukya, Taitiriya, Yetray, Chhandogya, Brihadaranyak and Shwetashwatar. The Yagnas that are mentioned in Brahman texts, their aim is to attain Heaven and the aim of Upanishad is to make aware of Supreme Knowledge and, attain salvation from the bondage of life and death.

All the four Vedas have emanated from the four mouths of Brahma. The four Vedas are the symbols of speech, mind, breath and eyes of god. Rigveda is a poetic Sahita. This is a Ved of praise, symbol of knowledge, speech is required for praise and knowledge. Therefore, Rigveda is equivalent to speech. Yajurved is a karma Ved. For the skillfulness of karma and its expertise, the concentration of mind is necessary. Therefore, Yajurveda is equivalent to the mind. Saamved is the mantra of music. Music is from the heart. Therefore, Saamved is equivalent to heart or breath. Atharvaved is a scientific Ved and if one wants to gain special knowledge in science, then the eyes have to be kept open. Therefore. Atharvaved is equivalent to the eyes.

As described earlier Ved means knowledge. At the end of Dwapar, Lord Vyas made four Sanhitas from the wealth of knowledge after selecting mantras from the various chapters and later on made his four disciples to deeply study the four Sanhitas. Rik Sanhita to pail, Yaju to Vaishampayan, Saam to Jaimini and Atharva to Sumantu were given for study. According to the Indian belief, in the beginning of creation, god had bestowed the knowledge of Vedas to four rishis. The knowledge of Rigveda to fire, Saamaved to wind, Yajurved to Sun and Atharvaved to rishi angira. After this many rishis who followed, went on to know about the meaning and myths of the Vedas through their deep study, thinking and devotion towards god. Those rishis who understood the myths of the mantras or tried to know the meaning of them, they became the rishis of those mantras. The Vedas were so deep and mystical that in the later period the Vedas were simplified Bahman, Aaranyak, Upnishad, Vedang, Smritis, Religious texts etc. for their disciplinary explanations. The mantras of Rigveda are poetic whose number is 10,580 Yajurved is related to yagna. This is in the form of a prose. In this, there are 40 chapters and 1915 mantras. This is the Ved of Karmakand. In this some mantras are similar to those of Rigveda. From the point of its size Saamved is the smallest among sanhita. In this, there are 1810 mantras. Richas when sung become saam. That is why most of the mantras here are from Rigveda. Some mantras have come twice. The beginning of Indian Music system is from Saamved. Atharvaved is both in prose and poetry. In it, there are 5987 mantras.This is the father of Ayurved, the storehouse of the deep knowledge of medicine.

In this large number of Ved mantras, one mantra is called Vedmata. Gayatri is the best among all mantras. There is the ritual of reciting this mantra every day three times-morning, afternoon and evening. This mantra has three stages. There are eight words, in each phrase. **'तत्सवितुर्वरेण्यम्'** is the first phrase. **'भर्गो देवस्यधीमहि'** is the second phrase and **'धियो यो नः प्रचोदयात्'** is the last phrase. The phrase of the poem is the charan. In this mantra one prays for purification of the mind to god Savita. 'Om' in the beginning of the mantra is the enlightened form of the Almighty and **'भूर्भुव स्वः'** are the great three spaces simultaneously the earth, the sky and the heaven, and the giver of this life. God is reminded to salvage from sorrows and give joy and happiness. In short, in this mantra we all meditate on the pure form of that god, who is worth worshipping and who is the parent of all living beings, the form of knowledge and light, who guides our intelligence to work on the right path.

Ved means knowledge. The acquirement of knowledge is not possible without a guru. There are many gurus. To acquire different types of knowledge on has to learn from many persons. Indians are grateful in nature hence if one letter knowledge is received, we give the position of guru to him. In this big crowd of gurus, three persons are called Atiguru or extra ordinary gurus. These three Atigurus are mother father and teacher. It is a dharma to do their service, to obey them and to take care of them with respect, others are adharma. It is a principle to follow their advice without a second thought **'आज्ञा गुरुणाम् अविचारणीया'**. There is no fault even if one follows their indifferent advices also. This is the reason Parshuram did not have the sin of killing his mother and because of the advice of guru, king Dhrupad does not have enmity towards Arjun, although he wins over Dehrupadi, more so makes him his son-in-law.

A disciple has three qualities-Politeness, Curiosity and Service. One has to go before a guru with politeness and after being faithful, one should show curiosity towards knowledge. If one wants to acquire something from a guru, one should render service to him and make him happy. After the completion of education a disciple had three paths before him in ancient times. 1. To stay forever with his guru as *brahmachari* for his entire life. 2. To return to his home to become a householder. 3. To become a *sadhu* in the jungle. These persons living in the jungle were called Vanprasth. From the word pandit it would naturally mean Brahmin but actually a pandit is a person with the knowledge of Brahma. Such pandits are supposed to have three characteristics according to the Ideologists.

मातृवत् परदारेषु परद्रव्येषु लोष्टवत्।
आत्मवत् सर्वभुतेषु यः पश्यति स पंडितः॥

Pandits are those who consider other women as mothers, others' wealth as a lump of mud and all living being as his own. After the creation of this universe the self-originated god, divided into Trilok or Trijagat which are known by the names of heaven, earth and super nature. All the gods reside in heaven. Super nature is the place of ascetic or holy souls. Vamanavatar of Vishnu gave the king of charities Bali the super nature kingdom after being pleased. Even after the greatness of heaven, human beings living on the earth do not get a permanent residence there. Human to go heaven to enjoy the fruits of their good deeds, but after that they have to again return to the earth. Even sometimes gods come to this earth for its welfare or they come to do penance for their faults and misgivings.

Life is of three types-1. Fit for salvation. 2. Always in the world and 3. Engulfed in darkness. Those who are fit for salvation are gods, rishis, kings and the best people. According to one's karma, each living takes different body forms, enjoying both heaven and hell, are clutched in this bondage of this routine world. Demons, monsters and evil human beings come in the category of dark souls.

A weak person is suppressed by three-King, one who is provider and the strong and able:-

'कहैं इहैं स्त्रुति सुमृति, इहै सयाने लोग।
तीन दवावत निसक ही, राजा पातक रोग॥

Although the holy Ganga rises from the Himalayas and falls into the Bay of Bengal for the students of geography but for the religious minded Indians arises from the nail of Vishnu, and after getting its space in Brahma's kamandal, traverse through the long tresses of Lord Shiva and finally comes to the earth. This is how Ganga is connected to three Gods. So it is three-paths or three streams. It flows in all three worlds. The Milky Way, Bhagirathi or Punyatoya and Patal Ganga- these three names are its three images believed and accepted by the aethist. In Adiparva of the Mahabharat, Ganga has three names- Alaknanda in the land of gods, Vaitarni in the land of father and on land Ganga. Ganga is the other name of holiness. It relieves us from all types of sins. In different countries of the world, there are many centres of religious faith, but there is no attraction like the Ganga in any temple, mosque, gurudwara, river, lake or pilgrimage. Ganga is unique. One get pious by bathing in Ganga anywhere, but at three places bathing in Ganga is of prime importance

'सर्वत्र सुलभा गंगा त्रिषु स्थानेशु दुर्लभा।
गंगाद्वारे प्रयागे गंगासागरसंगमे।।

It is the effort of everyone in this world to eradicate one's sufferings and sorrows. Many types of sufferings are divided into three parts. The rulers of India also aimed that their people should free of these sufferings, the king of Ayodhya, Rama is the ideal of kings. In his kingdom, no one had any suffering, it is said by Goswami Tulsidas in his Ramcharitmanas-

दैहिक दैविक भौतिकतापा। राम राज काहू नहिंव्यापात।।

–रामचरितमानस

Physical catastropes are-physical suffering, pain of the senses, diseases in the mind and body, Material catastrophes are-robbery, dacoits' loot, kidnapping, harm by wild animals, and Godly curses are-famine, flood, earthquake etc. those who are protected are supposed to be more happy than others. These sufferings are also known as super natural, super physical and super godly. Actually all these sufferings are due to lack of knowledge and committed mistakes like falling sick by eating wrong food or remain disturbed after being jealous or be unhappy after doing bad deeds etc., such are the first type. Super materialistic physical suffering are those which are inflicted by other animals-like somebody loots your property or any animal attacks you etc. Natural disaster are super godly. Similarly in this world, there are three main hindrances or obstacles. 1. Happiness in the external world, 2. Hope for immortality in the world of body and 3. Hope for truth in the world of the mind. In the world, man has three stages of life birth, work period and death. This is his three phased life and this is the wheel of coming and going. To free oneself from these circle, one wishes to submerge in the Triveni. Ganga, when it meets its two friends saraswati and Yamuna, then it takes the name of Triveni Sangam. At the Triveni Sangam, where the devotees are unable to see the Saraswati, while standing on the banks of it, they can very clearly see the white Ganga and the blue Yamuna mingle together to be one. Due of three qualities, a person due to his qualities, habits and behavior are affected by three deficiencies or faults-Lust, Anger and Greed. These three are the most vital and strong among many mental deficiencies. Even the greatest of saints, or those with high profile antecedents and also the learned are not able to free themselves from it. Even the migratory saint Narad is engulfed by lust, just like ordinary beings and becomes the person of mockery. Rishis and saints also curse due to anger. Even after being the son of the best Rishi Atri, Durvasa is very famous for his anger. Kings were already in the fear of possible anger of Parshuram. The greed of golden skin, gave Sita lot of suffering and sorrow, this is the fact. The importance of all these three are described by Tulsi as-

सात तीन अति प्रबल खल, काम, क्रोध अरु लोभ।
मुनि विज्ञान धाम मन करहिं निमिष मुँह छोभ।।

-तुलसी दोहवली

Mahabharat calls them as gates to hell.

त्रिविधं नरकस्येव द्वारं नाशनमात्मनः।
कामः क्रोधस्तथा लोभस्तमादेतत्ययं त्यजेत्।।

-भीष्मपर्व-40-21

According to the ideology of Vidur other three destructive deficiencies or faults are described. The entire Kaurav dynasty ended due to the greed of other's wealth. Bali was killed because he had relations with other's woman. We find lots of people who are ruined after alienating from a true friend. Dharma is dead when one has relations with other's wife. Age is dead when one extorts other's wealth and reputation is dead when one leaves his true friend-

'हरणं च परस्वानां परद्यराभिमर्शनम्।
सुहृदश्च परित्यागस्त्रयो दोषाः क्षयावहाः॥

-विदुरनीति-1-70

One who is controlled by Tridosh (three faults) is encircled by Trimad (three attractions) Lost in the attraction of family, Ravana loses everything. People who are mad about wealth are seen everywhere. It is seen that the worshippers of Saraswati are bloated with pride due to their high knowledge. It is prevalent to put the titles of one's education before one's name, as the high sign of education. Those who are afflicted with and are full of Trimad and Tridosh, they become the three gates of hell for them. Lust, Anger and Greed are such gates, by entering these three gates one travels straight to hell. Three types of human beings-low, medium and best, according to their levels and standards take shelter of three ways-low, medium and the best and try to reach to their destinations or goals. To be free from all these faults and attractions, in Indian culture one needs to perform Sandhya three times a day according to the ritual, which is performed in morning, noon and evening. By doing this Sandhya, one gets the knowledge of Tripath. Karma, Knowledge and Worship named Tripath take the person towards good path. They can also be stated as Karma, devotion and knowledge. Lord Krishna has described these three paths in chapter 18 of Gita. First six chapters teach Karmayog, middle six chapters teach Bhaktiyog and the last six chapter teach Gyanyog. A person may take the shelter of any path the end result is the benefit of closeness to the Almighty. If one walks in life amalgamating all these three, then there is welfare for all. Its neglect is not favorable. Great poet Jai Shankar Prasad writes-

ज्ञान दूर, कुछ क्रिया भिन्न है, इच्छा क्यों पूरी हो मन की।
एक दूसरे से न मिल सके, यह विडम्बना है जीवन की॥

-कामायनी

Mind has three powers-Power of Desire or Ambition, Power of Work and Power of Knowledge. First the desire is born then the mind works towards the fulfilment of that desire but to see the right fruit or result of that work the mind requires the power of knowledge.

Gods, demons and humans are the children of the Almighty. After the penance of Brahmacharya, all the three went to their father at different times and asked for his advice and guidance. The father said only 'D' and asked them what they understood. All three found separate answers the gods said with the word 'Daman', that one should have control over one's desires and requirements. Humans gave the meaning as 'Daan' (charity) and the demons gave the meaning as 'Daya' (Saympathy). All these three should be owned by one for best life. Guru Nanak put three ideals before his disciples. 1. To work hard. 2. To share and eat and 3. To chant the name of god. There are three main reasons of man's sorrows-1. Ignorance 2. Indifferent behavior and 3. Lust for sex and others. Due to ignorance we deviate from our paths or due to indifferent behavior fall for sorrows in relationships. Different types of lusts also compel us to fulfill them despite tolerating the sorrows. Selfishness has three differences personal, group and national. Low type of human beings are limited to their own selves, whereas the medium type of human beings also keep in mind the interest of the self along with the interests of community and nation. Those are the best human beings who work keeping the national interest in the forefront.

Those persons who wish to get anything need to do three kinds of karmas- 1. Routine work, 2. Temporary work and 3. Desired work. Routine works are those which are to be done on daily basis like Sandhya, bath, worship etc. that work which is done as being present on some unusual occasions. Temporary karma is like birth and death in somebody's house and yagna being performed for sutak and patak occasions. Desired work is that which is done with societal or other responsibilities such as pilgrimages, keeping awake at night for devipuja, fasting or penance etc. Those works in which one has no self-interest and which are done for the welfare of others, are the karmas of the highest category-dig wells, to build temples or rest houses, build schools etc. Karmas are further divided into three- 1. Sanchit (accumulated), 2. Prarabdh (Own's effort) and 3. Kriyaman (Present), these are associated with all human beings. The collection of the result of karmas done by a person is Sanchit karma. The results may be both good and bad. These good or bad karmas do not get their results together. Therefore from the Sanchit the Karma that has to be undergone that all is called Prarabdh karma. That karma which is done in the present is called Kriyam or karma. All these three depend on Kriyaman karma. If Kriyaman is good then everything improves. Kriyaman becomes Sanchit. The culture that is inculcated through knowledge and then accumulated these are only called Sanchit karma, and the good and bad results of this Kriyam which adhered that is only Prarabdh karma. Therefore, if the present is right then past and future are automatically set right.

Like the three karmas, there are also three charities. The highest category of charity is to give charity to those who are dependent on us, these who serve us and those who come to our door for begging. Charity for any occasion is life giving at the time of marriage, birth or on the occasion of getting any success or honor. Any charity when done with hope of getting something elusive or for the accumulation of piety is called Kamya-daan. But, three charities are given the name of Mahadaan (great charity) like Godan (charity of cow), Bhumidaan (charity of land) and Vidyadaan (charity of knowledge). They are said to be the best for the reason that from a cow one gets food and wealth from the land. Crops are procured and from education one gets knowledge. Man passes through three stages. According to philosophers there are no stages than Wakefulness, Dreams and Unconscious. During wakefulness, man works and his senses are all active. In dreams the body and senses are silenced but the mind keeps on working and it is felt, apparently, that body and its other parts are active. In the state of unconsciousness neither we have the feeling of the body nor the senses that is the state beyond happiness and sorrow. Yogis also state about a fourth stage and that is Turiyavastha. Turiyavastha is the complete eradication of death of life's lusts and a state of pure awakening. After attaining this state man rises above all worldly sorrows. Due to ego the feeling of happiness and sorrow is awakened and dreams are there in both the stages.

In awakened state the mind, senses and intelligence all are active in their tasks whereas in dreams there is only the world of the mind. Although the senses are quiet in our dreams, we still experience them. In unconscious state, the mind is lost in the soul, its relation to the world is cut off. This is also the state of Samadhi but there is the difference of feeling. In Samadhi, the mind knowingly and decidedly breaks its relationship with the worldly matters, but the life feeling is there. After awakening from the unconscious state a person again become worldly whereas after Samadhi, he attains Buddhatva enlightened and becomes a Paramhans (Supreme Swan Soul).

Every person who comes to this world is bound by three debts or obligations. Everybody desires to be free from it. The success of this life is to be free, from father's debt, rishi's debt and god's debt. Our parents have given us birth it is not possible to repay their debt, but by serving them and by forwarding their progeny, where we express and show our gratitude, at the same time we fulfill the desire of god's creation. The solution freedom from this debt is to procreate able children, who work for the welfare of people. As heredity, we get attained knowledge from the rishis. To acquire that knowledge one should study while following the path of chastity, and one should give that knowledge to others through teaching, lectures and discourses, and advice. Then only we can be free from rishi debt. By the blessing of god we get food, water, air, fire, vegetable, flowers and fruits all these things for our beneficial use. Through the medium of yagna we express our obligation to the gods. Fire is the mouth of the gods. By putting Ahuti(offering) into it we return their charity. **'त्वदीयं वस्तु गोविन्द तुभ्यमेव समर्पये।'** By this statement, we express the same feeling. By satisfying the gods by performing yagna, modern scientific minds should take the assumption that the pollution we create in this clean environment of nature, we should try to end it or reduce it by performing yagnas. Actually, service done for the welfare of people or for the nurture of body, as a means are all yagnas. In a yagna, the most important is the Ahuti (offering). Through karma also, one gives offering of his knowledge and strength. By the offerings in yagna, the atmosphere becomes scented. The fragrance of karma of a person also remains for long. Some learned have also quoted a fourth debt which is called human debt. By being kind to all the living, one ban be free from this debt.

Having come to this world, one needs wealth for one's discharge of duties. In Varnashram system the householder is only the owner of wealth. A householder has three types of wealth. Shukla (white) wealth is that which is attained according to one's varna or work division and in legal way. In today's reference it is called white money. Shabal wealth is that which is attained through other's work or just extorted, procured from wrong means or procured as a means of generosity or obligation. This wealth is immense with today's leaders of state and administrative officials. Illegal or black wealth is that which is earned through dishonesty, cheating, robbery, looting, kidnapping, mixing bad things, false interest on money. This is black money is English dictionary. All these three types of wealth are the Best, the Medium and the Worst respectively. The householder is said to be the owner of wealth, but three are kept away from its right of owning. Wife, servants and son cannot be the owners of wealth, because the wealth that is earned belongs to the one under whom these are there. The husband is the Swami of wife, the servant is the wealth of the owner and the wealth of a son is his father.

'त्रय एवाधना राजन् भार्या दासस्तथा सुतः।
यत् ये समधिगच्छन्ति यस्य ते तस्य तद्धनम्।।

–विदुरनीति–1–69

Many things are got when we come to this world. But three things almost remain elusive-1. Birth of man, 2. Desire for salvation and 3. Closeness of good people. According to Indian belief, after taking birth in 84 Lakh wombs, one gets the birth of a human being, but offer that also man is encircled by desires, ambitions and lusts, and then death arrives. Human life ends. There are very rare human-beings who have the awakening of the cycle of travel and freedom from its bondage in their minds. This is one kind of cycle. One gets human form of life due to the result of pious deeds in the previous birth. When one craves for the freedom of bondage and when there is an awakening then he seeks the third rare thing as his goal, the search for the close company of good person. Goswami Tulsidas considers good company above heaven and salvation

'तात स्वर्ग अपवर्ग सुख धरिअ तुला एक अंग।
तूल न ताहि सकल मिलि जो सुख लव सतसंग।।

When the desire for salvation arises, if a person gets the privilege of the good company of a saint, then there is the possibility of getting freedom from the bondage of arrivals to the world. For this one should have kindness towards all living things love towards god and service to all humans, these three best dharmas should be followed. In this world, people are of three complexions- Fair, Dark and Yellowish. All the three types have the desire for prosperity. Prosperity are of three types- Best, Medium and Worst. As mentioned earlier, the three means to acquire wealth, according to that the prosperity is also of the same category. Three things are expected to be kept in mind on acquiring the best of category of wealth. 1. Not to have the intention of exhorting other's wealth. 2. To be constantly pursuing to fulfill one's duties and 3. To protect what one has earned. Rishi Davel sees three types of sparks in a man-Offspring, Karma and Knowledge are the three sparks or light. When one has these three at its best, he achieves greatness and after death also these three sparks get recognition.

It is natural to remember Gandhiji's three monkeys, when we mention three. The simple meaning of them is-Don't see evil, Don't hear evil and Don't speak evil. In the Indian context, this is not their meaning but the monkey with closed eyes says-don't see outside, all that is outside is an illusion and false, see the god existing within you. Concentration to any thought is by closing the eyes. Second monkey says-don't hear the noise and humdrum outside, listen to the Almighty within your heart, listen to your heart, listen to your soul. Heart never tells the untruth and evil. Normally it is said- 'Do whatever your heart tells you. Listen to what you heart tells you. Great poet Kalidas justifies the same fact and says- **'सतां हिं संदेहपदेषु वस्तुषु प्रमाणमन्तःकरणप्रवत्रयः'**. In things that are of suspicion, the heart is the only proof. Third monkey says-Speak that comes from within, what the inner self says, not with the mind. When we listen to the mind, the heart saying becomes the mantra when it is seen and heard from the heart, then it is mantra. Therefore, rishis are the creators of mantras not their listeners nor seers. Rishis did not hear the mantras from outside. Nobody has spoken the mantra to rishis but were seen through the heart that is why they are mantras.

Where Vedatrayi (three Vedas) are mentioned for knowledge, Prasthantrayi is also very important. In Prashthantrayi, Gita, Upanishad and Brhamasutra are included. In these ancient scriptures we find the best philosophical experiences written with intense description. The entire Indian philosophy is included in these three scriptures. It is compulsory for the Indians saints to study all the three of them. In Indian Puranas with Tridev (3 gods) there are three goddesses also- Lakshmi, Saraswati and Parvati. Lakshmi is the goddess of wealth. By her blessings there is wealth, food and attainment of prosperity, Dressed in white and the player of Veena, Saraswati is the giver of knowledge. Goddess Parvati the consort of Lord Shiva, the great and generous god, is deeply touched by the sorrows of others. Her blessings are invaluable. The Almighty who has given three gods and three goddesses expresses himself by three mediums-Truth, Thought and Joy. His image is ever joyful.

For Indians three places- Kashi, Prayag and Gaya are specially important, but Goswami Tulsidas believes Tristhali as Haridwar, Prayag and Ganga Sagar connects all three of them to Ganga and says:-

'गंग अवनि थल तीन बडेरे। एहि किए साधु समाज घनेरे।'

In these cities, Kashi is the city of Lord Bhootnath. It is one of the seven holy cities which gives salvation. By giving the offering of Pind, ancestors get salvation, this is so believed by Indians. Prayag is the king of pilgrimages because of the confluence of Ganga, Yamuna and Saraswati rivers. In Haridwar, first time Ganga comes out of the tresses of Shiva and touches the earth. Submerging all rivers and small tributaries within itself it gives its shape of Ganga and finally it immerses its existence in the sea near Gangasagar. Therefore the famous saying **'सारे तीरथ बार-बार, गंगासागर एक बार'**. It is also believed that those who believe in the importance of these Trishthali (three places) for them. There is no suffering or sorrow from three families-Father's family, Mother's family and In-law's family. With relation to family, a person is connected to this father, mother and in-laws families. It is expected to visit the Trishtati for their family rituals. We feel happy when there is the presence of three qualities in the wind-Cool, Soft flowing and Fragrant, this makes anyone joyful. When three persons-Secretary, Doctor and Guru speak the untruth because of some fear or are afraid to tell the truth, then three things are sure to be destroyed-State or Country, Body and Religion.

A minister, without any fear must give the king advice which may be the most unpleasant but beneficial. A doctor should not shy away from giving to his patient any bitter medicine. A guru should keep on making his disciple aware of his shortcomings Goswami Tulsidas writes-

'सचिव बैद गुरु तीन जौं प्रिय बोलहिं भय आस।
राज धर्म तन तीन कर होइ बेगहीं नास॥

In India, we come across many images of a triangle. Proof is the basis of truth. Proofs are of three types-Real, Assumption or Proof of word, Real or Actual proof is the witnessed, incident seen through the eyes of a person. By seeing the smoke, the information about a fire is through the assumption proof. Word proof are the statements of the learned persons of Ved and ancient scriptures and the religious, truthful, obliged persons, also the statements in religious scriptures are also supposed to be Word proofs. Where we have the Satva, Raja and Tama as the three qualities, we have three main objective of these three qualities. They are service for religion, Accumulation of wealth and Feeling of lust respectively, they are the characteristics of Satva, Raja and Tama qualities. Where which quality is there, its decision can also be done through three things, the karma which gives us the feeling of shame, suspicious and fear, that is Tamas karma. To desire to gain fame, even in poor and pitiful condition when one gives charity to the Charan-Bhat who showers praises is the characteristics of Rajas quality. The attitude through which one can get the purity of the soul, one is not shamed of one's karma, one is always curious, that karma is of Satva quality. The mental and physical differences of karma were discussed in the previous chapter. But in these three each three karmas are considered to be bad or of worst category. The thought of robbery, to have evil thoughts or keep jealousy in mind, these are the worst type of mental category karma. There are three types of physical category of karma, to rob, to cause violence, or going to prostitutes. One who relinquishes pride as drinking wine, honor as absolute hell and prestige as the shit of a pig, he remain happy.

अभिमानं सुरापानं गौरवं घोररौरवम्।
प्रतिष्ठा सूकरी विष्ठा त्रयं त्यक्त्वा सुखी भवेत्।।

In a man's life, there are three strong feelings which are called as Trividh Ishna. The ambition of son, wealth and prestige is the strongest. Through a son a person is living, even after his death. With wealth all worldly amenities and happiness and the hunger for success is always among the best of people. In Buddhist religion there are three gems-Buddha, Buddhist Religion and Community. Those who believe in Gautam Buddha, can have their faith in Buddhist religion and the propagation and extensive broadcast was done through the medium of community (Sangh). That is why they say– **'बुद्धं शरणं गच्छामि, संघं शरणं गच्छामि, धम्मं शरणं गच्छामि।'** No wealthy man is ever mentioned in the four centuries of history of India. We do find the names of meditators, learned, religious, valiant, kings and emperors. But from Satyug till today in the history, no wealthy persons are remembered. In Kaliyug one wealthy person, gave in charity his entire wealth, then his name became immortal in history. Such a charitable man, Bhama Shah had kept three things for himself from his boundless wealth-

'भामाशाह राखी निज संपत्ति में वस्तु तीन।
कीर्ति, इकलौती धोती, लोटा जल पीवे को।।

In three means-Religion, Money and Emotions. These are the three means or Trivarg, and salvation is the god. Money and emotions are good and pure according to religion. Only the householder has the right on money other three ashrams do not possess the right to it, but many a times, even sanyasis are drawn towards money. If a recluse sanyasi goes to a king, there are three reasons behind it. Taste of the tongue, desire for honor or desire for wealth-

राजदुआरे साधु जन, तीन वस्तु को जाय।
कै मीठा कै मान को, कै माया की चाय।।

In the three varnas Brahmin, Kshatriya and Vaishya are two groups. Even after the four varnas, on the basis of, Upanayan ritual or thread ceremony, two become three varnas. Brahmin, Kshatriya and Vaishya should respectively have their Upanayan ceremony at the age of 8, 11 and 12. The age for Upanayan is approved both from womb and age. Even though there are four Yugas, Satyug, Dwapar and Treta are known by the name of Triyug. Three respects come under the faith and devotion towards God, Brahmin and Guru. When three things are under control, a person is called Jitendriya. These three are- Mind, Intelligence and five senses. Senses are activated through the mind. Therefore the mind should be first under control. Strong intelligence can only control the mind. Therefore, after controlling the three one can become Jitendriya. Worship has also three types- The worship for which the services of a karmakandi Brahmin is taken, that worship is commercial. To pass time in old age, to read religious books or perform puja is the worship which is like a profession. To collect some mantras, rote them by heart and to teach karmakand according to the procedures and principles is the worship of earning. The entire living world and the Almighty are included in three. Physical body and nature are mortal or destroyable. Enlightenment and Soul are immortal. Almighty or the immortal soul are imminent.

In India, three rights are of special importance. The time of birth of Krishna on the dark night of Bhadrapad, when all guards guarding the prison of Kansa became unconscious due to supernatural attraction. So it is called Mohratri. The king of Ayodhya Ram returned with his wife Sita and younger brother Lakshman to Ayodhya after 14 years of exile in the jungle. On their arrival all rejoice the whole night as a celebration of joy. Therefore, the dark night of Kartik is called Maharatri. One of the names of Lord Shiva is Mahakal. In Ujjaini, there is a famous temple of Mahakal the dark night of Falgun is called Mahashivratri. It is to be pondered that these three nights are the dark fortnight nights. In the midst of despair alone, hope takes birth. After the birth of Krishna, cruel Kansa will be killed and after the return of Rama ideal Ramrajya will be established. Only through the worship of Shiva benevolence is attained.

In India's religious epics, Ram Katha has special importance. The first singer of Ram Katha is the ancient poet great rishi Valmiki. In this story also, number three has its own special place,

Ram Katha is connected to three places in particular. These three places are Ayodhya, Vindhachal or Pampapur and Lanka, on which the story is centred. In this story, there is meeting and struggle of three communities. The humans of Ayodhya meet the bears and monkeys of Vindhyachal and then both these have a war with the demons of Lanka in the end of the story, it is the meeting point or sangam of three cultures, because in the end the friend of humans, Vibhishan, becomes the ruler of Lanka. Ayodhya is north India, Vindhyachal is middle India and Lanka is in the south of India. This is a story of the unity of India. This story has three heroes.

Ram is the hero of human story. Hanuman is the hero of bears and monkey's story and Ravana is the hero of the story of demons. Among all these three heroes Ram is the great or star hero. Ram perform three main duties in the entire story. His first duty is to protect the good people. To protect the yagna of Vishwamitra, to give assurance to the rishis of Dandkaranya of fearlessness to help to Sugriva and Vibhishan. To suppress the bad people is his second duty. The killing of Subahu, Tadaka, Khar, Dushan, Trishira, Bali and Ravana with his entire family. To establish humanity is his third duty. He did not accept the throne even after Bharat's requests and persuasion, he made Sugriva and Vibhishan as kings, he honored Jatayu, Shabari and Nishad.

Truth also has three condition-Apparent truth, Practical truth, Heavenlytruth. Whatever is seen in magic or dreams is not true, so it is apparent or is seems like truth. Philosophers may call this world untrue, but in practical terms, the things in nature are true. To feel thirst is true and after drinking water, thirst is quenched is also true. This can be seen in all worldly things and relation. Heavenly truth is the only Brahma truth. Ved as the Brahma form is considered as Heavenly truth. Aman comes into the category of a great man when three things happen to him-1. When he has the highest knowledge, 2. When he has a strong inclination to do good work on the strength of his knowledge and 3. When he does extreme struggle to fulfill that desire. Three types of people get the best gift from this earth-Brave, Knowledgeable and those who know their duty. They receive the golden flower from the creeper like earth. Three are so capable and bold that they do not have any accusations. Goswami Tulsidas says-

'समरथ को नहीं दोष गुसाई।
रवि पावक सुरसरि की नाई।।

The sun absorbs both good and bad things-Fire burns sandalwood and even manure. Even if many rivers and tributaries fall and mingle into Ganga or dead bodies are thrown in them, all these three are called holy.

Fathers are of three types. All are aware of the father who gives us our body. He is called the procreator of the body. If any time, there is disaster on one's life, and at that time whoever happens to protect our life from that disaster, he is called the protector but his position is like the father one who provides hand nurtures in the absence of one's own father who is the procreator is called the Annadata or provider of food-

शरीरकृत् प्राणदाता यस्य चान्नानि भुञ्जते।
क्रमेणैते त्रयोऽप्युक्ताः पितरो धर्मशासने।।

Tulsidas has mentioned three types of persons like three fruits Patal, Mango and Jackfruit **'संसार महं पुरुष त्रिविध पाटल रसाल पनस समा।'** Patal or Padar is such a tree on which bloom white and red flowers. They have only flowers, no fruits. In the same way some people only say but they don't go. On a mango tree both flowers bloom and fruits appear. In the same way some people say and also do. On a Jackfruit tree only the fruit appears. In the same way they do not say but only do. Those persons who have faith in stars and planets are afraid on the arrival of the planet Saturn or Shani but if one remembers Gadhi, Kaushik and Piplad, the curse of Saturn is eliminated-

'गाधिश्च कौशिककश्चैव पिप्लादो महामुनिः।
शनैश्चरकृतां पीडां नाशयन्ति स्मृतास्त्रयः।।

As such there have been many saints in this country, but three saints (muni). Panini, Katyayan and Patanjali are well recognized. These three saints are the topmost in their own fields of grammar. Grammar is the root of all knowledge. Therefore, after studying lot many things, one should study grammar, it is so said.

यद्यपि बहुनाधीषे तथापि पठ पुत्र व्याकरणम्।
स्वजनः श्वजनो मा भूत् सकलं शकलं सकृत् शकृत्।।

In the absence of knowledge of grammar, such possibilities are there of misinterpretation. Fire is also of three types. The worldly things that we do in the fire is called the home fire (Grihagni). This fire is also called Davagni. The fire of hunger or gut is downed by the hard work of a person, he takes the help of good and bad means, that is called Jatharagni (Fire of the gut). When this becomes slow and weak one has to go to the rescue of doctors and when it becomes extremely hot, then one suffers from the disease of ashes. Even huge rocks are reduced to mere grains of sand and also there, is the power of lightening in it the fire in water is known by the name of Badavagni. All services which were done or which will be done, for that one has to take the shelter of the three doers (Trikaran)- Mind, Speech and Body. If the periods are divided in three parts, then a day is also divided into three time periods- Morning, noon and evening. Time has no limit. Period cannot be killed still three parts of it are believed- Beginning, Middle and End. This is mentioned by historians as an Ancient period, Medieval period and Modern period.

Lord Buddha may not have been able to believe in three Vedas or three Gods, but after his death his followers divided his advises in three parts which were the three Pitak- Sutrapitak, Vinaypitak and Abhidhammapitak. Like the Tripitak, the followers of his thoughts divided into Triyan- Mahayan, Heenyan and Madhyayan, the three divisions of Buddhism. In Jain religion also, the travel from self-realization to self-knowledge, there are three principles. Through Samyak faith, Samyak knowledge, and Samyak service (karma) it is possible to attain Kaivalya (salvation). These are Samyak darshan, Samyak gyan and Samyak charitra (character) respectively. To give up three types of foolishness is Samyak faith or darshan. To give up human foolishness or the foolishness of the fake mind is Samyak darshan or faith. It is foolish to think that we become pious if we bath in the rivers or the blind faith in the powers of gods and goddesses, or the belief in the miracles of saints. Samyak karma (service) are non-violence, truth, chastity and detachment. Samyak gyan (knowledge) is the belief of the mortality of this world.

Ayurved cannot be neglected or over-looked with reference to three. Among the four Upvedas, Ayurveda is one of them. Ayurveda's entire work is fortified in Tridosh (three facts)- Vaat, Pitta and Kapha or based on Trimalam (three excreta)- Mal, Mutra and Kapha. If there is any conflict between these three then Triphala-Harad, Baheda and Amla is said to be useful, or sometimes Trikut-Sonth, Peepal and Black pepper's use is suggested. From Trikutam-Gokharu, Trishul and Tridhar many medicines are prepared, where even Dhanvantri will be incomplete without Trikshar-Javakhar, Sajji and Suhaga-Trijatak-Cardamom, Cinnamon and Tejpatta are not limited only to medicines and are used for one's prestige and honor also. If Trilavanam (Salt)-Rock salt, Plain salt and Black salt is the basis of all salty medicines, then in drink, avaleha etc. have Trimhadhu (Three sweteners)– Ghee, Honey and Sugar, which cannot be ignored but sometimes do the work of option are Trisharkara – Gur, Sugar and Misri.

Services or duty is rendered in three ways- 1. Like animals 2. Like humans and 3. Like Gods. The category of the human-being is decided according to the feelings he has while doing his duty. The first category of service is done in the fear of suppression or the basis of a stick. This type of service is taken from the animals. The second category of service comes when one is under the clutches of selfishness and greed, and serves others. The third category of service is when one gives up greed and attraction and takes it as his duty in a natural way. In such persons alone there is the existence of god. Swami Vivekanand said that the greatness of a nation depends on its people and to make a person great, he needs to imbibe three qualities- 1. Faith in good powers 2. Freedom from jealousy and doubt 3. To help those who are trying to be good and doing good. During the three time-periods of the day, there is the principle of doing three things. One should do meditation in the morning. In the noon he should work for his earning and in the night one should make love. It is believed to be good if a woman has three parts as prominent- Voice, Heart and Navel. With the heart being deep, there is sweetness of emotions. Deep and sweet voice is attractive. The depth in the navel increases the beauty of the body.

While describing three in the context of Indian culture, there are three swaras (notes) of music – High, Low and Immediate, which have been named as Dirgha, Hraswa and Plut and they cannot be ignored. The notes of music can be divided into three scales on the basis of their pitch- Komal or Mandra, Madhya and Taar. Similarly Indian literatures have talked about three qualities – Prasad, Oj and Madhurya, which express the feelings of Simplicity, Greatness and Softness. The principal, teachers, in the context of love, have mentioned elaborately the description of the nayikas (lover) as Swakiya, Parakiya and Samanya, who wish to meet their lover at a chosen place for love, they are seen as Divasabhisarika, Shuklabhisarika and Krishnabhisarika, in these three forms. Swakiya is one's own wife, Parakiya is unmarried or other woman and Samanya is the state woman. Designated or chosen place is the place of meeting where Parkiya nayika meets the Parkiya nayak. One who goes to the chosen place during the day is called Divasbhisarika. During the nights of Shukla (Moon) Paksha and Krishna (Dark nights) Paksha, the nayikas are called Shuklabhisarika and Krishnabhisarika respectively.

Three should not be left even in the times of distrees- 1. Devotee 2. Servant and 3. One who says I'm yours. This devotee can be of god or even of a human. Servants are dependent on us hence they cannot be abandoned in troubles. Third category is of the one who comes to our refuge. There is elixir in three qualities – 1. Control, 2. Sacrifice and 3. Consciousness of duty. The control of senses is control. In Mahabharat, 18 deficiencies or faults are mentioned. The sacrifice of these faults are the qualities of control of the senses that means one who sacrifices small faults, he has controlled his five senses. These deficiencies are – 1. Contradictory thoughts about duty and no duty 2. False lecture or speech 3. Finding faults with qualities 4. Lust for women. 5. To be always in the action of earning wealth. 6. To have lavish needs. 7. Anger. 8. Sadness. 9. Thirst. 10. Greed. 11. Habit of gossiping. 12. Hurting. 13. Violence. 14. Mourning. 15. Disinterest in texts. 16. Forgetfulness of duty. 17. Useless talks and 18. To think oneself great. Sacrifices are many but six types of sacrifices are said to be of the best category. 1. Not to rejoice after getting wealth. 2. To spend wealth in yagna and in the creation of gardens, lakes and wells. 3. To give up lust having attained Vairagya or detachment. 4. Not to feel sad if unpleasant things happen. 5. Not to crave for a woman or a son and 6. To give charity to a deserving person. Third quality is Apramad that means to be conscious towards duty. In such a person, eight qualities are there- 1. Truth 2. Concentration 3. Holistic thought 4. Compromise (Lack of doubt and Digression in one's heart) 5. Feeling of detachment (Lack of feeling of any attraction) 6. Not to rob 7. Chastity (Lack of eight types of intercourse) and 8. Feeling for least possessions (Lack of accumulation of things). So it is clear that if these three qualities– Control, Sacrifice and Consciousness towards duty, with their many differences come into any person, then always there will be elixir raining on him.

Victory and success have four means- Saam, Daam, Dand, and Bhed but there are three stages of victory acquired from them. Saam or peace, Daam or charity, which means not to confront anybody and make them fearless, the victory achieved through these two means is the best. Through the principle of divide or Bhed, like dividing the enemy and army, this type of victory is of medium category. After a war, the victory achieved after slaughtering is the low or worst category of victory. Three bows are considered to be godly- 1. The bow that Arjun got from fire king, the Gandiva of Varun, which was burnt in the Khandav jungle 2. Indra's victory which Rukmi got and 3. Shanrga which was with Krishna. Behind every work there is some inspiration. This inspiration is also of three types- 1. Inspiration of God. 2. Inspiration due to accidental co-incidence, and 3. Inspiration of our past karmas. Because of them a person sets himself to work.

On the 10th day of the Mahabharat war, Dronacharya had talked about the three ill-fates of the citizens- 1. Anger of Yudhisthir 2. Fight between Bhishma and Arjun 3. To sell the various weapons of war by me (Drona). As a commandant of the Army, one day Dronacharya decided to hold Yudhisthir as a prisoner. Arjun tried to console Yudhisthir and asked him to be fearless. Seeing Yudhisthir's doubt Arjun had said- I don't remember three things- 1. Whether I have even told a lie 2. Whether I have ever been defeated. 3. Whether I have not fulfilled after taking an oath or making a promise. After the Mahabharat war only three brave hearts of Kaurava side were alive- Ashwathama, Kripacharya and Kritverma. Among them Ashwathama and Kripacharya were long living but Kritverma died in the Yadav struggle.

Japa is of three types- 1. Readable when the words of mantra are clearly heard. 2. Upanshu- in which the sound of speech is not heard, only the lips move. Throat is used. 3. Manas- the Japa in which the flow of the meaning is in the mind. According to category Upanshu is better than Vachik (readable) and Manas is better than Upanshu, and is the best. One should not meet these three persons empty handed- Brahmin, King and Woman. One should not go in disguise to these three persons – King, Brahmin and Devoted wife. On being cheated all these three through their curse can destroy the cheater. One who desire for success, should go to them with simple feeling. Indra had to bear the curse of Gautam due to his disguised appearance and Ravana was completely destroyed. Three persons do not have the right to know or listen to the supreme secret mantra- 1. One who is not compassionate? 2. One who is compassionate but not learned 3. One who is both compassionate and learned but his mind is not under his control. These three increase when they remain static. Therefore, these three should never be left to remain in the least. These three are- Debt, Fire and Enemy.

'ऋणशेषं रोगशेषं शत्रुशेषं न रक्षयेत्।

-शुक्रनीति-3-104

In some texts, along with debt and fire, the third is mentioned as disease. Therefore a disease should also be taken out from the roots.

ऋणशेषमग्निशेषं शत्रुशेषं तथैव च।
पुनः पुनः प्रबर्धन्ते तस्माच्छेषं न धारयेत्।।

-महाभारत। शान्तिपर्व 140-58

The interest increases on the debt, due to the wind, the fire lights up, an enemy gathers strength. For all the ashrams there are three types of tapa- Non-violence, Truth and patience. The human beings of this world come under three categories- Enemy, Friend and Indifferent person.

According to Srimad Bhagvad Gita, man is divided into three categories- 1. Mortal person- this world is an example of the mortal person. 2. Immortal person- the soul is the immortal person and 3. The best or the Highest person-the root of this world is the name of that Supreme Element or the Supreme Person. Three sins are considered equal to the murder of Brahma- 1. A wrong judgment or wrong witness given by a judge. 2. To gossip wrongly before a king and 3. Deceitful behavior with a guru. There are three things to see any object in person or reality- Images, Eyes and Light. Images is the object, eyes are the medium and light is the surrounding or the atmosphere.

There are three antonyms of friendship and enmity. Friendship of good people is like a scratch or line on a stone and enmity is like a line on water. The friendship of crooked, mean and bad persons is like the line on stone and enmity is like a line on a stone. Friendship and enmity with common or ordinary people is like a line drawn on sand. Friendship has three levels are Best, Medium and Worst are like the lines drawn on stone, sand and water respectively:-

'उत्तम मध्यम नीच गति पाहन सिकता पानि।
प्रीति परिच्छा तिहुन की बैर बितिक्रम जानि॥

–दोहावली

Earlier, the description of religion as common special and immediate have already been done. On the basis of attitude, religion can be further divided into another three types- 1. Vedokt dharma- Ved are the roots of religion, therefore whatever is written therein, it should be believed as religion. 2. Shastrokt dharma – The following of Vedic religion according to religious texts or their new patterns. 3. The religion which is followed by disciplined people in society, which is also called Samaj dharma. A kshatriya has three duties towards a Brahmin- 1. To protect a Brahmin like a son. 2. To respect him like a guru and 3. To do its service and worship like fire. Three types of persons are capable of getting charity- 1. Those who are unknown earlier. 2. One who has stayed lifelong and 3. One who has come from a far off country? Three things are only for Kshatriyas- Wealth, State and Treasury. Wealth earned through ethics should be divided into three- 1. Through one part one should promote religion and economy. 2. Second part should be used for oneself and 3. Third part should be used for the progress of future generation's incumbent.

Festivals are of three types- 1. Regular 2. Occasional and 3. For desire. The festivals whose time is certain are the regular festival like Deepawali, Holi, Ekadashi etc. Those festivals or celebration that come due to some occasion like the birth of son, marriage, house warming etc. those celebrations that are done for fasting, pilgrimages for puja or for any new venture's inauguration are the celebration of desire.

Kabir believes that it is easy to give up the greed of gold and the love of a woman but it is very difficult to give up desire for prestige, to hear one's praise and jealousy-

कंचन तजना सहज है, सहज त्रिया का नेह।
मान बड़ाई ईरषा, दुरलभ तजनी येह॥

Kabir also says that one who begs, loses his lustre, honor and the feeling of love towards him.

आब गई आदर गया, नैनन गया सनेह।
ये तीनों जबहिं गए, जबहिं कहा कछु देय॥

To make friendship permanent, one should bear three things in mind- 1. No to play tricks on a friend 2. Not to exchange money with him 3. Not to talk to his wife in his absence. While teaching or giving knowledge, out of the three one must at least keep in mind that one benefit is reaped otherwise it is like sowing a seed in a barren land. These are the three benefits- 1. Honor or service 2. Attainment of religion and 3. Attainment of money. Knowledge also has three differences- 1. Trayi 2. Education or Varta and 3. Principle of punishment. Trayi is the knowledge of three Vedas. Education is related to knowledge of farming, animal husbandry, other subjects and sciences. Law and its study comes under the principles of punishment or Dandneeti. Thetreatment of Ayurveda has three differences- 1. Daivi or godly 2. Manushi or Human and Rakshasi or Demonic. Treatment with liquids and light medicines is Daivi, whereas treatment with herbs, flowers and fruits is Manushi. Those treatments which are done after cutting, operation is considered demonic. A body also has three differences- Sthool, Sukshma and Karana. Actual body in its form is sthool. This body is related to the awakened state. Under sukshma body, breath, mind and intelligence are included. The state of dream is related to this. Body in actual form is seen. Its activity is through sukshma(micro) body. Through this micro body we travel in the dream world. Karana body is a state ahead of it.

Advice is of three types- 1. Parents like god, advice given by a guru or king 2. Advice given by a close friend, and 3. Advice politely given by a wife. All three are advices but there is difference in their presentation. Among the many specialties of Indian culture, there are three important symbols- , Ganga and Gayatri, while preparing the birth chart, the born child has one of the three categories-God, Human or Demon. In these three categories all human beings are divided. Similarity there are three nadis- Adi, Madhya and Anta. While fixing the marriage of the sons and daughters of a Brahmin, it is to be ascertained that their nadis are different. Pilgrimages are of three types- Trotter (Jangam), Manas (mental) and Sthavar (Permanent). All saints, Brahmins and sanyasis who travel all around the world are the globe trotters. Because of their good advice, we get the peace of mind and piety in attitude. Mental pilgrimages are truth, forgiveness, control of sense, kindness, simplicity, sweet language, chastity, charity, patience, good service and cleanliness of mind, speech and karma. All pilgrimages situated on this earth are existing as permanent pilgrimages their number is many. There are the seven cities of salvation, the king of pilgrimages Prayag, Pushkar, Kashi and four dhaams etc. One who gets praise from three persons gets immediately destroyed. One should protect oneself from the praises of gambler, funboyist and prostitute. After death, the human body has three rituals-Turn to ashes after burning, turn to mud after being cremated and turn to waste after being eaten by birds and animals.

In a country where the honored are neglected and put to shame and undeserving people are elevated and honored, three happenings are imminent-Famine, untimely death and Atmosphere of fear:–

अपूज्या यत्र पूज्यन्ते पूज्यानां च विमानना।
त्रीणि तत्र भविष्यन्ति, दुर्भिक्षं मरणं भयम्॥

In Skand puran its narration thus–

अपूज्या यत्र पूज्यन्ते पूज्यानां न पूज्यते।
त्रीणि तत्र प्रवर्तन्ते दुर्भिक्षं मरणं भयम्॥

The basic colors are three-Red, Yellow and Blue. On their mixing other colors are formed. Like purple from red and blue, green from yellow and blue, orange from red and yellow. There are three ways to accept a thing-Hearing, thinking and Thinking with depth (Nididhyasan). Hearing is an activity of the mind whatever we gain by hearing, reading and seeing comes in the first category. Thinking is the activity of intelligence. After reading, hearing and seeing that which we ponder about is the deep thought. After hearing or to deeply think about a subject is Niddhyasan. If a Brahmin does something which is sinful, then his guilt is punishable, then he should be punished in three ways and released that is his kill-1. To shave off his hair 2. To take all his wealth and 3. Remove him from the place. Yagna are also of three types. Satvik (pure) yagna is the one performed according to the rituals without any expectation. Rajsik yagna is the one performed with the attitude of ego and with the hope or fruit of any desire. Tamasik (dark) yagna is that which is performed without any rituals without any mantras, without offering and without faith. Like yagna, tapa and daan (charity) are also of three types each- Satvik, Rajsik and Tamasik. Tapa related to body is worship of gods, Brahmins and the learned, piety, simplicity, chastity and non-violence. Tapa related to speech is no excitement, true and beneficial talk, reading of Veda texts, and japa (chanting) of the name of god-Tapa related to the mind is simplicity of mind, sombre nature, thought of god, control of mind and the piety of the heart. All these three tapas are Satvik (pure). Rajsik tapa is the one which is done to get felicitation and honor, from this desire there is the fulfillment of selfish means. Tamasik tapa is the one which is done out of stubbornness and foolishness of the mind, body and speech and all the three are under pain and it gives unwanted pain to others also. Charity is also of three types. The Satvik (pure) type of charity is that which is given to the rightful person and for the situation or consequence in a country. That charity is Tamasik which is given as obligatory and with an attraction of getting a reward or gain on the basis of the things given in charity, it is divided into three-Best, Medium and Worst. The best type of charity is that of food, cow, land, gold, elephant, horse etc. The medium type of charity is that of education, medicines, household things etc. The worst type of charity is that of shoes, carpet, lamp, wood and fruits and flowers. This charity also has three differences. Such as- Regular, Occasional and Desirable.

Like Tridev (three gods) three goddesses are also important. Laxmi is the goddess of wealth, Saraswati is the goddess of learning and Durga is the goddess of killing. The tri froms of creation is believed to have three reasons- Upadan, Nimit and Sadharan. If we take the example of an earthen pot, then mud is Upadan reason, one who moulds it. The pottery man is the Nimit reason. The wheel, axle, water and thread are Sadharan reason. Similarly in the creation, nature is the Upadan and rising reason, God is the Nimit or consequential reason and the five elements are Sadharan or ordinary reason. As such, in this country there have been many rulers with the tittles of Vikramaditya, but among them are Trivikram the three who are known by their names. First was Skandgupt, Vikramaditya who was the grandson of Chandragupt II Vikramaditya second was, the king from Chalukya dynasty, Vikramaditya-VI. The book of Welhan-Vikramankdevcharitam was written on him. He established the new name of era for Chalukya dynasty's period. Third is the Chol dynasty king Rajendra Chol, who started the era of Vikram Samvat.

Three things have to be kept a secret from a king- 1. One's weakness 2. One's advice and 3. One's skills and expertise yoga has three forms- Gyan yoga, Karma yoga and Bhakti yoga. Gyan yoga or knowledge yoga is that by which one detaches from known unknown, detachment from desires and the strong feeling of service. Karma yoga is that by which one gives up the desire for fruit or result and renders his services to this world. Bhaktiyoga or yoga of devotion is that by which one does not see anything except god, and by experiencing him be considers himself only a part of him. The basis of this is faith. Wealth in itself is a fault. In a poor person, there is only one fault the poor person, there is only one fault the lust for wealth but in a rich man there are three distinct faults- 1. To have wealth 2. Pride of wealth and 3. Craving or thirst for wealth.

Three 'Ps' always need dedication or sadhana- 1. Pada 2. Paisa and 3. Pratishtha. Pada is position, Paisa is money and Pratishtha is prestige. If a person maintains a balance of these three, then there is gradual increase in all three. Three faults destroy the life-

1. The extortion of other's wealth 2. Relationship with other woman 3. Absolute lack of faith on one's good friends.

परस्वानां च हरणं परदाराभिमर्शनम्।
सुहृदामतिशंका च त्रयो दोणाः क्षयावहाः।।

-बाल्मीकि रामायण 6-81-24

In context to the world, it is seen with three perspectives- Indriya (senses) - the world is before the eyes 2. Vichar (thought) - this world is ever changing 3. Vivek (thought discrimination) there is some power at the foundation of this world. According to Vyas, a woman is always to be protected:-

पिता रक्षति कौमारे भर्ता रक्षति यौवने।
पुत्रस्तु स्थविरे भावे न स्त्री स्वान्त्र्यमर्हति।।

-महा. आदि पर्व (सम्भवपर्व) 73-6

On the fourth stage of the shloka, today's woman have deep disagreement, but the truth about the first three stages cannot be ignored. There are three means to do a karma- 1. Body 2. Speech and 3. Mind. Today speech is considered one with the body. So body, mind and wealth together as a unit is talked about, actually to attain a desired goal in karma one needs to unite these three means. Death is of three types- 1. Accidental 2. Before time and 3. Natural. Accidental death are caused by, snake bite or bites from poisonous living things, drowning, and accident or due to heart-attack, suicide is a death before time. Any kind of death after an age is reached, due to any reason is natural death. Actually, for a death one has to show some kind of excuse.

For the attainment of god, three things act as hindrances- 1. Have some desire for one's own self. 2. To have the feeling of possession of any worldly object 3. Not to think god as one's own. Devotees after detaching themselves from this world should attach personal relations with god. Kabir says **'हरि मेरो पीउ मैं राम की बहुरिया'** Tulsi calls himself the slave of Ram and Meera makes an outright confession.

मेरे तो गिरिधर गोपाल दुसरो ना कोई।
जाके सिर मोर मुकुट मेरो पति सोई।।

To attain god at the earliest, three things are useful- 1. Kindness toward all living beings 2. Satisfaction in all situations and 3. To have control over one's senses.

Three of them are those respected who can be addressed as 'Tu'- 1. God 2. King and 3. Mother. Nachiketa's son Vajshrava had asked Yamraj (god of death) for three boons- 1. Let my father be free of anger, peaceful in mind and contented. 2. Explain to me the knowledge of fire through which one can acquire godliness and immortality in heaven. 3. Give me the self -knowledge that whether after death the soul exists or not. In our bodies there is constant wars between gods and demons. In this war gods, asur and demons take part. If the body is considered a battle field then (satva) good qualities are gods, medium qualities (Rajo) are asur and the dark (tamo) qualities represent the demons.

In different books, three reasons have been mentioned for man's sorrows, may be with different names. Some have said as- Ignorance, Split intelligence and Lust and some have said as- Time or Period, Karma and Behavior. One should gift something on meeting with these three- 1. King, 2. Guru and 3. Pilgrimage.

In this world three things are very rare. They can be achieved through god's grace-

दुर्लभं त्रयमेवात्र दैवानुग्रहहेतुकम्।
मनुष्यतवं मुमुक्षुत्वं महापुरुषसंश्रयः।।

–विवेकचूडामणि–3

It is not easy to be born as a human being, desire for getting salvation and the company of great and good souls. It is got by only these on whom god showers his blessings.

In the discussion of charity, it is necessary to state that is has be further divided into three- 1. Best, 2. Medium and 3. Small. Eight things such as-House, education, temple, land, cow, well, life and gold are the best charities. Compared to other charities it is considered the best. The medium charities are food, clothes, horse or vehicle, and gardens. The small category of charities are that of shoes, umbrella, utensils, curd, honey, carpet, lamp, wood, stones etc. but there is regret or charity to the undeserving and ill feeling, then there is no good result of all these three charities. In the life of every Sikh there are three gurus- 1. Guru, 2. Gurudwara and 3. Gurbani, which have prime importance. For an ideal life, every Sikh has three main principles- 1. Do japa of name, 2. Do work with honesty and 3. Do the service of langar, that is, give away the 10th portion of you earning as charity for langar.

One who considers three as small, destroys himself- 1. Child of a Brahmin, 2. Spark of fire and 3. A snake. The first is to be understood with intelligence. Three are either always and mostly neglected- 1. Home physician, 2. A poet friend and 3. One's wife. Wealth has three fates

दानं भोगो नाशः तिस्रो गतयो भवन्ति वित्तस्य।
यो न ददाति न भुड.क्ते तस्य तृतीया गतिर्भवति।।

–भर्तृहरि नीतिशतक–43

One who does use his wealth or give it in charity destroys his wealth. Those who feel that this world is meaningless, consider only three things as meaningful- 1. Residing in Kashi, 2. Service of the good people and 3. Meditation at the feel of good-

काश्यां वासः सतां सेवा मुरारिपदचिन्तनम्।
असारे खलु संसारे सारमेतत् त्रयं स्मृतम्।।

Three are not under the control of anybody- 1. Young maiden, 2. Texts or scriptures and 3. King

'शास्त्रे नृपे च युवतौ च कुतो वशित्वम्।।

–शुक्रनीति।

राखिय नारि जदपि उर माहीं।
जुवती सास्त्र नृपति बस नाहीं।।

–रामचरितमानस

Those whose three things are pure like- 1. Education, 2. Family and 3. Karma. They should always stay in the service of saintly persons. To have the company of such persons is far better than the study of texts.

येषां त्रीण्यवदातानि विद्या योनिश्च कर्म च।
ते सेव्यास्तैः समास्या हि शास्त्रेभ्योऽपि गरीयसी॥

–महाभारत, वनपर्व

Devotees are of three types- 1. Arta-Those who are always keen to meet god, like Surdas, Tulsidas and Meera. Those who look upon god in the times of crisis also come in the same category, like the Gajraj, Prahlad, Draupadi and Narsi etc., 2. Jigyashu- One who is worryless nor does he desire anything for himself. He just wants to know god, like Nachiketa, 3. Artharthi-He is patient, faithful and hard working. He only pleads for his mere existence and its development to god. He believes in Gita's **'योगः कर्मसु कौशलम्'** like king Harishchandra and Yudhisthir.

A man is encircled by three faults and killed by them- 1. Greed, 2. Lust and 3. Belief.

लोभप्रमादविश्वासैः पुरुषो नश्यति त्रिभिः।
मस्माल्लोभो न कर्तव्यः प्रमादो नो न विश्वसेत्॥

If three- 1. Kshatriya, 2. Snake and 3. Learned Brahmin are even weak, one should not insult or derogate them, if they wish for their own progress in future-

क्षत्रियं चैव सर्पं च ब्राह्मणं च बहुश्रुतम्।
नावमन्येत वै भूष्णुः कृशानापि कदाचन॥

Mahabharat is the reason of the insult of Pandavas due to their weak circumstances. King Dhrupad had to bear the punishment of giving half his kingdom for insulting.

Dronacharya who had gone to him to beg for his living. Snake is known for taking revenge. According to one eritic, there are only three poets in Hindi, others are like the collectors of seeds from the land of the poetry like farm-

कविता करता तीन हैं, तुलसी केसव सूर।
कविता खेती इन गुनी, सीता बिनत मजूर॥

The 18 chapters of Gita have been divided in three parts. First six chapters are said to be connected to Karmayog.

7-12 chapters are believed to be of Bhaktiyog and last six chapters are related to Gyanyog.

When Gopichand took the tutelage of Gorakhnath, then Gopichand's mothers asked his son to follow three things- 1. Stay within the strong fortress, 2. Eat tasty food and 3. Sleep on a soft and comfortable bed. Gopichand's mother was a philosopher by her actions and was of religious thinking. So the son could not understand his mother's advice and said to his mother-Mother, I have now taken sanyas. A sanyasi gives up all these three things, so, how can I follow your advice. The mother explained the deep secret hidden in her statement.

Fortress is that living inside it one is absolutely safe. For a sanyasi, the closeness to a guru is like a fortress because in his closeness, bad thoughts can never erupt. So to be away from bad thoughts and stay protected, always stay close to your guru. Food is tasty, when one is really hungry and till there is hunger, the taste remains, so eat only when you are hungry and eat less so that your hunger remains. The body and mind remain healthy when one cuts when he is hungry and also eats less. For a good sleep one needs a soft and comfortable bed but a sanyasi cannot get this and this is a stark truth that one who works very hard can have good sleep even on stone. So you should work very hard for a good sleep. Then you will realize like at home you had good sleep on a soft bed, that sleep you can have.

Three things- 1. Education, 2. Wealth and 3. Strength or Power can have different impact on the good and bad persons-

विद्या विवादाय धनं मदाय शक्तिः परेषां परपीडनाय।
खलस्य साधोर्विपरीतमेतद् ज्ञानाय दानाय च रक्षणाय।।

Three types of human beings- 1. Low, 2. Medium and 3. Best may have three different types of thoughts for the work.

पारभ्यते न खलु विघ्नभयेन नीचैः
प्रारभय विघ्नविहता विरमन्ति मध्याः।
विघ्नैः पुनः पुनरपि प्रतिहन्यमानाः
प्रारभ्य चोत्तमाजना न परित्यजन्ति।।

One does not go to a doctor if one does three things- 1. Take milk before going to sleep, 2. Take water after getting up in the morning and 3. To drink butter milk after taking food.

निशायां तु पिबेद दुग्धं निशान्ते शीतलं जलम्।
भोजनान्ते पिबेत्त्क्रं किमन्यद् भैषजं नृणाम्।।

This shloka is also mentioned this way-

दिनात्ते च पिबेद दुग्धं निशान्ते च जलं पिबेत्।
भोजनान्ते पिबेत्तक्रं वैद्यस्य किं प्रयोजनम्।।

One should be contented with three and discontented with three things-

सन्तोषस्त्रिषु कर्तव्यः स्वदारे भोजने धने।
त्रिषु चैव न कर्तव्योऽध्ययने जपदानयोः।।

One should be contented by one's wife, food and wealth but should not be contented with study of Vedas, Japa of god's name and charity.

One should be contented with what god has given and how much he has given us and should always be for good deeds. When there is an attack on one's motherland, there is religious oppression or the pride and honor of woman is at stake, then one should give up one's life fighting. This is the sole duty of a king or a commoner-

घर जातां धर्म पलटतां त्रिया पडन्ता ताव।
ये तीनों दिन मरण रां कोण रंक कोण राव।।

There are three faults of a wealthy man- 1. Wealth, 2. False pride of wealth and 3. Lust for wealth for punishment, there are three ways:-

मौनानीहानिलायामा दण्डा वाग्देहचेतसाम्।
न ह्योते यस्य सन्त्यंग वेणुभिर्न भवेद् यतिह।।

-भागवत 11-18-17

Silence for speech, unconsciousness for body and Pranayam for the mind are the three punishments. One who does not have these three punishments, does not become punished by the striking of bamboo on his body. God, good people and father are happy due to excellent behavior-

स्वभावेन हि तुष्यन्ति देवाः सत्पुरुषा पिता।

There is no pilgrimage as Ganga, there is no god greater than Vishnu and there is no better varna than Brahmins as said by Brahma-

न गंगासदृशं तीर्थे न देवः केशवात् परः।
ब्राह्मणेभ्यः परं नास्ति एवमाह पितामहः।

–महाभारत, वनपर्व 85–96

Some curse befalls the person who kills Brahmins, one who slaughters a cow and one who leaves the person who comes to his rescue or refuge:-

यो हि कश्चिद् द्विजान् हन्याद् गां वा लोकस्य मातरम्।
शरणागतं च त्यजते तुल्यं तेषां हि पातकम्।।

–वही 131–6

The charities of Cow, Land and Education are greater than any charity, so they are called Atidaan. One who does Atidaan becomes free of all sins and these charities are beneficial for the giver:-

त्रिण्याहुरतिदानानि गावः पृथ्वी सरस्वती।
तारयन्ति हि दातारं सर्वपापादसंशयम्।।

–बृहस्पति स्मृति 18–19

The devotee, the servant and the one who says 'I'm yours', three types of persons who come to your rescue should not be left alone:-

भक्तं च भजमानं च तवास्मीति च वादिनम्।
त्रीनेतांश्छरणं प्राप्तान् विषमेऽपि न संत्यजेत्।।

–विदुरनीति 1–73

These three are the best means of well-being and happiness:-

तन पवित्र सेवा किये धन पवित्र कर दान।
मन पवित्र हरिभजन कर होत त्रिविध कल्यान।।

There are three facilities- Trayi, Varta and Principles of law. Three Vedas are called Trayi Farming and Cow protection come under Varta:-

यः प्रीणयेत्सुचरितै पितरं स पुत्रो
यद् भर्तुरेव हितमिच्छति तत्कलत्रम्।
तन्मित्रमापदि सुखे च समक्रियं यद्
एतत्त्रयं जगति पुण्यकृतौ लभन्ते॥

–भर्तृहरि नीतिशतक 69

These three are got as the fruits of boon- 1. S son who gives joy to his father for his best behavior, 2. A wife who cares for the welfare of her husband and 3. A friend who is always there with you through thick and thin.

According to one's karma a living had three types of fate- 1. The attainment of heaven or Upper flight, 2. To be born as a human or medium fate and 3. To be born as animal or birds, that means Low flight-

तिस्रो वै गतयो राजन् परिदृष्टाः स्वकर्मभिः।
मानुषं स्वर्गवासश्च तिर्यग्योनिश्च तत् त्रिधा॥

–महा० वनपर्व 181–9

Cleanliness is of three types- 1. Vakshauch (Piety of the speech), 2. Karmashauch (Piety of work) and Jalshauch (Cleanliness of the body with water). Those who are prosperous with these three types of cleanliness they are the rightful persons for heaven and there is no doubt about it-

वाक्शौचं कर्मशौचं च यंच शौचं जलात्मकम्।
त्रिभिः शौचेरुपेतो यः स स्वर्गी नात्र संशय॥

–वहीं 200–82

Once a daughter is of marriageable age, if she is not married off by the father it is very shameful. During the pregnancy period of a wife, a husband who does intercourse is very shameful and after a husband's death a son who does not take care or protect his widowed mother is most disgusting-

अप्रदाता पिता वाच्यो वाच्यश्चानुपयन पतिः।
मृते भर्तरि पुत्रश्च वाच्यो मातुररक्षिता।।

–वहीं 293–35

The way three is described in Ved- Smriti, Puran and religious texts and literature and its different faculties, similarly it is described in folk-literature also. Three people have to face insult- 1. One who does worldly social work after taking loan from somebody, 2. Being the owner of a one who keeps it locked and 3. Who sends his sister somewhere along with his wife's brother, they all come under crucial circumstances-

उधार काढ़ि व्यवहार चलावै, छप्पर डारै तारो।
सारे के संग बहिन पठावै, तीनों को मुँह कारो।।

Three persons are fools in the eyes of folk poet- 1. One who walks in spite of having a horse at home, 2. One who shools his arrows count by count without a quiver and 3. One who keeps his wealth at his son-in-laws house as treasure, all of them are called fools-

घर घोड़ी पैदल चलै, तीर चलावै बीनि।
थाती धरै दमाद घर, जग में भकुआ तीनि।।

One folk poet has seen three qualities on shaving head- 1. The irritation of scalp vanishes, 2. Address them as Maharaj thinking them to be a sanyasi and 3. Maharaj has no shortage of sweets in society:

मूँड़ मुड़ाइ तीन गुन, सिर की मिटजा खाज।
खाने कू लड्डुवा मिलै, लोग कहें महाराज।।

It is a famous saying that the beetle does not sit on a Champa, fold poet saw that the flower of Champa has all the three qualities- beauty, colour and fragrance, then why does the beetle stay away from Champa. So, he asked Champa-

चम्पा तो मे तीन गुन, रूप रंग अरु बास।
अवगुन तो में कौन हौ, भ्रमर न आवै पास।।

For poets animals, birds, creepers and leaves all speak. So, champa then replied-

चम्प बरन है राधिका, भ्रमर स्याम को दास।
जननी अपनी जानि कै, भ्रमर न आवै प्यास॥

In the end, I am not Tripathi-reader of three Vedas nor Trivedi-one who do not know three Vedas, still I meditate on Trayambak Lord Shiva, I prey to the 3-legged god of wealth, I seek the blessings of Dattatreya, the god with three heads, while doing the japa of three words 'Om'. I give my introduction as Trigambhi (one whose behavior, voice and navel is deep) and conclude the praise and description of the greatness of three.

❐

4 (Four)

The creator of this nature Lord Brahma is Chaturanan or four faced. The four basic Vedas of Indian tradition have emanated from his mouth. With context to Vedtrayi, brief introduction of all four is already done in the last chapter. So with four kind of sacredness we begin the description of four.

1. To gain godly qualities by being in the company of good people.
2. To get the benefit of creative thoughts by being in the company of creative people.
3. To gain good faith by pondering deep about the welfare of the people of this earth.
4. To gain worship of the Almighty through praise and prayer.

All these four are the givers of sacredness. In the hands of Lord Krishna, there are four war related weapons- Conch, Wheel, Grit and Kind of Sickled Sword. In the same way, Garuda or the vehicle of Shani, the son of the Sun also has four arms, who hears-Bow, Arrow, Pricking weapon and Shield in his hands.

Indian traditions and culture is based on divisions of caste system. So four castes have been determined, they are Brahmin, Kshatriya, Vaishya, and Shudra. In the beginning, the caste system was according to the work division, but with the periods of time it became ascertained by birth. In the earlier times, Parshuram and Dronacharya were Brahmins by birth, but Kshatriya by work and became a Brahma rishi like the Brahmins. With reference to the subject of birth of these varnas or castes, it is said that they were produced from the body of Brahma.

ब्राह्मणोऽस्य मुखभासीद्बाहु राजन्यः कृतः।
उरु तदस्य यद्वैश्यः पद्भ्यां शूद्रोऽजायत॥

–यजु० 31–11

From the mouth of the ruler Brahma evolved Brahmin, from the hands Khsatriyas, from the middle of body Vaishya and from the legs Shudra. The meaning of this subtle image is that the foundations of the four varnas are- Knowledge, Country, Economy and Labour respectively. The work of Brahmins was teaching and learning. For this very reason Brahmins are called the mouth of Brahma that means Brahmins should have knowledge about Vedas. Kshatriyas have been given the responsibility of defense. **'शस्त्रेण रक्षिते राष्ट्रे'** This statement can only be meaningful when one group of the society is deeply involved in the defense of the company with due arms. The Vaishyas got the business of farming, trade and cattle-rearing. The shudras got the responsibility of serving these three varnas. This was the combined picture of the society. A person chose his own business or task according to his own ability. From this point of view, a Brahmin had six duties- To perform yagna, To help others in performing yagna, To give in charity, Learning, Teaching and To take in charity. The Kshatriyas have five duties- Charity, Study, Yagna, Law and Punishment and War. The Vaishyas have four duties- Charity, Study, Yagna and Farming and Business. Shudras had only one duty, to serve all of them as described in the texts.

Like the caste bonds were not related to birth, similarly the bonds of work were also not difficult. One could easily accept the duties of other varnas or caste, time and again, and they were approved and accepted by the society. In the end a legislation was also there that the discharge and rating of duties will depend on four things, they are- Varna (Caste), Ashram (Stages of life), Swabhav (Behavior) and Paristhiti (Situation or Enviornment). One who does not perform his duty according to all these four is actually misusing his rights. Even after the mention of different duties by different varnas, for the four varnas Manu has mentioned the dharma for all of them. They are- Non-violence, Truth, Non-stealing, To control the senses. These are the duties for all. The most praiseworthy and revered in the four varnas are- Brahmin by knowledge, Kshatriya by strength, Vaishya by the power of wealth and Shudra by the age.

In all the four varnas, the order of excellence is from the top to bottom. Brahmin is at the head of excellence but on attaining a certain age Shudra also becomes eligible for polite and respectful greeting. This following shloka is clearly visible:-

बलंज्येष्ठं स्मृतं क्षयं मंत्रज्येष्ठा द्विजातयः।
धनज्येष्ठाः स्मृता वैश्याः शूद्रास्तु वयसाधिकाः॥

–महा० उद्योगपर्व 168–17

With respect to excellence one more parameter is narrated:-

ब्राह्मणो द्विपदां श्रेष्ठो गोर्वरिष्ठा चतुष्पदाम्।
गुरुर्गरीयसां श्रेष्ठः पुत्रः स्पर्शवतां वरः॥

–महा० आदिपर्व 74–57

Among the human beings, brahmin is the best. Among the four-legged animals the cow is the best, among the glorious persons guru is the best and the best person to be touched is the son. Kalidas tells about a son, in the manner **'पुत्रस्पर्शात सुखतरः स्पर्शो लोको ने विद्यते।'** In today's scientific era, some Indian political leaders of state, express their resentment to this structure of the caste system. Sometimes their unpleasant dictions also seem to be right, but most of the times their attitude changes on the basis of votes. The basic or main caste system's four categories have now been divided into thousands of social or sub-social classes and their divisions are increasing. So many innumerable differences are further being made like- Upper, Lower, Dalit, Scheduled caste, Scheduled tribe, Adivasis, among the backward classes also the more Backward, among the Dalits also more Dalits. By not adhering and keeping in mind- Varna (caste), Ashram (stages of life), Swabhav (Behavior) and Paristhiti (Situation), in every field delict is being created. One who could become a good teacher, he became a ruler or administrator, one who was capable to defend the country, becomes a businessman. So the importance is not laid on his specialties of attitude and behavior. Actually the four varnas are the body parts of the entire society. If one of the parts is distorted or invalid, it will make the whole society distorted. When there is disorder in any part of the body, the whole body experiences pain. The mouth takes the food and the whole body gets energy. The tilak (spot mark) of sandal wood is put on the forehead but the head bow down on the feet. Those who have unbound strength in their hands, can seek the blessings only after touching the feet with their hands. Ganga having erupted form the nail of the toe of feet finds place in the head of Lord Shiva.

Actually this body itself is Brahma and the four varnas are within it. This varna system is based on culture. A person with good and pure qualities in prominence can only be Brahmin. The mind, eyes, ears, tongue, speech all are the basis of work. Everybody accepts the dominance of the senses and the heart and mind. In the society of the form of body, these are Brahmins. The hands not only defend our own body as a whole but also are the first to defend other bodies. The word Khsatriya is meaningful with the fact that the hands defend the attack coming upon the head. The knowledge or easy knowhow of energy of the entire body rests on the muscularity of the thighs. So Vaishyas have the responsibility of maintenance of not only the entire mankind but also the living world. The middle part of the body represents Vaishya. The body that stands erect on the strength of its feet that represents Shudra which is the whole foundation of all the three varnas. If the feet had the feeling of abjection or lowliness. We would not touch the feet to seek blessings and would not call ourselves the servants of the feet. Actually, on dividing the body into four parts, the relevance of the body can be known. Brahmin or the intelligent group is above the neck, the centre of which is the mouth. Hands are the symbol of strength, this is Khsatriya. The intelligence of the mind and the strength of hands is always seen. If there is muscularity in the lower body and thighs, then the legs are the foundation without them there is no possibility of any strength to stand or walk or have any movement or speed. Even today, whether it is the expert of shastras or knowledge or a harnessed warrior of defense or a master of any industrial or commercial institution, the labour group is the main foundation of every one's work. To consider the base as small or low or useless is our mistake. Shudra are better compared to others. The dharma that Brahmins follow, that dharma is the giver of salvation. While following one's own dharma Kshatriya collect the means of enjoyment for himself. The dharma of Vaishya is to collect wealth and protect economy. The dharma of Shudra is service. The first three varnas do for themselves first, then for the others. A Brahmin will first acquire knowledge himself, then alone he can share, the Kshatriya will first save energy and strength, then alone he will defend somebody, the Vaishya will first save money for himself, then he can give in charity. Shudra first renders his services, then receives something in return. He gives more and receives less. Service to others is the highest dharma **'परहित सरिस धर्म नहीं भाई'** Every varna or caste has its own dharma also. Those who follow their own caste dharmas get to the Prajapatya Lok, Indra Lok, Vayu Lok and Gandharva Lok respectively. Like the four varnas, four ashrams are accepted as the ashram- systems in India. So, we pray to god that, **'कुर्वन्नेह कर्माणि जिजीविषैच्छतं समाः।'** by doing or Karma or work we may live upto 100 years. These 100 years of age has been divided into four parts, 25 years of each, and 25 divided into four ashrams which we know by the names of Brahmacharya (Conduct or mode of behavior), Grihast (Householder), Vanprasth (Going to forest) and Sanyasi (Hermit). The main task of Brahmacharya stage is mainly to Study, but during this period, the brahmachari has to serve his guru, perform sandhya and also earn food as bhiksha. Grihastha is the base of all the three ashrams. The needs of the people of other three ashrams, this duty is the responsibility to be fulfilled by the Grihastha. The main duties of this ashram is hospitality of guests, yagna, charity and worship of god. Grihasth ashram also has two differences: 1- Sadhak (Seekar) and Udaseen (indifferent). A Grihasth, who is constantly engaged in the maintenance of his family is of the category of a devotee, and there is the other kind who is free of three obligations, who relinquishes wonan and wealth, has a deep desire for salvation, and he walks alone on the path of life, such a person is called Udaseen. In the Vanprashth Ashram, there is the importance of tapa and self-study. A Vanprasth person should take tubers, roots and fruits every day and perform yagna. A hermit has to do quiet meditation by tapa, deep thought and knowledge. By bearing a vow of silence, a hermit depends on bhiksha or begging. Sanyas ashram is only for the Brahmins.

These four things are important respectively-Food, Bath, Charity and Remembrance of god. One should find time to remember god, leaving aside the thousands of work. One should give the desired charity by sacrificing lakhs of personal needs. Even after thousands of busy chores, bath should be given importance and one should take food, leaving aside hundred tasks. Today only we will put forth the topic of good. In this relation, there is a shloka:-

शतं विहाय भोक्तव्यं सहस्रं स्नानमाचरेत्।
लक्षं विहाय दातव्यं कोटिं त्यक्तवा हरिं स्मेरत्॥

Disease, illness, wounds and death are not kind on anyone. Lord Ram had to take Jal-Samadhi (Meditative consciousness under water). Krishna was killed at the hands of Baheliya. The Pandavas had to rot on the Himalayas. Jesus Christ was put on a Cross. Sukrat (Socrate) was given poison, Panini, the writer and maker of the texts of grammar was eaten by a tiger. The great rishi Jaimini, the writer of the texts of Mimansa (ritual traditions rooted in the Vedas) was killed by an elephant crushed under his feet. A crocodile swallowed the teacher, Pingal, who wrote the Chhnad Shastra (text for poems). Chanakya died due to the fire in his hut. Gautam Buddha died as he ate the meat of a pig's infant. Adya Shankaracharya suffered from fistula or piles. Abraham Lincoln was assassinated. The hands and legs of Mansur were cut, his eyes blinded and he was pierced in the body with hot iron rods. Dayanand Swami died of poison.Swami Ramtirth died due to drowning in water. Mahatma Gandhi was shot dead. Ramkrishna Paramhans, Maharshi Raman, Hanuman Prasad Poddar founder of Kalyan, all died of cancer. Yogi Aurobindo died of diabetes. A disciple of Udiya Baba hit a chopper on his head and he died immediately. Pandit Nehru suffered from Paralysis. Swami Shradhdhanand and Indira Gandhi were assassinated. Trayambak Shastri of Ahmedabad had known 18,000 shlokas of Bhagvad by heart, he died of leprosy.

Varnashram system is based on religion. Dharma or religion is a unit which has four important divisions. They are- Tapa, Knowledge, Yagna and Charity. In accordance with the classical dictionary, they are the four divisions or four Paad. In the Satyug, dharma stood on its four paad (feet), but in the Tretayug, tapa had decreased and in the Dwaparyug, knowledge had decreased and so dharma was left with only paad. In Kaliyug, the paad of yagna also ended and finally now only the paad of charity is existing Goswami Tulsidas writes-

प्रगट चारि पद धर्म के कलि मँहु एक प्रधान।
जेन केन बिधि दीन्हें दान करइ कल्यान॥

From this metaphor one can infer that with the progress of the yuga or era, tapa, knowledge, yagna went on decreasing gradually. In Kaliyug, dharma has many characteristics or in other words in modern era, charity is of prime importance. Because of charity, the first paad of dharma is seen in this era. Those who have achieved something on the basis of their hard work or deep meditation, have contributed greatly to knowledge, or have made the atmosphere of life picturesque or beautiful, they contribute all the accumulated tapa, knowledge, and yagna for the sake of charity and the welfare of others. In this, where the economic dissimilarity reduces, the light of knowledge spreads. For these four eras, there are their own religious ethology, from which they seek their right directions. In satyug Manu, Maharishi Gautam in Tretayug, Maharishi Shankh in Dwaparyug and Parashar in Kaliyug had written and described in detail the religious ethology. These four paad are also called Yug dharma. Every yug or era has a prominent god. Brahma during Satyug, Sun during Tretayug, Vishnu during Dwaparyug and Shiva during Kaliyug. Just as the gods, in every yug, one pilgrimage is also given importance. In Krityug, there were many pilgrimages, but the best pilgrimage for Tretayug was Pushkar, for Dwaparyug it was Kurukshetra and for Kaliyug the prominent pilgrimage is Ganga.

सर्वं कृतयुगे पुण्यं त्रेतायां पुष्करं स्मृतम्।
द्वापरेऽपि कुरुक्षेत्रं गंगा कलियुगे स्मृता॥

–महा. वनपर्व 85-90

According to the Puranas, pilgrimages have four categories: 1- Dharma tirth (Religious pilgrimage), 2- Artha tirth (Economic pilgrimage) 3- Kam tirth (Pilgrimages for fun and frolic), 4- Moksha tirth (Pilgrimage for salvation). Pilgrimages on the bank of lakes and rivers are called the places to ethical benefits. These are Dharma tirth. The fairs or festivals where there is the trade of animals are the Artha tirth like the trading of donkeys in Gadh Mela. The places where we go for fun, frolic and enjoyment are called Kamtirth like the Olympic, Asiad, IPL etc. The places where people meditate for the desire of salvation, it is called Moksh tirth like Benaras.

According to Indian belief the period of Satyug was 17 lakhs, 28 thousand years, Tretayug was 12 lakh 96 thousand years, Dwaparyug was 8 lakh 64 thousand years and now Kaliyug is 4 lakh 32 thousand years. The entire period of this Chaturyug (4 eras) is 43 lakh 20 thousand years. It is believed that after 1000 chaturyug, there is going to be.

In today's scientific mind, the divisions of these 4 Yug and the calculation of their time periods may seem absurd. For them, Manu has presented a solution. According to Manu, these eras are the attitudinal behavior of the king, that means, the yug takes shape as the king rules. Actually the king is called the yug or era or in other words he is the creator of the era:-

कृतं त्रेतायुगं चैव द्वापरं कलिरेव च।
राज्ञो वृत्तानि सर्वाणि राजा ही युगमुच्यते।।

When a king shows indifference in his stately discharge of duties, then it is Kaliyug, and when he follows his duties consciously, then that is Dwaparyug and if he always remains proned to the thoughts of welfare of his subjects, then that period is called Tretayug. If any king tries to know the sorrows of his subjects and tries to be always ready to eradicate them, finishes all plans to give happiness to his subjects, then it is Satyug:-

कलिः प्रसुप्तो भवति स जाग्रद् द्वापरं युगम्।
कर्मस्वभ्युद्यतस्त्रेता विचरंस्तु कृतं युगम्।।

In the generality of religion, four is mentioned a number of times like in the case of varna, ashram, ved, paad, which have four divisions each, so there are four divisions of religion also: 1- Ved 2- Smriti 3- Sudachar and 4- To feel happy with one's soul. Smriti is memory and Sadachar is good behavior.

वेदः स्मृतिः सदाचारः स्वस्य च प्रियमात्मनः।
एतच्चतुर्विधं प्राहुः साक्षाद्धर्मस्य लक्षणम्।।

The name of Indian religion is Vedic dharma. In India only those religions have prospered and bloomed, who had their faith in Ved. One who does not have faith in Ved is called an aethist **'नास्तिको वेदनिंदकः'**

The Smirit strongly establish the principles of religion and they rate the rules of religion. So to follow them or not to follow them decides whether one is religious or non-religious. These characteristics are directly related to the physical and mental behavior of the person. Manu has said that manners or behavior is Paramdharma or supreme religion. **'आचारः परमो धर्मः'** To do the work that is joyful to our soul is the fourth characteristics of dharma. The soul never permits for adverse behavior. It is quite different, that one kills or suppresses one's soul and being influenced by the mind, people tend to move towards a wrong path. So the test of good work is also the behavior and work according to the guidance of soul. **'आत्मनः प्रतिकूलानि परेषां न समाचरेत्'**। The great poet Kalidas says when there is doubt to decide between the suitable and unsuitable, or there is difficulty to decide between right and wrong, then the statement of the soul should be considered, as the proof. King Dushyant, in his mind, has an attraction on seeing Shankuntala in the ashram of Kanv rishi, but at the same time Dushyant thinks that it will not be the right thing, for him as a Kshatriya king, to have the daughter of a Brahmin rishi as his wife. But he becomes sure and worry less after thinking, that the statement of the heart is the proof **'सतां हि संदेहपदेषु वस्तुषु प्रमाणमन्तः करणप्रवृत्तयः।'**

Culture is related to religion. Sometimes it becomes difficult to draw a line between them to separate them. A culture can be decided by seeing these four things together. There are four tenors for on the basis of which the cultures can be differentiated, they are- Language, Costumes, Food-habits and character. Although we may accept foreign language or food habits, but our character or manners and behavior cannot become like the foreigners. Every culture has its own language like Sanskrit is the language for our auspicious occasions and celebrations. So the ones who vouch for secularism, are seen to make use of Sanskrit in also government planning. Young girls wearing pants and jeans, prefer to become brides by adorning themselves in the traditional red saree costumes also clarify the difference. Hindus and Muslims are normally differentiated by their costumes. Every language has its own nature, which is seen among the people who speak that language.

The softness and complacency of Sanskrit and the sweetness of Braj have gained fame. Ancient form of Hindi language or the hard hitting stark language of Bangru cannot be hidden.

In every religion, there is the descriptive mention of god or revered. Indians believe in 33 crores gods, but four real or actual or living gods are there- Mother, Father, Teacher and Guest. We are blessed with this body because of our parents and the body is the first base of dharma **'शरीरमाद्यं खलु धर्मसाधनम्'**, After getting the life form in the body, it is the teacher who makes us well educated and groomed human beings by imparting knowledge to us. Thus, a teacher or guru is at some places compared to Brahma, Vishnu and Mahesh or at others is supposed to be the first to be saluted before god. The arrival of a guest is considered the symbol of good fortune. Hospitality extended to a guest is the fifth yagna called the Manushya yagna. One who does not offer food to a guest is dead even though he breathes.

A person becomes powerful by four types of powers. The four types of powers are: 1- Strength of the body. 2- Strength of the mind. 3- Strength of the way or opportunities. 4- Strength of friends. With the strength of the body, determination of the mind and sharpness of the power of intelligence increases. 'One who has intelligence, has power' – this is a famous statement or saying **'बुद्धिर्यस्य बलं तस्य...'**।

The strength of ways or opportunities is the strength of means. A person who is equipped with means, remains powerful in spite of the lack of any strength that he does not possess. A person also becomes powerful due to the strength and support of his family, friends and relatives. In some places, a fifth strength, called Pragyabal or Power of intelligence is also mentioned. This should be understood as the power of character or Charitable. In Mahabharat, this power is said to be the best power. Therein, some slight difference is there in the names of four powers. According to Vyas there is Physical power and Economic power in terms of a nation, the strength of the ministers with characters of a monk and the fourth is the strength of traditions and culture:-

There are similarities in man and animal:-

आहारनिद्राभयमैथुनं च समानमेतत्पशुभिर्नराणाम्।
धर्मो हि तेषामधिको विशेषो धर्मेण हीनाः पशुभि समानाः।।

Food, sleep, fear, and sex, all four have their importance. Human beings and animals both need food. For food both work hard. Sleep is also essential for both of them. The strongest of the strong man, and the king of animals, Lion also is fearful. To have sex with the opposite sex to have the desire to stay with them, these feelings are there in both animals and man. Religion is the only factor which differentiates man from animals. The perspective of religion of man is very wide. For example, however poor a householder may be, there and four things that are always there-Carpet to sit, floor to sleep, water to drink and words for hospitality. Animals are dependent, without any speech, are not the masters of property, so they are incapable to follow any religion. To protect oneself from any situation, human being are guided to follow the religion. These four phases are - Lust, Anger, Greed and Life.

In the context of similarity and dissimilarity, one fact is to be thought that in the following of four similarities animals have had a better record than the humans. Animal takes note and care of edible and inedible, vegetarian cows and buffaloes do not become non-vegetarian. A non-vegetarian lion will die of hunger but will not eat grass. An animal, completely gives up his food when unwell of sick. Even after the doctor's advice, man does not follow the rules that a doctor prescribes. Animal awaken from sleep at a definite time. Birds awaken the human-beings by chirping and twittering early in the morning. Man is irregular in terms of his sleep habits. An animal is scared of the present situation of fear, whereas a human-being becomes fearful and is disturbed by the sad incidents, which are possibly as doubts in his mind. With regard to sex, animals have more control. There are no cases of rape, only during the mating season, they copulate and have sex for conceiving for pregnancy. In this situation, man's condition is pitiable. If duty is considered as dharma, then also animals are less useful compared to humans.

Every philosophy has four basic steps of thoughts, they are – World, Living, God and Salvation. Some call this world truth, some untruth and some call it unreal, the living things are called as the part of the Almighty or perishable, god may be called one who is in form or formless, everybody's aim is to seek salvation. All philosophies move around these four main things. Words have four phases – Para, Pashyanti, Madhyama and Baikhari.

These are called Vaak. The tiniest of the tiny knowledge is Paravaak. That is called the Veda. This Veda has been visualized by the rishis. So it is called Pushyanti vaak, it is the words, in actual form which is seen as Veda in the form of knowledge. So this form is 'Madhyamavaak. Bhaikarivaak is the language of the common people. While performing yagna, Hota, Udgata, Adhwaryu and Brahma are respectively used as mantras in Rik, Sam, Yuju and Atharva ved. Yog is also of four types – Hath yog, Raj yog, Laya yog and Mantrayog. A hathyog tries to distract his attraction from the five senses. Ashtangyog is Rajyog which will be described in the eighth chapter. Layayog is to completely denounce all worldly matters and the japa of Gaytri is Mantrayog. Through yog one regains self-confidence and also one experiences the joy of self-realization.

If these four persons pull down your esteem, they should not be returned with the same action. They are Teacher, Mother, Father and Elder brother. We should bear in mind the first three are the living real gods and after the death of father the elder brother is as revered as father. Similarly, great persons do not do four things-self abuse, self-appreciation, other's abuse, other's praise.

'आत्मनिन्दाऽऽत्मपूजा परनिन्दा परस्तवः।

–महा० सभापर्व 44-24

There is the feeling of degradation due to self-abuse and there is the feeling of false pride due to self-appreciation. So one should keep away from them. Gossiping about others invites lot of troubles. False praise of others is synonymous to false behavior. There are four principles for the human endeavour- Dharma, Artha, Kam and Moksha. They are ascertained in the same order. A person has to be spiritual first, then only he can think about money or wealth, because it is expected that money should be earned rightfully through fair means. Among all pious things clean economy is the greatest asset, **'सर्वेषामेव शौचानां अर्थशौचं विशिष्यते।'** earned through pious means is used for good and pious work. Such a person will also have spiritual love life. These three are the means of endeavour, the last endeavour, salvation, is the goal. The final aim of all pious karma is the freedom from the cycle of life, in other words the attainment of Moksha or salvation. To accomplish these four endeavours, the basic thing is the body to be free form any ailment or disease.

धर्मार्थ काममोक्षाणामारोग्यं मूलमुत्तमम्।

Four things burn- Fire with its flames and intensity, Sun with its rays, King with his punishment and Brahmin with his anger. A person faces lot of problem in his life. All the solutions to face and overcome them, there are four principles which are called Sam, Dam, Dand and Bhed. It is good if the work is accomplished by peace and good behavior, otherwise it is better to take the support of money and get the work done. If both the solutions fail then the principle of bhed or divide should be utilized or to create division among the enemies. Punishment should be the last solution or resort. Punishment is a synonym of war. It is best to keep away from it.

Four are the best with due reasons- Brahmin among humans, Cow among four legged, Guru among the glorious and Son among the ones who can be touched among the living and the non-living. Brahmin is the symbol of intelligence and knowledge. It is not right to consider a Brahmin on the basis of his birth because from birth everyone is Shudra. With culture, deep study of the Vedas and with the knowledge of Vedas.

जन्मना जायते शूद्रः संस्काराद् द्विज उच्यते।
वेदपाठाद् भवेद् विप्रः ब्रह्मसानाच्च ब्राह्मणः॥

Such a Brahmin's greatness will be recognized by all. Cow is the basis of wealth. Its milk is as good as nectar. Its body and all its parts are sacred and useful. Nobody can be more glorious and praiseworthy than a guru. He is supposed to be worshipped like god, he opens our doors to knowledge and makes us capable to acquire the title of guru. A son is our very own, our soul takes birth as our son. Even after death, we live in the form of our son. A son, saves his father from the name of 'Pum', the other word for hell.

पुम्नाम्नो नरकाद् यस्मात् पितरं त्रायते सुतः।

Four worldly and unworldly or supernatural fruits are to be preserved. In the absence of wife, son, wealth and home, one cannot get the fruits of both worldly and supernatural fruits in life. For the success of worldly tasks, the contribution of all these four are important and beyond doubt. By fulfilling and following the worldly dharma, one can confirm one's supernatural dharma. A sanyasi does not have these four, but to take sanyas without the consumption and enjoyment of Grihasth ashram is the disturbance in the cycle of ashram system.

Sanyasis are of four types- Kutichakra, Bahudak, Hansa and Paramhans. A Kutichakra snayasi is the one who relinquishes all worldly attachments, gives up all attractions, lives with his sons in his small but with a sense of detachment. A Bahudak sanyasi is always engrossed in the japa of Gayatri Mantra, relinquishes his family, takes trident kamandalu and a begging bowl or bhikshu-patra, wears a sacred thread and a saffron robe. A Hans sanyasi remains engrossed in fast and austere living, wears sacred thread and bare minimum clothes to cover his body and carries a dand, just these are his belongings. The Paramhans sanyasis are the ones who wear only a loin and a piece of cloth to cover the body and carries a dand. He experiences oneness with god by renouncing all worldly materials.

Four things should always find shelter at home- An old relative, sorrowful person of good family and noble descent, poor friend, and childless sister. Ram had performed the last rites of Jatayu with the same feelings as a father does for his son. History is witness the fact that, many people have sacrificed themselves by giving refuge to persons who are of noble descent and have been faced by adversity. Guru Arjun Dev had given shelter to Jahangir's son Khusro and sent him on his plea by giving him rupees 5000. Jahangir had imposed rupees two lakhs as penalty on him. Guru did not consider it a crime to provide shelter to a sorrowful noble person, so he refused to pay the penalty and finally sacrificed his life after undergoing lot of torments. A friend is a dear one of our heart, his indifferent attitude is very painful. Krishna gives shelter to his poor friend Sudama, and there is joy on both sides. King Dhrupad does not give shelter to his poor friend Dronacharya. As a result Dronacharya feels hishonored and insulted and Dhrupad has to face defeat. A sister is adorable, due to this very thought Ravana had given shelter to his childless sister Shrupnakha, as his religious duty and thus invited enmity with Ram.

No weapons are used on these four- woman, Cow, Brahmin and the one who has provided food or the one who has given shelter.

With a slight difference, Goswami Tulsidas, has mentioned these four as- सुर महिसुर हरिजन अरु गाई। हमरें कुल इन्ह परं न सुराई।। He considers it against the Indian culture and traditions to show strength or bravery on the four. According to Indian traditions woman, cow and Brahmin are considered inviolable. It is ungrateful to use weapons on person who has provided food. Ingratitude is the greatest of all sins. Gods and devotees of god are in the category of worship.

According to the Indian culture, a human life is divided into four part: 1- Development of qualities. 2. Limited consumption. 3- Service and 4- Sacrifice. A person can be useful to society only after accomplishing within himself the proper assets. The one who believes in limited consumption will be away from the evil quality of greed. The highest service is to serve the other living beings. For this kind of duty one has to take the help of sacrifice. Diseases are of four types- Sudden, Bodily or Physical, Mental and Natural.

Sudden illness are to meet with an accident by a vehicle or to be struck by a weapon or stone. Physical illness are due to imbalance in the body due to eating and drinking habits. The reasons for mental illness are anger sorrow, disease, fear, excitement, Jealousy, sex, greed and hatred etc which disturb the mind. The natural illness are arising due to hunger, thirst, old age or sleep. There are four things which give pain like the spike Rame tells Sugreev- **'सेवक सठ, नृप कृपन कुनारी। कपटी मित्र, सूल सम चारी।।'** One who has a foolish servant, when one has to work with a miserly king, when one has a promiscuous woman in the house and one has an insincere or deceitful friend, he can only be protected by god. Four karmas show their influence immediately- Pledge of gods, Brilliance of the intelligent, Politeness of the scholar and Destruction of the sinners.

देवतानां च संकल्पमनुभावं च धीमताम्।
विनयं कृतविद्यानां विनाशं पापकर्मणाम्।।

–विदुरनीति–1–77

There are four tasks which when done with due rites make one fearless and when done against rites create fear. The four tasks are- Agnihotra, Classical silence, Study and Yagna.

It is beneficial to give up four bad qualities- Violence, Untruth, Stealing and non- renunciation. There are four bad habits or addictions normally found in kings- to hunt, to drink, unpleasant kind of play or sexual consummation and too much attraction to it. A person who is attracted to such bad addictions forgoes and neglects all duties and starts behaving according to his whims. One gambled puts Druapadi on stake and the other insults her in a big congregation. In the evening, four things are forbidden- Food, company of women, sleep and self-study. In a gurukul, during study period, a student should follow four principles- Yagna, Bhiksha, Service of guru and Sleep on the floor. Four things are forbidden for even a strong and powerful king. A king should not consult or discuss with fools, senseless enthusiasts, long standing designers and servants. One cannot get right suggestions or advice. People who are jealous and passionate cannot think about the pros and cons, long standing designers cannot complete the plan due to their laziness and servants can only by yes masters. He will only falsely praise the king without giving any opinion or decision about good or bad. There are four such great sins from which one should remain protected- like killing of a Brahmin, Drinking, Stealing and Going to the wife of a guru. One should not keep any relation with such people, otherwise that person will also partake in the sin. So it is clear that there will be the influence of bad company and one should save oneself from it.

Four things are always dissatisfied. Wood from fire, Sea from rivers, Death from the living things and Women from men:

नाग्निस्तृप्यति काष्ठानां नापगानां महोदधिः।
नान्तकः सर्वभूतानां न पुंषां वामलोचना।।

You may go on putting wood in the fire, it will keep on burning. There is no turbulence in the sea even after taking in the waters of many rivers, it still remains calm. From the beginning of creation death has been crushing and destroying all living beings and this will be the course in future also. It seems that whatever the writers of scriptures have said about women that must be a statement in some special context, which has been generalizes. It is normally seen, the fault or crime of one person is imposed on the entire community. Such injustice has been done to women, when one women has committed the crime, the entire woman community was defames and denounced. Goswami Tulsidas took the whole women community into its clutched while writing about Manthara, Kaikeyi and Shurpnakha.

There are four types of immoral of unrighteous speech- Harsh speech, Untrue speech, To tell tale, To spread rumours knowingly. One should keep away sand stay protected from such immorality. This causes pain to others. To instill pain to others is the greatest adharma **'पर पीडा सम नहिं अधमाई'** Intelligence or the mind has four tasks. They are- Logic, Thought, Investigation and Mediations or compromise. A person with intelligence does not accept anything without proper thinking. First he tries to find the truth by logic and analysis, for which one has to be thoughtful. Only the thoughtful person can take decision of profit and loss through his investigation and after passing through all these three processes, one can find solutions to the problem or come to a conclusion. Speech has four special feature- Silence, To speak the truth, To speak dearly, To speak righteous. To keep silence is better than to speak. Silence has more impact. If one has to speak according to the time and circumstance then one should speak the truth, but the truth should not be unpleasant, but one should not speak against righteousness on the pretext of speaking pleasant or untrue. It is best that one should speak both pleasant and righteous. All these four qualities of speech gradually increases in excellence.

Beauty depends on four elements. These four element generate attraction. Beauty is that which attracts. Attraction is related to mind, intelligence, determination and thought. In spite of having physical beauty, if these four good qualities are not there, then that beauty is useless. People who have physical beauty but have sly and malignant mind are exactly like poison filled in a gold urn.**'मन मलीन तन सुंदर कैसे। विषरस भरा कनक घट जैसे'** That is why it is believed that a person with physical beauty are also good in their mind. The great poet Kalidas, tries to prove this fact and says-**'न तादृशा आकृतिविशेषा गुणविरोधिनो भवन्ति'।** With the hermit like attitude of intelligence and determination, there is increase in beauty. Because of beautiful thoughts, even the ugly seem to be beautiful. If these qualities are lacking then that beauty is no praiseworthy. For example, there is beauty in prostitutes but that beauty is not good and desirable.

Everybody has the desire to have a son with good qualities. Every father's wish is that his son should be more genius and worthy, more powerful and intelligent than him. Sons are of our types- Jaat, Anujaat, Atijaat and Apjaat. The son of Jaat category is like mother in qualities and that of Anujaat category is like his father. A son who has more qualities than his father is known as Atijaat. A son who is with brute and low karmas and is the most unworthy or vile is called Apjaat. Among the common people this word has changed its image and is termed as Kamjaat. One who pays salutation and the one who render services to old people have four things which increases with them- Age, Knowledge. All good qualities and Strength. Such people keep on getting blessings good wishes and appreciation.

अभिवादनशीलस्य नित्यं वृद्धोपसेविनः।
चत्वारि सम्प्रवर्धन्ते कीर्तिरायुर्यशो बलम्॥

- महा० उद्योगपर्व-39-74

In the exhibition of bravery, the ability to face risk is tested. So bravery is also of four types. Because of this, the brave hearts are of four categories. We find lot of examples of Yudhveer (Brave at war), Daanveer (Brave at charity), Dharmaveer (Brave at righteousness) and Dayaveer (Brave at kindness) in Indian history. If Chandragupt Maurya is Yudhaveer then Karna and Harishchandra are Daanveer. Fateh Singh, the son of Guru Govind Singh who was trapped in the walls and Joravar Singh are examples of Dharmaveer. King Shivi is a unique example of Dayaveer, the one who gave away pieces of flesh from his own body to the bird who came in his refuge.

Who is that Indian who would not go to the Kumbh and earn deep and special benevolence? There are four Kumbh places-Haridwar, Prayag, Ujjain and Nasik, where the gods had tussle with Rahu and in snatching and getting the nectar urn after the churning of the ocean, some few drops had fallen in these places. Now in these places every twelve years the Kumbh festival is held. In Haridwar at the banks of Ganga, in Prayag at the Sangam, the meeting point of Ganga Yamuna Saraswati rivers in Ujjain at the banks of Shipra river and in Nasik at the banks of Godavari river. At these places crores of Indian people dive and immerse themselves in these holy rivers when Aquarius comes under the influence of Jupiter, then there is Kumbh in Haridwar in Prayag when Taurus comes under the influence of Jupiter in Ujjain when Scorpion comes under the influence of Jupiter and Purna Kumbh in Nasik when Leo comes under the influence of Jupiter along with these, Ardha Kumbh are organized every six years at Haridwar and Prayag.

Four places established by Adi Shankaracharya are famous as the four Peethas. In the north Badrinath (Uttaranchal) called Jyotishpeeth, in the south, on the banks of Tungabhadra river Shringri math Shardapeeth, in the east Jagganathpuri - Govardhanpeeth and in the west Shardapeeth of Dwarka is for all the people of different varnas and ashrams, but some special features are also mentioned, like Shringri is the main Peeth for Brahmins and Sanyasis. Badrinath is the main spiritual centre for Kshatriyas and Brahmacharis. The chief priest there is an unmarried Kshatriya who is related to the Raval of Tihari state. Dwarka is the principal Peeth for the householders and Vaishyas. Jagganathpuri is the principal Peeth for the fourth varna vanprasthis. Here there is a priest of Bhil community besides priests from other communities. Adi Shankaracharya had taken up the task of preservation of the Vedic religion. To keep up the light of knowledge, he established four Peethas or institutes in four directions of the country, which have been enunciating the unity and integrity of this country for thousands of years. This is also a matter of co-incidence that even after the partition of the country, all these four Peethas are in India. Adi Shakaracharya also has completely assessed the sphere of functions, teaching the branch of Veda etc. He has lot of instructions for discipline and strict discipline. The instruction for strict discipline is that teacher should not leave his path of righteousness and enter into another field. They should remain busy in their own field of propagation of religion and culture and teaching activities. The situation of different fields are- Ang (Bhagalpur), Bang (Bengal), Kaling (Magadh-Bihar), Utkal (Odisha), are in the fields of Govardhan Peeth of Jagganath Puri. Sindh, Marwad, Saurashtra, Gujarat, Brij and its central area are in the field of Shardapeeth of Dwarka. The state of Kuru, Delhi and surrounding places, Jammu and Kashmir, Kamboj or Punjab, Panchal (West Uttar Pradesh) are in the fields of Jyotishpeeth of Badrinath. Andhra, Dravid and Karnatak are in the fields of Shringeri Peeth.

Indians consider four cities as the holy cities- Ayodhya, Mathura, Kashi and Haridwar. Ayodhya is the birth place and main

Karmabhoomi (field of work) of Ram, the incarnation of Vishnu. Krishna was born in Mathura and the destruction of injustice was seen here. Kashi is the city of Lord Bhootnath. Mahadev lives here. The land of Haridwar has had the fortune of first touching the sacred and holy Ganga. Lord Shiva had left Ganga on this earth from his tresses and then she moved ahead behind the chariot of Bhagirath.

The body is the first medium to earn life's deep broad benevolence. **'शरीरमाद्यं खलु धर्मसाधनम्'।** The body is the basis of the life. Life has four phases- Birth, Growth, Degeneration and Destruction. During the time of birth the child has a very small form which develops gradually into the form of a strong and huge body. As the middle age approaches the body gets degenerated slowly. The hair starts falling, one stoops from the waist, teeth fall, eyes, ears, hands and legs stop working. The young body of youth becomes very thin and light in old age and one day death comes and puts an end to life. These are the four halting phases of travel from birth to death.

In Indian environment, there is special importance of four months – Chaturmasya from moon Ekadashi of Ashadh to dark moon Ekadashi of Kartik. These are the four months of Shravan, Bhadrupad, Ashwin and Kartik.This is the sleeping period of gods. So during this period auspicious occasions are not there. During these months devotees are engrossed in following their own vows. In our farming country, these months are the root support of our economy. During this period travel and war are stopped. The completeness of Indian army used to be in its four colored divisions. Indian rulers used to proceed and march for war by taking elephants, chariot, horses and infantry together. It will not be irrelevant to mention Chatushpadam in context of the Indian war techniques. They are Grahan, Dharan, Prayag and Pratikar. After learning these only one could get the right to use the weapons and arms. Acharya Drona had procured weapons from Parshuram after attaining these four special assets.

Woman, Son, Servant and friend start doing things of their choice without asking then they hurt us like thorns-

तूठहिं निज रुचि काज कर रूठहिं काज बिगारि।
तीम तनय सेवक सखा मन के कंटक चारि।।

A woman should follow her husband's precept, a son his father's, a servant his master's advise. If a friend does not follow well-disposed advice, then naturally he has to face pain and sorrow. They earn disrespect who are ill since long time, are very poor, who speak harsh language and are greedy.

दीरघ रोगी दारिदी कटुबच लोलुप लोग।
तुलसी प्रान समान तउ होहिं निरादर जोग॥

A person who is ailing since a long time, his dear ones desire for his death. Even friends do not respect one who is poor. King Dhrupad had told his friend Drona **'मैं तुमको एक दिन का भोजन दे सकता हूँ'** People wish to avoid closeness with the one who speaks harsh language. Everyone hates a greedy person. In Buddhist religion much stress has been put on sorrow, which is remembered four times- 1. There is sorrow, 2. There is reason for sorrow, 3. There is solution or way out for sorrow and 4. The path through which sorrow is salvaged. It means that this world is sorrowful, one show experience and know this. Also one has to think about the reason of sorrow. Ignorance and attachment to love are the reasons of sorrow. If there is sorrow, then there are ways to eliminate them also and when a person tries to bring those remedial ways in his behavior, then he is known to have taken the right path.

मातरं पितरं विप्रमाचार्यं चावमन्यते।
स पश्यति फलं तस्य प्रेतराजवंश गतः॥

One who neglects parents, Brahmin and guru, he comes under the control of Yama, the god of death and endures the fruit of sin.

Even after the four divisions in varnas and ashrams,in Kamshastra, woman are of four types- Padmini, Shankhini, Hastini and Chitrini. All want to save themselves from Hastini who has thick lips, thick fingers, heavy hips, large breasts, dark complexion and is full of Lust.

स्थूलाधरा स्थूलनितम्बबिम्बा स्थूलाङ्गुलिः स्थूलकुचा सुशीला।
कामोत्सुका गाढरतिप्रिया च नितान्तभोक्त्री नितम्बखर्वा खलु हस्तिनी स्यात्॥

This is called Hastini or Karini. All desire for a woman whose eyes are like lotus, incessant beautiful breasts, one with beautiful hair, popular, one with a soft voice, talented in music and instrument playing, good tempered and well disposed, adorned with beautiful clothes, such is a beautiful Padmini Woman.

भवति कमलनेत्रा नासिकाक्षुद्ररंध्रा अविरलकुचयुग्मा चारुकेशी कृशांगी।
मृदुवचनसुशीला गीतवाद्यानुरक्ता सकलतनुसुवेशा पद्मिनी पद्मगंधा॥

Compared to Hastini Chitrini is more beautiful and talented. Chitrini woman is also dear to all, who knows the desires and pleasures of love, with neither big or small nostrils, eyes like the blue lotus, one with hard and close breasts, adorned with all such qualities is the Chitrini woman.

भवति रति रसज्ञा नातिखर्वा न दीर्घा तिलकुसुम सुनासा स्निग्धनीलोत्पलाक्षी।
धनकठिन कुचाढया सुंदरी बद्धशीला, सकलगुण विचित्रा चित्रिणी चित्र वक्य॥

The Shankhini woman also cannot be ignored, she who has big eyes, exquisite beauty, is talented and well disposed, one who takes interest in sexual pleasures, with three lines in her neck, one who loves company and playfulness.

दीर्घातिदीर्घनयना वरसुंदरी या कामोपभोगरसिका गुणशीलयुक्ता।
रेखात्रयेण व विभूषतकण्ठदेशा संभोगकेलिरसिका किल शंखिनी सा॥

As such, the whole world is a theatre but acting is of four types. Angik Abhinay (Body acting) is done by using different parts of the body, similarly Mukh Abhinay (Speech acting) is done by the speech which is called Vachik.

Costumes also have importance in acting. Any dark complexioned person is made Krishna with a peacock feather crowned, wearing a yellow robe (pitambar) and holding a flute. This is a palpable category of acting. Satvik acting is a thing beyond our control. This acting is not to be performed but it automatically happens. This can be visualized in these lines when Kanv's Satvik acting was at the time when Shakuntala was leaving the ashram.

आज शकुन्तला जायेगी, मन मेरौ अकुलात।
एक वाणी गद्‌गद्‌ गिरा, निकसि न मुख सों बात॥

Satvik Abinay is when the voice stops, when the heart and throat are full and when no words come out as speech. In the context of Indian performing Arts, it is natural to remember four types of plays- Dheerodatt, Dheerprashant, Dheer lalit and Dheerodhatt. That cannot be a play where there is no patience. The category of Dheerodatt play starts with high notes and generous feelings. The son of Dashrath, Ram is this type of an actor. The Dheerprashant actor can be a Brahmin only. He should be a content person. It is a bad quality for a Kshatriya to be content 'असंतुष्टा द्विजा नष्टाः सन्तुष्टश्च महीपतिः।' Brahmin Charudutt is an example of Dheerprashant actor. Dushyant and Udayan are the actors of Dheerlalit category, the one of love. One who is not suppressed by anyone, like Bheem is Dheerodatt category of actor. The Dheerlalit actor with the mentality of love can be of the southern direction. They are of four types by Knave and trickster types of persons. One who follows homogenity with one wife and one who takes care of his wife come in Anukul or favorable and pleasant category. The actors of the poets of fixed periods of time are normally Knaves and tricksters who do transcend into another body or Parkaya Gaman. They become humiliated and shamed sometimes and at other times when their mystery is exposed they start acting the same way as before.

When Bali was attacked by Ram to death, Bali had asked Ram- O master, which is that reason that you took Sugreev as your friend and have taken me as an enemy and killed me. Then Ram had replied him that it is not a sin to kill the one who looks upon, these four with evil intentions- Brother's Wife, Sister, Daughter-in-law and the one like a daughter.

अनुजवधू भगिनि सुत नारी। कन्या सम सुन सठ ये चारी।।

When four sentiments are the same then a fool and learned scholar are the same.

काम क्रोध मद लोभ की जब लगि घट में खान।
कहा मूरख कहा पंडिता, दोनों एक समान।।

The four characters of Mahabharat, are known by the name of Chandal Chowkadi because of their misdeeds. These four are-

Shakuni, Duryodhan, Karna and Dushasan Shakuni makes a plan, Duryodhan approves it and Karna and Dushasan start preparing for its implementation. The message that Arjun gave to the Kauravas, he had said 'I will fight a war with the wish to acquire a state after bowing to the four persons-Bhishma, Drona, Krip and Ashwathama. The four horses which were attached to the chariot of Krishna were-Shivya, Sugreev, Meghpushp and Balahak. The color of Shaivya was green as a parrot's wings. Sugreev was red as a Palash flower. The glow of Meghpushp was like the clouds and Balahak was of white color. In Dwapar yug god had taken four forms by the prayers of Lord Brahma to destroy the evil forces. They are Krishna, Sankarshan (Balram), Pradumana and Anirudhdh, such is the belief of religious people. The test of these four- Patience, Religion, Friend and Woman are only during objectionable or difficult times, otherwise all show themselves as patient and good souls from the outside image. All show friendship even the wife or woman expresses love-

धीरज धरम मित्र अरु नारी। आपतकाल परिखिअहिं चारी।।

There are different forms and practices of worship in four different 'yugs'. In Satyug it is 'meditation'. In Treta Yug it is 'Yagya'. In Dwaparyug it is the ability to worship and in Kalyug it is the ability to remember.

While going to the Forest, Shri Ram, Sita and Lakshaman also went to the ashram of Atrimuni. Over there, the wife of Atrimuni told four types of womanhood to Sita while preaching her.

जग पतिव्रता चारि विधि अहहीं। वेद पुरान संत सब कहहीं।।
उत्तम के अस बस मन माहीं। सपनेहुं आन पुरुष जग नाहीं।।
मध्यम परपति देखई कैसें। भ्राता पिता पुत्र निज जैसें।।
धर्म विचारि समुझि कुल रहई। सो निकिष्ट त्रिय श्रुति अस कहई।।
बिनु अवसर भय ते रह जोई। जानेहु अधम नारि जग सोई।।

Weapons are of four types — Mukt, Amukt, Yantramukt and Muktamukt. Those weapons which are struck at the enemy from the bow are called Mukt like arrows etc. Those which are held in hand and struck at the enemy , the are called Amukt, like sword, spear.

Those which are struck with the help of an instrument is called Yantramukt, like bombs. The weapon that is struck on the enemy but returns to the striker, is called Muktamukt, like the Sudarshan Chakra of Krishna and Vajra of Indra.

There are four ways to gain the success of the desired- 1. Attachment, 2. Yog or Union, 3. Expertise and 4. Prudence or moral code. Raag is the attachment towards things. On the awakening of the desire to attain it, one moves ahead with means and property, which is called yog or union-Expertise or proficiency is very important for progress in this field. In proficiency we can see the zeal, strength and skill or craft of a person. After having and acquiring all these three, the support of prudence is taken even then the fruits are in the hands of god. It is not possible for one to atone four types of sins- Rebel against friend, Ungrateful, Woman killer and Killer of guru. About an ungrateful person, it is written in detail in the first chapter. This is also said earlier that a woman in inviolable in any state. One who rebels against a friend and one who kills a guru have to bear for two consequences.

गुरू से कपट मित्र से चोरी। या हो निर्धन या हो कोढ़ी।

In four situations, one can tell a lie- 1. When life is in danger, 2. During Marriage, 3. To protect somebody else wealth or property and 4. For the protection of religion.

Four places are not under any master or owner- Forest, Mountains, Rivers and Pilgrimages. All these four are public. There are four bases of control or self-restraint- karma, mind, speech and eyes. A person does undesirable things when out of control, has evil thoughts in mind, makes undesirable use of speech and sees through evil eyes. Therefore, a person can be self-restraint only after controlling these four aspects. The four varnas can have glory from these four things- Brahmin from tapa, Kshatriya from defense and following Vaishya from hospitality of guests and Shudra from service to others. There are four things which distract the mind-Youth, Wealth, Knowledge and Prosperity. Therefore, the legal persons have mentioned four with a slight difference- Youth, Wealth and property, Dominance and Indiscretion.

यौवनं धनसंपत्तिः प्रभुत्वमविवेकता।
एकैकमप्यनर्थाय किमु यत्र चतुष्टयम्।।

These four although being relatives, become enemies due to one fault or sin- A father who is a debtor, a mother who is promiscuous, beautiful wife and a foolish son.

ऋणकर्ता पिता शत्रुः माता च व्यभिचारिणी।
भार्या रूपवती शत्रुः पुत्रः शत्रुरपण्डितः॥

The guarding or following of non-violence is through four means-Not to be violent through mind, speech and karma and not to eat meat. These four are the top of knaves and tricksters-A barber among humans, a crow among birds, a jackal among animals and a gardener's wife among woman.

नाराणां नापितो धूर्तः पक्षिणां चैव वायसः।
चतुष्पदां श्रृगालस्तु स्त्रीणां धूर्ता च मालिनी॥

On the basis of birth process, vegetation, insects and worms, animals and birds and human beings are divided into four types- Udibhaj, Swedaj, Andaj and Jarayuj. Grass, creepers, trees are Udibhaj. Bed bug, lie and mosquitoes are Swedaj. Birds are born out of eggs, so they are Andaj. Andaj have wings and a hole in place of ears. Animals and human beings are Jarayuj. According to Mahabharat four things are enhanced or increased-Age, Renoun,Glory and Power **'ब्राह्मण प्रति पूज्यामायुकीर्तियशोबलम्'**. A Religion has many forms but four are for eternal or constant religion- Non-violence, Truth, Freedom from anger and charity. Four make up the conscience- Mind, Heart, Intelligence and Pride or Arrogance.

In human body four parts should be with reddish lustre-Palms, Palate, Lips and Nails. One can get discharge or salvation if one has the knowledge of Brahma, funeral rites in Gaya, death in a cow ranch and home or residence in Kurukshetra.

ब्रह्मज्ञानं गयाश्राद्धं गोगृहे मरणं तथा।
वासः पुंसां कुरुक्षेत्रे मुक्तिरेषा चतुर्विधा॥

As according to western tradition there is holiday on every Sunday in a month, similarly according to Indian tradition four days are holidays- Ashtami or eighth day of new moon and dark moon, dark night and full moon night. From these four one cannot get any benefit- 1. Wealth in the hands of a miser, 2. Accumulated knowledge by evil and intransigent person, 3. A person without quality and zest and 4. From an averse friend during bad times. Four persons can be satisfied in four ways- 1. By giving money to a greedy person, 2. Greetings to a generous person with folded hands, 3. By praising the fool and 4. By elemental discussion with a scholar or pundit. It is appropriate to punish the four with four kinds of punishment-1. Punishment for a thief is slaughter, 2. Punishment for an evil friend is short talk, 3. Punishment for women is to sleep on separate bed and 4. Punishment for Brahmin is not to send him invitation.

Among many worries, four worries are very sharp like the one of a sword- 1. The worry of humiliation from a low and brute person, 2. Worry of a wife suffering from hunger, 3. Worry of a wife who is without love and passion, 4. Worry of barrier which comes naturally in work. Four things go a waste-1. Rain on the sea, 2. Importunity to have more food to a satisfied person, 3. Charity to a well to do prosperous person, 4. Good work done for the low cast person. Wind, Fire, Water and Indra are known as Mangalik Chatushtya. One who takes four under one's control, he is called Susanyat or well controlled. Those persons are well balanced and controlled whose hands stay away violence, gamble, other's belongings and kidnapping one who has not aligned his genitals with other women or one who does not have lustful feelings for other women, one who does not eat more and take care of stomach and one whose speech is true beneficial and well-wished. One is self-restraint if one has control over hands, genitals, stomach and speech. Four things should be kept as secrets-Age, Wealth, Mantra and Value or Prestige with the help of four, four things are protected-

सत्येन रक्ष्यते धर्मो विद्या योगेन रक्षयते।
मृजया रक्ष्यते रूपं कुलं वृत्तेन रक्ष्यते।।

With truth religion is protected, with yog knowledge is protected, with cleanliness the image is protected and with ethics family is protected.

The four dhams or pilgrimages of Uttaranchal- Badrinath, Kedarnath, Gangotri and Yamunotri are the centres of faith for the faithful people. In four yug or eras four things or places are forbidden. In Satyug, the country where there is sin, in Tretayug, the village where there is sin, in Dwaparyug, the family where there is sin and in Kaliyug, the only person who commits sin should be left out. Wealth is gained in four ways- 1. From family lineage, 2. Due to god's grace, 3. With the success of work, 4. Due to help from a friend. Because of four, a person becomes respectable and praise worthy-Happiness in Countenance, Compassion in the heart, sweetness of speech and Philanthropy in Karma or action.

वदनं प्रसादसदनं सदयं हृदयं सुधामुचो वाचः।
करणं परोपकारणं येषां केषां न ते वन्द्याः॥

'Ramcharitmanas' of Goswami Tulsidas is no less than a religious text for religious people. No other text has this sort of huge respect among texts written by men. In the story of Manas narrator and listener are four. Lor Shiva is narrating the story to goddess Parvati. Yagyavalkya is the narrator and Bharadwaj is the listener, Kakbhushundi is narrating the story to Garud and Goswami Tulsidas is narrating Ram's story to the saint community. In the story of Ram gods, rishis, birds and humans are four categories of narrators and there are four categories of listeners.

That king, who keeps his subjects happy with four things like prospective look, heart, speech and karma like giving charity, his subjects are happy with him in return-

चक्षुषा मनसा वाचा कर्मणा च चतुर्विधम्लल।
प्रसायति यो लोकं तं लोकोऽनुप्रसीदति॥

-महा. उद्योगपर्व 34-35

A king should always perform four types of duties- 1. To earn wealth through just means, 2. To protect the earned wealth, 3. To increase the earned wealth and 4. To deposit that wealth to good and deserving persons. In the homes of gentlemen four things are never lacking- 1. Food, 2. Floor to sleep, 3. Water and other drinks and 4. Pleasant and truthful speech. These four should never be neglected by human beings-Snake, Fire, Lion and Aristocrat person. When four occasions occur, a person feels as if he has acquired ambrosia or nectar. Like- Fire in extreme cold, The sight of one's loved person, Special award or honor by the state and Food prepared from milk are like the nectar.

अमृतं शिशिरे वहिनरमृतं प्रियदर्शनम्।
अमृतं रासम्मानं अमृतं क्षीर भोजनम्।।

Karma are of four types- Prashast (Expansive), Aprashast (Non-expansive), Shreshth (Foremost) and Shreshthtam (Superior most or Best). To help our parents, friends and relatives is the Prashast category of work. The Aprashast category of work are robbery, kidnapping, loot-despoil, bribery, adulteration etc. Shreshth category of work are service of the poor and destitutes, erection of religious sanctuary or dharamshala, hospital and temple etc. for the welfare of people. Under the Shreshthtam category of work come the performing of yagna approved by the holy texts. Although the number of Brahmins is in multitudes, even so four Brahmins are especially famous. They are Sanak, Sanandan, Sanatan and Sanat Kumar. God had incarnated as avatar in these four forms and fulfilled the vow of unbroken celibacy. Knowledge has four steps-Adhiti, Bodh, Acharan and Prachar. Knowledge is first studied, from that we gain cognizance. Then it has to be brought in practice or patristic role and after that it is propagated and publicized. Like the gold is tested by friction, beating, heating in the same way a man's knowledge is also tested by Adhiti, Bodh, Acharan and Prachar.-

यथा चतुर्भिः कनकं परीक्ष्यते निघर्षणच्छेदनतापताडनैः।
तथा चतुर्भिः पुरुषः परीक्ष्यते अधीतिबोधाचरणप्रचारणैः।।

External cleanliness is of four types- 1. Cleanliness of the body by water or mud (nowdays with soap etc. also), 2. Cleanliness of Behavior by proper behavior and good manners, 3. Cleanliness of food is by having food from the money earned through clean means and lastly, 4. Cleanliness of matter by earning wealth through pure means which is also called Arthshauch. Edible food are of four types- 1. Bhakshya (Chewable), which can be chewed and eaten like chapatti, fruits, dry fruits etc., 2. Bhojya (Drinkable) which can be swallowed like milk, juice etc., 3. Lehya which can be licked like honey, Chutney etc. and 4. Choshya which can be sucked like sugarcane, mango etc. These are also called four types of foods. One desiring release or salvation from this worldly transmigration, should desirably, possess for primary characteristics- 1. Purity of nature, 2. Cleanliness of thoughts, 3. Chastity of life and

4. Purity of Behavior. Only after becoming prosperous with these four qualifies a devotee has the awakening of Brahma knowledge and curiosity for salvation. For the fulfillment of it, four means are assimilated which is called Chatushtya, like-Discretion, Renunciation, Six quality property and God's regard and attention. In Shadgun Sampatti there is Sham (Peace of mind), Dam (Control of soul), Titiksha (The strength to face conflicts), Uprati (To cease from worldly activities) Shraddha (Faith in guru, texts and god) and Samadhan (Faith in one's pure inner self). By god's attention or grace means to acknowledge god at the highest existence and surrender oneself before him. A person who has four qualities- Celibacy, Patience, Courage and Renunciation, it is not impossible for him to achieve anything.

Saints are graceful due to four qualities- Control, Sacrifice, Renunciation and Cessation. Control is to keep the mind and senses under one's restraint. Sacrifice is detachment or lack of attraction towards worldly things. The complete lack of interests towards worldly things is renunciation. The state of Upramta comes when one does not pay attention to worldly valuable things and thinks it as useless like pebbles and stones or grass and hay. These four stages gradually move towards the direction of progress and success. First, it is necessary to have control, then sacrifice is possible. Therefore the importance of control is more than sacrifice. After the union of control and sacrifice renunciation is born or generated. Uprati is the highest state. Vajragya or renunciation is the name in the absence of attachment but when work does not move towards the profession, it is Upramta. To contract and distract the mind from the senses and from all other matters is Uprati.

When Krishna came to meet the Pandavas in exile in the forest, Draupadi had said- O Krishna! You should protect me always because of four reasons-

चतुर्भिः कारणैः कृष्ण! त्वया रक्ष्यास्मि नित्यशः।
सम्बन्धाद् गौरवात् सख्यात् प्रभुत्वनैव केशव॥

As per relation you are my brother, you give me adoration and respect, you are the friend of my husband, Arjun and you are capable enough to defend. For the benefit and welfare of human beings four things are scarce- 1. Charity with pleasant words,

2. Knowledge without pride, 3. Velour with forgiveness and 4. Wealth with sacrifice. These have been called Chaturbhadra. In the stories of ancient times the mention of Somras is often found. This Som is of four types-1. Cereal, 2. Juice of Somlata shrub, 3. Nectar and 4. Chandramandal. A famous saying is–

'चतुर्विधात्मक सोमं ये पिबन्ति च सर्वदा।'

Similarly a yagna has four parts- 1. Bath, 2. Charity, 3. Offering and 4. Tapa. In Mahabharat, Soot community is mentioned many times. A child born out of the union of Brahmin mother and Kshatriya father is called Soot. In the order of varnas it is considered after Kshatriya and before Vaishya. Four soot have been famous- 1. Sumant was the minister and charioteer of Dashrath, 2. Sanjay was the minister and charioteer of Dhritarashtra, 3. Kochak was the brother-in-law of king Virat and 4. Karna the king of Angdesh.

After the death of Acharya Drona, Ashwathama shows Duryodhan four types of friends-

वदन्ति मित्रं सहजं विचक्षणास्तथैव साम्ना च धनेन चार्जितम्।
प्रतापतश्चोपनतं चतुर्विधं तदस्ति सर्वं तव पाण्डेवेषु॥

Scholars mention four types of friends. One are simple friends with whom one has natural friendship. Others are those who become friends by treaty of alliance. The third are the ones who have been made friends by giving money to them. The fourth type of friends are the ones who come into the shelter themselves due to someone's very strong majestic influence. With the Pandavas one could have all kinds of friendship. Four gods have four famous weapons- 1. Shiva has bow, 2. Varun has loop, 3. Indra has thunderbolt and 4. Kuber has an arrow.

Once or the other a person is burnt by four means- 1. Fire burns with its flames, 2. Sun heats up through its rays, 3. King victimizes by imposing punishment and 4. Brahmin makes one tremble with his anger.

अग्निर्दहति तेजोभिः सूर्यो दहति रश्मिभिः।
राजा दहित दण्डेन ब्राह्मणो मन्युना दहेत्॥

The four ashrams have been said to have four blemishes- 1. Not to follow the vow of celibacy, 2. Not to do karma on being a householder, 3. To stay in the village although being a vanprasthi and 4. To remain entangled in matters of passion although being a sanyasi or hermit.

Saving oneself from these, one should follow four paths or ways in four yug-

कृते यद् ध्यायतो विष्णुं त्रेतायां यजतो मुखैः।
द्वापरे परिचर्यायां कलौ तद्धरिकीर्तनात्॥

In Satyug through meditation, in Tretayug through yagna, in Dwaparyug through worship one gain Paramgati or ultimate goal or destination, the same can be achieved in Kaliyug by only naamkirtan or singing god's praise.

Those persons who desire for salvation have four guards on the four gates of salvation, who work as gatekeepers, they are- 1. Sham (control), 2. Vichar (thought), 3. Santosh (satisfaction) and 4. Sadhusangam (union with saints), all these should be deliberately assimilated. **'शमो विचारः संतोषश्चतुर्थः साधुसंगमः।'**

These four get the person out of the worldly ocean and are also the best solutions for destroying matters from the root. There are four faults of speech- 1. To speak in the form of order, 2. To shout and speak, 3. To speak abusive words and 4. To speak harsh. To save oneself from these faults it is best to take the refuge of silence. Silence is also of four types. First type of silence is to have control on one's speech. The second type of silence is to control the senses from lust and passion through chastisement. After the renunciation of all lusts and passions a state which is lacking all efforts and endeavors is called Kashta Maun or silence like the wood. When a person full of life constantly remains engrossed in the nature of god that state is called Sushupt Maun or dormant silence.

For the purification of mind, four means, Chatushtya have been shown or directed- 1. Constant discretion that is the perpetual state of god and the knowledge of the unperpetual state of his world. 2. The total feeling of detachment of worldly pleasures and the pleasures of the supernatural world. 3. To face conflicts and sorrows, being worry less, and titiksha (without complaining and with endurance). Uprati sanyas (completely in peace with one's mind, thoughts and actions), Sham (control of one's mind), Dam (control of one's senses, Shradhdha (faith in guru and texts) and Samadhan (to have concentration and focus on Brahma thought) and 4. Mumukshtva (a strong feeling for salvation). These are the four Chatushtya means.

A house holder who dines alone in pure bronze vessel, has increase in his age, intelligence, honor and strength.

एक एव तु यो भुङ्क्ते विमले कांस्यभाजने।
चत्वारि तस्य वर्धन्ते आयुः प्रज्ञा यशो बलम्।।

There are four ways of efforts to think- 1. Religious viewpoint. 2. Economic viewpoint. 3. Sensual viewpoint and 4. Salvation viewpoint. In Ravana one can see all these four viewpoints. Ravana is the devotee of Lord Shiva, is a scholar of Vedas, has faith in yagna, know the laws of prudence. This is the religious out look of Ravana. Ravana's Lanka is erected on gold, he snatches the estate and Pushpak viman of Kuber that is his economic outlook. In his palace Hanuman had seen many beautiful women. These group of women were the medium to satisfy his passionate feelings. So that is his sensual and passionate outlook. Ravana is the devotee of Ram. He decides-

सुर रंजन भंजन महि भारा। जो जगदीस लीन्ह अवतारा।।
तो मैं जाए बैर हठ करऊँ। प्रभु सरचाप हने भव तरऊं।।

He is keen to die at the hands of god and so he antagonizes him as an enemy to save his entire family. This is his salvation outlook.

It's beneficial to kill four-

मानं हित्वा प्रियो भवति क्रोधं हित्वा न शोचति।
कामं हित्वार्थवान्भवति लोभं हित्वा सुखी भवेत्।।

So after killing ego, anger, passion and greed, we will find our dear ones, will remain without mourning and sorrow will find wealth and prosperity, and life will become happy and joyful. As such power has many forms, but four prominent ones are called Mahashakti or Super power- 1. Power of wealth 2. Power of humans or mankind. 3. Power of state or country and 4. Power of self. Actually, these four are related to each other. Only on the basis of wealth and manpower, today, power of state is achieved and one who has both of these, automatically get self-confidence or power.

In the history of India, the names of four sons of Guru Gobind Singh are taken with deep respect. The four sons of the guru- Ajit Singh, Jujhar Singh, Joravar Singh and Fateh Singh had sacrificed their lives in the defense of the country. On their martyrdom their father's pride has been expressed in this way-

इन पुत्रन के कारणे, बार दिए सुत चार।
चार गए तो क्या हुआ, जीवित कोटि हजार॥

The sacrifice of Joravar Singh (9 yrs) and Faterh Singh (6 yrs) sends goosebumps even to this day. Persons who bear these four in their hearts, get released from the cycle of several births, they are the four with the letter 'G'-Ganga, Gita, Gayatri and Govind.

गीता गंगा च गायत्री गोविंदेति हृदि स्थिते।
चतुर्गकारसंयुक्ते पुनर्जन्म न विद्यते॥

– महा० भीष्मपर्व 43-3

Parampad or to attain salvation, four means have been suggested-

रागद्वेषविर्निमुक्तः सर्वभूतहिते रतः।
दृढ़बोधश्च धीरश्च स गच्छेत् परं पदम्॥

Raga is to be detached from worldly attachments and attraction, to be always into the welfare of all other beings, to have full faith on the almighty and to be constantly patient, such a person can have the rightful authority to salvation. With a desire for salvation and for its success, a person has to assimilate within himself four mantras- 1. Patience. 2. Resourcefulness. 3. Intelligence and 4. Efficiency. A person with all these four qualities is never become unsuccessful.

While fasting one has to take care. With four reasons a fast can be destroyed-

असकृद् जलपानाच्च सकृत् ताम्बूलभक्षणात्।
उपवासः प्रणश्येत् दिवास्वापाच्च च मैथुनात्॥

(By drinking water again and again, by chewing betel once, by sleeping during the day and by sleeping with a woman)

For all the four varnas one each remedy is shown. These four remedies are-

कै जूझिबौ कै बूझिबो दान कि काय कलेश।
चारि चारु परलोक पथ जथा जोग उपदेस॥

-दोहावली

The path to attain another world or heaven for a Brahmin is acquisition of knowledge, for a Kshatriya to fight a war, for a Vaishya to give charity and for a Shudra to render services to others even by bearing agony and anguish. Today there is dispute and controversy on these preachings. So it is better to know and consider them as the synonyms of scholar, combatant, businessman and labourer.

According to Indian tradition, religious texts are called Scriptures. Scriptures have four parts- 1. Shruti 2. Smriti 3. Puraan and 4. Tantra. Shruti is Veda. Ved is the voice of god, which has been heard. That is why it is termed Shruti. Smritis are those stories which have come all along by the listening of people and have been put in writing during time lapse. The meaning of the word Puraan is ancient. These are the compilations of different type of knowledge stories. Their number is 18. Tantra are the scriptures which describe the procedures related to ritualism. One can know the procedures of religion and karma or their proceedings through the knowledge of tantra. One gets close to death, with these four persons

दुष्टा भार्या शठं मित्रं भृत्यश्चोत्तरदायकः।
ससर्पे च गृहे वासो मृत्युरेव न संशयः॥

-गरुड़ पुराण 108-25

Death will definitely come to the house where the wife is of promiscuous behavior, friend is sly and knave, the servant replies back and there is a snake. A person can experience the feeling of living in heaven, although he is on earth, is by four things- 1. Charity 2. Pleasant speech 3. Worship of gods and 4. Honor of Brahmins

स्वर्गस्थितानामिह जीवलोके चत्वारि येषां च वसन्ति देहे।
दानः प्रसंगो मधुरा च वाणी देवार्चनं ब्राह्मणतर्पणं च॥

There are four thing which can be a failure- 1. Rain on the sea. 2. Feed a person who is satisfied. 3. Give charity to a powerful and able person and 4. To light a lamp during the day.

वृथा वृष्टिः समुद्रेषु वृथा तृप्तस्य भोजनम्।
वृथा दानं समर्थस्य वृथा दीपो दिवापि च॥

At four places or situations four unrighteous things are there like-gambling, violence, woman's company and wine, along with them are lie, cruelty, passion and lust are respectively there. A person is always afraid of four fears- 1- Fear of death. 2. Fear of old age. 3. Fear of poverty and 4. Fear of one's dear ones. These four are the best in their categories-

चतुष्पदां गौः प्रवरा लोहानां कांचनं वरम्।
शब्दानां प्रवरो मन्त्रो ब्राह्मणो द्विपदां वरः॥

–महा. शान्तिपर्व 11–11

Cow is the best among four legged animals, among metals gold is the best, mantra is excellent among words and among humans Brahmin is the prime Agnihotra, Silence, Study and Yagna- These four actions can free man from fear, but if they are not done properly or are performed with insensitivity and false pride, then they create fear otherwise

चत्वारि कर्माण्यभंयकराणि भयं प्रयच्छन्त्ययथाकृतानि।
मानग्निहोत्रमुत मानमौनं मानेनाधीतमुत मानयज्ञः॥

–वही आदिपर्व 90–24

Among the four varnas for bases are there for being sublime among Brahmins, that person is sublime who is great in knowledge, among Kshatriyas one who is the most powerful, among vaishyas one who is very wealthy and rich and is acceptable to all and among Shudra on who is aged. They are all sublime-

ज्ञानवृद्धो द्विजातीनां क्षत्रियाणां बलाधिकः।
वैश्यानां धान्यधनवान् शूद्राणामेव जन्मतः॥

Due to these four reasons one faces physical pain and sorrow- 1. Disease 2. Bad incidents 3. Hard labour and 4. Separation of the loves ones.

व्याधेरनिष्टसंस्पर्शाच्छ्रमादिष्टविवर्जनात्।
दुःखं चतुर्भिः शारीरं कारणैः सम्प्रवर्तते॥

-वही वनपर्व, 2-22

Lord Vishnu's complexion keeps on changing according to the yug. He himself says- In Satyug my complexion is white, in Tretayug yellow, in Dwaparyug red and in Kaliyug black-

श्वेतः कृतयुगे वर्णः पीतस्त्रेतायुगे मम्।
रक्तो द्वापरमासाद्यं कृष्णः कलियुगे तथा ॥

-वही 189-32

Four persons or things see through four means- Cows from scent, Brahmins from Vedas, Kings through detective and ordinary persons through eyes-

गन्धेन गावः पश्यन्ति वेदैः पश्यन्ति ब्राह्मणाः।
चारै पश्यन्ति राजनश्चक्षुभ्यामितरे जनाः॥

-वही -34-34

Lord Ram tells Lakhsman- A king has four types of patronistic role- To earn wealth through legal or just means, To increase the earned wealth, To protect the increased wealth and To employ and distribute that wealth among good deserving persons.

न्यायेनार्जनमर्थस्य वर्धनं रक्षणं तथा।
सत्पात्रप्रतिपत्तिश्च राजवृत्तं चतुर्विधम्॥

Four have four types of strengths- Evil men have the strength of cruelty, the strength of kings is to punish, the strength of women is service and the strength of worthy persons is forgiveness-

हिंसा बलमसाधूनां राज्ञां दण्डविधिर्बलम्।
शुश्रूषा तु बलं स्त्रीणां क्षमा गुणवतां बलम्।।

-महा. उद्योगपर्व 34-75

There is a constant relationship of Yagna, Charity, Study of scriptures and Tapa with good and gentle persons and the saints follow these four paths- Detachment of passions, Truth, Simplicity and Tenderness

यज्ञो दानमध्ययनं तपश्च चत्वार्येतान्यन्ववेतानि सद्भिः।
दमः सत्यमार्जवमानृशंस्य चत्वार्येतान्युयान्ति सन्तः।।

-वही 35-35

In the homes of good and gentle people, these four things are never in shortage- Carpet of grass, floor, water and pleasant speech.

तृणानि भूमिरुदकं वाक् चतुर्थी च सूनृता।
सतामेतानि गेहेषु नोच्छिद्यन्ते कदाचन।

-वही 36-34

Vidur tells Dhritarashtra- O! King, one who has had opposition with a strong person such a weak and poor person and who has lost everything he gets into the bad habits, robbery and keeping awake at night-

अभियुक्तं बलवता दुर्बलं हीनसाधनम्।
हृतस्वं कामिनं चोरमाविशन्ति प्रजागराः।।

-विदुर नीति 1-13

Four things are incomparable- Kartik among months, Vishnu among gods, Ved among scriptures and Ganga among pilgrimages-

न कार्तिकसमो मासः न देवः केशवात्परः।
न वेदसदृशं शास्त्रं न तीर्थं गंगया समम्।।

-पद्मपुराण

In Skandpuram the second chapter on praises is changed and said- **'न कृतेन युगं समम्'**. Devotees are of four types-

चतुर्विद्या भजन्ते मां जनाः सुकृतिनोऽर्जुन।
आर्तो जिज्ञासुरर्थार्थी ज्ञानी च भरतर्षभ।।

-गीता 7-16

The kings who are in the imprisonment of king elephant, Draupadi and Jarasandh are the devotees of Aarta category- Sugreev and Vibhishan are the devotees of Atharthi category. Parikshit and Uddhav are devotees of Jigyasu category. Shukdev, Bhishma, Prahlad and Sanakadi are the devotees of gyani category. With the four, the other four can be destroyed-

वमनं कफनाशाय वातनाशाय मदर्नम्।
शयनं पित्तनाशाय ज्वरनाशाय लंघनम्।।

Vaat (wind), Pitta (bile) and Cough cause trouble often. So a person afflicted with cough should spew or vomit through water therapy. One who is suffering from vaat will benefit by oil message and a relief from pitta will give good sleep. If one has fever, one should fast, fever will disappear. Relationship between a father and son, in this context, sons are of four types- 1. Excellent 2. Medium 3. Ignoble and 4. Combined form of excreta

उत्तमः चिन्तितं कुर्यात् प्रोक्तकारी तु मध्यमः।
अधमोऽश्रद्धया कुर्यात् अन्य उच्चरितं पितुः।।

Excellent sons do exactly what their fathers think. The medium category of the son is the one who works according to his father's words and instructions. The ignoble category of sons are the ones who follow their father's instruction without any faith. After this, rest are just sons for name's sake. Those who are Raghuvanshi do not show courage on these four because on their killing one commits sin and one gets defamation on defeat. So Lakshman tells Parshuram-

सुर महिसुर हरिजन अरु गाई। हमरें कुल इन्ह पर न सुराई।
बधे पाप अपकीरति हारे। मारत हूँ पा परिअ तुम्हारे।।

One should praise at the feet of god, Brahmin, devotee and cow. In the context of four, folk poets have said tactical things. Four faults cause four bad results. Excessive sleep due to laziness will bring bad results to farming. So a farmer should take precaution against it. Due to excessive coughing four are unsuccessful in their work. One who has excessive greed to earn interests will be destroyed and a widow who passes smiles will become a traveler of ill paths-

आलस नींद किसानइं खोबइ चोरइ खोबइ खांसी।
टका ब्याज बैरागी खोबइ रांड़ई खोबइ हांसी॥

However, number of people with us, we should take care of the four ourselves- Businessman, Guest, Woman and Horse. When they go in the hands of others, they will create trouble and nuisance-

व्यापारी अरु पाहुना, तिरिया और तुरंग।
अपने हाथ संभालिए, चाहे लाख हो संग॥

There is a greater possibility of the businessman going out of one's hands and developing closeness with others. Sometimes relationships can be tarnished in the hospitality of guests. So one should treat the guests on their own. It is natural for a woman to become delineated from the path, if she comes in contact with another man. A horse has to be trained. There will be doubt if other person trains it.

Devotional worship has nine forms, which will be described in the ninth chapter but there are four forms of devotional worship of our own duty- Dasya (Slavery), Sakhya (Friendship), Vatsalya (Fondness or affection) and Madhurya (Loveliness). To consider and believe god as one's master is the devotional worship of dasya feeling. Goswami Tulsidas considers himself as a servant-

हम तो चाकर राम के पटौ लिख्यौ दरबार।
अब तुलसी का होयंगे नर के मनसबदार॥

In the second type of bhakti, one establishes a relationship of friendship. This friendship is of equals. In this friendship, there is no feeling of big or small. The cow herds of Surdas have an equal relationship with Krishna. They even tell Krishna that-

जाति-पाति तुम ते कछु कय नाहीं, नाहिं बसत तुम्हारी छैयां।
अति अधिकार जतावत या ते, अधिक तुम्हारे हैं कछु गैयां॥

To accept god as their son Dashrath-Kaushalya and Nand-Yashoda have a bhakti feeling of Vatsalya or fondness. The mother worries about her child for his food but sometimes she binds him to the log also. To consider god as one's husband is the bhakti of madhurya feeling. Kabir, Meera and the gopis of Krishna are of this bhakti category. Kabir says-

हरि मेरो पीऊ मैं राम की बहुरिया।

Meera also openly acknowledges and accepts-

जाके सिर मोर मुकुट मेरो पति सोई।

In the end, by trodding at the pace of a tortoise, a person who gathers information through four eyes or detectives, by performing four karmas as an authority or leader, by attaining the seat on Chaturdat Eirawat (elephant) with the desire of four kinds of wealth (Land, Cow, Knowledge and Wealth). I pray to the four dwarpal or guards of directions (Indra of east, Varun of west, Kuber of north and Yam of south) that may grant me co-operation to make me adequate, so that the goddess with four hands (Saraswati) has her blessings on me for life-long.

❑

5 (Five)

Indian philosophers have described the five elements of Panch Mahabhoot as – Sky, Wind, Fire, Water, and Earth in the creative cycle of this nature.

महाभूतानि खं वायुरग्निरापस्तथा च भूः।
शब्दः स्पर्शश्च रूपं च रसो गन्धश्च तद्गुणा।

–महा० वनपर्व 210–17

The qualities of these five basic elements are world, touch, image, flavor and scent respectively. According to this opinion, wind arises from the sky and fire outbreaks from wind, from fire water and from water earth has emerged. The philosophical life takes this cycle on this body of man is the combination of sky, wind, fire, water, earth, medicine, food and semen. These five elements have a major quality. The quality of sky is word. Every word goes from one place to another through the medium of sky. The major quality of wind is touch. We know it only through touch although its subsidiary quality is also word. Fire's major quality is form which is expressed in the form of brightness and heat, whereas word and touch are the general qualities of fire. The major quality of water is flavor. Form, touch and word are its general qualities. Scent is the major quality of earth. The major qualities of other elements, word, touch and flavor are also found there as subsidiary forms. Among all these elements the earth has primness. Among the five elements, the sky is the most subtle. Wind is more subtle than all others but the sky. In wind, fire and water are also embodied. Fire has more form than wind. Those elements are only those seen all over the world in which there is fire element. In which there are no fire elements, they cannot be seen like the sky, wind, mind, soul,

Almighty water has more form that fire. Earth has more form than water.

In the human body, these five great elements represent the five senses. Hearing, Skin, Eyes, Tongue and Nostrils bear the qualities of sky, wind, fire, water and earth respectively. These senses are related to the five elements. Hearing is related to words, skin with touch, eyes with form, tongue with flavor and nostrils with smell. The qualities of these five elements are called Panch Tanmatra. Every element has a main task. The sky gives opportunity to integrate within itself, there is space for everyone. The work of wind is motion. It keeps on flowing. Fire does a holy task. It makes everybody pious and cooks everything. The nature of water is to congregate. It collects drop by drop. The earth bears the inanimate, the living, the moving and the static.

The human body has been built with the matching and combination of these five elements. That is why, these five great elements remain in existence in the body with their qualities. The body erected with the help of five elements, remains sheer dead when the soul element goes away. Its five elements go and meet with their basic or root elements. These five senses also have five gods. The god of hearing is direction or dik, touch or twak is wind, eyes chakshu is sun, flavor is varun and nostrils is Ashwini kumar. Like the five senses there are five work senses like- Hands, Legs, Mouth, Ass and Urinary. These five senses of work also have gods. The god of hands is Indra for legs is Upendra, for vak or mouth is fire, for genitals Prajapati and Ass is death.

Like the five senses in this body, there are five types of winds which are called as Panch Pran. They are Pran, Apan, Vyan, Udaan and Samaan because of this Panch Vayu or Panch Pran a man is living. The residence of Pran Vayu or breath is the heart. The residence of Apan Vayu is near the ass. It works to eliminate urine, excreta and semen. Vyan Vayu wonders through the entire body. Because of Vyan Vayu, there is the circulation of blood in the tiniest of blood vessels, arteries and veins. Samaan Vayu remains in the central part or navel of the body and digests the food. Due to its disorder one suffers from dyspeptic and diarrhoea. The residence of Udaan Vayu is in all the joints of the body.

This lifts the body and after death takes the subtle body to another world. The dwelling of breath has been described according to Yug. In Satyug the breath was in the bones. In Tretayug it was in the flesh, in Dwaparyug it was is the blood and in Kaliyug it is in food etc. that means in Kaliyug if one does not get food, breath is destroyed. Theist persons, prior to taking their food, take five morsels by reciting the mantras as **'प्राणाय स्वाहा, अपानाय स्वाहा, व्यानाय स्वाहा, उदानाय स्वाहा और समानाय स्वाहा'** Like the Panch Pran, there are Panch Uppran like- Nag, Kurm, Krika Devdutt and Dhananjay. In the body, their places are not defined and definite. Due to Nag one can spit, cough, sneeze and burp. Kurm does the work of shrinking the body. Through Krikal one has the desire to eat and drink. The work of Devdatt is sleep and Dhananjay does the work of Sustenance or nurturing. The wear and tear cuts and wounds of the body are cured by it.

God always has five enemies who always pound human-beings- King, Thief, Heir or Successor, other animals and Disease King imposes tax on the wealth of the rich and wants to acquire it. A thief snatches by robbery. The heir are attracted towards the wealth. Other living things want wealth through some excuse on the other. Tuberculosis is the representative of all diseases. There are diseases of the accomplished people have the capability of its treatment, that is why it has got the name of Rajyakshma. For the acquisition of one's adored god, there is the importance of Panchgni Tapa. Panchgani tapa is to light the sun doing tapa. There are five rites to acquire paranormal power or sidhdhi. They are birth, medicine, mantra, tapa and samadhi. Some people come to this earth with conspicuous excellent talent. Some gain some exclusivity by the use of some special medicine. It is a classical belief that paranormal powers can be achieved through the technique of mantra and penance. A person who acquires the state of samadhi or trance rises much above all desires. According to the desires of man, there are five categories-1. Those desirous of a long happy consummate life. 2. Those who are worried about wealth more than their age and life. 3. Those desirous of fame and name more than life wealth. 4. Those who have the thirst for knowledge more than life, wealth and fame and 5. Those desirous to know the self, sacrificing their ego, arising due to wealth, fame and knowledge.

In the body of Brahmin, there are five flames. It's the duty of the king that by desired things and complacent environment, try to extinguish those flames. Flames at mouth or speech are calmed by welcome gesture and words of respect. Flames at the feet are calmed by washing the feet with provided water. Flames at the twak or touch are calmed by decoration with beautiful clothes and ornaments, flames in the heart by satiation or libation, and flames in the genitals by giving full freedom at home. In today's environment, it is not possible to agree with the remedy to calm the fifth flame but in the ancient stories there are many such examples when kings have given their daughters to the sages and hermit as gifts. In eight types of marriages, in Dev-vivah, the bride is gifted to the Brahmin as wife, who comes to perform yagna. The Panchsheel of Budhhist religion-Asteya (not stealing), Ahinsa (non-violence), Brahmacharya (Celebacy), Prohibition of intoxicating drinks and Truth. This is known and acceptable to all.

The divisions of birth and work, there are five God, Humans, Celestial musician, Snake and Pitar or the five varnas- Brahmin, Kshatriya, Vaishya, Shudra and Nishad, this is the order. Among the five varnas, Brahmin is said to be the best and foremost but this excellence is gained by the Brahmin who studies the types of Vedas in five ways-1. He should study the Veda from the speech of a guru. 2. He should ponder on the mantras of Veda. 3. He should study them repeatedly, because **'अनभ्यासे विषं विद्या'** 4. He should do japa of ved mantras and 5. His disciples should study the vedas. For the theist and religious people, the five chapters of tenth skand of Srimad Bhagvat is very important. From chapters 29 to 33 in these five, there is the description of Raas Leela. So the devotees of Srimad Bhagvat consider it as the body and the five chapters as their Pran or breath.

In human body, there are five thesaurus-1. Food thesaurus. 2. Vitality thesaurus. 3. Mind thesaurus. 4. Scientific thesaurus and 5. Joyful thesaurus. They are also called as Brave and royal body, Vitality body, Mental body, Intelligent body and Self-joyful soul.

The food thesaurus body is the form which reduces and increases with food. Comprising under this are five senses of karma and five other senses of knowledge and the inclusion of seven metals. The food thesaurus is cleansed and purified with washing and bathing. The vitality thesaurus operates the food thesaurus. Under this form with subtle vitality five uppran are also there. The bath after touching a corpse, purifies the vitality thesaurus with fire and gold. The mind thesaurus is the one which balances and operates the vitality thesaurus. Vitality thesaurus is made with the Rajogun (quality of fun and frolic) and mind thesaurus is made with Satvagun (virtuous quality of moral goodness). All the business thoughts, resolutions, alternatives etc. are assimilated and stored in the mind thesaurus. The pollution that comes into the vitality thesaurus after the eclipse of sun and moon can be cleansed through bathing, charity, japa etc as the statute ritual. The scientific thesaurus is to pave the path of the mind by good or evil thoughts. The intelligence gets to work with its instructions and guidance. The impurities or pollution that creep into this thesaurus through bad company can be overcome by good company and study of classical excellent scriptures. The joyful thesaurus is the supreme and sublime and is beyond intelligence. This is unlimited and infinite joy and happiness. Here one can feel the joy within oneself to remove the impurity of this thesaurus one should perform selfless work and sacrifice, devotion to god, devotion to guru and to acquire knowledge. These have the sole importance. The impurities that come into these five thesaurus are- Mal (excreta), Vikar (perversion or disease), Vikshep (aberration), Aavaran (wrapping) and Asmita (pride and egotism). Excreta means unholy or impurity, perversion is deformation or defacement, vikshep is restlessness or self-consciousness, aavaran is the ignorance of the mind and asmita is ego or excessive pride.

In our culture yagna has special importance. For every auspicious and inauspicious occasions, there is a statute ritual of yagna. Yagna is just not an offering to the fire, but different texts have mentioned them with five different names-1. Lok yagna. 2. Kriya yagna. 3. Sanatan grihayagna. 4 Panchbhoot yagna and 5. Manushya yagna, these yagnas have been mentioned by the writer of Mahabharat. On the basis of a house holder person. There are five types of yagnas. The basic foundation of varnashram system is the stage of the house holder. In every home of the house holder there are four places of violence- Stove, Four-mill, Broom, Pounder and a water pot. During their use, there is always the fear of the death, burns or crushing of small living things or insects. To save oneself from the sin of this violence, every house holder has to perform five great yagnas or Mahayagna-Brahmayagna,

Pitrayagna, Bhootyagna or Manushya yagna. Self study of Vedas every day is Brahma yagna. This learning and teaching can be curbed confined to one's convenience. One may as well study two or four mantras but karmas like the worship in the evening (Sandhya upasana), is necessary for this yagna. Pitra yagna is the Shraddh of the ancestors with tarpan (libation) or Shradhdh pind and charity and being hospitable and doing the services of living parents and provide them with food and shelter. Dev yagna is the adoration and worship of one's desirable god, the worship of the Almighty, to give offering to the gods through the fire by yagna and havan. Dev yagna is also just shared offering in fire. Bhoot yagna is to provide morsel of food or pind for worms, flying insects, crawling insects, animals, birds and living things. The cooked rice which is offered in bhoot yagna or balivaishvadev yagna, when taking out the six parts of it. If some guest arrives, then one should offer that food to him. So from this fact, it means that man is first entitled to that food. If there is no person before us who is afflicted with scarcity, then others should get it. It is also to be noted what Indians think about- from a word to god? Is it possible in any other religion that worms, crows and dogs get some food from a house holder. Manushya yagna or Atithi yagna is to render services to a guest, to feed the guest, to give food to Brahmins, poor and destitute. Some texts have mentioned Panch Mahaygna as- Worship of parents, Service of husband, Feeling of respect for all, Not to rebel against friends, and Hymns of praise for Vishnu.

A guest who comes home should be given dakshina (rightful offering)- 1. To see with loving eyes. 2. To wish him well from the heart. 3. Use of sweet speech. 4. To serve till he stays at home and 5. To go with him a few steps when he leaves.

चक्षुर्दद्यान्मनो दद्याद् वाचं दद्याश्च सुनृताम्।
अनुव्रजेदुपासीत स यक्षः पंचदक्षिणः।।

–महा. वनपर्व 2-6

Maharishi Vyas says- Those never see the gates of Yam who give five things to their guests- 1. Water to cleanse his feet. 2. Oil to massage his feet. 3. Lamp for light. 4. Food to eat and 5. Place to reside. Guests are in the category of gods. One who does not offer food to these five- God, Guest, Servant, Ancestor and Soul is dead even if he is breathing. Kapila, the wife of Rishi Kashyap has five children, who are important in their own fields. These five are- Nectar, Brahmin, Cow, Celestial singer and Celestial nymph.

Yagyuvalakya Smriti dharma has four evident characteristics- Ved, Smriti (Memory), Sadachar (Morality) and Atma (Soul) which is joyful, one more mediating pledge connects it. They call all these five as the root of religion. Manusmriti lays stress on yam- niyam (To follow regulation). The five yam are- Truth, Non-violence, No stealing, Celibacy and Lack of attachment and collection (Aparigraha) and the five niyam are- Shauch (cleanliness), Santosh (satisfaction), Tapa (sacrifice of desires), Swadhyaay (self-study) and Ishwar Pranidhan (surrender before the supreme and the highest ruler-god)

अहिंसासत्यास्तेयब्रह्मचर्यापरिग्रहा यमाः।
शौच संतोष तपः स्वाध्यायेश्वर प्राणिधानानि नियमाः॥

But Skand Puran has shown the number of yam and niyam as 10-

सत्यक्षमाऽऽर्जवं ध्यानमानृशंस्यमहिंसनम्।
दमः प्रसादोमाधुर्यं मृदुतेति यमा दश॥
शौचं स्नानं तपो दानं मौनेज्याध्ययनं व्रतम्।
उपोषणोपस्यदण्डौ दशैते नियमाः स्मृताः॥

The ten yams are said to be Truth, Forgiveness, Simplicity, Meditation, Lack of cruelty, Total lack of violence, Control of mind and senses, To always be joyful, To behave pleasant and To have tender feelings for all. The ten niyams are said to be Shauch (Cleanliness or purity), Bath, Tapa, Charity, Silence, Yagna, Self-study, Vow or pledge, Fast and Control of the genital senses

अहिंसा सत्यमस्तेयमसंगो हीरसंचयः।
आस्तिक्यं ब्रह्मचर्यं च मौनं स्थैर्ये क्षमाभयम्॥३३॥
शौच जपस्तपो होमः श्रद्धाऽऽतिथ्यं मदर्चनम्।
तीर्थाटनं परार्थेहा तुष्टिराचार्यसेवनम्॥३४॥
एते यमाः सनियमा उभयोर्द्वादश स्मृताः।

-भागवत 11-19-33-34,35(पूर्वाद्ध)

Non-violence, Truth, No stealing, Inconsistency, Modesty, Non-collection, Theism, Celibacy, Silence, Stability, Forgiveness and Fearlessness are yam and cleanliness Japa, Tapa, Havan, Faith, Hospitality to guest, Worship of god, Travel to pilgrimages, Effort to help others, Satisfaction and Service to guru are niyam. One can save oneself from five great sins by following the five features of religion and also the five yam-niyam. The five greatest sins are-Murder of Brahmin, To drink wine, To steal, To go to guru's wife and the closeness or affinity to all these four. Actually a person should guard against five reasons and pay attention to save oneself from immorality-1. Fear of god. 2. Dominance of texts. 3. Fear of the loss of family's boundary. 4. Law of the state and 5. Fear of physical and economic contretemps, stops one from going on the immoral path. Among these the first two bases are faith. In the third the entire family and environment is connected. The fourth is based on punishment and the fifth depends on personal decision. Sins committed can be destroyed in five ways- 1. To acknowledge that sin. 2. By doing good work. 3. By atonement of penance. 4. By giving in charity and 5. By meditating.

Good persons imbibe moral work, love, prestige, gain and the paths of welfare, but evil persons desert these five qualities-

पुण्य प्रीति पति प्रापतिउ परमारथ पथ पाँच।
लहहिं सुजन परिहरहिं खल सनुहु सिखावन साँच॥

Actually, there is nothing life good or bad, but are accepted as good or bad. By the closeness or the environment it gets into. Home, Medicine, Water, Wind and Clothes become good or bad due to their company. Clothes become excellent by the closeness of bride and bridegroom. Wind becomes fragrant when it is scented by the touch of roses but becomes polluted by the dirt and impurity. Goswami Tulsidas writes-

गृह भेषज जल पवन पट पाइ कुजोग सुजोग।
होहिं कुबस्तु सुबस्तु जग लखहिं सुलच्छन लोग॥

The strength of men are of four types **'बल पंचविधं नित्यं पुरूषाणां निबोध में'** The power of hands, the strength of excellent acquisition of ministership, strength of wealth, the strength of being born in aristocratic high family and the strength of intelligence. There is excellence in each gradually. Strength of the hands is deficient strength and that of wisdom and Prudence is excellent strength. That is why the logical persons say **'बुद्धिर्यस्य बलं तस्य'**. Some texts have slightly made the change of name in strength and have mentioned five strengths- 1. Physical strength. 2. Strength of intelligence. 3. Strength of wealth. 4. Strength of status and 5. Strength of beauty or looks. Actually there is only difference of words in strength of hands and physical strength. Strength of intelligence is actually self-confidence. One gets the strength of status, normally when one is born in high exquisite family. Today the importance of the strength of beauty is known worldwide.

It is considered good if the woman has small or subtle parts- fingers, hair, hair on skin, nails and skin. Five parts of the body are considered good if they have red glow- Palms, Under the feet, Eyelids and Nails.

सूक्ष्माण्यंमुलिपर्वाणि केशरोमनखत्वचः।
पाणिपादतले रक्ते नेत्रान्तौ च नखानि च।।

–महा. उद्योगपर्व 116–3

It is good to have five small parts of the body- Sides of the eyes, Under the feet, Tongue and both lips. It is good to have prominent and sharp parts of the body- The middle of breasts, Both hands, Teeth, Eyes and the Nostrils. Five types of untruth are without sins-

विवाहकाले रतिसम्प्रयोगे प्राणात्यये सर्वधनापहारे।
विप्रस्य चार्थे ह्यनृतं वदेत पंचानृतान्याहुरपातकानि।।

–महा. कर्ण पर्व 69–33

During marriage, occasions of women, when somebody's life is in danger, when everything is extorted or looted and for the welfare of Brahmin if one tells the untruth, there is no sin. In Srimad Bhagvat Mahapuran it is slightly changed-

स्त्रीषु नर्मविवाहे च वृत्यर्थे प्राणसंकटे।
गोब्राह्मणार्थे हिंसाया नानृतं स्याज्जुगुप्सितम्।।

–19–43

Vyas says thus-

न नर्मयुक्तमनृतं हिनस्ति न स्त्रीषु राजन् न विवाहकाले।
न गुर्वर्थे नात्मनो जीवितार्थे पंचानृतान्याहुरपातकानि।।

-महा० शान्ति पर्व 165-30

On should leave on knowing the truth if these five, disciple, friend, servant, minister and beautiful women start impressing and pleasing others-

शिष्य सखा सेवक सचिव सुतिय सिखावन सांच।
सुनि समुझिअ पुनि परिहरिअ पर मन रंजन पाँच।।

-दोहावली

If one does five things, he becomes unhappy- 1. To do farming at a place far from one's residence. 2. To get attracted to a person while on a way. 3. Debt on big interest. 4. Farm near a road and 5. Our expectation and enmity with elder.

पाही खेती लगन बट रिन कुब्याज मग खेत।
बैर बड़े सों आपने किए पाँच दुःख हेत।।

Sons are of five types- 1. One born with one's wife. 2. One born with another woman. 3. One who is purchased. 4. One who is fostered and 5. One who is well cultured with upanayan (sacred threat ceremony).There are five types of fathers also said to be- 1. One who gives birth. 2. One who gives knowledge. 3. Elder brother 4. Father-in-law and 5. Provider. In the last chapter we have mentioned edible things, are of four types, where we have described- Bhakshya, Bhojya, Lehya and Chaushya but in some texts the fifth one is mentioned as Peya. They have not considered Peya things under Chaushya. According to them only those food which are eaten with tongue are Chaushya like porridge, halwa and kheer, and milk, juice etc which can be drunk are Peya food. There are five types of distress are- 1. Ignorance, 2. Pride, 3. Attachment, 4. Malevolence or Spite and 5. Persistence. One should save oneself from these. Pride is ego and persistence is obstinacy. Everybody in society is keen to have value and respect. There are five reasons to gain prestige, they are- 1. Wealth accomplishment, Family friend, Having elderly status and age, all three increase prestige. These are external reasons, but there are two such reasons which are seen as both external and internal reasons-1. People who gain prestige through their karmas according to Ved-Smriti and 2. Also, the scholars who get the authority for gaining prestige always. One gets prestige through wealth, friend, age, karma and knowledge but one gain this more gradually.

धनं बधुर्वयः कर्म विद्या भवित पंचमी।
एतानि मान्यस्थानानि गरीयो यद्यदुत्तरम्॥

For cleanliness and purity, mud is used but the mud of five places is not admissible-1. Mud under the water, 2. Mud of the temple, 3. Mud of Valmiki or Bambi, 4. Mud collected by rats, 5. Mud used during cleaning excreta. In Varnashram system, the duties of different varnas are mentioned. Therein, the five duties of Kshatriyas are shown-1. Guarding the subjects, 2. To give charity, 3. To perform yagna, 4. Study and 5. Not to have greed towards materialistic things. For gaining worldly happiness, wealth, property and knowledge, one should worship the five gods of Panchayatan-Shiva, Shakti, Ganesh, Sun and Vishnu. Among them Shiva is the provider of happiness and auspiciousness. Shakti is the mother of the world. Ganesh is the god of speech and knowledge. Sun is god, who is evident and conspicuous and Vishnu is omnipresent and the cherisher and nurturer. The reason of having faith in any one of the five gods five sects have been formed- Vaishnav, Saur, Shaakt, Shaiva and Ganpatya. The relation of these five gods are also described to the Panch Mahabhoot. Vishnu is said to be the master and ruler of the sky, Sun is that of wind, Durga is that of fire, Ganesh is that of water and Shiva as the master of the earth.

When prosperous people get wealth and prosperity, they should divide their earned wealth in five parts while making good utilization of it. It is therefore conducive and auspicious to divide the wealth as-Righteous or religious work, For fame and glory, For livelihood, For life's luxuries and For one's family. According to Srimad Bhagvat that division should be after deducting the share of the state. A king can take one sixth portion in the form of tax which is a legislation. As such Mahrishi Vyas had imparted the knowledge of all the Vedas and Puranas to all his students but in the traditional order of his disciples five are principal or main disciples-Pail, Vaishampayan, Jaimini, Suamntu and Sukhdev. Some scholars consider fifth disciple as Lomharshan. Shukhdev was the son of Vyas. Lohmharson and Shukhdev both are connected to the Puranas.

All the different parts of the body do their own work, but the whole work of the body is divided into five parts. These have been called as five work places. 1. up to the mouth- thoughtful group Hands-defense group, Stomach- nutrient group, Legs-servant group and opening for excreta-cleaning group. They can be called as head, hands, stomach, legs and private parts respectively. In this work, there is no discrimination of big and small. One who does not do its duty is the one who is sick. That is the one which is small and at a smaller state. This must have been the basis of the imagination Panch varna or Panch Jan.

Acquisition of empire is through five qualities- Victory on enemy, Cherishing the subjects, The power of tapa, Wealth and good fortune and Excellent prudence of moral code. On the strength of these alone an empire can stand. There is ban or forbiddance to use weapons against five persons-Woman, Cow, Brahmin are all inviolable. It is also forbidden to raise arms these one who has been the provider and the one who has provided shelter. It is expected that in this world for the sake of wellbeing and for good livelihood, there should be mutual balance and agreement between five types of living beings- they are-god, rishi, ancestor, man and others. They all to co-operate with each other for human welfare. The gods give the desired fruits to all the living of this entire world. The treasure of knowledge is acquired through sages and hermits. Fathers take care of the sustenance and the thought of well-being of their children. A man becomes wealthy and prosperous on the basis of his power and knowledge, which is approved by all. The field of others is wide...Bird and animals, the gratuity of nature, all in the forms of means of comforts respond and totally submit themselves. The rituals of five Mahayagna is the response of their services.

In the whole of India, Prayag is considered to the king of pilgrimages but in Uttarakhand there are five Prayag. In this pilgrimage, there is the evident union of two rivers. In Uttrarakhand also, at five places, two rivers have union. That is the reason of the existence of Panch Prayag. Here, there is the place of union of rivers or Sangam at Vishnuprayag, Nand Prayag, Karnaprayag, Rudraprayag and Devprayag. The union of Alakhnanda and Dhauli Ganga or Vishnu Ganga is at Vishnuprayag, the union of Alaknanda and Garud-ganga (Mandakini) at Nandprayag, Alaknanda and Pindar ganga united at Karna prayag, Alaknanda and Mandakini united at Rudraprayag, and Alaknanda and Bhagirathi united at Devprayag. Alaknanda meets other rivers and submerges all within itself but when it meets Bhagirathi at Devprayag it loses its existence and here its name bocemes Ganga. Pryag is the king of pilgrimages of entire India and Pushkar is the king of pilgrimage among the five pilgrimages in Rajasthan. The main pilgrimages of Rajasthan are Chaar Bhujaji, Nathdwara, Eklingji, Kankroli, Karoli and Pushkar.

In the same way, in Assam, about 32kms far from Guwahati, there are five pilgrimages-Haygreev Madhav, Kandareshwar, Kameshwar, Kaleshwar and Ganesh Mandir. The meaning of Haygreev Madhav is Vishnu the head of a horse. In Kandareshwar temple, there is a Shivling of Ardhanarishwar. This image of Shiva is nowhere to be found. This Ling has been formed naturally. This is not an image which is sculptured. In the circular form of ling, there is the image of Parvati in a Vacant place. On the forehead, there is the sign of the third eye. On the right side is the place of Ganga, at the back there are three tresses of Shiva which are the symbols of sat, raj and tam.

Cow has been the foundation of India's economy and in another way, it has been important part of religion. After Veda, Cow is important. One gets Panchgavya from a cow. Accepting these, one feels purified. There are very few who have faith in Pachgavya and its consumption prepared from milk, curd, ghee, urine and cowdung, but all have the desire to have the mixture of Panchmrit or Madhapark prepared by the combination of milk, curd, ghee, honey and sugar. Lord Shaligram is ordinated with this Panchamrit. In pachgavya, besides cows urine and cowdung, milk of white cow and curd of the milk from black cow and also ghee extracted from the milk of blue cow are included. Cow is worshipped among the five. They are cow, Gita, Ganga, Gayatri and Gopal (Govind). All these five are praiseworthy and sublime.

One should take the help of five remedies for acquisition of the intended thing. They are- 1. Blessings of the parents,

2. Kindness and courtesy of guru, 3. Enterprise, 4. Pre ordination and 5. Kindness of god. It is expected to follow the righteous path to acquire the intended. Manu has shown 10 characteristics of dharma and Narad has shown 30 characteristics. The five characteristics shown by Yagyavalakya are- Ved, Smriti, Ethics, One which is lovable to the soul and mediating pledge or vow has already been described earlier. But when Manu discusses four varnas he lays stress on the necessity to follow the five common characteristics of dharma. These five characteristics are- Non- violence, Truth, Non-stealing, Cleanliness and Control on senses. Mahavir has also stressed on five Mahavrats which are to be followed in Jain religion. The five Mahavrats are-Non-violence, Truth, Not to steal, Non possessiveness and Celibacy. According to Vidur the five agni or fire are- Mother, Father, Guru, Fire and Soul. He also said that if one desires happiness and fame, one should always revere these five. These five are worth reverence-god, ancestor, man, hermit and guest.

If the five senses are under the control of the mind then one is joyful and if these five senses disturb and tumult the mind, distract it, then the result is sad. The desire to get beauty, on seeing the wish to fullness to hear pleasant voice on hearing the yearning for tender and enjoyable touch, the wish to taste the flavor, the deep desire to fill the soft, senescent. These are all because of sense.

Victimized by five senses, these five animals are the symbols of senses. A deer gets caught by a tiger being under the control of hearing. The elephant becomes a hostage in the greed of the sense of touch. The moth is attracted by eyes towards flame and gives up its life. In the desire to satisfy flavors, the fish gives up its life. The poet which is greedy for the sense of beauty remain locked the whole night in the lotus flower. The attraction of senses steals the mind of its intelligence but that situation comes when mind is aligned with the senses. So the religious texts give the teachings to control the mind.

Word (speech), touch, beauty, scent and flavor, attracted by one of these deer, elephant, moth, bee and fish respectively either fall pray and get into bondage or fall into the trap of death. But these five attractions entice human beings. He enjoys and consumers with all the five senses why will he not be killed?

कुरंगमातंगपतंगभृंगमीना हताः पंचभिरेव पंच।
एकः प्रमादी स कथं न घात्यो य सेवते पंचभिरवे पंच।।

In the context of five, it is natural to remember Draupadi. In the history of the world, possibly, she is the only such woman who is the wife of five husbands, Her five husbands are the five Pandavas-Yudhishthir, Bheem, Arjun, Nakul and Sahadev, are all known to all. For the subsistence of a wife's duty with all these five husbands, there was an arrangement. The rule was that Draupadi used to stay for one year in each brother's house. The five brothers had also decided when any of the brothers enjoyed sex with her in private, if the other saw him he would have to live in the forest for 12 years. Arjun had to go in exile to the forest for breaking the rule. From these five husbands Draupadi had five sons whose names are in order of their father-Prativindhya, Sutsom, Shrutkarma, Shatnik and Shrutsen. These five brothers were killed by Ashwathama while in sleep.

The five Pandavas had separate wives also. Yudhishthir had married the daughter of Govasan the king of Shividesh from whom Yodhyey was born. Bheemsen had married Balandhara the daughter of Kashiraj whose son's name was Sarvag. From Hidimba, Ghatotkach was born to Bheem. Subhadra the sister of Krishna was Arjun's wife. Abhimanyu was their son. Nakul was married to Karenumati, the daughter of the king of Chedi from whom he got the son named Narmitra. Sahdev was married to Dyutimaan, the princess of Madra. Their son's name was Suhotra. All the five Pandavas had proficiency in the five fields of the techniques of warfare. The five Pandavas proficiency in Tomar, Mace, Bow and Arrow, Dhal and Sword respectively. They got their training from the king Shak, who performed penance on the Shatshring mountains, before they came to Hastinapur. On coming to Hastinapur, Pandavas got training from Kripacharya, Ashwathama and Dronacharya. While staying in exile in the unknown palace of king Virat, the five Pandavas had five names respectively. They were- Kank, Ballav, Brihanala, Grathik and Tantripaal, who used to work respectively as princess, cook, music and dance teacher, trainer and expert of horses and cowherd. Draupadi stayed as Sairandhri. Sanjay, the messenger of Dhritarashtra to give Yudhishthir five villages, whose names were- Avisthal, Vriksthal, Makandi, Varnavat and the fifth any other village

अविस्थलं वृकस्थलं माकन्दीं वरणावतम्।
अनसानं भवत्वत्र किंचिदेकं च पंचमम्।।

–महा. उद्योगपर्व 31–19

In some texts, the names of five villages are mentioned as- Tailprasth, Tilpat-close to present Delhi, Indraprasth-Delhi, Vyaghraprasth-Bagpat, Swarnaprasth-Sonepat and Parnaprasth-Panipat. Five generations were taking part in the war of Mahabharat. From the elder brother of Shantanu Vahlik, and Abhimanyu and the son of Duryodhan Lakshman are five generations. All the five Pandavas had five conches whose names are- Anant vijay, Paundra, Devdatt, Sughosh and Manipushk respectively.

As such, 64 forms of arts have been mentioned, but five forms of art is known by the name Lalit Kala-Art of poetry, Art of music, Art of Painting. Art of sculpture and Art of Vaastu. Among these the order of excellence is from the top, that means the art of poetry is the best and vaastu in the end. That art which takes more material from the outside it becomes of low level or grade Punjab or Panchnad is because of five rivers. These five rivers are- Vitarta, Chandrabhaya, Irawati, Shatadru and Vipasha whose modern names are- Jhelum, Chenab, Ravi, Sutlaj and Vyas. With the waters from other four rivers Sutlaj meets the river Sindhu. For the pronunciation of words, by five types of various efforts, five- five words are pronounced which are called as varga. These vargas are also five- K-varga, ch-varga, t-varga, t-varga and p-varga. The places of their pronunciations are also five-Throat or Kanthya, Palatal or Talavya, Upper palate or Moordhanya, Teeth or Dantya, and Lips or Oshthya. Basically, notes are also five-A, Ee, Ri and Lri. Other notes are either higher or subdued. With relation to the body five have special importance. The body is built of five elements in which there are five sensory organs and five work organs. Five Pran or breath or five wind are present in the body at all times. There are also five uppran. Five attractions makes a man a sufferer. There are five fingers and five toes in hands and legs. The names of the fingers of hands are- Kanishthika (Pointer), Madhyama (Middle finger), Anamika (Ring finger), Tarjani (Little finger) and Angushth (Thumb). Divine sufferings are of five types- **'दैवपीडनमग्निरुदकं व्याधिर्दुर्भिक्षं मरक इति'**

They are in the forms of fire, water, disease, dearth and epidemic. That person is also called guru who gives the knowledge of even one word. From this point of view the number of gurus is very large. A very large number of the relatives on the sides of father and mother come under this group of gurus. Many come in the category of gurus of the sides of husband and wife. Teacher, king, mother, father, elders of mother, mother-in-law, father-in-law, elder brother, uncle, elder uncle, wife of guru, sisters of father and mother etc, all come in the category of guru, but among these five, gurus are the most important. Kurm Puran makes changes in this order. According to this there is no god as a father. For women the only guru is her husband. A guest is a guru for all meetings or congregations. The number of greetings and salutations are also related to five. We bow before somebody for five reasons-1. The respectful person who is expected to be more scholarly and learned, 2. He has done excellent work, 3. He is older in age, 4. He is more wealthy and 5. He is one's relative. Paternal and maternal uncles are offered salutations only because of relations, although they do not have the first four specialties.

In the five arrows which are found in the quill of Pushpdhanva Kamdev are- Unmadan (Maniac), Taapan (heat), Shoshan (exploitation), Stambhan (astriction) and Sammohan (fascination or infatuation) or also known by the names of Rochan (likeness) Harshan (joyful), Mohan (hypnotic), Shoshan (exploitation) and Maaran (killing)

हर्षणं रोचनारव्यं च मोहनं शोषणं तथा।
मारणं चेति संज्ञाभिर्मुनि मोह कराण्यपि॥

They hypnotize the minds of hermits also. There are changes in the body due to the effect of sensuality and excessive desire like- Madness or being Maniac, irritation, to be lost, to be hypnotized, to be lovable, to be joyful, to be controlled by sexual desire and to be in a situation like death, are because of these arrows. Kamdev himself has five different names- Kam, Manmath, Kandarp, Makardhvaj and Meenketu, The arrows of Kamdev is of flowers and these five flowers are of five tress- Arvind (lotus) Ashok, Amra (Mango), Navmallika and Neelkamal (blue lotus).

अरविन्दमशोकं च आम्रं च नवमल्लिका।
नीलोत्पलं च पंचैते पंचवाणस्य सायकाः॥

Today Ashok is without any flowers but in Sanskrit literature there is vivid mention of its flowers. Possible, the Ashok tree with flowers has disappeared today.

For all those who take the form of the body, five things are definite and destined for them- Age, Karma, Wealth, Education and Death prior to their birth in the womb.

आयुः कर्म च वित्तं च विद्या निधनमेव च।
पंचैतानि हि सृज्यन्ते गर्भस्थस्यैव देहिनः॥

Even after this, for the protection of age, knowledge and money five types of things are forbidden or prohibited- Drink, Meat, Sex, Fish and Currency. These attractions are not good. In the texts we find the description of many forbiddance of rites for the success of work. But in Bhagvad Gita Lord Krishna considers five reasons for the success of any work. They are Ashishthan (palce) Karta (doer), Sadhan (means), Prayatna (effort) and God. These are there in the root of success of every work.

According to the Puranas, five women are considered virgins, even after their marriage and having relations with other men due to some or the other reason. They are Ahalya (wife of Gautam), Draupadi, Tara (wife of Bali), Kunti and Mandodari, whose memory is considered saintly or holy.

अहल्या द्रौपदी तारा कुन्ती मंदोदरी तथा।
पंचकन्या स्मेन्नित्यं महापातकनाशानम्॥

With their memory, all sins are destroyed. The relationship of Ahalya and Indra, the five husbands of Draupadi, after the death of Bali, Tara becomes the wife of Sugreev, Kunti bearing sons from sun, Dharmaraj, Vayu (wind) and Indra, after the death of Ravana Mandodari becomes the wife of Vibhishan. These are the behavior contrary to the validness of society. Even then, Puranas have given them importance. Many ethical persons do not like these incidents. The devotee of Ram, Goswami Tulsidas also writes thus-

जेहि अध बधेउ व्याध जिमि बाली। सोई सुग्रीव पुनि कीन्ह कुचाली।
सोई करतूति विभीषन केरी। सपनेहुँ राम नेकु नहिं हेरी॥

One who protects five fathers like Father, Teacher, Father-in-law, Provider and Fear, he follows the path of five non-possession or Aparigaha of five Mahavrat (great vows)- Non-violence, Truth, Non-stealing, Celibacy and Detachment. God is always pleased with the one who remembers god by foregoing the five attending things like- Scent, Flower, Incense, Lamp and offering for worship and by accepting the importance and greatness of five leaves-Jamun, Kaith, Aam (mango), Bijaura and Bel (golden apple). Taking all these and while worshipping before the five nirajan – Lamp, Lotus, Clothes, Betel leaf and Mango. In any religious occasion of the urn establishment (Kalash-Sthapna) Panchvat, cannot be possibly avoided. These are- Aam, Peepal, Vat, Paakad and Gular.

If one has to perform any auspicious occasion from birth to death, then one has obviously to see the almanac or Panchang in which there is information about date, day, stars or planets youg and karan. Two miles away form Nasik in Dandkaranya where Ram had made his Parnakuti in Pachvati, this name of Panchvati was due to the five types of trees of the fig genus of plants like the-Peepal, Bel, Badh, Harad and Ashok. Some scholars have mentioned the name of Amla (gooseberry) instead of Harad. The purity of the bark of, Pachbakkal in Vedic religion is acceptable to all. They are Badh, Peepal, Gular, Plaksh and Vetas. The dictionary meaning of Plaksh is Badh and Gular. So its is not clear as to which tree is counted separately in pachbakkal. Before taking food, the the theist persons take out Pachkaval- five portion or food for-Dog, Downtrodden, Ill person, Leper and Crow, this is followed in symbolized way.

India is a country of hermits, beneficent or donors and martyrs. Among them are five donors- Bali, Shivi, Dadiehi, Karna and Harishchandra are the supreme. In spite of being cautioned by his guru Shukracharya, Bali gave donation to Lord Vaman and in spite of being deceived is considered the foremost among donors. Shivi cut the parts of the body one by one and put it on the balance for the protection of the dove which had come to his rescue. Dadhichi donated his bones for the protection of gods. Karna presented an excellent example of his generosity by giving his breastplate and spiral.

Great kind Harishchandra underwent agony as he gave away all his belongings in his dreams which he thought as real or genuine, the fact is known to all.

As such the number of nakshatra or lunar houses is 27 but among them five of the asterisms are considered inauspicious. So it is a contraband to perform any auspicious occasion in this Panchak. They are- Dhanishtha, Shatbhisha, Poorvabhadra pad, Uttarachadrapad and Ravati. Along with the nature the five types of work that god or the divine powers have to do is called Panchkritya which are-Creation, Conjuncture, Extermination or Carnage, Disappearance and Mercy. Everybody has the yearning to bathe in Panch ganga, the five holy rivers namely- Ganga, Yamuna, Saraswati, Kirna and Dhootpapa. In Kashi there is a place where Kirna and Dhootpapa rivers meet the river Ganga. At present both these rivers are vanishing. The Ganga flowing in Kashi brings along Yamuna and Saraswati with it.

This Indian land co-ordinated with the knowledge of Vedas, there are five kinds of sounds-Veda sound, Sound of detainee or convict, Sound of crowd, Sound of conch and Sound of mark are considered sublime. Also the right of Panch Mahashabd has been limited to kings and emperors in which Shring, Khanjadi, Shankh (conch), Bheri (kettle drum) and Jayghanta (bell of victory). These used to make great tumult sound or Mahatumulnaad. Whether there is the performance of worship or there is yagna, a pundit (learned or skilled) gives the instruction to bring five types of flowers such as- Champa, Mango, Shami, Lotus and Kaner together with five types of dry fruits- Almonds, Dates, Raisins, Soft pistachio and soft coconut. In Vedic religion the importance of Brahmins is acknowledged. Brahmins have divided themselves as Gaud and Dravid and both of these have five distinctions. Among the Panch Gaud are- Gaud, Saraswat, Kanyakubj, Maithil and Utkal and among Panch Dravid are- Maharashtra, Telang, Karnatak, Gurjar and Dravid. These are the cognition of Brahmins as per their place. So it is irrelevant to have their distinction of small and great.

The five things of Sikhs are- Kanghi (comb), Kachha (loin cloth), Kada (bangle), Kripan (sword) and Kesh (hair), this is the introduction of all. But the Panch Pyare Guru Gobind Singh are- Dayaram Khatri of Lahore, Dharamdas Jat of Delhi Hastinapur,

Mohammad chand Dhabi of Dwarka, Sahabchand Nai of Bidar and Himmatraj Kahar of Jagganathpuri. It is necessary to remember them for the sovereignty, integrity, love for one's country and love for the power of religion-These Panch pyare of five dear ones are from five provinces respectively as- Punjab, Uttar Pradesh, Gujarat, Karnatak and Odisha who covered all the four directions of the country and express the country's unity integrity and largeness. These Panch Pyare demonstrate to the divisive forces that sacrifices are given by persons not place or any patch of province. Among these five none are from the present Punjab. The Sikhs have five Takhts (throne) where the problems of Sikh religion are solved. Among these five takht, Amritsar is the highest place. The five takhts are-1. Akaal takht at Amritsar, 2. Shree takhat- Harimandir Sahib at Patna, 3. Keshgadh Sahib takht at Anandpur, 4. Hajoor Sahib takht at Nanded and 5. Damdama Sahib takht at Bahtinda. Like the Panchakkars there are Panch Jakars which are scarce-

जननी जन्मभूमिश्च जाह्नवी च जनार्दनः।
जनकः पंचमश्चैव जकाराः पंच दुर्लभाः॥

–सुभाषितरत्नभण्डागार 157/170

They are Janani (mother), Janmabhoomi (motherland), Jahnavi (Ganga), Janardan (god) and Janak (father). The natural images of the king is of five types because he protects the lives, wealth, prestige, health and law and order of his subjects. For this cause and situation a king takes the form of five according to time. A king works as- fire, sun, death, wealth or kuber and yama from time to time. When sinners deceive the king with the attitude of pretense and deception, then he takes the form of fire and becomes brilliant and with his intense heat burns all the sinners. When a king is furious with anger due to the actions of unrighteous and immoral people, he destroys their son, their grandson and assistants or accomplices, then he takes the form of death. When a king looks after and protects his subjects through detectives together information, then he takes the form of sun. When a king lavishes wealth for the beneficent and punishes the non-beneficent by taking away their wealth, that time he is in the form of Kuber. When a king is kind and benevolent to the religious souls and gives severe punishment to unrighteous people to bring them on the path of rectification, then he is in the form of Yamraj or the god of death.

These five things sustain on the basis of humility, like-Religion, Truth, Ethics, Power and Wealth. Where there is humbleness, these five come their on their own. Three reasons of enmity are famous- Jar, Wife and Land. But the writers of Mahabharat show five reasons of enmity- 1. For a woman, 2. For house and land, 3. For harsh speech, 4. Due to communal hatred and 5. Offence committed a sometime. In the modern times the number of reasons have increases to quite some extent. However more or less may be the number of friends of a person but five natural friends are always close to them and are always with them and they also come to rescue in times of crisis. These five are- Knowledge, Valour, Proficiency, Strength and Patience. Before eating food, five should be washed with water. They are both hands, both feet a mouth. Already five types of prohibition have been mentioned on their line five positive things are-Similar nature or likeness, Simplicity, Closeness (of guru and disciple), Freedom and self-restraint, give salvation and power of psychic ability.

समभावोऽथ सारल्यं सामीप्यं गुरूशिष्ययोः।
स्वाधीन्यं संयमश्चैते, सकाराः पंच मोक्षदाः।।

In the ashram procedural system the children of king and commoner study together in the same environment. This is the example of Sambhaav. When a king's son also went going about begging then one could see the likeness between a king and a commoner. Even the kings and emperors went about begging in Brahmacharya ashram and went to the forest in Vanprasthashram. This is the image of simplicity. For the sake of gaining knowledge a disciple has to go close to a guru. Freedom is to protect one's self-respect and without the control of the mind and senses, no psychic power or success can be gained. So it is advised to imbibe these five things. In the hands of a person there are five pilgrimages, as believed. The devotees of Sandhya prayer, accept the importance of these pilgrimages. At the tip of the finger is Devtirth. At he base of Kanishtha and Anamika fingers is Rishitirth which is also called as Arshtirth, Karyatirth and Prajapatyatirth. In the middle part of thumb and Tarjani is Pitratirth. At the base of thumb is Brahmatirth and at the middle part of palms is Vaishnavtirth. Vaishnavtirth is considered to be the best among all tirth.

If these five persons go to somebody house after a gap of one year they should be worshipped with Madhupark (a mixture of milk and honey). They are king, priest, bachelor, guru and father-in-law. Some texts have mentioned their number as six and in these have included- Teacher, Priest, Relative, Bachelor, Friend and King. If one recollects five holy places in his mind and takes bath at home, he becomes free of sins. These are the memorable place-Kurukshetra, Ganga, Gaya, Prabhas and Pushkar. There are five such unprincipled persons who are never freed from burdens, they should be renounced from a far. They are- Murderers, Unfaithful or aethist, or one who is dependent on a woman for one's livelihood. Donation is also said to be of five types- 1. Righteous donation-The donation with the desire fame, respect and prestige in this world and happiness in another world. 2. Wealth based donation-A donation given to hear one's renounced name from the mendicants, 3. Fear based donation- A donation given with a feeling of fear, that if it is denied then one will be humiliated or one will malign reputation. With this feeling donation is given to leaders and high officials, 4. Desire based donation- In this types of donation one's desires are connected and 5. Mercy based donation-when one is melted by somebody's poverty and gives a donation.

Five types of persons are considered deficient- 1. One who tells lies, 2. One who is jealous of good work, 3. One who does not perform sandhya, 4. One who is argumentative and obstinate, 5. One who humiliates a person who has come with an invitation for five types of purification shuddhi or expiation is required. The expiation of mind, karma, family, body and speech brings purification.

मनःशौचं कर्मशौचं कुलशौचं च भारत।
शरीरशौचं वाक्शौचं शौचं पंचविध स्मृतम्॥

An another ethical person has shown five other types of piousness. They are-Follow truth, purify mind, Control senses, Compassion and benevolence for all living and washing with water. They are the five types of cleansing-

सत्यशौचं मनःशौचं शौचामिन्द्रयनिग्रहः।
सर्वभूते दयाशौचं जलशौचं च पंचमम्॥

In spite of being a fiancée, a woman can have another husband for five reasons as per rule-1. If the future husband had gone to another country, 2. If he dies, 3. If he becomes a sage, 4. If he is infertile and 5. If he is sinful. Five have to face five tests at five occasions-1. Friend in times of crisis, 2. Hero in war, 3. Sacred woman in a secluded place, 4. Wife when glory, wealth diminished and 5. Hospitality to guests daring famine. These are the identification of their being very lovable

आपत्सु मित्रं जानीयाद्रणे शूरं रहः शुचिम्।
भार्या च विभवे क्षीणे दुर्भिक्षे च प्रियातिथिम्।।

This shloka is also found with some changes-

आपत्सु मित्रं जानीयाद् युद्धे शूरं धने शुचिम्।
भार्या क्षीणेषु वित्तेशु व्यसनेषु च बाँधवान्।।

These five ruin the longevity of age- 1. The heat of morning sun, 2. Excessive sex, 3. Going to a cemetery, 4. To warm palms in fire and 5. To see a woman during menses. Another ethical person has cautioned people who desire for long age- 1. Heat of bright sun, 2. Smoke of funeral fire, 3. Old lady, 4. State curd and 5. Dust from a broom. In some texts its number is shown as six, they are- Dry meat, Old lady, Hot sun, Use of curt at night, Sex in early morning, Sleep at early morning, These six ruin the life. Some texts have show five qualities to increase the longevity of age- 1. Tender feelings and behavior towards all living being, 2. Not to see faults in qualities, 3. Tolerance, 4. Patience and 5. Not to be trusted-1. River, 2. Animals with nails and horns, 3. Man armed with weapons, 4. Woman and 5. Family of king. These five can destroy the chaste behavior of a woman- 1. Company of knave and scoundrel person, 2. Separation for a long period, 3. Excessive respect and prestige, 4. Affection towards other and 5. To live in others house. These five tasks are supposed to be done slowly- 1. Acquisition of knowledge, 2. Accumulation of wealth, 3. Mountaineering, 4. Desired psychic powers and 5. Righteous behavior. It is not proper for a scholar to live in a place where these five are not found in ones country or village. These five are- Wealthy, Kshatriya, King, River and Doctor.

धनिकः श्रोत्रियो राजा नदी वैद्यस्तु पंचमः।
पंच यत्र न विद्यन्ते न तत्र दिवसं वसेत्॥

– चाणक्यनीति 1-19

At some places, they are called as prophet, king, river and gentle person. Actually they fulfill the entire needs of life. The king protects, one gets financial help from a wealthy person during financial crisis. Pundit or learned persons get to perform and accomplish religious rites. A river will always provide water and with that water agriculture and wealth will grow and prosper. Doctors treat physical ailments. From prophets we gain knowledge the king whose five persons are not careful towards their duties, his state cannot be stable. They are- Son, Servant, Minister, Priest and Senses. One should take special care of Snake, Horse, Woman, King and Low community armed person. These do not take time to change-

उरग तुरग, नारी नृपति, नीच जाति हथियार।
रहिमन इन्हे संभारिये, पलटत लगै न वार॥

These five can be controlled by five means- 1. Child with sweet things, 2. Gentleman with humility, 3. Woman with wealth, 4. Gods with meditation and 5. All people with good conduct. These five are not considered as exact or accurate- Wind, Fire, Gold, Sea and Nectar drunk by the gods. Lakshmi the goddess of wealth leaves persons for five reasons- 1. One who wears dirty clothes, 2. One who does not keep clean teeth, 3. One who eats more, 4. One who speaks harsh words, and 5. One who sleeps during sunrise and sunset.

कुचैलिनं दंतमलोपधारिणं बह्वाशिनं निष्ठुरवाक्यभाषिणम्।
सूर्योदये ह्यस्तमयेऽपि शायिनं विमुंचति श्रीरपि चक्रपाणिम्॥

One should not walk in between these five- 1. Between Brahmin and fire, 2. Between two Brahmins, 3. Between husband and wife, 4. Between master and mistress and 5. Between horse and bull. With these five actions, even the prosperity and wealth of Indra comes to an end. They are- 1. To eat others share of food, 2. To use others wealth, 3. To sleep on others bed, 4. To have sex with or to enjoy with other woman and 5. To live in others house.

Five persons remain unsuccessful in their own work- 1. Negligent businessman, 2. Egoist servant, 3. Voluptuous beggar, 4. Poor who has numerous desires and 5. Prostitute with harsh language. Five karmas or actions are the bad characters of man- 1. To be donor in poverty, 2. To be miserly although being wealthy, 3. Not to be the obedient son, 4. To be in the service of bad persons and 5. To die while doing ill to somebody else. Five things burn a person without fire- 1. Separation from wife, 2. Humiliation by Kilns or own people, 3. Remaining debt, 4. Service of rogues and 5. Aversion of friends due to poverty. But if these five are acquired then all sorrows are destroyed from roots. They are- 1. Compatible son, 2. Education which gives money, 3. Healthy body, 4. Good company and 5. Controlled wife.

Gold, silver, pearl, lapis lazuli and coral are called gems. Some texts have mentioned five gems as- Sapphire, diamond, emerald, pearl and coral. Five types of Brahmins, in spite of being scholarly like Brahaspati are not worshipped like-1. Without patience, 2. Rough and harsh in nature, 3. Immobile, 4. Wearing dirty clothes and 5. Being present in a meeting or assembly uninvited. There is no stability in these five- 1. Shade of a cloud, 2. Love of a rogue, 3. Company of strange woman, 4. Youth and 5. Wealth. A student shows ideal image when he possesses five qualities- 1. Curiosity like a crow, 2. Concentration like a crane, 3. Sleep like a dog, 4. One who eats less and 5. A student who stays away from home.

काक्चेष्टा बकोध्यानं श्वाननिद्रा तथैव च।
अल्पहारी गृहत्यागी विद्यार्थिनः पंचलक्ष्मणम्॥

Hindranees ministers are of two types but each of them have five distinctions like- fire, floods, spreading of disease, famine and epidemic are natural disasters. Other disasters are manmade like- fear from the states officials, robbers, enemies, persons dear to king and the king himself. The five divine trees are- Madar, Parijat, Santan, Kalpvriksh and Harichandan. The world renowned famous text of Panchtantra, famous for its simple stories in which the three sons of king Amarshakti, Bahushakti, Ugrashakti and Anantshakti were made scholars in six months by the teacher Vishnu Sharma. This Panchtantra has five distinction-1. Friend, 2. Attainment of friend, 3. Kakolukiya, 4. Labdhpranash and 5. Aparikshitkarak.

There are many pilgrimages of his country among which Pachnath has special importance. In the north Badrinath- Badrikashram in Uttaranchal, in the south Rangnath- Shrirang in Madras or Chennai, in east Jagganath- Neelanchalpuri in Odisha, in west Dwarikanath-Dwarka in Gujrat and in the centre Govardhannath in Rajasthan are called Panchnath.

One should be extremely careful to do the services of five, because if any of them becomes furious then there will be a catastrophe. These five are-Mother, father, guru, soul and fire. Pure air, pure water, pure land, pure light and pure food are Panchamrit. Persons who are careful about five things live for 100 years.

वामशायी द्विभुंजानो षणमूत्री द्विपुरीषकः।
स्वल्पमैथुनकारी च शतं वर्षाणि जीवति॥

(One who sleeps turning on left side, one who takes food two times a day, one who goes for small natural calls six times a day, one who cleanses the body twice a day and on being a house holder has very little sex, such persons live for hundred years). The love relationship happen with someone due to five reasons-1. Birth, 2. Relative, 3. Association or acquaintance, 4. Selfish motive and 5. Ethics and culture. Love relationship with parents, son and daughter and brother and sister is because of the reason of birth. Love grow when one is connected by relation like husband, wife, mother-in-law, and father-in-law. Friendship happens due to association. Sometimes one tries to be close with a motive of selfishness and one does not know when it changes to love. Sometimes we love a person by hearing or knowing about him. Then it is due to the reason of ethics. The discussion of Ashtasiddhi will be done in the eighth chapter. Among the Psychic powers, two more have been mentioned, which will be discussed in chapter 10, but in this chapter, apart from the 10, there are five such Psychic powers are attained by the yogis or spiritual sage-1. Yogis know about the past, future and present, 2. They are not under the control of cold-heat, joy-sorrow, attachment-malevolence, 3. They have the power to know other peoples mind and thoughts, 4. A yogi can benumb and shock even the powers of fire, sun, water, poison etc. and 5. He is invincible for all. The entire army of Vishwamitra was defeated before the yogic power of Vashishth. At that time Vishwamitra has commented thus-

धिगबलं क्षत्रियबलं ब्रह्मतेजोबलं बलम्।
ऐकेन ब्रह्मदण्डेन सर्वास्त्राणि हुतानि मे।।

The woman whose husband has gone to a foreign land, five things are forbidden for her- Games, Make-up, and Participation in Social functions. Fun and frolic and go to a stranger's house. In five things, five evil and unrighteous things reside like in Gambling- Lie, Drinking- Anger, Company of woman- Passion or lust, Violence- enmity and Gold- Rajagan. So those who are keen to have their welfare and well-being should stay away from always. There are five characteristics of touch are Tender, Hard, Cold, Hot and Touch of wind. In Mahabharat war by challenging Arjun and keeping him away from the main area of war, were the five warrior. They were the king of Trigart state Sanshaptak and his five brothers whose names were- Satyarath, Satyaverma, Satyavra, Satyeshu and Satyakarma. One should not be friends of feelings are missing- Livelihood, Fear, Modesty, Cleverness and Sacrifice.

लोकयात्रा भयं लज्जा दाक्षिण्यं त्यागशीलता।
पंच यत्र न विद्यन्ते न कुर्यात् तत्र संगतिम्।।

–चाणक्य नीति 1–10

In the tradition of Indian worship, there is very great importance of Panchopchar (five cures). In worship one has to have-Fragrance, Flowers, Incense, Lamp and Offering as Prasad. Panchamrit made for a guest or for the worship of god is made of five things, by mixing them together. They are- Milk, Curd, Ghee, Honey and Sugar. For the bath of god, Panchganga is used. They are Ganga, Yamuna, Saraswati, Godavari and Narmada. Many who worship goddesses have five Mahadevi who are worshipped. They are called- Durga, Parvati, Savitri, Saraswati and Radha. The Mahamantras of Shaiva and Vaishnav cults are also of five letters- **'ऊँ नमः शिवाय'** and **'ऊँ विष्णवे नमः'** Mother, father, teacher, guest, husband and wife are patristic and customary gods. Their worldly behavior is proved. Hence the should be dignified and greeted after the war of Mahabharat Krishna had accepted himself that it was not possible to kill these five warriors due to righteousness in war. These five were- Bhishma, Drona, Karna, Bhanishrava and Duryodhan. One cannot acquire knowledge due to five reasons- Arrogance, Anger, Carelessness, Disease and Laziness.

Those who are prosperous and are generous, such persons should divide their earned wealth in five parts and spend it.

धर्माय यशसेऽर्थाय कामाय स्वजनाय च।
पंचधा विभजन् वित्तमिहामुत्र च मोदते॥

These five divisions are for- Religious purposes, Ones fame and prestige, Economy (business and livelihood) Kam (comforts of life) and family or dear ones. Such a person enjoys happiness in this world and in the other world. Five things disappear as soon as one asks for something.

मान बड़ाई प्रेम रस गुरुवापन और नेहु।
ये पाँचों तबहि ही गये जबै कही कछु देहु॥

In this context the following shloka is also ponderable-

देहीति वचनद्वारा देहस्था: पंचदेवता:।
सद्यो निर्गत्य गच्छन्ति धीश्रीह्रीशान्तिकीर्तय:॥

The moment one utters these words- ‘Give me something, five gods present in the body leave. They are- Intelligence, Fortune or wealth, Modesty, Peace and Renown name. In the last chapter for words with ‘G’ were discussed- Gita, Ganga, Gayatri and Govind. In some texts the five ‘Gs’ are called the Panch Pran of the culture of Hindu religion. Among these cow is the fifth one. Among the five types of expiations (shudhdhi), the purity of the heart is the ultimate.

मन: शौचं कर्मशौचं कुलशौचं च भारत।
शरीरशौचं वाक्छौचं शौचं पंचविधं स्मृतम॥
पंचस्वेतेषु शौचेषु हृदिशौचं विशिष्यते।
हृदयस्य च शौचेन स्वर्गं गच्छन्ति मानवा:॥

These five types of expiations are called as- The purity and cleanliness of the heart, Flawless and untainted karmas the tradition of purity of family and lineage purity of the body and purity of speech. Among these five expiations the most outstanding is the purity of the heart. By the purity of heart, one attains heaven speech has five qualities- 1. To speak conducive or beneficial, 2. To speak less, 3. To be silent, 4. To speak sweetly and 5. To speak pleasant. Five types of people do not get the fruits of pilgrimage, even though they go on a pilgrimage-

अश्रद्दधानः पापार्तो नास्तिकोऽच्छिन्न संशयः।
हेतुनिष्ठश्च पंचैते न तीर्थफलभागिनः।।

They are- 1. One who has no faith in pilgrimage, 2. One who is a sinner, 3. One who is an atheist, 4. One who is doubtful and 5. Argumentative. One should eat after washing both hands, both feet and face-

हस्तपादे मुखे चैव पंचार्द्रो भोजनं चरेत्।।

Such a person lives long. When the devotion of god awakens in the heart of a devotee, he does not like five things- 1. Worldly comforts, 2. Sleep, 3. To lark about, 4. Affection in the world and 5. Excessive talking.

नारायण हरि लगन में यह पाँचों न सुहात।
विषय भोग निद्रा हँसी जगतप्रीति बहुबात।।

A man gets dignity with five words. These five are- 1. Education, 2. Body, 3. Speech, 4. Clothes and 5. Wealth and prosperity.

विद्यया वपुषा वाचा वस्त्रेण विभवेन च।
वकारैः पंचभिर्युक्तो नरः प्राप्नोति गौरवम्।।

After taking ones food, one should move ones hand three times on ones stomach and with this mantra remember the five- 1. Agastya, 2. Garud, 3. Shani, 4. Badvanal and 5. Bheem-

अगस्तयं वैनतेयं च शनिं च वडवानलम्।
अन्नस्य परिणामार्थं स्मरेद् भीमं च पंचकम्।।

The mutual relationship of a person are of five types- 1. Friend, 2. Enemy, 3. God hearted, 4. Mendicant or stoic and 5. Moderator. Friend is mutually kind and favorable and enemies are the opposite.

A good-hearted person is are beneficial from their side. A stoic does not side with either our friend or enemy. A moderator is keen for the benefit of both the sides. Only after procuring the proper receptacles one can develop; ones talent. These five are- 1. Weapon, 2. Implements of war, 3. Text, 4. Veena and 5. Woman. Five karmas become resultant when one had tilak (holy mark) on the forehead. They are- 1. Bath, 2. Charity, 3. Tapa, 4. Yagna and 5. Worship of god.

स्नान दानं तपो होमो देवतापितृकर्म च।
तत्सर्वं निष्फलं याति ललाटे तिलकं विना॥

In ancient India a ruler was of five types on the basis of his powers, they were- 1. King, 2. Sovereign, 3. Samrat or emperor, 4. Chakravarti and 5. Universal.

One who respects father, mother, fire, guru and soul, these five he wins over this world and the other world.

पिता माता तथैवग्निर्गुरूरात्मा च पंचमः।
यस्यैते ते पूजिताः पार्थ तस्या लोकावुभौ जितौ॥

–महा. वनपर्व 159–14

A person who desires progress has five gurus-

पञ्चैव गुरवो ब्रह्मन् पुरुषस्य बुभूषतः।
पिता मातग्निरात्मा च गुरुश्च द्विजसत्तम॥

–वही 214–27

In the above two shlokas same thing is said. The five Mahayagnas (great service) are- 1. Worship of parents, 2. Service of husband, 3. Same feelings for all, 4. Not to rebel against friends and 5. To praise Lord Vishnu and sing for him.

पित्रोश्चाथ पत्युश्च साम्यं सर्वजनेषु च।
मित्राद्रोहो विष्णुभक्तिरेत पंच महामखाः॥

–पदमपुराण

A person commits sin due to ignorance but it can be destroyed by 1. Acceptence, 2. Doing good work, 3. By repentance, 4. By giving donation and 5. By meditation.

धनंजय कृतपायं कल्याणेनोपहन्यते।
ख्यापनेनानुतापेन दानेन तपसापि वा।।

–महा. शांतिपर्व 7.36

A man has five natural friends. They are- 1. Knowledge, 2. Bravery, 3. Cleverness, 4. Power and 5. Patience, because intelligent people live by them.

विद्या शौर्यं च दाक्ष्यं च बलं धैर्यंन पंचमम।
मित्राणि सहजान्याहुर्वतयन्ति हि तैर्बुधाः।।

–शुक्रनीति सार 4.13

A king is supreme in his state. A person who has performed Rajsuya yagna after victory in all directions is called Maharaja. Samrat is the title for those who perform Ashwamedh yagna after becoming a Maharaja. One who has performed Ashwamedh yagna again and again and has widened his territory beyond oceans, gets the title of Chakravarti. The rule of Chakravarti is within the boundaries of India. That Chakravarti ruler went beyond the oceans outside the boundaries of India, he used to get the title of universal ruler. In the expansion of the state, horse has a lot of importance. Actually horse is a symbol of state. A running horse was the pointer of the progress of state. It was considered a hindrance for the progress of state if a horse was stopped and held in custody. Such a hindrance would be got rid of by a king through his strength and intelligence. The five things that a house holder expects are- 1. Illusion, 2. Home, 3. Wife, 4. Land and 5. Worldly attitude. These are acquired by saints when god is against them.

माया मन्दिर स्त्री धरती अरु व्यौहार।
वे सन्तन को तब मिलें कोपे जब करतार।।

In the end I pray to god Panchanan that the five parts of Nimb (Neem)- Leaves, Flowers, Fruits, Bark and Roots along with five modes of treatment- Vaman (vomit), Reehan (more excretion), Nasya (sneeze), Anuvasan (massage with oil) and Nirooh (massage without oil) should be protected from and provide shade of five trees- Mandar, Parijat, Santan, Kalpavriksh and Harichandan.

❐

6 (Six)

India is the only country in the world where there are six seasons. In Chaitra- Vaishakh, Vasant (spring), in Jyesh-Asadh, Grishm (summer), in Shravan-Bhadrapad, Varsha (rain), in Ashvin-Kartik, Sharad (autumn), in Agahan-Paush, Hemant (early winter), and in Magh-Falgun (winter). Every season has its own specialty and attraction. Vasant is the king of seasons. It attracts every living being, the world and plants with its beauty and intoxication. In this season, one is free from extreme cold. Also, there is no excessive heat at this time. The first clouds of the rain attract the lives who have been scarched by the heat of summer. Sharad is enjoyable for both wealthy and poor. The winter of Hemant and Shishir makes one experience of both joy and sorrow.

This is Kaliyug. The various facets of religion had disappeared. Even after this scholars of religion have asked to follow, in this yug, six compulsory rules, they are- Sandhya, Bath, Japa, Worship of gods, Hospitality of guests and Yugdharma. These are called Nitya Karma (routine work)

सन्ध्या स्नानं जपो होमो देवतानां च पूजनम्।
आतिथ्यं वैश्वदेवं च षट् कर्माणि दिने दिने।।

In the last chapter hospitality to guests and Balivaishvadev, Yagna have been described. With bath the body is expatiated whereas sandhya and japa are the means of mental expatiation. By the worship of gods, we express our gratitude to them. Some texts have made slight changes six desirable karmas are mentioned. They are- Agnihom, tapa, swadhyay, constant obedience to the orders of Vedas, hospitality to guests and Balivaishvadev yagna, these are the six karma rituals. Our culture is predominant of yagna. For every auspicious occasions yagnas are performed.

The foundation of religion is Veda. So one should follow its command as an obligation.

Six pious karmas are supposed to be done by a person- 1. Construct a large well, 2. To dig wells, 3. Construction of water bodies, 4. To construct temple, 5. Charity of food and 6. To groom gardens. These are six such tasks which gives happiness and satisfaction to famished people and refugees. First three tasks is to provide water to human being animals and birds. God's temple gives peace to the mind. Food satisfies and calms the pansy of hunger. Woods and gardens are those that give manifold happiness. Six good qualities make a person graceful. They are Tenderness, Kindness, Patience, Good behavior, Control on senses and Control on mind. Some texts have mentioned them as- Bravery, Brilliance, Morale, Donation, Politeness and Prosperity, the six qualities. Six types of devilish feelings should be crushed by hard implements like stones. These three mental frames are compared to animals and birds like- 1. That of owl or doubt and uncertainty, 2. That of wolf or attacking, 3. That of dog or parasite, 4. That of sparrows or unsocial, 5. That of garud or arrogant and 6. That of kite or greed. Here there is description of the mental frames representing anger, envy or jealousy, passion, lust and greed. These six internal group of enemies is called Shadvarg.

Veda may have four parts but the number of Vedang are six. Among these Vedang astrology is called the eye, terminology ears, education nostrils, grammar mouth, period hands and verse are called legs. Astrology was basically a physical science. Now there are no texts available for Vedic astrology. It is the work field of astrology to ascertain time and period for culture for occasions and yagna proceedings etc. In astrology there is description of lunar houses of asterisms (nakshtra), date, fortnight, month, season and personified year and all its phases one can know the derivations of the vedic words and the meaning of mantras and their differences in knowledge from the terminology. Terminology is the encyclopedia of Vedas. Now-a-days the terminology of sage yaska is available on which many commentary and expositions have been written. The primary knowledge of mantra is the field of education. Education is the approach and procedure for the cause of practice of Vedmantras and their right and adequate pronunciation.

This is called the art of pronunciation. In this teaching the procedure of yagna is explained. To prepare the platform, to cook, the bait. The teaching has relation to both bait and god. Grammar is the introduction of the right perception of office. The basic text of grammar is Panini's Ashtadhyayi grammar on this text also there have been comments, and criticisms. Grammar stabilizes the rules of language. It also stabilizes the meaning rules and the image of form. Through grammar one gets to know the words and introduction to meaning. It is the work of grammar to stop unsoundness in Veda. The importance of grammar is expressed thus-

यद्यपि बहुनाधीषे तथापि पठ पुत्र व्याकरणम्।
स्वजनः श्वजनो मा भूत् सकलं शकलं सकृत् शकृत्।।

Although you have studied enough, even then, O! Son study the grammar because without studying grammar you will not understand the discrimination of pronunciation. So a swajan (relative) may not be pronounced as shwajan (dog) or Sakal (all)- Shakal (piece), Sakrit (once)- Shakrit (excreta).

In Kalp, the appropriation precept is described. This is the text of karmakand (ritualism). Thus the procedures of yagna are described in Kalp Vedang. The expatiation of the vessels of yagna, the collection of the materials of yagna etc. These things are explained in this text. This is written in poetry form. So from every prosody or verse, one gets to know the rishi of god of every verse. It is necessary to have the knowledge of every verse for the right pronunciation of Ved Mantras. Without the right knowledge and study of verses and pronunciation of mantras, one cannot have the proper image of Vedas. The entire Vedang Ved is the means to comprehend the real meaning of Ved mantras.

Like Vedang, Ved has six Upang which are called Shaddarshan. Philosophy is the text which expresses, its viepoint on the genesis of nature's creation, the reason of birth and death of the living being and its pace, state and condition. There are six theist philosophy. They are- Critical investigation (mimanshu), Vedant, Atomic theory (Vaishashik), Justice or propriety (nyay), Spiritual reality (sankhya) and yoga. One who has faith in Veda is called a theist. Mamansa and sankhya do not believe in god, but because they believe in Ved, they are they are theist philosophy. 'नास्तिको वेद निन्दकः' On this saying there are six atheist philosophy, who have no faith in Ved and so they also say 'त्रयो वेदस्य कर्तारो धूर्तभाण्डनिशाचराः।' persons who are the defamers of Shaddarshan Ved are- Charvak, Jain, Vaibhashik, Sautrantik. Yogachar and Shoongavad. Normally there is no support for person who do not have faith in Ved, God and Sanskrit. So there are six founder spiritual teachers whose names are- Jaimini for Mimansa, Vyas for Vedant, Kanda for Vaisheshik, Gautam for Nyan, Kapil for Sankhya and Patanjali for yog. There are six such enemies who should not be under estimated 'रिपुरुज पावक पाप्र प्रभु, अहि गनिअ न छोट करि' So always be cautioned when an enemy will gain more power and cause among when a disease will take a monstrous form, when fire will spread with the help of wind, sin shows itself sometime or other, a master may take a reverse attitude and snake is the pest of death. Nobody can be the same as a mother, even then six women are considered as mother in context to relationship. So they are called upmata. They are- Mother, Sister, Sister-in-law, Aunt, Father's sister, Mother-in-law and Mother's sister-in-law come under this category. In this world we come in touch with many people but these relationship are connected by six types of feelings. These six feelings are- Passion, Anger, Fear, Affection, Consensus or agreement and Camaraderie. A person connects for the sake of satisfaction of passionate feelings. When one is angry one gets mentally connected with him. Due to fear one keeps on thinking about one's enemy one connects to one's relatives with affectionate feelings. To be connected to an organization or party is due to camaraderie is due to the closeness of the hearts.

For a king six qualities are expected. A capable rulers should be-Expert in logic, Accomplished in moral code, should be mature and magniloquent and the art of oratory, keeping the memories of past and looking forward to the future. A king has to have six types of relations with the other rulers. These six relations are- Treaty, Separate or independent, Seat, Coach, Doubtful attitude and Aimed foreign policy. Treaty is done with two intentions or purposes. Treaty is done with another king to attack enemy king or by making a treaty with the enemy king for not attacking and establishing friendship with him. Treaty is also best, medium and low-down or unworthy. The treaty that is done after taking money is Vitt Sandhi and is considered the best category. Treaty that is done due to fear is considered of low-down category. In today political relations the form of treaty has changed. In a treaty there is also the consolation of mutual co-operation that is inherent. In vigrah or separation one has to fight with the enemy king or as today one has to curtail relations. In this category also there is the effort to create conflict or bicker between two enemy kings. Aasan is to sit at one's place and express the feeling of neutrality in the expectation of waiting for an opportunity. In aasan, one tries to understand the weakness of one's partisan, one waits for the opportune time. Yaan is to attack the enemy. In this four tasks have to be done. They are- 1. To increase ones friends, 2. To fill one's treasury, 3. To destroy the friends of enemies and 4. To deprive enemies treasury. In Dvaidhibhav, One achieves the goal by dividing the army in two parts and fights under the leadership of the king and the commander. To sow dissension among enemies or express friendship from outside but nature enmity from inside, comes under this category. One should take the refuge of some strong king, when the enemy is stronger than us one has the appreciation of one's defeat or one has to face the agony of the enemy king, then through aimed foreign policy or and kinship harness one should seek the refuge.

Woman is the most beautiful of all god's creations. It increases her beauty if six parts of her body are raised and prominent. These six parts are- 2 hips or buttocks, 2 breasts, one forehead and one nose **'श्रोण्यौ ललाटमुरू च घ्राणं चेति षडुन्नतम्'**। In Mahaudyog Parva-116-131, Vyas has mentioned thighs or urn in place of breasts. One who eats less, gains six qualities-Health, Longevity, Strength, Happiness, Best progeny and the Lack of Sarcasm of eating more.

The six body parts of a cow are considered good if they are big and sturdy and strong. These six parts are-Neck, Thighs, Back, Tail, Head and Teats. There are six types of persons who disturb the peace of the society.

अग्निदो गरदश्चैव शस्त्रोन्मत्तो धनापहः।
क्षेमदारहरश्चैतान् षड् विद्यादाततायिनः॥

–शुक्रनीतिसार 3–40

1. One who set fire. 2. One who gives poison. 3. Killers with weapons in hand. 4. Onw who extorts wealth, 5. One who hijacks

field of land and 6. One who kidnaps woman. These are called the six types of desperate people. In the modern world, they are plenty in number. Newspapers are full of such types of information. One does not commit sin if such desperate people are killed, this is the authenticity of texts. Six types of people are always miserable. They are-1. Those who envy others. 2. Those who hate others. 3. Those who are discontented. 4. Those who are angry. 5. Those who are always doubtful and apprehensive and 6. Those who live on the destiny of others.

ईर्ष्यी घृणी न सन्तुष्टः क्रोधनो नित्यशंकितः।
परभाग्योपजीवी च षडेते नित्यदुःखिताः।।

-विदुरनीति 1-15

Six types of diseases in a person cannot possibly be those who are envious of others wealth, beauty, valour, nobility, happiness, privilege and fame.

य ईर्षुः परवित्तेषु रूपे वर्ये कुलान्वये।
सुखसौभाग्य सत्कारे तस्य व्याधिरनन्तकः।।

-महा. उद्योगपर्व-34-42

There are six reasons for ruining of wealth-To take any type of intoxicating things, To loiter around at the cross roads, Interest in music and dance, Gambling, Company of bad friends and be immersed in laziness, Their wealth is definitely bound to be ruined. Six types of bad qualities develop inferior character in women. They are- Consuming intoxicating things, acquaintance with men and women of bad or evil characters, To stay away from one's husband, To loiter around here and there aimlessly, To sleep at odd times, and To stay at other's house, this brings the situation of a woman's fall or retrogradation of character.

पानं दुर्जनसंसर्गः पत्या च विरहोऽटनम्।
स्वप्नोऽन्यगेहवासश्च नारीसंदूषणानि षट्।।

It is beneficiary to renunciate these six persons-1. Teacher who does not teach. 2. Desired family priest. 3. King who does not protect. 4. Wife who speaks harsh language. 5. Shepherds or cowherds who are keen to stay in village and 6. Barbe who wishes to go to the forest, these should be left alone-

षडेतान् पुरुषो जह्याद् भिन्नां नावमिवार्ण वै।
अप्रवक्तारमाचार्यमनधीयानमृत्विजम्।।
अरक्षितारं राजानं भार्यां चाप्रियवादिनीम्।
ग्रामकामं च गोपालं वनकामं च नापितम्।।

–महा. शान्तिपर्व 57–44–45

One should leave these six like one leaves a broken boat in the sea. The enemies which stay in the mind- Passion, Anger, Greed, Enchantment, Jealousy and Egotism. These are always grievous. It is always conducive and good to remain protected from them.

There is a rule or precept for six karmas or duties of a Brahmin. They are- Learning, Teaching, To perform yagna, To help in performing yagna, To give donation and to take donation.

अध्यापनमध्ययनं यजनं याजनं तथा।
दानं प्रतिग्रहं चैव ब्राह्मणानामकल्पयत्।।

–मनुस्मृति

Among these six duties of Brahmin, the three duties are duties of elevation-To study, to perform yagna and to give donation. To teach and to perform yagna for others and earn one's livelihood are good duties. To live one's life by taking donation is not good. If due to any reason, a Brahmin is not able to maintain his livelihood, then there are six other rules for his earnings. They are-To collect food scattered in the fields, to arrange for some donation, to beg, to do some odd business or by farming and cattle rearing, he can carry on with his livelihood. Yudhishthir is well-known for his six qualities- Tenderness, Mercy, Patience, Humbleness, and Control of senses and Control of mind.

आनृंशस्यमनुक्रोशो धृतिश्शीलं दमश्शमः।
पाण्डवं शोभयन्त्येते षड्गुणाः पुरुषोत्तमम्।।

Six qualities should never be abandoned- Truth, Charity, Activity, Free from envy, Forgiveness and Patience.

षडेव तु गुणाः पुंसा न हातव्याः कदाचन।
सत्यं दानमनालस्यमनुसूया क्षमा धृति॥

-विदुरनीति 1-18

Everybody desires for six types of happiness in this world. They are-Health, Lack of debt, Lack of travel, Good company. Independent livelihood and a fearless home. Six persons are dependent on six other persons like-Robbers on negligent and heedless persons, Doctor on patients, Women on passionate men, Claimant or beggar on Parishioner (yajman), King on fighters and pandit on the fools-

षडिमे षटसु जीवन्ति सप्तमो नोपलभ्यते।
चौराः प्रमते जीवन्ति व्याधितेषु चिकित्सकाः॥
प्रमदाः कामयानेषु यजमानेषु याजकाः।
राजा विवदमानेषु नित्यं मुर्खेषु पण्डिताः॥

-विदुरनीति 89-90

Due to carelessness or non caution for sometime, these six can be destroyed, they are-Cows, Service, Farm, Woman, Knowledge and Righteous Company, they should be carefully protected. These six neglect their prior beneficiaries- 1. A student neglect the teacher from whom he has attained knowledge. 2. A son neglects his mother after marriage. 3. A woman neglects after her passions are satisfied. 4. A needful person after his need are fulfilled. 5. A protector or a boat is neglected after one crosses over jungle and water, and 6. A patient neglects his doctor.

षडेते ह्यबमन्यते नित्यं पूर्वोपकारिणम।
आचार्यं शिक्षिताः शिष्याः कृतदाराश्च मातरम्॥
नारीं विगतकामास्तु कृतार्थाश्च प्रयोजकम्।
नावं निस्तीर्णकान्तारा आतुराश्च चिकित्सकम्॥

-विदुरनीति 1-92-93

Six bad qualities decrease the longevity – Excessive egotism, Lack of sacrifice, Anger, Desire of one's own livelihood and Rebellion towards friends. On the basis of family relations, sons are of six types- 1. Born from one's own wife 2. Grandson of one's daughter 3. Pranati or son born out of one's wife through the grace of another man. 4. Paunarbhave or the son born out of second marriage. 5. Kaneen- when a daughter is marriage the condition put forth is that the first son born out of her womb will be of her father and 6. Sister's son. There are also six types of sons outside the family- 1. Adopted-the son whom his parents have dedicated. 2. Kreet-One who has been purchased after giving money. 3. Kritrim-One who has come close as a son. 4. Sahodh-One born out of unmarried daughter. 5. Gyatireta-One born out of low caste than oneself and Manas-One who is believed to be a son from one's heart.

Six Manas Putra of Lord Brahma are famous as great rishis. They are-Marichi, Atri, Angira, Pulastya, Pulaha and Kratu. Only the most extraordinary are gifted with six types of properties. They are- 1. Sham (Intelligence/mind constantly with god), 2. Dam (Control of sense), 3. Uprati (To be away from bad people), 4. Titiksha (To tolerate all kinds of conflicts including agony), 5. Shraddha (Faith on Vedas, texts, guru and their teachings as a direct seer or on looker) and 6. Samadhan (Lack of doubt and apprehension and aberration in one's heart), Sham is the feeling to involve and immerse one's soul and heart in righteous attitude or control one's self. Dam is said to be the control of senses and working organs and the mind in good karmas. Uprati is the feeling to stay away from people who do evil things and to control the activities of the mind. Titiksha is the feeling to abandon feelings like compensation, worry, lamentation etc., and to bear all sorrows with repose. Shraddha is the faith on teachings of guru, trusted teachings and statements of sages and hermits and religious texts. Finally, Samadhan is the feeling of lack of all doubts and concentration of the mind on Brahma. In there, six there is the lack of stability-

यौवनं जीवितं चित्तं छाया लक्ष्मीश्च स्वामिता।
चंचलानि षडेतानि ज्ञात्वा धर्मरतो भवेत्॥

-शुक्रनीति सार 1-138

One should be engrossed in righteous path considering youth, life, mind, shadow and domination as inconsistent and fickle. Baths are of six types- 1. Brahma Snan- One with the utterance of mantras and water drops spring led with the help of kush or blade of grass. 2. Agneya Snan-Coating of the entire body from head to foot with the ashes from fire. 3. Vayavyay Snan- to be grizzled or strewn with dasi from the dust arising out of cows feet. 4. Divya Snan-To bath in the rain when the sun is also there. 5. Vaaran Snan-To jump into the water and bath by immersing in water and finally. 6. Yogic Snan-It is to bath in the contemplation of the soul and that of god's memory. Some texts have also shown them as- Vaarun, Mantra, Bhaum, Agneya, Vayavya, Divya and Manas. Great rishi Shankh has described these six types of baths as-Nitya, Naimitik, Kamya, Kriyang, Malakarshak and Kriyasnan. Nitya snan is done every day in the morning Rajaswala or menstruating woman who is taking the bath or when one touches a corpse or any untouchable thing. That is Naimitik snan, the bath that is taken on the rising of holy lunar asterism (nakshatra) is called Kamya snan, like the bath on Somvati Amavasya or Purnima etc. on the banks of rivers and lakes. Kriyang snan is the one which is done with japa of holy mantras for the worship of gods and dead ancestors. That is also Kriyang bhoot snan. Kriya snan is the combined community bath taken at the pilgrimages banks of holy rivers, banks of ponds, small water body with the aim to gain benevolence and purity. Kriya snan is done on the occasions of Kumbh, Kartik and Purnima etc.

For a house holder six persons are meant for reverence- 1. Parents, 2. Teacher, 3. Wife, 4. Friend, 5. Servant and 6. Brahmin. There are six means to attain final liberation- 1. Study of Vedas, 2. Dedication to vow or tapa, 3. Knowledge of true learning, 4. Control of senses, 5. Following religion and 6. Meditatin and contemplation of god. These six are incomparable in comparison- 1. Veda among texts, 2. Shiva among gods, 3. Brahmin among the humans, 4. Varanasi among cities, 5. Shadakshar or six lettered mantras among all mantras and 6. Guru among protectors. Among gods, Shiva is said to be incomparable and Shadakshar is the mantra for his worship. 'Om Namah Shivay' is the one to save everyone from the distress of Kaliyug. These six should be abandoned- 1. A wife without qualities. 2. A rascal friend. 3. An unrighteous and immoral king. 4. Bad son. 5. A daughter without qualities and 6. A dirty country. In texts, Mahatma has been shown to have six characteristics-

विपदि धैर्यमथाभ्युदये क्षमा सदसि वाक्पटुता युधि विक्रमः।
यशसि चाभिरुचिर्व्यसनं श्रुतौ प्रकृतिसिद्धमिदं हि महात्मनाम्॥

One who has patience during adversity, one who is forgiving during one's elevation or rise, one who has eloquent oratory in meeting, one who is victorious in war, one who is interested in fame and honor, one who is addicted to the knowledge of texts, he is a Mahatma or great soul.

In India Shaddarshan or six philosophy Yog has special importance. Yog talks about the control of minds faculties- **'योगश्चित्तवृत्तिनिरोधः'** The Hathyogi seeker describes the Shatchakra or six cycles which are-Muladhar, Swadhishthan, Manipurak, Anahat, Vishudhdh and Agya. They considered the position of Brahmarandhra or Sahasrar above all these chakras, above the palate in the brain, in the middle higher part of the head. Here there is the belief or hundreds of lotuses. According to them there is the residence of Shiva in Shasrar. The seeker considerate their duty that by Yog Sadhana, the cycles are to be penetrated to let the meeting of the power of muladhar with that of Shiva existing in Shasrar. Once they are meeting as one or are in oneness then the nectar flow out from mahamukh. These seekers remain engrossed and immersed in meditation to drink the nectar by awakening the down faced sushumna in muladhar to rise to upfaces sahasrar and through it to the meeting point. Due to similarity of their images, these chakras are also called lotus or kamal. Muladhar has four groups of chakras, Adhishthan has six, Manipura has ten, Anahut has twelve, Vishudhdh has sixteen and Agya has two groups cycles. Actually the chakras, that the yogis talk about, are in subtle form or minute form in body not the material body. In Atharvaveda **'अष्टचक्रा नवद्वारा देवानां पः'** the eight chakras that are mentioned are different from Shatchakra or six cycles. According to its belief, there are two chakras on this earth or land- Agya and Sahasrar. The internal has Parjanya chakra, Bhhotgram and Brahma yagna chakra. In the land of gambling there are two chakras Agnisomatmak and Hiranyagarbh chakra and far from the land of gambling. That means far from this universe is the position of the Paramatma chakra or the cycle of the Almighty. So the summary is that at some places are mentioned as six and at others seven, but Artharvaved mentions about eight chakras.

Muladhar chakra lies at the bottom of the spinal chord, two fingers above the intestines between the intestines and sex organs. Its shape is of four petals and is comprised of the predominance of earth elements. Due to his excreta and polluted wind from body is emitted and controlled. In Adhishthan ling or penis base has six petals and is prodimant of water element. When it awakens, it destroys bad feelings like cruelity, pride, laziness, carelessness, contempt or disrespect. In the entire body, this chakra distributes the food material. Manipurak is positioned at the navel. This has ten petals. Who it is awakened feeling like craving for lust, jealousy, fear, hatred and enchantment disappear. This chakra makes the semen matured and ripe. There is a glow and brightness on the face of a person due to this. Anahat chakra positioned in the heart has twelve petals and it is predominant of wind element. On its awakening, fraud, deception, enchantment, arrogance, egotism, ignorance like bad qualities get destroyed. Vishuddh chakra is positioned at the lower part of throat. This chakra has sixteen petals. This has the dominance of sky element. This chakra controls the speech and breath the purification of blood, the concentration of mind and the purification of speech is controlled by this chakra. Here, there is dominance of contemplation. Agya is positioned in between the eyebrows and nose and is of two petals. On its awakening all the powers awaken. The concentration of the mind is done by focusing at this point. This is the gateway to reach upto Sahasrar, from muladhar chakra to all the other chakras and then to Sahasrar chakra, these are the rishis respectively- Kashyap, Atri, Gautam, Bahradwaj, Jamdagni, Vishwamitra and Vashishth.

Due to six reasons, six things get destroyed. 1. A recluse due to material possessions. 3. King due to bad consultation. 3. Knowledge due to attainment of fame. 4. Modesty due to drinking. 5. Love due to lack of humility and simplicity and 6. Virtuous and worthy due to egotism, all soon get destroyed. Shurpnakha tell Ravana-

संग ते जती कुमन्त्र ते राजा। मान ते ज्ञान पान तें लाजा।।
प्रीति प्रनय बिनु मद ते गुनी। नासहिं बेग नीति अस गुनी।।

Those who desire wealth and prosperity should abandon six bad qualities.

षड्दोषा पुरुषेणेह हातव्या भूतिमिच्छता।
निद्रा तन्द्रा भयं क्रोध आलस्यं दीर्घसूत्रता॥

-विदुरनीति 1-83

Pre-dominance of tamogun (delusion) in the mind is sleep, to be in a trance is tandra, lack of fearlessness is fear. When the mind is not controlled, then the feeling of anger arises Laziness lethargy is the greatest enemy existing in the body. **'आलस्यं हि मनुष्याणां शरीरोस्थो महानरिपुः'** To be deprived of the good company of learned men, delay in work and aberration of the mind is a long formula. These six qualities are not there in ignoble persons-Self-knowledge, Lack of anger, Tolerance, Devotion to religion, To stand by the word and Activity of charity. Six types of wives with extraordinary qualities is scarce to find. A wife with excellent qualities does six types of work-

कार्येषु मन्त्री करणेषु दासी भोज्येषु माता शयनेषु रम्भा।
धर्मानुकूला क्षमया धरित्री भार्या च षाड्गुण्यवतीह दुर्लभा॥

She is the minister when she counsels her husband for his work. A good minister is the one who gives the right and appropriate counselling without any fear, wife stands this test with confidence. She does the work of her husband like a true server with a feeling of complete faith and studiously. The wife has the same maternal affection, when the husband has his food, that feeling which is got from a mother. She satisfies her husband with passionate feelings, when she is on the bed with her husband and is like the celestial nymph Rambha. In religious rituals and karmas, she follows her husband like a partner and she is like the earth in forgiving.

After death, there are six destinations- 1. Wealth remains on the earth, 2. Wife comes upto the door of the house, 3. Friends and relatives come upto the burning ground, 4. Body comes upto the funeral pyre, 5. Cattle stay back in the plot and the life goes on the path of the other world with his own karmas.

धनानि भूमौ पश्वश्च गोष्ठे नारि गृहद्वारि जनाः श्मशाने।
देहश्चितायां परलोकमार्गे धर्मानुगो गच्छति जीव एकः॥

Although the experts of culinary arts have mentioned 56 types of cuisines but all of them get integrated under Shatras or six flavors. Normally, all are attracted towards sweet. All take the taste of acidic flavor in the form of pickles. All accept the necessary status of salt. The sizzle of the hot and the desire of pungent things are always there with the gluttonous. The bitterness of the bitter things is limited to medicines.

A living thing passes through six changes in its entire life-cycle, which have been names as- Genesis, Position, Change, Growth of body, Deterioration and Death. Maharshi Yaska has them, in Nirukt text, in these words **'जायते, अस्ति, विपरिणमते, वर्धते, अपक्षीयते, म्रियते'** Good people do not allow to come near them the pervert feeling of six changes or Shadbhav like-Ashamed, Proud, Hunger, Thirst, Delight and Disappointment. The six good qualities or Shadgun are- Prosperity, Knowledge, Yagna, Good omen, Detachment or renunciation and dharma. One who is co-ordinated with dharma or righteousness, he attains happiness and good fortune along with respect and fame. The six Kaurav warriors who had killed Abhimanyu, the son of Arjuna, their action is denounced. They are- Dronacharya, his brother-in-law Kripacharya, his son Ashwathama, Son of Radha-Karna, Kritvarma- a Yadava descendant and Brihadval had surrounded the incomparable heroic son of Subhadra, but his death was due to the strike of mace by Dushasan's son.

Even though there are many raga and raginis in music but Shatraga have their possessed importance. Music depends on the foundation of swar-sadhana and notes or swar have six sources- they are Nose, Throat, Chest, Tongue, Palate and Teeth. Where these physical organs and its positions are necessary for pure notes and clear pronunciation, there a singer should have the knowledge of the relation of different notes with different positions.

Acharya Mammat has told six purpose of poetry-

काव्यं यशसेऽर्थकृते व्यवहारविदे शिवेतरक्षतये।
सद्यः परनिर्वतये कान्ता सम्मिततयो पदेशयुजे॥

Through poetry one gets- 1. Fame like Rahim and Raskhan, 2. Poetry gives wealth like Bihari, Keshav, Gang etc. poets had got or the poets of today get money by various awards and felicitations, 3. Through poetry one gets the knowledge of custom-like the knowledge of various fields of the contemporary society from epics like Ramayan and Mahabharat, 4. Poetry is also written for the destruction of calamity. With this purpose Goswami Tulsidas had written the texts Vinaypatrika and Hanuman bahuk, 5. One gets immediate freshness from poetry. This is the subject of feeling of rising together, 6. Poems like Kanta also send pleasant advice or preachings. Because of one verse (doha) of Bihari the king got into the subjects welfare and the poet received the stated patronage. On the basis of one verse, Pravinray got the opportunity to return to her lover.

One should never have the company of six types of ignoble men- 1. One who does distressful things, 3. Very careless, 3. One who always tells lies, 4. Unstable devotees, 5. One who is not tender and 6. One who considers himself clever, it is the better to keep away from them.

संक्लिष्टकर्माणमतिप्रमादं, नित्यानृतं चादृढभक्तिकं च।
विसृष्टरागं पटुमानिनं चाप्येतान् न सेवेत नराधमान् षट्।।

Six types of persons are called Krur Karma or doers of cruelty. They are- Desirous or greedy, Cruel, Severe oppressor, Miserly, Angry and Self-Praise. To save Jaydrath from Arjun and for his protection, six great charioteers were appointed. They were- Karna, Bhunishrava, Ashwathama, Vrishsen, Kripacharya and Shalya. One gets progress in six ways- 1. One's own progress, 2. Progress of one's friend, 3. Progress of a mutual friend, 4. Impairment of one's enemy, 5. Impairment of enemy's friend, 6. Impairment of a mutual enemy.

आत्मवृद्धिर्मित्रवृद्धिर्मित्रमित्रादयस्तथा।
विपरीतं द्विषत्स्वेतत् षड्विधा वृद्धिरात्मनः।।

Learned men or scholars should not get attracted to six things because they are not constant-Beauty, Youth, Collection of wealth, Health and Living together of all dear ones'

Previously, the four parts or divisions of army have been discussed. But in Mahabharat, an army has six divisions. A collective form of an army is said to include at one place chariot, elephant, horse, infantry, cart and camel. At another occasion, the divisions of an army are said to be-chariot, elephant, horse, infantry, treasury and rich vaishya. A king should assimilate the qualities of these six divisions. A king should have the sweetness of a koyal, aggressive ability to stop like a pig, doggedness like Sumeru mountain and the feeling to be high, the ability to offer rescue like shunya-graha, maneuver like an actor and dedication to welfare like an enamoured camaraderie. These six have been called the most pious- Yagna, Charity, Ved, Truth and Good and holy work, Hunger, Thirst, Mourning, Enchantment, Old age and Death are called the six waves or surges. There are six genus of immovable living things- 1. Trees- Banyan, Peepal, Mango etc., 2. Copse- grasses, 3. Creepers-creepers and climbers on trees, 4. Balli- creepers spreading on the ground, 5. Tvaksar – bamboo, betelnut etc. and 5. Trin-grass and crops growing in the field etc. Some texts have distinguished them as vegetation medicinal, creepers, tvaksar, viroodh and drum. Vegetation or trees that have fruits without flowers like gular, banyan and peepal etc. Those plants which get destroyed after fruits are produced, those medicinal plants and plants of rice, wheat and peas and lentils. A creeper which grows with some support like brahmi, giloy etc. Tvaksar, whose bark is very hard like-bamboo, Viroodh- the creepers that sprawls and spreads on the ground like the creepers of musk melon and water melon, pumpkin etc. Drum-Trees that have flowers first and after that fruits borne on them like mango, guava, jamun etc.

Six things should be done every day- Sandhya, Bath, Japa, Hom, worship of god and Hospitality of guest. A server with six qualities is scarce in this world-

निरालस्याः सुसन्तुष्टाः सुस्वपनाः प्रतिबोधकाःल।
सुखदुःखसमा धीरा भृत्या लोकेषु दुर्लभाः॥

(One without idleness or indolence, very much contented, free from insomnia, always alert, stable in joy and sorrow, stable mind and a server full of patience is scarce to find in this world. Due to six reasons, a person's body becomes the home of diseases- 1. To drink excessive water, 2. To consume rich food, 3. Impairment of minerals, 4. To stop the speed or urgency of urine and excreta, 5. To sleep during the day and 6. To remain awake at night. These six things provide life-breath immediately- 1. Ghee (freshly prepared), 2. Grapes, 4. Young maiden, 4. Consuming milk, 5. Warm water and 6. Shade of trees.

सद्यः पक्वघृतं द्राक्षा बालास्त्री क्षीरभोजनम्।
उष्णोदकं तरुच्छाया सद्यः प्राणकराणि षट्॥

Six thing bring back the wealth lost since a long time- 1. To keep the head clean by washing with water, 2. By keeping the feet clean, 3. By not going to a prostitute, 4. By eating less, 5. By not sleeping naked and 6. To have sex with a woman on the days when there are no festivals. Six secret counselling preaching the ears get destroyed. So they must be limited to only four ears. Even Brahma is unable to know the secret counselling between two ears-

षट्कर्णो भिद्यते मंत्रः चतुःकर्णश्च धार्यते।
द्विकर्णस्य तु मंत्रस्य ब्रह्मप्यन्तं न बुध्यते॥

Among the many joys of the world, six joys are the prominent ones-

अर्थागमो नित्यभरोगिता च प्रिया च भार्या प्रियवादिनी च।
वश्यश्च पुत्रोऽअर्थकरी च विद्या षड् जीवलोकस्य सुखानि राजन्॥

-विदुरनीति-1-87

Vidur explains this to Dhritarashtra saying- O! king, the six happiness of this world are- Acquisition of wealth, to be always healthy, dear wife, wife who speaks sweetly. Sons who are under control and the knowledge that provides wealth.

For the upliftment of nation, six elements are compulsory to have- Honesty, Truth, Sacrifice, Labour, Dharma and Karma. Six persons are considered as the rightful and eligible to get madhupark (milk with curd and honey, ghee and sugar)- Graduate, Teacher, Priest, King, Son-in-law and Best friend. Six persons do not possess wealth- 1. One who is distressed and pained, 2. Careless, 3. Atheist, 4. Idle, 5. No self-restrain and 6. Without energy. Dhauti, Vasti, Neti, Nauli, Tratak and Kapalbhati are six types of Shatkarma. Dhauti cleans the entire path from throat to the stomach and destroys all cough related diseases by cleansing it. Through Vasti karma the cleansing is done for the kidneys and small intestines. It is for the removal of heat in the intestines, repair faults in it, constipation etc. Neti karma cleanses the path of the nostrils and purifies the forehead. It removes the diseases related to eyes, teeth, mouth, tongue, ears and head. Through Tratak, the deficiencies of the eyes are cured. Through Nauli diseases of the stomach are destroyed, there is increase of hunger. Through Kapalbhati, diseases arising due to cough in the body are removed.

Do not be friendly with six people- Child, Old person, Greedy, Fool, Ill person or convalescent and Impotent person. If six are pure then there is righteousness and if they are impure then unrighteousness occurs- Country, Period, Material, Doer, Mantra and Karma. The dharma of Kashi is service and that of Maghar is path towards hell. During birth one conveys congratulations but during death one expresses grief. As a doer to sell milk is dharma but for a Brahmin it is adharma. The closeness to a wife as a thing or material, for a householder, is dharma but for the other three ashrams it is adharma. The pure utterance of mantra is holy and bountiful but impure utterance is harmful. One who considers himself the doer of karma faces sin due to egotism but when it is dedicated to god it becomes holy.

Today, the field of history may be limited but Kautilya has included six texts in history they are- Puran, Itivritt, Akhayika, Udaharan, Dharmashastra and Arthashastra. Bhakti or devotion is of six types- 1. Devotion to father, 2. Devotion to guru, 3. Devotion to king, 4. Devotion to master, 5. Devotion to country and 6. Devotion to god. The first five are the duties of a person and the last Prabhu bhakti or devotion to god is his dharma. The devotion to god has nine distinctions which will be described later. According to Chanakya these six qualities-Truth, Knowledge, Dharma, Kindness, Peace and Forgiveness are respectively in the form of our six relatives- Mother, Father, Brother, Sister, Wife and Son-

सत्यं माता पिता ज्ञानं धर्मो भ्राता दया सखा।
शान्तिः पत्नी क्षमा पुत्रः षडेते मम बान्धवाः।।

–चाणक्य नीति

A mother provides help and support in every situation, a father protects, brother becomes a supporter, sister helps to save from sin, wife gives happiness and son increases the fame and prestige. One who possesses Endeavour, Courage, Patience, Intelligence, Strength and Adventure, six types of energy, even gods hesitate to malign him

उद्योगः साहसं धैर्यं बुद्धिः शक्तिः पराक्रमः।
षड्विधो यस्य उत्साहस्तस्य देवोऽपि शंकते॥

–गरुडपुराण। 1–32

Through renunciation six types of wealth is acquired- 1. Sham (to control the mind), Dam (to control the senses), Titiksha (patience), Upra (not to be attracted towards comforts and material, even when they are there), Shraddha (belief in Almighty, texts and saints) and Samadhan (end of all doubts and apprehensions).

Witchcraft and occult arts are also a six types- Quietness or peace, Black magic or bewitchment, Suppression, Enmity or hatred. Alienating or driving away and Killing. One can hear the stories or incidents enchanting by witchcraft or occult mantras even to the extent of destroying and killing. With this kind of influence of witchcraft, Usha the daughter of Bansur has taken away Anirudhdh, the grandson of Krishna.

The retention of six in memory, destroys all sins- 1. Bali 2. Vibhishan 3. Bhishma 4. Prahlad 5. Narad and 6. Dhruv. These six vaishnavas should be remembered.

बलिर्विभीषणों भीष्मः प्रहलादो नारदो ध्रुवः।
षडेते वैष्णवाः प्रोक्ताः स्मरणं पापनाशनम्॥

As such, there are many celestial nymphs in heaven, but six of them are the best among them- 1. Urvashi, 3. Purvachitti, 3. Sahajanya, 4. Menaka, 5. Vishwachi and 6. Ghritachi

उर्वशी पूर्वचित्तिश्च सहजन्या च मेनका।
विश्वाची च घृताची च षडेवाप्सरसां वराः॥

–महा. आदिपर्व 74–68

These celestial nymphs have broken the tapa of so many sages and hermits. So the texts caution-

अनित्यं यौवनं रूपं जीवितं रत्नसंचयः।
ऐश्वर्यं प्रियसंवासो गृध्येत्तत्र न पण्डितः॥

–महा. वनपर्व 2–47

A person with discretion should not get attracted and attached to these six things as they are not eternal- 1. Youth 2. Beauty 3. Life 4. Collection of gems and Jewels 5. Wealth and prosperity and 6. Sex with dear one.

In the assembly of king Janak, Shakalya had questioned Yagyavalakya, as to who are the six gods. Yagyavalakya replied saying their names as- 1. Fire 2. Earth 3. Wind 4. Sky or aerospace 5. Sun and 6. Gamble place. These gods can be attached to oneself by any dharma (religion), Sampraday (cult) and Jati (community). Believing them to be gods one can be saved from environmental pollution.

ब्रह्मचारी यतिश्चैव विद्यार्थी गुरुपोषकः।
अध्वगः क्षीणवृत्तिश्च षडेते भिक्षुकाः स्मृताः॥

Six are considered to be the claimants or beggars of dharma. They are- Brahmachari (celibate), Sanyasi (religious recluse), Vidyarthi (student), Guruposhak (investor in guru), Pathik (traveler on a journey) and 6. One whose livelihood is destroyed. These should be the dharmabhikshuk. In the body there are six signs:

अत्यन्तकोपः कटुका च वाणी दरिद्रता च स्वजनेषु वैरम्।
नीचप्रसंगः कुलहीनसेवा चिहनाति देहे नरकस्थितानाम्॥

Therefore, one should save oneself from anger, should bring sweetness in speech, should work to eliminate penury, one should not have enmity with one's own people. One should keep away from the people with evil or low activities and one should not serve the people of inferior descent. Six things should not be trusted-

नदीनां नखीनां श्रृंगीणां शस्त्रयाणीनाम्।
विश्वासो नैव कर्तव्यः स्त्रीषु राजकुलेषु च॥

1. Rivers 2. Whose nails are like weapons 3. Animals with horns 4. Armed men 5. Women 6. Persons from aristrocractic families. They can put you in trouble anytime, can strike you and can punish you. With six types of actions a person can be insignificant- 1. Friendship with children, 2. Laughing without reason, 3. Discussion with women, 4. Serving the ignoble, 5. Riding a donkey and 6. Scurrilus language

बालसखित्वमकारणहास्यं स्त्रीषु विवादमसज्जनसेवा।
गर्दभयानमसंस्कृतवाणी षडिभर्न लघुतामुपयाति।।

There are six materiality of this immaterial world-

विष्णुरेकादशी गंगा तुलसीविप्रधेनवः।
असारे दुर्गसंसारे षट्पदी मुक्तिदायिनी।।

These six are the ones that give freedom from this immaterial world they are- 1. Lord Vishnu, 2. Fast of Ekadashi, 3. River Ganga, 4. Tulsi, 5. Brahmin and 6. Cow. According to Srimad Bhagvat Mahapuran, there are six good qualities or virtues for good and truthful persons, but for the low persons these qualities become vice because of these qualities the persons become proud and egoist and their outlook becomes faulty, their discretory mind is destroyed. Everyone should chase away six conducts of actions.

उलूकयातुं शुशुलूकयातुं जहि श्वयातुमुत कोकयातुम्।
सुपर्णयातुमुत गृध्रयातु दृषदेव प्रमृण रक्ष इन्द्रः।।

1.Owl is fond of darkness so it is a symbol of ignorance. Its attitude is doubtful and uncertain, 2. Jackal is the symbol of anger and cruelty. A jackal is of attacking nature, 3. The attitude of a dog is parasitic, 4. In the attitude of sparrows there is dominance of sex, 5. A garud which flies very high has an attitude of pride and that is symbolic of arrogance and 6. In the attitude of vulture, there is gluttony. Therefore one should become courageous and chase away owl like enchantment and doubt, jackal like anger, dog like envy, sparrow like passion and sex, garud like pride and vulture like greed. As such, there are many pilgrimages in our country which are visited by theist travelers but there are six such pilgrimages in which one does not have to travel. They are available to all- 1. Bhakt Tirth- those who are devotees of god. They are like pilgirmages to others. Yudhishthir had called Vidur Mahatirth (great pilgrimage), 2. Guru Tirth- There is limitation in the light of sun, moon and lamp, but a guru always lights the heart of his disciple. A guru always evicts the darkness of ignorance. So he is the Paramtirth (supreme pilgrimage) for his disciple, 3. Mata

Tirth and 4. Pita Tirth- For children, there is no greater pilgrimage than mother and father. Both of them are living gods. Therefore, their service and worship is the greatest pilgrimages and is bountiful and benevolent. 5. Pati Tirth- According to India belief, a husband is the only guru of his wife. Service to one's husband gives the results of all the pilgrimages. 6. Patni Tirth- A wife having six qualities, Shadgunvati is rare to find, even then Indian women follow the dharma of pativrat or fidelity to husband and family. So a husband should look upon his wife as a holy pilgrimage for his own welfare and welfare of the family. According to Vishnu Puran one who has wealth and properity, righteousness, fame, politeness, knowledge and complete renunciation, he is like god-

ऐश्वर्यस्य समग्रस्य धर्मस्य यशसः श्रियः।
ज्ञानवैराग्ययोश्चैव षण्णां भग इतीरणा।।

Here all the adjectives are for the six. Their Shadvarg names are-Passion, Anger, Enchantment, Greed, Pride and Inebriety. This enemy Shadvarg should be abandoned. A king is happy by foregoing it-

कामक्रोधस्तथा मोहो लोभो मानो मदस्तथा।
षड्वर्गमुत्सृजेदेनमस्मिंस्त्यकते सुखी नृपः।।

–वही 1–143

These six persons are worthy and should be worshipped by offering arghya. They are-Teacher, Priest, Relative, Graduate, Dear friend and king-

आचार्यमृत्विजं चैव संयुजं च युधिष्ठिर।
स्नातकं च प्रियं प्राहुः षडर्घ्यार्हान नृपं तथा।।

–महा. सभापर्व 36–33

The above statement is for Yudhishthir from Bhishma. These six are very helpful during a travel to a foreign country- Wife without a child, Good vehicle, Able coolie to carry luggage, Guard to protect, the skill to eliminate other's agony and servant without idleness-

भार्याऽनपत्या सद्यानं भारवाही सुरक्षकः।
परदुःखहरा विद्या सेवकश्च निरालसः।
षडेतानि सुखायालं प्रवासे तु नृणां सदा।।

–शुक्रनीति सार 3-292

Foolish son, Widowed daughter, always angry wife, Penury, Service of brutes or scrubs and Always in debt, these six are painful and they do not give any happiness.

मूर्खः पुत्रोऽधवा कन्या चण्डी भार्या दरिद्रता।
नीचसेवा ऋणं नित्यं नैतत्षटकं सुखाय च।।

–शुक्रनीति सार 3-242

In this world of humans, there are six types of happiness. 1. To be healthy, 2. Not to be in debt, 3. Not to stay in a foreign country, 4. To have association with good people, 5. To earn one's livelihood through one's professions and 6. To be fearless.

आरोग्यमानृण्यमविप्रवासः सद्भिर्मनुष्यैस्सह सम्प्रयोगः।
स्वप्रत्यया वृत्तिरभीतवासः षड्जीवलोकस्य सुखानि राजन्।।

–विदुरनीति 1-94 ।।

In the end, after Shatsnan, by following six rules and doing holy work with the medium of Shaddarshan and Vedang, with the help of Shatneeti, destroying six enemies, to gain Shatsampatti, by seeking the blessings of Shadanan Kartikeya and after the penetration of Shadchakras, with this hope I wish the union and oneness of Shakti and Shiva and that all Indian be deeply adhered to six holy karmas.

❐

7 (Seven)

The importance of seven is the highest among the basic numbers one to nine. Seven is the sign of auspiciousness. In the field of religion and spiritual, the use of number seven is seen as strong. If we see from the viewpoint of calculation of time, according to the calculations of Indian rishis, at this time the seventh period is going on. Prior to this were Swayambhuv, Swarochish, Uttam, Taamas, Raivat and Chakshush these periods have passed. The name of the seventh Manvantar or period is Vaivasvat. Indian rishis have calculated the age of creation. In the context of four, four eras have already been discussed. The total period of all these four eras is called Mahayug. Four eras or one Mahayug is of 4320000 years. The ages of the four eras are 1728000, 12960000, 864000 and 432000 respectively. So a Mahayug is of 4320000 years. 74 Mahayug is equal to one Manavantar and 14 Manavantar is equal to one Kalp, as said by them. A creation's age is of one Kalp. The rishis of seven Manavantar are- Gautam, Bharadwaj, Vishwamitra, Jamdagni, Vashishth, Kashyap and Atri.

Gau means senses. So due to the reason of control of the senses, name was given as Gautam. By the power of meditation Gautami Ganga (Godavari) came to this and Bhardwaj is the thinker of the sixth mandal of Rigveda. Vishwamitra is the only rishi who became Brahmarshi from Rajarshi. He is the creator of Gayatri mantra. Jamdagni was the son of Satyavati and Richik. Satyavati was the sister of Vishwamitra. His wife was Renuka, the daughter of king Prasenjeet. Parshuram was the son of this couple. According to the Vedas, Vashishth is called the friend and son of Varun. According to the Puran he is the mental son or the son of thoughts of Brahma. The name Vashishth is due to the control of sense. He is the rishi of the 7th Mandal of Rigveda. He has accepted the duty of a purohit for the kings of Ayodhya. Kashyap was the grandson of Brahma and son of Marichi. Thirteen daughters of the ruler Daksh were his wives. Gods, demons, monsters, snakes are their children so one can address himself of being of Kashyap gotra, if one does not know his gotra. Atri is the son of Brahma. He was born from the eyes of Brahma. He is one of the 10 Prajapatis. Ansuya was his wife who was considered as the gem of piety. During the time of exile to the forest Ansuya had given advice to Sita about piety and pure religion. Atri is the thinker and creator for the 5th Mandal of mantras for Rigveda.

For the realization and actualization os Veda mantras, the continuous tapa that was going on among the families of the rishis, is called the rishi parivar or the Rishi families. Such rishis have 315 families, whose descendants are prominent and who have been called Saptrishis. Actually, they are those big families, whose descentants have been constantly engaged in tapa of this. Among them also only four families are considered as the main families. They are – Angiras, Bhargav, Kashyap and Atreya. Gautam and Bhardwaj joined the family of Angiras because Bharadwaj is the son of Brahaspati, who in turn is the son of Angiras, and Gautam is the son of Rahugam who in turn again the son Angiras Vishwamitra and Jamdagni got connected to Bhargav and Vashisth got connected to Kashyap family. Atreya family is independent. Richik was the son of Bhrigu. So the families of Vishwamitra and Jamdagni got included in the family of Bhargav. Marichi's son was Kashyap, Kashyap's son was Maitravarun, Maitravarun's son was Vashishth, Vashishth's son was Shakti and Shakti's son was Parashar. So Vashshth and Parashar families were considered among Kashyap family. The rishis of 6th Manavantar is also mentioned in the Mahabharat. The Saptrishi of the 6th Manavantar were-Marichi, Atri, Angira, Pulatsya, Pulaha, Krtu and Vashishth. They are the Manas Purtras of Brahma. The constellation the seven stars in the sky is also called Saptarishi. These seven stars represent the seven rishis of the 6th Manvanta. These seven stars are also called the Saptarishi Mandal or Constellation. Close to them is a small star which is known by the name of Arundhati the wife of Vashishth. This constellation Saptrishi, rotates around the Dhruv star or the North Pole star and is seen in the northern direction.

The wives of these Saptrishis are the seven Lokmatas whose names are- Sambhuti (Marichi), Ansuya (Atri), Kshma (Pulaha), Preeti (Pulatya), Sannati (Krtu), Lajja (Angira and Arundhati (Vashishth).

Speech is the medium of expression. Speech also has seven types- Sanskrit, Prakrit, Paishchi or Bad and slang, Apbhrash (broken or altered speech), Lalit (beautiful), Magadh and Prose. In some texts the seven different types of speech are- Medha (Intelligence), Dhriti (Stability), Shruti (Tonal), Pragna (Deep thinking), Buddhi (Knowledgeable), Yash (Honor) and Kshma (Forgiveness). Actually they are the qualities of the kind of speech and Sanskrit Prakrit are the languages. In nature, there are basically seven colors. They are Violet, Indigo, Blue, Green, Yellow, Orange and Red. The variety of colors is due to their mingling. In the previous chapter, the six qualities of a servant have already been described, but some texts have mentioned seven qualities of a servant- Trust, Piety, Pride, Patience, Hospitality, Love and Sweet Speech, one becomes the best servant if one has these qualities. Hanuman is the ideal example of a servant.

Every Indian has the desire to bath in the seven pious and holy rivers which are there in India. The strong faith towards these seven holy rivers- Ganga, Yamuna, Saraswati, Godavari, Narmada, Sindhu and Kaveri is so strong that the believers invoke the waters of these seven rivers in their bucket prior to their bath, in this way-

गंगे च यमुने चैव गोदावरि सरस्वति।
नर्मदे सिन्धु कावेरी जलेऽस्मिन् सन्निधिं कुरु॥

Ganga and Yamuna rise from the Himalayas and meet at Prayag. At present, there is no geographical existence or form of Saraswati. May be, it flowed through Punjab and then it went to Rajasthan. Today, it is believed that this disappeared Saraswati meets Ganga at the Prayag. On this fact, it is called Sangam Triveni. Kaveri and Godavari are the rivers of South India. Narmada arises from the Vindhya Mountains and then falls into the Bay of Cambay, Sindhu arises from the crown of India, Kashmir and goes towards Pakistan. The vreatores of Mahabharat have described the seven holy rivers and thus said- the person who drinks the water of Ganga, Yamuna and Saraswati (born out of the roots of Plaksha), Rathastha, Sarayu, Gomti and Gandaki, their sins are destroyed immediately

गंगां च यमुनां चैव प्लक्षजातां सरस्वतीम्।
रथस्थां सरयूं चैव गोमतीं गण्डकीं तथा।
अपर्युपितापापास्ते नदीः सप्त पिबन्ति ये।
इयं भूत्वा चैकवप्रा शुचिराकाशगा पुनः॥

–महा. आदिपर्व 169–20–21 ।

Similarly, like the seven holy rivers, there are seven holy cities, which have been called Mokshdayini or the Giver of Salvation. At least once in their life, these religious people have the desire to visit these holy cities and touch their holy mud-

अयोध्या मथुरा माया काशी काँची अवन्तिका।
पुरी द्वारावती चैन सप्तैता मोक्षदायिकाः॥

Ayodhya is the birth place of Ram, the great man chaste qualities, and Mathura is the birth place of Krishna and also his play field. The ancient name is Maya. It is this place where Ganga descended on land. Shiva had left Ganga down on the earth from his tangled tresses at Har ki Pauri. Kashi is the city of Lord Vishwanath. It stands on the Trishul or trident of Shiva, it is so believed according to the Puranas. Avantika (Ujjain) is the city of Lord Mahakaleshwar. Dwarka is the capital of Krishna. He is Ranchod ji, because of the reason of fleeing from war to Dwarka. Kanchi is called the Kashi of the South. Today it is known by the name of Kanchipuram. These seven holy cities depict the geographical unity of India. If Haridwar is in the north of India, then Kanchi is in south of India, Dwarka in the west and Ayodhya, Mathura, Kashi and Avantika are located in central India. Among these seven cities, three- Ayodhya, Mathura and Dwarka are Vaishnav cities or Vaishnavpuri. Haridwar, Kashi and Ujjain are Shiva cities or Shivpuri. Kanchi is Hariharatmakpuri. That is the reason it has two parts-Vishnukanchi and Shivkanchi.

If it is possible for one to attain salvation it is the best, but if due to the rotation of karmas it is not attained, then every person at least desires for heaven. In all the religious texts of the world, it is said about the attainment of heaven on doing good karma. In all these religious texts those joys and comforts of the heaven are mentioned, which cannot be achieved in this world but still a man desires to get them. In the imagination of the heaven or Jannat. There are a few topics such as- the fearlessness of death, freedom from worries, fulfillment of all desires, the company of beautiful and talented women. Even if somebody calls these women as angels or hoor. It is natural to imagine some other world for the attainment of worldly joys and comforts. Therefore, is the Indian Puranas there is the belief of seven worlds, which are known by the names of Bhu, Bhuva, Swaha, Maha, Jan, Tapa and Satya. This is for the persons who perform pious and good work for the people. This is better and better than the previous one. There are seven gates to Heaven. They are- Tapa, Charity Suppression, Control, Coyness, Simplicity and Kindness, through them alone one can get permission to enter Heaven. In some texts they are mentioned as- Bhu, Bhuva, Swarg, Tapa, Satya, Vaikantha and Golok. Below Bhulok also seven other worlds are described which is called Paataal. These worlds, compared to the previous seven worlds are of low status. Their names are- Paataal, Atal, Sutal, Vital, Mahatal, Rasatal and Talaatal. The number of Hell are also seven. Their names are- Avichi, Mahakal, Ambrish, Raurab, Maharaurav, Mahasutra and Andhtamishra. In this world there are seven continents- Jambu, Plaksh, Shalmali, Kush, Kronch, Shaak and Pushkar surrounded by the seven seas- Lavan, Ikshu, Kshir, Dadhi, Sura, Ghrit and Shudhdh.

By drinking the water of the seven river, sins are destroyed immediately. Among the holy rivers Ganga, Yamuna and Saraswati are already there. Apart from them there are four other rivers- Rathashtha, Saryu, Gomti and Gandaki. According to the Indian belief, the foundation of the earth's pivot or bearing are many. The popular beliefs are- the back of a tortoise, the fangs of Sheshnag or the horns of a cow. After this also, some common people believe that the stability or balance of this earth is due to some holy souls. The reasons for holiness are- Cow, Brahmin, Veda, Sati (pious woman), Truthful, Non-greedy and Generous, these are seven such bases because of which the earth remains stable.

गोभिर्विप्रस्य वेदैश्च सतोभिः सत्यवादिभिः।
अलुब्धैर्दानशीलैश्च सप्तभिर्धार्यते मही॥

–महाभारत

In Narad Puran, seven such women are mentioned who should not be considered as valid :-

भर्तृघ्नीं पुष्पिणीं जारां सूतिकां गर्भपातिनीम्।
कृतघ्नीं च तथा चण्डीं कदाचिन्नाभिवादयते्।।

They are- killer of one's husband, Crazy about wealth, One who has relations with other men, One who has just delivered a child, One who aborts her child, Ungrateful, and Always angry. One should not bow before someone by seeing his wealth.

Where a person acquires honor due to his Karmas, if the people surrounding him are also polite, then there is additions or increase to this glory and honor. In this world, that person is honored everywhere whose seven close persons are polite. They are- Disciple, Wife, Brother, Family members, Servant and The dependent. For a Vaishya or business man seven types of work are according to dharma- Cattle rearing, Charity, Yagna, Study, Business, Interest, and Farming. Among these charity, Yagna and Study is to improve for preparing for the other world after death and the remaining four are the means of earning livelihood. The seven persons who should never become a witness are- Palmist, Doing business on stealing, Gambler, Doctor, Enemy, Friend, and Dancer.

सामुद्रिकं वणिजं चोरपूर्वं शलाकधूर्तं च चिकित्सकञ्च।
अरिं च मित्रं च कुशीलवं च नैतान् साक्ष्ये त्वधिकुर्वीत सप्त।।

Mundak Upanishad had said about the seven lashing tongues of fire:-

काली कराली च मनोजवा च सुलोहिता या च सुधूम्रवर्णा।
स्फुलिंगिनी विश्वरुची चं देवी लेलायमाना इति सप्तजिह्वाः।।

The most dangerous and aggressive forms of fire are Kali and Karali. Monojava is like the exuberant lashes like the mind, Sulohita is the one with red flames, in Dhumravarna there is the prominence of smoke, Sphulingini is the sparking fire breaking with sound and crackling. The world of this universe is the form of fire.

The one who is protected from these seven are always happy: 1. Staying in a foreign country without reason. 2. Acquaint and meetings with sinners. 3. To go to another woman. 4. False Pride.

5. Stealing or Robbery. 6. Gossiping and 7. Drinking of wine. In the world famous epic of Ram Charitmanas, Goswami Tulsidas has written seven Kands or happening- **'सप्त प्रबन्ध सुलभ सोपाना'** The seven chapters of this epic are- Balkand, Ayodhyakand, Aranyakand, Kishkindhakand, Sundarkand, Lankakand and Uttarkand. In ancient poet Valmiki's Ramayana aslo there are seven Kands. There Lanka Kand is written with the name of Yuddh Kand. Here it is important to mention that the narrative story of Valmiki Ramayan get over with Yuddh Kand. Uttar Kand is an attachment writer by somebody else. One gets the result as per his own faith from these seven episodes:

मन्त्रे तीर्थे द्विजे देवे दैवज्ञे भेषजे गुरौ।
यादृशी भावना यस्य सिद्धिर्भवति तादृशी।।

Actually, faith is related with these things. Faith is a feeling of the heart. Those who have faith in- Mantras, Pilgrimage, Brahmin, God, Astrologer, Doctor, and Guru, they can see the some kind of influence. In some texts its number is said to be six.

मन्त्रे तीर्थे द्विजे देवे भैषज्ये वा गुरावपि।
यादृशी भावना यस्य सिद्धिर्भवति तादृशी।।

In this shloka, the foreteller astrologer is exempted. It can be thus said that the 7th shloka is appropriate seeing to the fact that the foreteller astrologers have great faith from the society. Goswami Tuldidas considers seven as auspicious in this case. They are- Nectar or Elixir, Saint, Kalpvriksh (Imaginary tree), Flower, Good Fruit, Nice talk and the Devotion to Ram.

सुधा साधु सुरतरु सुमन सुफल सुहावनि बात।
तुलसी सीतापति भगति सगुन सुमंगल सात।।

It is always better and happier that before the goodness is destroyed and before it becomes stale one should relinquish or give up- City, Woman, Food, Servant, Friend and House, otherwise when leaving them it causes great pain and remorse.

नगर नारि भोजन सचिव सेवक सखा अगार।
सरस परिहरें रंग रस निरस विषाद विकार।।

There are seven such qualities which increase the prosperity of a person- Patience, Peace, Control on senses, Purity in behavior, Compassion, Soft speech, Non-rebellion towards friends.

धृतिः शमो दमः शौचं कारुण्यं वागनिष्ठुरा।
मित्राणां चानभिद्रोहः सप्तैताः समिधः श्रियः॥

Anger is the worst horrible quality. The angry person loses the company of- Son, Servant, Dear one, Friend, Wife, Dharma, and Truth. The first five do not like his nature and behavior, and for the last two the angry person does not have any focus or concentration. Therefore, one should give up anger to have control on somebody, seven types of remedies should be taken as the means of help. These means are- Mantra, Medicine, Web, Sam, Dam, Dand and Bhed. The last four have been described in the fourth chapter. The greatness and importance of mantras is accepted even today. There are innumerable incidents described in newspapers practically every day, to control somebody by feeding some things or offering some drinks. The influence of Hypnosis and Black Magic is prevalent here and there, to this day.

Everyone confirms and approves the importance of earning money through four self-abilities or hard work. Before money comes dharma. So that money is the best that is in connivance with dharma. There are seven means for procuring wealth according to dharma, they are- Wealth received from parents or hereditary property, wealth received in the form of profit from business, wealth received from the sale of a property, Wealth received due to victory, wealth received from interest, wealth earned due to labor or hard work and wealth received in the form of charity, all these money are the one's earned through dharma. If the seven essential qualities are being followed. Then the generation prospers. These are- Tapa, Dam, Study of Vedas, Prestige, Traditions of the best type of marriage, Charity of Food and Good behavior contribute to the development and prosperity of the family and generation.

तपो दमो ब्रह्मवितं वितानां पुण्या विवाहाः सततान्नदानम्।
येष्वेवैते सप्तगुणा वसन्ति सम्यग्वृत्तास्तानि महाकुलानि।

–महा. उद्योगपर्व 36–23

Aristocracy or good breeding has seven qualities. Tapa is related to the body, and in this type of Tapa one should keep seven things in mind. To worship God, Brahmin, Guru or learned person, Purity or Piousness, Simplicity, Chastity and Non-violence are the Tapa related to body. Behavior is also of seven types- Vedic, Vaishnav, Shiva, Dakshin, Vam, Siddhant, and Kaul. Behavior that based on Karma is Vedic, based on devotion is Vaishnav, and based on knowledge is Shaiva. Dakshin based on Karma, devotion and knowledge. The persons to the path of Vam or opposite path are those who eat what is not edible, drink what is not drinkable, walk along with the undesired and all those who vouch for opposite things. They do not differentiate between good and bad and talk of demolishing the Almighty. Siddhant is that state when enjoyment and sacrifice rules and warnings and activity and retirement don't exist at all. This state is a godly state. Kaul is the highest state of the body which is without words. These seven forms of behavioral state are shown in the text of Shakt Darshan, Kularnav, People with good behavior keep themselves away from seven types of bad addiction. They are- Drinking wine, Gambling, To go to a prostitute, Hunting, Punish others. To use bad language or slangs and Corruption, that is earning money through illegal means.

The sun is called the Saptrashmi or the one with different colors. He sits on the chariot of seven horses. Seven rays are his seven horses. The names of the seven horses of the sun are- Gayatri, Brihati, Ushnik, Jagati, Pankti, Anushtup, and Trishtup. These are the basic seven poems and these poems as mentioned as the horses of the sun is one form of documentation or roopak. These seven poems have evolved from that Great Almighty and in Veda these poems have been used. Rest of the poems are described by Acharya Pingal. Seven days are also called the seven horses of the sun. The land which fertile by the seven rivers is called Sapt Saindhav. These seven rivers are Saraswati, Shatadru, Vipasha, Parushni, Ashivani, Vitasta and Sindhu. In these seven persons seven qualities are missing. They are- Piousness in crow, Truthfulness in gambler, Forgiveness in snake, Satisfaction of sex in women, Patience in infertile male, Thinking power in drunkard, Friendship in a king.

काके शौचं द्यूतकारे च सत्यं सर्पे क्षान्तिः स्त्रीषु कामोपशान्तिः।
क्लीबे धैर्यं मद्यपे तत्त्वचिन्ता राज्ञो मित्रं केन दृष्टं श्रुतं वा॥

In time division, day has its own place. Days are seven. All the calendars of the world show the number of days as seven. Day is related to the sun, also days are related to the planets. Days have been named on the basis of seven planets. They are- Ravi, Chandra, Mangal, Buddh, Guru, Shukra and Shani'. Seven types of people are in the category of 'not to be killed' or Avadhya. They are Brahmin, Cow, Family member, Child, Woman, Provider of food, and Refugee, should not be killed under any circumstances. The limitations of Veda or there are seven limitations of the work.

These are- Robbery, Unchaste behavior, Atheism, Abortion, Drinking wine, To commit bad things again and again and after committing any sin telling lies to hide it, is to outrage the limitations of Veda. So one should, not go close to these bad qualities. Seven painful qualities are supposed to be exempted by a king. They are attraction towards women, to punish very severely, To gamble, To hunt, To drink, Harsh speech and the ill use of wealth.

सप्त दोषाः सदा राज्ञा हातव्या व्यसनोदयाः।
प्रायशो यैर्विनश्यन्ति कृतमूला अपीश्वराः।
स्त्रियोऽक्षा मृगया पानं वाक्पारुष्यं च पंचमम्।
महच्च दण्डपारुष्यमर्थदूषणमेव च॥

–विदुरनीति, 1-96-97

The poet of Anand Ramayan had made slight changes of these bad qualities and thus said-

निद्रालस्यं मद्यपानं द्यूतं वारांगनारतिः।
अतिक्रीडाऽतिमृगया सप्त दोषा नृपस्य च॥

–आनन्द रामायण, राज्यकांड-16-7

That means the seven bad qualities of a king are- More sleep, Laziness, Drinking wine, Gambling, Love of prostitutes, Too much of play and Too much hunting.

Where the Indian great thinkers have accepted the positions of different gods, at the same time they have accepted the symbols of their power that is many goddesses also. At every auspicious occasion as a part of Navgraha worship, different gods are remembered. Similarly, with some pretest or other the goddesses are also worshipped as a regular ritual. At auspicious marriage occasions Sapt Matrikas or seven mothers are worshipped. The names of these seven mothers are – Brahmi, Maheshwari, Kaumari, Vaishnavi, Varahi, Indrani and Chamunda. These seven should never be allowed to stay at one's house- Good for nothing, One who eats a lot, One who hates all, More attached, Cruel, On who does not know about the time, country and the surrounding, One who dresses in shameful way. The basic mantras of progress are- Industrious, Patience, Accurate, Careful, Control, Memory, To begin work after thinking. Students should always keep away from- Laziness, Lust, Frivolousness, Gatherings, Rebellion attitude, Pride, Lack of Selfishness, these are the seven such bad qualities.

In this country from Prithu to this modern era, many kings, rulers and emperors have been there. History and Puranas are full with the stories of their bravery in wars, charity and services for religion. Among these hundreds of rulers the most renowned rulers are only seven. According to Indian belief the king whose chariot wheel moves beyond the seas was called Chakravarti. Only the Chakravarti king had the right to perform Ashwamedh and Rajsuya Yagna. Actually, who are counted in this category are those who bonded the whole country India in one bond. The seven Chakravarti kings are- Bharat, Mandhata, Nahush, Sagar, Bhagirth, Sahasrarjun and Yudhishthir. All these seven kings are famous because of their natural strength, strength of tapa, popular with the countrymen, victory on the enemies etc. qualities that were exceptional. At the time of discussion about kings, it is natural to remember the seven parts of the state. Today in the definition of a state or country, it is essential to have sovereignty, area and population, but according to the ancient Indian belief the seven essentials were- King, Minister, Friend, Country, Fort, Treasury and Army.

स्वाम्यमात्यश्च राष्ट्रञ्च दुर्गं कोशो बलं सुहृत्।
परस्परोपकारीदं सप्तांगं राज्यमुच्यते।।।

–कामन्दक नीतिसार

Due to their groups, the state is formed and due to their breaking, the existence of the state dies. In this belief, the king is the most important. The importance of others gradually, diminishes. The king should be protected even after scarifying everything.

If the king is alive, then other bodies can be created. The seven prominent heads of state or seven Prakritis are also there. They are- Durgadhyaksh (Head of Fort), Baladhyaksh (Head of Army), Dharmadhyaksh (Head of Religion), Commander, Pandit or Purohit, Doctor, and Astrologer.

Every king always has the virtue that his countrymen should not have any discomfort, they may not have to face any disaster. In Indian context disasters and catastrophes are called 'Iti.' These 'Itis' are also seven in number- Floods, Famine, Disaster of rats, Disaster of locusts, Harm by the Birds, Civil war and Foreign attack. It is the duty of the king to protect his countrymen or citizens from these seven disasters. Modern rulers also use the Prime Minister's Relief Fund for such disasters.

While describing the greatness of seven in the context of music, the number cannot be ignored. The notes on which the entire palace of music foundation stands, these notes are also seven. They are known by the names of Sa, Re, Ga, Ma, Pa, Dha and Ni. The note Shadaj or Sa evolves from the nostrils, throat, heart, upper jaw, tongue and teeth, these are the six locations of Sa. The reason for the evolvement of the other six notes also, respectively, this is called Sa. Re on Rishabh is the wind rises form the navel and strikes the throat and the head. Ga or Gandhar is the note after Re, it rises as wind from the navel, strikes the head and comes out through the nostrils. Ma or Madhyam is the note arising from the navel makes a sound in the centre after striking the heart and the chest. Pa or Pancham note touches the navel, heart, chest, throat, and head, these five places. Dha-Dhaivat note emanates or rises from the upper jaw. Ni Nishad is a very sharp note. Before this, the other notes become subdued. The body is the foundation of Sadhana for Music. The body too has seven basic elements of its total composition. They are known by the names of - Body fluid or Plasma, Blood Muscles, Fat, Bones, Sensory nerves and Sperms or Ova. In Srimad Bhagvad Gita, these seven elements are mentioned as-Skin and Inside of Skin, Muscles, Blood, Spaces, Sensory nerves, and Bones. The difference of Skin and Skin parts is unclear. In some texts instead of Plasma fluid, skin is mentioned. Med is Fats, Majja is called the intestines.

In India, the importance of seven is so much that one who walks seven steps with you is considered to be a life partner. During the marriage ceremony, to walk seven steps together with your life-partner is called Saptpadi, which is the most important tradition for the couple to become husband and wife. **'यावत् सप्तपदी न स्यात् तावत् कन्या कुमारिका'**, The seven stanzas or padas of Saptpadi have different meanings or connotations. The first step denotes that we both together will provide for food. Second step expresses the preservation of strength food and self-control. The third step denotes the provision of wealth. The fourth step is to attain soulful self-happiness. The fifth step denotes the prosperity of animal wealth. The sixth step denotes of staying healthy in all seasons and the seventh and last step is to walk together and to co-operate each other in all circumstances.

Earlier, we have already discussed the seven bad qualities which are forbidden for a king. It is expected that every king should possess seven good qualities. A king should be - Benevolent (Natural feeling or desire to make others happy), Sympathy (The feeling of sympathy on seeing other's sorrows), Compassion (To try to alleviate the sorrows of others), Lack of cruelty (Not to have any feeling of cruelty), Simplicity (Lack of fakeness), Forgiveness (Although being strong and powerful, not to have the feeling of retaliation for any crime) and finally Truth. The poet of Anand Ramayan has mentioned these seven good qualities of a king as the auspicious qualities.

सत्यं शौचं दया क्षान्तिरार्जवं मधुरं वचः।
द्विजगोयतिसद्भक्तिः सप्तैते शुभदा गुणाः॥

These seven qualities of the king are- Truth, Piety, Kindness, Forgiveness, Simplicity of nature, Sweet speech and Faith on Cow, Brahmins and Saints. In the Mahabharat war, the seven commanders of the Pandava army were- Drupad, Virat, Drishtadyumna, Shikhandi, Satyaki, Chekitan and Bheem. With the approval of Krishna Drishtadyuman was made the chief commander. Arjun was made the highest commander of all these seven commanders and Krishna was made the leader of even Arjun and also his charioteer.

In the war of Mahabharat seven brave soldiers used to sit on one elephant. Among them two would work as riders or mahavat with ankush, two of them would be the best archers, two would sit with swords and one would hold the shakti and trishul or trident.

In Mahabharat war, on the Pandava side only seven warriors were alive. The five Pandavas, Krishna and Satyaki.

In Mahabharat 14 (fourteen) viviparaons have been divided into two parts, as the animals that live in villages and animals that live in the forest, their number is seven each: Animals of the village are seven- Cow, Buffalo, Goat, Sheep, Horse, Dog and Donkey. Wild animals are also seven- Lion, Tigar, Jackal, Elephant, Monkey, Bear and Deer– Mahabharat Van Parva 134-4

The importance of sacrifice or desertion is described in virtuous qualities. Sacrifice is also shown as of seven types or seven stages gradually-1. Total sacrifice of forbidden actions, 2. Sacrifice of actions of lust, 3. Total lack of thirst for ambitions, 4. Sacrifice of the services to be taken from other's for one's own self-interest, 5. Total sacrifice in all actions from laziness, laxity and desire for a result, 6. Sacrifice of worldly material, its affection and attraction, 7. Total sacrifice of subtle lust and ego in respect to the world, body and all related actions. It is desirable for the messenger or ambassador of a king to have seven qualities. The messenger should be aristocrat, polite, humble, talkative, clever, one who speaks sweet words, conveying the message as it is and should be rich in his memory. The Brahmin who is chosen for funeral rites or donation should have seven desirable qualities-Aristocrat, Energetic, Literate in Vedas, Compassionate, Simple and truthful.

In Indian astrology, before starting on a journey, one should take note of the direction and the position of planets. To travel in all directions seven auspicious planets have been described. The numbers of lunar ecliptic (nakshtra) are 27. Therefore, Dhanishtha is said to be auspicious for west and north. For the journey of the east Kritika, Rohini, Mrigshira, Ardra, Punarvasu, Pushya and Ashlesha, for south Magha, Purva falguni, Uttara falguni, Hast, Chitra, Swati and Vishakha, for west Anuradha, Jyeshtha, Mool, Purvashadha, Uttarashadha, Shravan and Dhanishtha, for north Dhanishtha, Shatbhisha, Purvabhadrapad, Uttarabhadrapad, Revati, Ashwini and Bharani are auspicious lunar ecliptic. Due to seven reasons the sin of a sinner gets infected to another person-1. To discuss with a sinner, 2. By the touch of his body, 3. By union, 4. By dining together, 5. By sitting on the same carpet, 6. By sleeping on the same bed and 7. By travelling in the same vehicle.

Millet, Rice, Sesame, Kang, Moong bean, Gram (pulses) and Sawa are called seven cereals. In colloquial, it is called 'Satanja'. In donation 'Satanja' has an important legislation. Those sanyasis (hermits) who live in ashrams have seven reposeful eternal and inherent righteous behavior- Taking alms, Study of Vedas, Silence, Tapa, Deep thinking, Meditation, Knowledge and Renunciation. The holy sighting of seven things in early morning is considered as good omen. Among these seven any one should definitely be seen Cowdung, Sandalwood, Gold, Conch, Mridang, Mirror and Mani (gem). These are seven things for good omen. Seven tasks are very important for human beings. These should be performed in routine way daily. These are-Cleanliness of towels, Brushing of teeth, Bath, Meditation, Singing hymn (bhajan) and Sleep. It is necessary to offer obeisance and salutation to these seven-Mother, Father, Teacher, God, Sun, Fire and Guest. There are seven internal impurities-Envy, Hatred, Anger, Greed, Lust, Despise and Evil thoughts. One should always try to keep away from them. To protect and save oneself form these there are seven outer purification-Bath, Worship, Japa of mantras, Donations, Pilgrimage, Meditation and Yoga and to constantly attain knowledge which is beneficiary. By following thsese seven, there are seven exclusive benefits-Happiness in life, Peace, Destruction of fear, Protection from poison, Knowledge, Strength and Discretion, which are attained.

For brushing teeth, branches of seven trees should be used. These are Mango, Margosa, Bael, Acacia, Sycamore fig, Pongam and Spear. For brushing seven branches of trees are forbidden Gluten, Horse petal, Nee, Cotton, Dhav, Cannabis and Saccharum. Seven places are considered holy places-Kurukshetra (Haryana), Harihar kshetra (Sonpur), Prabhas kshetra (Veraval), Renuka kshetra (Uttar Pradesh), Bhrigu kshetra (Bharuch), Purushottam kshetra (Jagganathpuri) and Sukar kshetra (Soron), these are called seven kshetras (zones). Where seven get together, there is mostly quarrel among them. These seven among themselves-Brahmin, Barber, King, Dog, Co-wife (rival) and Cat.

बिप्र वैद नाई नृपति स्वान सौत मंजार।
जहाँ तहाँ ये जुरत है तँह तँह करै बिगार॥

There are seven friend of faith during untimely difficulties- Patience, Righteousness, Discretion, Good literature, Courage, Vow for truth and Faith in Ram. At seven places there is no untouchability- Temple, Journey of gods, Marriage, Yagna. Festival, War and Market place. In these places there is no question of untouchability. These seven should not be awakened while asleep-Snake, King, Lion, Wasp, Infant, Other's dog and Fool.

अहिं नृपं च शार्दूलं वरटां बालकं तथा।
परश्वानं च मूर्खं च सप्त सुप्तान्न बोधयेत्॥

On seeing Dronacharya's great outrage of Karmas, during the war of Mahabharat, the seven rishis- Gautam, Bharadwaj, Jamdagni, Vashishth, Kashyap, Atri and Vishwamitra, had told him that he fought the war with adharma. Now the time of year death has come. **'अधर्मतः कृतं युद्धं समयो निधनस्य ते'** You have killed, without the rules, in the war, those with the help of Brahmastra who do not know about Brahmastra **'ब्रह्मास्त्रेण त्वया दग्धा अनस्त्रज्ञा नरा भुवि'** One should always extend hospitality to these seven- 1. God. 2. Cow. 3. Brahmin. 4. Old person. 5. Doctor. 6. King and 7. Guest.

Bathing is of seven types-1. Bath with mantras or sprinkling water on the head by chanting mantras-

अपवित्रः पवित्रो वा सर्वावस्थां गतोऽपि वा।
यः स्मरेत् पुण्डरीकाक्षं स बाह्याभ्यान्तरः शुचि॥

To recite the mantras and have the feeling of purity. 2. Bhaum snan (Mud bath)- To put mud on the whole body. In nature cure, this bath has a lot of importance. 3. Angi snan (Fire bath)- To put ashes on the body. Naga sanyasis take this type of bath. 4. Vayvu snan (Dust from the feel of Cows)- To bath in the evening from the dust arising out of the feet of cows returning from the jungle. This is also called Godhuli snan. 5. Divya snan (Holy bath)- Bath when the sun is shining and also there is rain. To bath at this time in rain water is called Divya snan. 6. Vaarun snan- To bath by immersing in river, lake or sea and 7. Manasik snan (Mental bath)- To bath in one's own thoughts is also one type of bath.

गोभिर्विप्रैश्च वेदैश्च सतीभिः सत्यवादिभिः।
अलुब्धैर्दानशीलैश्च सप्तभिर्धायते मही।

–स्कन्दपुराण ।।

The Mahabharat has also shown the seven bearers of this earth, but with slight difference

धर्मः कामश्च कालश्च वसुर्वासुकिरेव च।
अनन्तः कपिलश्चैव सप्तैते धरणीधराः।।

–महाभारत

The seven bearing element of this earth are- Religion, Work, Period, Vasu, Vasuki, Anant and Kapil. In the heaven, there are many angels or beautiful ladies. In the last chapter, six most beautiful ladies have been mentioned. The king of gods. Indra has given special importance of seven beautiful ladies in his cabinet. These seven are- Dhritachi, Menaka, Rambha, Urvashi, Tilottama, Sukeshi and Manjughosha.

घृताची मेनका रम्भा उर्वशी च तिलोत्तमा।
सुकेशी मंजुघोषाद्याः कथ्यन्तेऽप्सरसौ बुधैः।।

There are seven things essential in worship- 1- Fragrance 2- Flowers 3- Dhoop or incense 4- Lamp 5- Offering 6. Water and 7. Betel.

The word Mahan or great has lot of importance. This becomes an adjective to noun and increases his greatness, but when attached before these seven, it diminishes or reduces its value:

शंखे चैव श्मशाने च तैले याने तथैव च।
यात्रायां ब्राह्मणे पात्रे महच्छब्दो न दीयते।।

1. Mahashankh is called unholy bone. 2. Mahasmashan is that place in the battle field where the corpses lie scattered hither thither. 3. Mahatel is to take out oil from somebody's body. 4. Death is Mahayan or Mahaprasthan. 5. Mahayatra is the funeral procession. 6. Mahabrahman and 7. Mahapatra- They are the lowest types of Brahmins who accept charity after someone's death.

A learned person should always keep in mind, to see these seven while walking always on one's right side. 1. Another learned 2. Temple 3. Chaityavriksh 4. Four cross-road 5. Educated old person 6. Guru and 7. God.

देवालयं चैत्यतरुं तथैव च चतुष्पथम्।
विद्याधिकं गुरुं देवं बुध कुर्यात् प्रदक्षिणम्॥

These seven tasks should not be done in haste. They should be done very very slowly:

शनैः कन्था शनैः पन्थाः शनैः पर्वतलंघनम्।
शनैर्भुक्तिः शनैर्मुक्तिः शनैर्विद्या शनैः तपः॥

1. One should stitch the rajai or gudadi slowly. 2. One should walk slowly on the path. 3. One should climb the mountain slowly. 4. One should eat food slowly. 5. The means of detachment or discharge should be done slowly. 6. Knowledge should be imbibed slowly and gradually, 7. Tapa should gradually be increased. Those persons who do not possess the following qualities, they move on this earth as a burden, they are animals in the form of human beings

येषां न विद्या न तपो न दानं ज्ञानं च शीलं न गुणो न धर्मः।
ते मृत्युलोके भुवि भारभूताः मनुष्यरुपेण मृगाश्चरन्ति॥

According to the Indian tradition, the world is divided into seven parts which are called continents. These seven are Jambudweep (Urasia), Plaksha (Japan, Greenland and Britain), Shalmali (North America), Kush (Africa), Krauch (South America), Shak (Australia) and Pushkar (Antartica). India is situated in Jambudweep. As such there are many pilgrimages in this country, but seven are considered as pilgrimages of the mind.

सत्यं तीर्थं क्षमा तीर्थं तीर्थमिन्द्रियनिग्रहः।
सर्वभूतदयातीर्थं तीर्थं च प्रियवादिता॥
ज्ञानं तीर्थं तपस्तीर्थं कथितं तीर्थसप्तकम्॥

By quoting Truth, Forgiveness, Control on senses. Compassion for all living things, Sweet and kind speech, Knowledge and Tapa, it is an evident endeavour to project them as pilgrimages of gentle chivalrous qualities of behavior. Those who immerse themselves in the river of pilgrimages of the mind do not have the necessity for going on the journey of geographical pilgrimages. Seven persons are considered long-lived.

अश्वत्थामा बलिव्यासो हनुमांश्च विभीषणः।
कृपः परशुरामश्च सप्तैते चिरजीविनः।।

The only son of maestro patriarch Drona Ashwathama, represents the feeling of vengeance. Maharaj Bali who is in awesome greed of power being cheated by Lord Vaman, the compilation and protection of knowledge by Vyas, the son of Parashar and Satyavati, Ram's extraordinary servant Hanuman, the epitome of allegiance to the aim of service, Vibhishan, the ruler of Lanka, who had sole affection for the benefit and the victory of righteousness for all Kripacharya, the teacher of the dynasty of Kaurva as for his excellence in worship and adoration and Parshuram, who represents as a symbol of retaliation for injustice. There are some who believe that even today Ashwathama moves around with a wound in his head. Dronacharya comes to temple of Dankaur once in a year and Vibhishan performs worship in the temple of Rangnath every day.

Sometimes, in magnificent also demerits or bad qualities creep in when bad qualities come into seven magnificent objects, they offend our mind-Moon without lustre, Woman without youth, Lake without lotus, Idiotic or foolish mind of handsome man, a king who is greedy and avaricious, the plight of a respectable person and the presence of wicked person in a king's court. These seven things prick the mind like a thorn and cause pain and anguish.

शशी दिवस घूसरो गलित यौवना कामिनी।
सरो विगतवारिजं मुखमनक्षरं स्वाकृतेः।।
प्रभुर्धनपरायणः सततदुर्गतः सज्जनो।
नृपशणगत खलो मनसिं सप्त शल्यानि मे।

–भर्तृहरि नीति–54–11

Monks show seven great gateways to the world of heaven, by which the living can enter. They are- Tapa, Donation, Stoicism, Subdue, Modesty, Simplicity and Mercy for all living beings.

तपश्च दानं च शमो दमश्च द्वाराणि सप्तैव महान्ति ही राजवं सर्वभूतानु कम।
स्वर्गस्य लोकस्य वदन्ति सन्तो पुंसाम।

-आदिपर्व-90-22

At the end by looking at the seven colored rainbow by the retention of the white colored seven faced highly praised god seated on the sea after the churning of the ocean. I study the entirety of Durga Saptshati and Srimad Bhagvat Geeta comprising of 700 shlokas with an ardent wish that our country may be the most excellent in seven zones and we journey through the seven mountains.

❐

8 (Eight)

The modern century is of consumerism, but the government is promoting industries and also advocating the same to a great extent. So aptly a modern and progressive person discusses 'Yoga' in his talks. So the beginning of number eight is done with eight types of the consumerism of yoga. The word 'Yog' is pronounced as 'Yoga' is being fakely interpreted as only the exercises of the body or being a foreign system of wellbeing, that Yog is and eight fold philosophy in Indian philosophy. The propagator of this philosophy is the great rishi Patanjali. This has been mentioned in sixth chapter. Yog is completely an Indian procedure or tradition of meditation and it has eight parts. This is not just exercises of the body but is actually a holistic external and internal Sadhana. According to yogdarshan (philosophy of yog) one has to control the five senses and that is yog. **'योगश्चित्तवृत्तिनिरोधः'** and according to Srimad Bhagvad gita, efficiency and skillfulness in karma is yog **'योगः कर्मसु कौशलम्'**

The eight parts of yog are- Yam, Niyam, Asan, Pranayam, Pratyachar, Dharna, Dhyan, and Samadhi. The first five are the external means. The number of Yam is mentioned as 5, 10 and 12 in different texts, Niyam also have been shown the same way. According to Yogsutra **'अहिंसासत्यांस्तेयंब्रह्मचर्यापरिग्रहयमाः'** the number of Yam is five, but in some texts Yam is believed to be Non-violence, Truth, Non-stealing, Chastity, Kindness, Rectitude, Forgiveness, Patience, Taking less food and Cleanliness as the 10 qualities. The texts that have shown Yam as 12 have mentioned them as- Non-violence, Truth, Non stealing, No accord, Modesty, No accumulation, Belief in god, Chastity, Silence, Stability or Balance, Forgiveness and Fearlessness. These are very magnanimous qualities and the first chapter of Yog Sadhana.

By imbibing the best qualities of Ashtang Yog, such as- Non-violence (Giving up hatred), Truth (To have faith in truth from mind, speech and karma), Non-stealing (To give up stealing totally), Chastity (Control of the existing senses), Non misbehaviors (To be free from ego and extravagance), Rectitude (The simplicity of the heart with mind and body), Kindness (Compassion towards the sorrowful and destitute), Forgiveness (In spite of having power and strength not to punish the one who has committed crime), Patience (Control on one's tongue and private or sexual organs), Eat less, Cleanliness (The purity of bath and lack of lust in karmas), No accord (Lack for any attraction), Modesty (Hatred towards sins), Believing or Belief (Belief in Vedas and god), Silence (Control on speech), Stability (Not to lose one's balance), and Fearlessness (Lack of any kind of fear totally), a person can cross the part.

'शौचसंतोषतपस्वाध्यायेवश्वरप्राणिधानानि नियमाः।' In Yogsutra the number of Niyam is also five. Some texts have shown to Niyam such as Tapa (way), Satisfaction, Belief, Charity, Worship of god, listening to principles, Modesty, Intelligence, Japa and Firm pledge. Those who have mentioned the number of Niyam as 12 have quoted as- Cleanliness of body, Mental purity, Japa, Tapa, Havan (offering in mortar), Faith, Hospitality, Devotion to god, Travel to pilgrimages, Try to help others, Satisfaction and service to guru. A devotee acquires the second part of yog by inculcating these good qualities- Cleanliness, Satisfaction, Lack of lust totally, by performing religious tasks even when one is facing difficulties, Self-study (Study and pondering of good books and texts), Submission to god (Feeling of total surrender before god's paramount rule), Charity, to make everyone fearless, Pare Japa for intelligence (To read holy mantras again and again), and Firm Pledge etc. By these Niyam or rules, the body, the senses and the heart is cleansed from all sorts of impurities and thus the life can be made righteous, pure and godly.

In this process the breath, the breath has to be stopped or to be taken with a space or difference. Purak is to inhale the breath from Chandranadi Ida (left nostril) to retain the same breath is Kumbhak and is Rechak to exhale the breath from Suryananadi Pingla (right nostril). It has been described to have special importance to control the mind. To distract and divert the senses from their topic and make them introspective is a climbing down action (Pratyahar). It is the control of senses. Through this, the senses are brought under control. Sitting for a deep purpose meditation and deep contemplation are internal privy disciplined and dedicated practice. Dhaarna is a state to protect the mind from dissatisfaction and materialism and highly ambitious feelings, from ignorance and concentrate. In this, the mind is bound to any particular part of the body or to a special aim. Patanjali says- **'ध्यानं निर्विषयं मनः'** through his writing. Actually, Dhyan the synonym of being completely joyful delighted and immersed in the thought of the Almighty. In this state, there is only the glimpse of aim, Samadhi is the synonym of ultimate concentration and self-immersion. In the highest excellent state of Dhyan, then distinction between the doer the action and the purpose disappears. This is the highest state of the concentration of mind. This can be said as unalternative Samadhi or the state of face to face with god.

Gautam Buddha has propagated eight follow path to control the mind and for the suppression of desires, which is called as Ashtangik Marg. This is also called Madhyam Marg (medium path). This is a medium middle path to severe meditation and make merry life. Samyak Drishti (medium sight), Samyak Sankalp (medium vow), Samyak Vak (medium speech), Samyak Karmant (medium action), Samyak Jeevika (medium livelihood), Samyak Udyog (medium industry), Samyak Smriti (medium memory) and Samyak Samadhi (medium state of intense concentration). He had given these eight principles for those humans who neither have excessive luxury nor ardous penance. This is to keep in mind that like is full of suffering and there are reasons for grief. By finding absolution from those reasons one can forgo those pains. That is Samyak Sankalp (medium vow). Samyak Vachan (medium speech) is to be safeguarded from taunt or satire and lies. Samyak Karmant (medium action) is to be protected from excessive luxury or materialism and violence. Samyak Ajeevika (medium livelihood) is to earn through honest and righteous means. Samyak Udyog (medium industry) is to abstain from vice and contemplation of good thoughts. Samyak Smriti (medium memory) is to destroy lust considering the body to be ever changing. Samyak Samadhi (medium meditative state), is the effort to know oneself through repose and concentration.

The opposite of yog or union is bhog or luxury. There are many distinctions and alternatives of luxuries. Five words beginning with 'm' are the forms of luxury. But according to Indian tradition meat, madira (alcohol) and maithun (sex) are not existing according to the best luxuries. Even while living a luxurious lifestyle, our traditions have some ideals and restriction. There is mention of eight luxuries for people living with top luxuries-Necklace, Perfume, Clothes, Music, Betel leaf, Food, Vehicle and Ornaments. Ordinary life is limited to food and clothes only. A luxurious life increases ambitions in life. Therefore, after many types of intensive spiritual practices (Sadhana), it is a natural desire to acquire eight spiritual powers. Anima (to be the most subtle) Mahima (to be large and larger), Laghima (to be light and lighter), Garima (to be heavy), Prapti (to be the ruler of all senses), Prakamya (to attain the power of all fulfilling desired enlightenment), Ishitva (to have the power to control over all) and Vashistva (to have the power to control over all). Among these eight spiritual enlightenment, first three are related to the body. Sursa, the powerful evil monster, must have wide her mouth hundred times, due to the force of Mahima Siddhi and Hanuman must have shrunk to subtle and tiniest form due to Anima Siddhi, that is could come out of Sura's mouth even after entering into it. Prakamya is the synonym of spiritual knowledge experiencing cosmic and ultra-cosmic things. Ishita is the word for the spiritual enlightenment to conduct and execute all actions according to one's will. Usha took Shri Krishna's grandson, Anirudhdh into her palace, due to her power on Vashitva Siddhi. Hanuman could fly due to his spiritual power of Laghima and would take the shape of a huge mountain due to his spiritual power of Garima.

To achieve spiritual powers and luxury a person has to bring in virtuous qualities in his life-Great saint Atri has mentioned eight characteristic of virtuous householders. They are- Unenviousness, Cleaning of bowels, Propitious, Ease, No craving for ambition, Subduing, Donation and Compassion. These eight characteristics truly defines a virtuous householder. One can easily get praise from people, but one who has unenvious gesture, surely the person who praises others' good qualities and does not ridicule others' faults. The reason of cleanliness is that of purification of mind and actions.

To alleviate the body from frivolous frolic, laziness and faults, physical exercises come under asan. In any exercise position where the doer can stay for the maximum time that is asan. This thing has been confirmed by the great rishi Patanjali thus 'स्थिरसुखमासनंम्'। To keep the various parts of the body beautiful and healthy there are many asanas. Pranayam is the effort to make the breath pure.

To follow the culture and traditions, to avoid bad company and to decide what is edible and what is not come under cleanliness. It is beneficial to do good and excellent work and to avoid doing shameful karmas. Automatically one gets the feeling of simplicity unwarranted and undesirable sadhana or causing pain to the body, is opposite of being spontaneous. A person who is full of detachment remains contented and happy with what he gets. The feeling of Aspriha or detachment is not to desire for other's wife and other's money. Dam is the control on one's senses and equanimity between happiness and sorrow. It is a feeling of Dam when one does not have opposite feeling or is not distorted, although being able and strong. Charity is to give something as per one's means and with pleasure, and kindness is the feeling of oneness and close with the entire living world.

These are the eight means of happiness and the abstract or summary of joy. They are- Meeting with friends, Having more wealth, Embrace of a son, To have intercourse, To speak sweet words on occasions, Progress among one's group, To acquire things that is desired or intended and honor in society. Eight qualities increase the fame of a man- Intelligence, High breed or aristocracy, Control on senses, Knowledge of texts, Strength or power, To talk less, Charity according to means and Gratefulness. These eight qualities are not found in bad people or evil souls- Not to see faults in qualities, Simplicity, Purity, Contentment, To speak good and sweet, To have control on the senses, To speak the truth and Natural disposition. These are the qualities of good person. Everyone gets these eight things, Joy, Sorrow, Trouble, Destruction, Harm, Benefit, Life, and Death. The army may have four or six divisions, but its eight divisions' importance is very much there since the ancient times. They are- Dhanrakshak (Protector of wealth or treasury), Dravya-Sangrahak (Collector of things), Chikitsak (Doctor), Guptchar (Spy, or Secret agent), Paachak (Digester), Sevak (Servant), Lekhak (Writer) and Prahari (Guard), without which no army can fight.

Eight types of marriage traditions are also prevalent at our place. They are — Marriage with the consent of parents, in the same caste, and the marriage of bride and bridegroom as per their wishes. This is called Brahma Vivah. This is a form of Swayamvar vivah, Dev vivah is to give one's own daughter in marriage to the brahmin after the Yagna who comes to the house to perform Yagna. Like the son of Angira and the brother of Devguru Brahaspati, Samvarta was performing Yagna at king Marut's place. After the Yagna, the king gave his daughter, Yajak in charity. When one cow and one bull are taken as exchange for a bride, such marriage is called Arsh vivah. By searching for an appropriate bridegroom, by the parents, for their daughter and marrying her off with traditions is called Prajapatya vivah. To take immense wealth from the bridegroom for the price of bride and to marry off the daughter against her wishes is Asur vivah. A marriage without any mantras, by the wishes of bride and bridegroom and accepting each other as husband wife is called Gandharva vivah is said to be the best.

क्षत्रियस्य हि गान्धर्वो विवाहः श्रेष्ठ उच्यते।
सकामायाः सकामेन निर्मन्त्रो रहसि स्मृतः॥

When a man and woman love each other and in solitude, a relationship develops secretly without mantras, it is called Gandharva vivah. The marriage of Shakuntla and Dushyant was of that category. The kidnapping of the bride forcibly and marrying the crying and weeping bride is Rakshas vivah. And after a war forcibly marrying the bride after victory is Peishach vivah. Among them, the first six types of marriages are considered to be righteous and according to dharma and the last two against dharma. According to the caste point of view Brahma, Dev, Aarsh and Prajapatya marriages are the best for Brahmins. These four and Asur and Gandharva vivah are according to dharma or righteous for Kshatriyas. A king can do Rakshas vivah also. Among the Vaishya and the Shudras Asur vivah is considered worthy or acceptance. After marriage, when a bride becomes a wife she protects eight things — Wealth, Children, Body, Travel, Dharma, Heaven, Rishi and Ancestors. All of these are protected by the wife.

The dharma or right religion has eight paths. They are — Yagna, Self study, Charity, Tapa, Truth, Forgiveness,Kindness, and Generously or lack of greed. Among them, all the paths go towards dharma. With very slight changes these are said to be the eight qualities which show us the heaven. These qualities which show us the heaven. These qualities are — Yagna, Charity, Study of holy texts, Tapa, Control of senses, Truth, Simplicity, and Softness. With a few changes here and there eight qualities are there to glorify and enlighten a man:

अष्टोगुणाः पुरुषं दीपयन्ति प्रज्ञा च कौल्यं च दमः श्रुतं च।
पराक्रमश्चाबहुभाषिता च दानं यथाशक्ति कृतज्ञता च।।

-विदुरनीति, 1-104.

These eight destroy eight-Old age of form and appearance, Hope of patience, Death of life, Seeing faults in other's qualities of righteous behavior and manner, lust of shame or modesty, service of vile men of ethics and good behavior, anger of wealth and arrogance destroys whole property

जरा रूपं हरति हि धैर्यमाशा मृत्युः प्राणानधर्मचर्यामसूया।
क्रोधः श्रियं शीलमनार्यसेवा ह्रियं कामः सर्वमेवाभिमानः।।

-महा. उद्योगपर्व 37-8

One should not have relations of transaction with these eight-Extremely kind king, Liberated woman, State personnel, Son, Younger brother, Widow with children, Soldier and that person whose rights and power have been snatched and restricted. In fasting, one should take care of food factor, that is edible and non-edible, otherwise there are chances of fast being broken, but the following eight do not break the fasting-Water, Roots or tubers, Fruits, Milk, Devotional offering after yagna, to take food on the request of a Brahmin, to take food due to guru's command and to take medicines.

अष्टौ तान्यव्रतघ्नानि आपो मूलं फलं पयः।
हविर्ब्राह्मणकाम्या च गुरोर्वचनमौषधम्।।

-महा. उद्योगपर्व 39-70

A person who is contained with eight qualities should be made a messenger or ambassador-Free of egotism, Free from cowardice,

One who is not affected by other's instigation, Healthy, One who works fast, One who has a pure heart and gentle and generous speech-

अस्तब्धमक्लीबमदीर्घसूत्रं सानुक्रोशं श्लक्ष्णमहार्यमन्यै।
अरोगजातीयमुदारवाक्यं दूतं वदन्त्यष्टगुणोपपन्नम्॥

–महा. 37–27

The designation of an ambassador is very dignified. Ram had chosen prince Angad, Pandavas had chosen Shri Krishna and Dhritarashtra had chosen Sanjay the ambassadors only on the basis of these qualities.

It is expected of a king, for the increase and prosperity of his wealth or treasury, eight types of means. First, to develop the land suitable for agriculture for growing cereals and food-grains. Second, to develop business, the businessman should be protected. Third, forts should be built and there should be provision for their defence. Fourth, bridges should be built and have defined provision for defence. Fifth, the king should be the protector of rare and valuable birds and animals. Sixth, he should have the possession of authority of the mines of gold and diamond. Seventh, the taxes should be collected properly and eighth, to settle the subjects in solitary and deserted areas and make that area populated and prosperous.

In the battle of Mahabharat the commander of army on Pandava's side was the son of Drupad, Dhrishtadyumna, but while taking any decision, eight big warriors were consulted. The eight big warriors on Pandava side were Dhritadyumna, Satyaki, Shri Krishna and the five Pandava. Even Duryodhan was impressed by the mutual love among these eight warriors. He tells Dhritarshtra-

धृष्टद्युम्नः पाण्डवाश्चैव सात्यकिः केशलोऽष्टमः।
सत्वस्था वीर्यसम्पन्ना ह्यन्योऽन्याप्रियदर्शनाः॥

Arrogance is one of the five types of bad quality. It is also of eight types. These eight types are-One's intelligence, Religiousness. Family race, Caste, Moral strength, Miraculous powers, Yog, Penance and Beauty. To relinquish these types of arrogance is in the interest of human kind. From the birth of a life to its salvation period the doer of eight stages is the Almighty. All these eight stages are in the hands of that supreme regulator these eight states are- Birth or origin, Position, Destruction, Regulation, Knowledge, Cover, Bond and Salvation. These eight names of Lord Vishnu are specially giving ease and comfort among the many goddesses and gods-

अच्युतं केशवं विष्णुं हरिं सत्यं जनार्दनम्।
हंस नारायणं चैव एतन्नाभाष्टकं शुभम्।।

They are Achyut, Keshav, Vishnu, Hari, Satya, Janardan, Hans and Narayan. These eight names shower good omen and auspiciousness. Some texts have considered-Brahma, Cow, Fire, Army, Ghee, Sun, Water and King as the eight which are of good omen.

Among the gods, Lord Shiva has eight statues Fire, Sun, Moon, Earth, Water, Wind, Parishioner and Sky are said to be the statues of Mahadev. There is a precept to a Sashtang Pranam (Prostration on the ground) for gods and respectable and venerated persons. This Sashtang Pranam is done by laying down eight parts of the body on the ground. Ashtang arghya (eight offerings) are prepared. When Milk, Nimble grass, Ghee, Honey, Curd, Red sandalwood, Red flowers of Karbeer for the special offerings to goddesses and gods.

In some texts, Ashtang Arghya or eight offerings are- Water, Milk, Curd, Ghee, Blade of trident grass, Rice, Jow (a cereal) and Mustard. According to some texts to worship god or to perform Kriya for one's ancestors, in the water for the Arghya or offering, eight things should be put- Curd, Unhusked rice, Blade of trident grass' upperpart Milk, Dry blades of grass, Honey and white mustard. If all the things are not available, then put all that is possible to get. So the availability is also been considered. A person who desires for salvation has to gain control on the eight types of nature and also behavior. After having control one should detach oneself from the five senses which are attracted towards the qualities of the five elements, one should control the mind, intelligence and false ego and then alone such dedicated persons can have the right to salvation. After ending the attraction of the senses of beauty, flavor, scent or fragrance, speech and touch controlling the mind, one can do wisdom with whatever good intelligence and without false ego that will take him towards salvation finally. Actually land, water, fire, wind, sky, mind, intelligence and ego are considered as eight forms of nature. Nature is that which creates from itself. By these eight things, nature is formed.

Lord Shiva is with eight idols and Ashtatarini Bhagvati is also of eight idols. By the praise of these eight forms of devis or goddesses, one can be relieved from all types of troubles and difficulties. These eight forms are- Tara, Ugra, Mahogra, Vajra, Kali, Saraswati, Kameshwari and Chamunda. In any type of sadhana or tapasya or vrat eight auspicious things are of special importance. They are lion, bull, elephant, urn or pot, fan, dhol, garland of vaijayanti and lamp. We pray to the Almighty for wisdom. Wisdom is also of eight types. They are- Desire to bear, Understand, Heart, to bear in mind, to investigate after advocacy and discussions, to know the opinion, to know science and Philosophy. After attaining these eight types of wisdom one can acquire actual or real knowledge. These are the gradual steps to knowledge.

Anger is one among the five bad qualities, but when it is awakened, it brings along eight other bad qualities. These bad qualities come after the eruption of anger- to tell tale, to rape, to rebel, Jealousy, to see faults in qualities, using wealth for evil work, Harsh speech, Hard punishment. Even though, there is similarity between man and animals with regard to food, sleep, fear and sex, but a man has sex in eight ways

स्मरणं कीर्तनं केलिः प्रेक्षणं गुह्यभाषणम्।
संकल्पोऽध्यवसायश्च क्रियानिर्वृत्तिरेव च॥
एतन्मैथुनमष्टाङ्गं प्रवदन्ति मनीषिणः।

Thought of woman, Talk about women, Play with women, To watch women, To have secret talks with women, To decide to meet woman, Try to meet woman and Physical contact with woman are all types of sex. In context to a bachelor these eight types of sexual acts are a little different. A bachelor should avoid these types of sexual acts such as- Memory, Listening, Talking, Watching, Love, Secret talks, Keli or play and Touch. To remember the beauty grace, looks and behavior or insinuation of a woman or to remember the dirty pictures is the sexual act of the first kind. To read the poem of love which excite sex, to listen or listen to the discussion on sex, to listen to the description of beautiful women about their beauty and grace or their dispositions, to talk or listen to porn, that is Kirtan. To watch the sexually exciting body parts of women or to see pornographic things is called Prekshan sex. To laugh and mock with women, to dance and sing with them, to play in water with them, to play holi is called Keli sex. To adorn oneself by grooming and decorating use of oils and perfumes is called Shringar sex. To touch a woman with sexual approach and thought, to kiss, to embrace is called Sparsh sex. In their spinster life woman also should avoid these eight things with respect to men.

Ashtadhata is the combination of eight metals from which the idols of gods are created or prosperous people make rings. Ashtadhata is famous for its strength due to the mixture of eight metals like-gold, silver, bronze, red colored metal, lead, zinc, mercury, and iron. These metals are also important in food. This is the reason that kings and emperors used to eat in silver and gold utensil-ware. All are well aware of the importance of water in a bronze container. There is special importance of gold ash or iron ash in Ayurveda. Doctors talk about the deficiency of iron.

Far from the geographical belief according to the Indian Puranas, the work to hold the earth upright is done by Sheshnag, Tortoise and Kamdhenu or Cow. Also, the work of taking care of the entire solar system and to keep it in control are done by the eight directions- East, Agneya (South-East), South Nairitya (South-West), West, Vayavya (North-West), North and Ishan (North-East). In these directions there are eight directions there are eight gigantic Airawat, Pundarik, Woman, Kumud, Anjan, Pushpdant, Saarvabhaum and Supratik, are there respectively. According to Indian astrology, in eight directions, eight planets work as the rulers of those directions. They are- Sun, Venus, Mars, Rahu, Saturn, Moon, Mercury and Jupiter and eight gods are known as the guards of these directions. They are- Indra, Agni, Yama, Nisriti, Varun, Marut, Kuber and Shiv. The following chart shows their relations:-

	Direction	Giants	Rulers	Gaurdians
1.	East	Airawat	Sun	Indra
2.	South-East	Pundarik	Venus	Agni
3.	South	Woman	Mars	Yama
4.	South-West	Kumud	Rahu	Nirriti
5.	West	Anjan	Saturn	Varun
6.	North-West	Pushpdant	Moon	Marut

7.	North	Saarvobhaum	Mercury	Kuber
8.	North-East	Supratik	Jupiter	Shiva

The number of directions and its respective guardians are also 10. Two other directions and their guardians will be further discussed in chapter 10.

Those who have faith in gods and goddesses make the idols and while establishing it they prepare a glue or gara, in that there are eight fragrant things. They are called Ashtagandha and are- Sandal, Agaru, Pine, Saffron, Camphor, Shailaj, Jatamasi and Grouchan. A land well-known for the prominent yagna. Indians use eight things for Yagna. They are Peepal, Ashwath, Gular, Pakarvat, Sesame, Mustard, Milk and Ghee, these all are included. But in some texts, these eight things are mentioned as- Peepal, Gular, Sikar, Vat, Sesame, Mustard, Kheer and Ghee. In Indian tradition, eight main mountains are there- Neel, Nishad, Malyavan, Malay, Vindhya, Gandhmadan, Hemkut, and Himalaya. Eigth Vasus had taken birth from the womb of Ganga, Shantanu's wife, among the eight, seven has immediately attained salvation, the eighth incarnation of Vasu Bhishma had attained a very long life. These eight Vasus were born because of the daughters of Daksh and because of dharma. Being cursed, these Vasus had to take birth on this earth from the womb of Ganga.

According to the Indian view-point, Lord Dhanvantari, divided the entire medical science into eight parts-Surgery, Mouth, Throat, Nose and Ears comes under the Shalakya category. Modern ENT is the form of the same. In general body treatments, body related diseases are there like fever diseases of the stomach, cold and flu, paralysis, water in the stomach, diseases connected with wind, bile juice and cough. Modern physician sees these aspects. Persons who are afflicted by witches and ghosts or evil spirits are treated by another department related to the ghosts or the supernatural. All the diseases of woman, system of pregnancy to delivery and child care come under Kaumarbhritya treatment. Diseases related and caused by poison are treated under the Agad system of treatment. The treatment of lack of minerals and to avoid infertility in males is treated through the Vajikaran system. The system of Ashtang treatments is also shown as eight, they are- Veins and arteries, Stool, Urine, Tongue, Eyes, Beauty or Face, Words and Touch. Narad mentions these eight sections to Yudhishtir.

'कश्चिद् वैद्यश्चिकित्सामाष्टांगायां विशारदः।'

From the nature itself eight treatments are available, Air, Food, Water, Fasting, Sun, Exercises, Thoughts and Sleep, all these keep us healthy. Air is in our body in the form of life-breath. So a walk in the morning is very much beneficial for health. The intake of this fresh morning air is called, 'The elixir or nectar of Brahman period.' With the freshness and nutrition in food, it is good for a person to eat less and in proportion, by this the mind and the brain remain joyful. Water is most important for health. With bath, there is physical healthiness and freshness and one gets active and spontaneous, also drinking water in the morning, works as medicine. During the day also one must drink water in enough proportion. All should fast. Through fasting the digestive system gets a relief and break. The mind and soul get happiness. People who fast do not have any diseases of the stomach and one whose stomach is good, other diseases also keep away from him. The sun also has a great contribution on our health. By the touch of the sun's rays, many physical diseases are, eliminated. That is why in Indian religious texts there is precept, only for this reason. By exercising every day the body parts become strong and flexible. Also the immunity power to fight against diseases increases, there is reduction, one gets the old age late. There is also great influence of good and pure thoughts on the body as well. So one should try and keep away from polluted thoughts, and should stop them from coming. For good health deep and adequate sleep is also required. One should regularly take 6-7 hours of sleep as daily routine, which gives freshness to the body. If the adequate benevolent services of these eight treatments provided by nature are being taken then one need not go into the eight treatment aspects of Dhanvantri. It is necessary that to take the treatments from nature, it should also be that nature is pure in its eight forms. In nature, there should be purity in Water, Fire, Sun, Moon, Earth and Air. Water, Fire and Sun cure many diseases due to their influence. The human being is the doer of his own Karmas. So, to remain healthy, one should always remain engaged in the yagna of Karma. The clearness of the sky, the availability of clean and fresh air, the cool rays of the sun and the touch of the earth saves us from many diseases. Rishi Chyavan once again regained his youth from old age after eating

Avaleha made from eight things prescribed in Ayurveda. Today also, this Avaleha, prepared from eight ingredients is of great importance. It is made of Jeevak, Rishmak, Meda, Mahameda, Kakoli, Ksheer kakoli, Riddhi and Vridhdhi. The eight main queens of Krishna were- Rukmini, Satyabhama, Jambvati, Shinshupa, Vishoka, Lakhshmna, Sumitra and Ketuma. According to Manu, there are eight rishis as propagator of Gotra or antecedents by heredity.

जमदग्निर्भरद्वाजो विश्वामित्राभिगौतमाः।
वसिष्ठकाश्यपागस्तयो मुनयो गोत्रकारिणः॥

They are (Janadagni, Bharadwaj, Vishwamitra, Atri, Gautam, Vashishth, Kashyap and Agastya are the only propagators of Gotra). At another place Manu has mentioned 24 Gotras. In the text of Dhanjay as Dharma pradeep there is mention of 40 Gotras. Today the number of Gotras is in hundreds.

In the Bhakti revolution of the Middle ages, Vallabhacharya has an important place. According to the Vallabh cult or tradition Lord Krishna has eight forms or roop, who are called as Ashtanath by the names of Shrinath Navneetpriya , Mathuranath, Madanmohan, Vitthalnath, Gokulnath, Dwarkanath and Gokul Chandrama. In context with Vallabhacharya and his son vitthalnath, it is natural to remember and recollect the names of eight devout poets of Krishna who are well known as poets of Ashtachhap. They are known by the names of –Soordas, Nand das, Paramanand das, Kumbhandas, Chhittaswami, Krishnadas, Govind das and Chaturbhujdas. Among the hundreds poets writing peoms on Krishna, these eight poets of Ashtachhap have the most importance. In context to the contempory literature of shringar or love, the eight types of nayikas also cannot be forgotten or over looked. Even after the distinctive differences written in many texts there are eight types of nayikas, who are mainly prominent. They are called as Swadheenpatika, Vasaksajja, Virahotkanthita, Abhisarika, Vipsalabdha, Khadita, Kalahantarita and Proshitpatika. Swadheenpatika is one whose husband is under her control, Vasaksajja is the one who decorates herself with clothes and jewellary on learning about the return of her lover from travel, Virahotkanthita is the one who is desperate due to the separation of her lover who has gone to a foreign country. Abhisarika is the one, who make love to her lover by meeting him at a definite place,

Vipralabdha is the one who is feverish or disappointed on reaching the destined place decided by the nayak or lover, the one who is known to the relations of the nayak or lover with another woman is Khandita, Kalahantarita is the one who is angry or annoyed due to quarrels in love and when her lover goes to a foreign land, she is called Proshitpatika. The Abhisarika nayika or lover has to go and meet her other lover during the day or dark night or on a moonlit night in light fortnight or Shukla paksha to a predestined place. These destined places are also of eight types, they are-farm-field, garden, ruins of a temple, house of the messenger, jungle, place of pilgrimage, cemetery and the bank of a river. These are the places described as the meeting places of nayak and nayika.

In literature eight such Satvik or good feelings on which one does not have any control. These eight feelings are- Stambh (To be static or rooted), Ashru (Tears), Swed (Perspiration flowing from the body without any reason), Romanch (To have shivering in the body or hair raising in the body), Swarbhang (Breaking or crackling of voice), Kamp (To have sudden tremble in the body), Vaivarnaya (Change of body colour to almost yellow or white) and Pralay, that means to be unconscious. Among the 60 daughters of the king Daksh, eight daughters were accepted as wives to the king Kashyap. These eight daughters were- Aditi, Diti, Danu, Kalka, Tamra, Krodhvasha, Mana and Anala. Among them Aditi bore as the mother of Aditya, who is known as the 33 gods (12 Aditya, 8 Vasu, 11 Rudra and 2 Ashwini Kumar). From Diti were born monster and from Danu were born demons. That means gods, monsters, and demons are step borthers.

Sanyasis should follow eight vrat or pledges. These pledges are- Non-violence, Chastity or Celibacy, Truth, Simplicity, Lack of Anger, Sacrifice to find faults, Control of the senses and not to gossip or tell tale. With the desire of enjoyment and salvation, the worshippers of Tripurbhairavi, also worship eight bhairavs and eight matrikas. The eight bhairavs are- Asitang, Ruru, Chand, Krodh, Unmatt, Kapali, Bheeshan and Sanhar. The eight matrikas are- Brahmani, Maheshwari, Kaumari, Vaishnavi, Varati, Maahendri, Chamunda and indomitable or Aparajita Durga. Eight Matri goddesses are also mentioned. They are- Jaya, Vijaya, Jayanti, Aparajita, Siddha, Rakta, Alambusa and Utpala. In philosophical dictionary proofs are of eight types- Evidence, Assumption, Similarity, Word, Interrogation, and Presumption from an answer, Possibility and Lack. Evident proof is when one personally and evidently experiences anything or any object at any time or any place. The second type of proof is, in the absence of the evident, to find out or know that is non-evident like the assumption of fire on seeing a smoke. On the basis of famous direct thing to attain knowledge, like to recognize neelgai on the basis of a cow. The advices given by the learned, truthful, religious and helpful or altruistic person. For them faith is the proof. Lie it is mentioned in the Vedas, Religious texts, Memory, the Puranas, and the Law. The incidents of any great man's life are the evident proofs. The resultant proof is to attain knowledge from reason or work experience, like rain due to the clouds and the falling of water due to rain under the proof of possibility are all those things which are possible in the sequence of nature and to have faith on them. And those things which are against the cycle or sequence of nature, like the proof that is beyond like the horns of a rabbit. The lack of evidence or proof is to find out from its available place in absence of the thing.

In our caste system Brahmins have occupied an important place. So there is an indebt belief that if there are eight types of bad feelings against Brahmins moves towards his calamity. They are-one who is heartily jealous of a Brahmin, one who opposes him through karma, one who snatches his wealth, one who desires to hit or kill, one who condemns them, one who doesn't like their praise one who doesn't remember them at proper or due times or occasions and one who looks down upon them when he pledge to them, such persons go towards their destruction.

अष्टौ पूर्वनिमित्तानि नरस्य विनशिष्यतः।
ब्राह्मणान् प्रथमं द्वेष्टि ब्राह्मणैश्च विरुध्यते॥
ब्राह्मणस्वानि चादत्ते ब्राह्मणांश्च जिघांसते।
रमते निन्दया चैषां प्रशंसा नाभिनन्दति॥
नैनान् स्मरति कृत्येषु याचितश्चाभ्यसूयति।
एतान् दोषान् नरः प्राज्ञो बुध्येद् बुद्ध्वा विसर्जयेत्॥

-विदुरनीति 1-98-100

Showing the eight paths of religion Vidur says-

इज्याध्ययनदानानि तपस्सत्यं क्षमाः दमः।
अलोभ इति मार्गोऽयं धर्मस्याष्टविधः स्मृतः॥

–महा. वनपर्व–2–75

The eight paths of religion are said to be- Yagna, Study, Charity, Tapa, Truth, Forgiveness, Kindness and Sacrifice of greed. No intelligent person will have trust on these- Women, Kings, Snakes, Self-study, Master, Enemy, Enjoyment and Age. They may change anytime.

स्त्रीषु राजसु सर्पेषु स्वाध्यायप्रभुशत्रुषु।
भोगेष्वायुषि विश्वासं कः प्राज्ञः कर्तुमर्हति।

Women and kings are frivolous by nature. To sting is the nature of a snake. One tends to forget the lessons of self-study without its revision again and again- **'अनभ्यासे विषं विद्या'**. When a master's mind will change, nobody knows. Enemies can strike anytime. Enjoyments are going to be destroyed within no time and age may get over anytime. So it is not a logical thing. To believe in them and stay without any worries.

The daughter of Yashoda whom Kansa killed presuming it to be the child of Devki, was a Jogmaya or a miracle. When she escaped from Kansa and was seen in the sky, then in her hands she had eight weapons- Bow, Trident, Arrows, Shield, Sword, Cohen, Wheel and Grit. God has created a king with eight parts- Indra, Air, Yama, Sun, Fire, Varun, Moon and Kuber. According to Srimad Bhagvad Mahapuran, idols are made of eight things- Stone, Wood, Iron, Sandalwood, Gods and goddesses are also painted in pictures. Ram had established the idol of Lord Shiva from Sand. All idols can be created from valuable metals without any hard or actual element one can create an idol through the mental feelings of the sketches. In Matsya Puran, idols made from lead and bronze are also considered. Every year lakhs of devotees go to the cave of Amarnath for the darshan of Shivling from snow.

Great rishi Atri has shown eight best characters for a householder- 1. Free from envy and jealousy 2. Cleanliness 3. Good will and Prosperity 4. Spontaneous 5. Detached 6. Control 7. Charity and 8. Kindnes. These qualities should be followed in daily routine life. With some slight change in their names great rishi Gautam has called them as the personal qualities such as- 1. Kindness 2. Forgiveness 3. Free from envy and jealousy 4. Cleanliness 5. Spontaneous 6. Good will and prosperity 7. Sacrifice and 8. Detachment. In the Ashtang Pranam of sacred or revered persons and also before gods, there are eight types of greetings or bows- 1. Thighs 2. Fleet 3. Hands 4. Chest 5. Mind or intelligence 6. Head 7. Speech and 8. Sight, all these are coordinated. For the greeting one has to lie down on the floor with both hands stretched in front and in this sequence the head, glabella, nostrils, chest, heart, stomach, knees, palms and the toes of leg are made to touch the ground. After that with both hands the feet should be touched. Then by sitting on the floor on one's knees one, should touch one's hands to one's eyes and heart.

Shukra principle has eight instructions for the behavior of kings, like- To punish the evil persons, To give charity, Compliance of his subjects, To perform Rajsuya yagna, To increase the treasury justly and legally, To impose tax on other kings, To demean the prestige of enemies, and constantly increase the borders of one's state or country. These eight types of karmas are the behavior of kings.

दुषनिग्रणं दानं प्रजायाः परियासनम्।
यजनं राजसूयादेः कोशानां न्यायतोऽअर्जनम्।।
करदीकरणं राज्ञां रिपूणां परिमर्दनभ्।
भूमिरुपाज्रनं भूयो शजवृत्तं तु चाष्टधा।।

-शुक्रकीतिसार-1-123-124

According to the principles of Shukra women have eight natural bad qualities or blames- To tell lies, False courage, Maya, Foolishness, Intense greed, Sacredness, Cruelty and Ego or Pride.

अनृतं साहसं माया मूर्खत्वमतिलोभता।
अशौचं निदर्यं दर्पः स्त्रीणामष्टो स्वदुर्गणाः।।

-शुक्रनीतिसार-3-162

Goswami Tulsidas translates the same feeling in 'Ramcharitmanas'

नारि स्वभाव सत्य कवि कहहीं। अवगुन आठ सदा उर रहहीं।
साहस अनृत चपलता माया। मम अबिबेक अशौच अदाया।।

-रामचरितमानस 6-16 क

In India there are eight main religious communities or groups 1. Hindu 2. Muslims 3. Christians 4. Sikhs 5. Buddhists 6. Jains 7. Parsis, and 8. Jews. Some religions have evolved due to the difference in the procedures of worship. Actually Sikhism, Buddhism and Jainism have been born out of Hindu religion and all these four religions have many similarities. Christianity is the new form of Jew religion. In India the number of Parsis and Jews are very few.

Eight types of snakes that all are afraid of- Anant, Vasuki, Padam, Mahapadam, Takshak, Karkotak, Shankh and Shesh. So we pray to the Ashtakarna Lord Brahma, that he may give us such wisdom that we may join in the eight duty services of Lord Shrinat ji, as – Mangal darshan (Seeing), Shringar (Decoration), Gocharan (To go to the fields with cows), Rajbhog (Kingly food), Uthapan (To rise from nap), Bhog (Food), Sandhya (Evening prayer) and Shayan (Sleep or Rest), we gain the strength and wisdom. To study Panini's Ashtadhyayi (eight chapters).

❐

9 (Nine)

In basic numbers where nine is big, it is also very auspicious. It is the elder brother of basic numbers. For auspicious numbers 7 and 9 are acceptable. Nine has come from the Sanskrit word Nava. Its meaning is new. In the counting of numbers, wherever there in nine there will be newness afterward. It comes with the message of change. In religion predominant India, to do or no to do, successful or unsuccessful, secret or open, it has special importance. The basis of religion is the body **'शरीरमाद्यं खलुधर्मसाधनम्'** All religious performances are through the body. A body also has nine stages-

निषेकगर्भजन्मनि बाल्यकौमारयौवनम्।
वयोमध्यं जरा मृत्युरित्यवस्थास्तनोर्नव।।

–भागवत–11–22–46

Pregnancy, Increase of foetus, Birth, Childhood, Youth, Adulthood, Old age. Death are the various stages. The first two stages are prior to coming to his world. Death is the last destination of this travel, rest of the stages are that of karma field. After getting nine stages, one can follow the nine differences of dharma, which have been described by the great father, Bhishma in Mahabharat. Manu has mentioned 10 characteristics of dharma which will be described in next chapter. In the Mahabharat, Bhishma's nine characteristics are thus shown-

अक्रोधः सत्यवचनं संविभागः क्षमा तथा।
प्रजनः स्वेषु दारेषु शौचमद्रोह एव च।।
आर्जवं भृत्यभरणं नवैते सार्ववर्णिकाः।।

–महा. शान्तिपर्व 7–8

(Not to be angry on someone to speak the truth, to use wealth after sharing, to have compassionate feelings, to bear children from one's own wife, to be pure from outside and inside, not to confront with others, to have a simple behavior, to nurture and feed deserving people, this is the same for all varnas to follow)

To live an ordinary religious life, there are nine such necessary karmas which is desired to be done by every Brahmin. They can be said as nine to be done or Karaniya karmas.

Sandhya, bath, japa, hom, study, worship of god, hospitality of guests offerings and one's services to (god, father, men, poor and destitute, sanyasi, parents etc.), to give food and drinks as per the rules are the nine karmas. Similarly, there are nine-Not to be done karmas. Like Untrue speech, to eat other's share, to eat that is not eatable or forbidden, to go to a place which is not proper, to drink that which is not drinkable, violence, stealing, karmas and behavior beyond veda, not to be friendly to other religions, these are the nine which are called resentful or shameful. The adoption of ordinary or common religion, to be busy in Karaniya Karma and to keep away from akaraniya karma, this takes man towards humanity. These things are not for any religion, caste or country, but are as the consequence of the welfare of entire human kind.

Nine things are hindrances to the road to heaven. These bad qualities are-1. To gossip, 2. To utilize other women, 3. Rebellion, 4. Anger, 5. Maya (cheat), 6. False speech, 7. To speak ill and bad, 8. Jealousy, 9. False ego. For a house holder there are nine means for religious karma. 1. Truth, 2. Cleanliness, 3. Non-Violence, 4. Forgiveness, 5. Charity, 6. Kindness, 7. Control on senses, 8. Not to steal, 9. Pratyahar (To distract senses from evils and settle it within)

These nine should not be believed, 1. Woman 2. Vagabond 3. Lazy 4. Fearsome 5. Angry 6. Chauvinist 7. Robber 8. Unfaithful and 9. Atheist.

स्त्रीधूर्तकेऽलसे भीरौ चण्डे पुरुषमानिनि।
चौरे कृतघ्ने विश्वासो न कार्यो न च नास्तिके॥

There are nine things which should be kept secret. To express or show them is not beneficial

आयुर्वितं गृहच्छिद्रं मंत्रमैथुनभेषजम्।
तपोदानावमानौ च नव गोप्यानि यत्नतः।।

In Shukra neeti the last line is thus-

दानमानापमानं च नवैतानि सुगोपयेत।

-शुक्रनीति सार-3-126

It is proper to hide one's age, wealth, home secret, mantra, sexual acts, medicine, tapa, charity and discredit. Their expression can be disgraceful, harmful, painful or meaningless. Also, there are nine things which are good to express and also beneficial. To take loan to return loan, thing received in charity, thing sold, giving daughter in marriage, study, shameful acts and committed in solitude, it is better to express them. Vrish means a bull. To make a mark on a dead man, bull should be set free. That is called Vrishotsarg. Vaishnavs have nine idols-Vasudev, Sankarshan, Pradyumna, Aniruddh, Narayan, Hayagriva, Varah, Narsinh and Brahma.

One becomes successful and destroyable who gives to nine types of people-mother, father, guru, friend, polite person, benevolent person, poor, orphan and saintly or good persons, these are the best but there are other nine types of people to whom whatever is given becomes useless or a waste-shrewd person, prisoner, fool, undeserving, bad doctor, gambler, wicked, gossiping person, gypsy and robber, all that is given is without utility-

धूर्ते वन्दिनी मंन्दे च कुवैद्ये कितवे शठे।
चाटुचारणचौरेभ्यो दत्तं भवति निष्फलम्।।

There are nine such things which should not be given in emergency also- property of the people, money that is collected as honorarium, wealth of the land, things of relationship, jewelry of one's wife, wealth of debt, thing of treasures, one's own wealth, even when one has his own son. These nine things should be given to the deserving persons. If one gives away these things, then be can become pure only after doing penance.

According to Indian tradition a guest is like god. On the arrival of the guest, the house holder should perform nine things as omens and is expected and should keep in mind-Kind heart, kind outlook, kind face, kind words, to get up and greet the guest, then after exchanging welfare, talk gently and sit close to the guest and when the guest goes, one should go after him for some distance, apart from these nine things, one should bear in mind nine special things on the arrival of the guest-offer a seat to the guest and give him water, give a carpet to sit and wash his feet, to offer place to stay and have bath, offer a bed and food and also give him mud and water.

In modern times due to scientific progress, the world may seem very small but its vastness is accepted since the ancient times. Great poet Bhavbhuti has expressed its vastness through **'विपुला च पृथ्वी'**. Among the seven big continents of this vast earth one huge continent has nine parts of land. All around Meru mountain among seven islands, one is a huge island. These are the nine big islands or lands by the names of Bharat, Kimpurush, Hari, Ilavrit, Ramya, Hiranya, Kuru, Bhadra and Ketumal. While doing worship, pandit calls this huge land as Bharatkhand to show its existence geographically. To take somebody as a disciple, three qualities are required

अमान्यमत्सरो दक्षो निर्ममो दृढसौहृदः।
असत्वरोऽर्थजिज्ञासुरनसूयरमोघवाक्॥

The are-1. Free from ego 2. One who does not intend bad for another 3. Skilled at work 4. Free from attachment, 5. Dedicated in guru's love 6. Not hasty at work 7. Desire for learning for the welfare of others 8. Free from envy or jealousy and 9. One who does not talk irrelevant. These nine need to be cared and nurtured by us-1. Mother 2. Father 3. Guru 4. Wife 5. Child 6. One in refuge 7. Guest 8. One who comes with fear and 9. Fire. One should consider one's duty for their food and other amenities. Abhyagat is invited and a guest is one who arrives suddenly.

In the context of nine, the nine doors or openings of the body is necessary to be mentioned. Vyas calls it- **'नवद्वारं पुरं पुष्यम्'** In the body there are two eyes, two ears, two nasal holes, one mouth, one anus, one opening both for urine and genitals, there are nine holes of different senses. Travellers on the path to meditation always ask or the necessity to guard these five senses. The desire for beauty, speech, smell and touch is through them and that desire is the main reason to destabilize the mind. Actually these nine openings are the means to throw out the excretory dirt from the body and the five elements of the body also go out of the body on death. That is why yogis talk about the guarding of these nine doors. The first stage of sadhana is to control these nine doors. At some places there is mention of a tenth door. Joyasi Brahmarandhra is called the 10th door

नवपौरी पर दसम दुआरा। तेहि पर बाज राज घरियारा॥

Some texts have called navel as the 11th door. In context to the earth, it is natural to remember the nine planets. It is believed in astrology that the residents of this earth are affected by the movements and speed of Sun, Moon, Mars, Mercury, Jupiter, Venus, Saturn, Uranus and Neptune. This belief is justified because before any auspicious moment there is the ritual of the worship of the nine planets. For their worship, their idols are also made as a principle. Sun is made with bronze, Moon with crystal, Mars with red sandalwood, Mercury and Jupiter with gold, Venus with silver, Saturn with iron, Rahu with lead and Ketu with german silver. According to geography also the number of planets are nine, but Sun is not a planet, but, it has its family and that solar system has nine planets-Mercury, Venus, Earty, Mars, Jupiter, Saturn, Neptune, Plato and Uranus. In English, they have these names whereas in astrology they are called as-Buddh, Shukra, Prithvi, Mangal, Guru, Shani, Arun, Varun and Yama. All these nine planets move around the Sun. According to the experts of geography the earth is a planet, whereas Rahu and Ketu are not planets, but mere reflections. On this earth there have been nine such kings who are well recognized and famous for their wealth and prosperity. They are- Rantidev, Nabhag, Mandhata, Manu, Pritha, Bhagirath, Yayati, Nahush and Yudhishthir. Like the seven holy rivers some texts have considered nine rivers to be holy.

गंगा सिन्धुश्च कावेरी यमुना च सरस्वती।
रेवा महानदी गोदा ब्रह्मपुत्र पुनातु माम्॥

There are nine bad qualities of the mind-Lust, Anger, Attraction, False pride, Attachment, Greed, Repentance, False intention and Jealousy, all texts advice to keep away from them and stay protected. Nine daughters of Kandarbh Devhuti-Kala, Ansuya, Shraddha,

Havirbhu, Gati, Kriya, Khyati, Arundhati and Shanti became the wives of nine rishis- Marichi, Atri, Angira, Pulastya, Pulaba, Krtu, Bhriga, Vashishtha and Athrva respectively. Among them seven of them are the acclaimed Suptarishis and are the adopted sons of Brahma.

In Indian tradition, whenever a man has felt of his helplessness is sad or distressed, at those times he has gone to the refuge of woman, although due to his ego, he may have called her weak. In their helpless state, the goddesses whose refuge man has taken, they are known by the names of Navkumari, Navdurga or Navshakti. For their worship, nine days are decided as Navratri, the Vikram era starts from the Chaitra new moon. So the first nine days of the New Year and again after six months in the month of Ashwin new moon, for nine days, Navdurga fasting worship and meditation is the auspicious occasion. Among the Navkumaris are nine goddesses- Kumarika, Trimurti, Kalyani, Rohini, Kali, Chandika, Sham bhavi, Durga and Subhadra. The nine goddesses Navdurga who are worshipeed during the months of Chaitra and Ashwin are Shailputri, Brahmacharini, Chandraghanta, Kushmanda, Skandmata, Katyayani, Kalratri, Mahagauri and Siddhida. In the Puranas, these goddesses are described as the form of nine powers- Prabha, Maya, Jaya, Sukshma, Vishuddha, Nandini, Suprabha, Vijaya and Sarvasiddhida. A goddess is actually the power of Shiva, who has been described in two form soft and horrible. In soft forms they are- Kumarika, Mahagauri, Siddhida, Jaganmata, Bhavani, Parvati and in angry form they are known as- Kali, Durga, Chandi or Chandika, Bhairavi. In the Angry form of the goddess for its devotees and worshipers has an element of disaster in food, drinks and clothing and decoration. In Kali's image, this goddess is happy with meat, wine and animal sacrifice. She has been shown as drinking the blood of defeated demons. Actually, Navdevi or Navdurga are the different images of the wife of Shiva. Some of her names are according to her work and some other names are her husband's surroundings. She is the daughter of the Himalayas, so Shailputri, she is also Brahmacharini having won over Lord Shiva due to her meditation, having half-moon in her neck, so she is Chandraghanta and taking the three world's sorrow within oneself, she is Kushmanda, Skandmata being the mother of Skanda, the one who is a warning to terror for time is Kalratri, making the works of gods as successful and rewarding, she is Katyayani, and being very fair and glowing due to meditation, she is Mahagauri, bestowing success and salvation, she is Siddhida. Actually the power of the Almighty has become manifold in different forms as his wife.

Behind the worship of all gods and goddesses, there is the prayer and pleading of desires of the worshippers. There are very few or marginal worshippers who fast or perform worship with a selfless or devoted feeling. Normally, a person desires for wealth and prosperity, Worldly credits are growing in the possession of gold and silver. Metals are of nine types now. Common people know them as bronze, copper and stainless steel. There are other metals also known but on scientific basis they are yet not accepted. This is not in the perspective of our discussion. Our emphasis is that every wealthy person, on being prosperous, wants to own the nine types of gems or precious stones. They are more precious compared to metals. They are-Pearl, Jade, Ruby, Moonstone, Diamond, Sapphire, Emerald, some of them are as stones in the ring which increases their look, this type of desire practically every wealthy and prosperous person has. To adorn them is to get away from the bad influence of the nine planets, which is the sole reason and the intention. They affect some birth charts with good or auspicious and others with bad or inauspicious effects. So to adorn them is as per the astrology. In some texts, navratna or nine gems are mentioned as- Hirak, Muktik, Manik, Panna, Neelam, Pukhraj, Parvat, Moonga and Feroza. In some Vaidurya is also mentioned among navratna (nine gems) but everywhere their total number is nine. A person who is prosperous with these nine gems and after relinquishing these be desires for Navnidhi. Devotees ask for Ashtasiddhi and Navnidhi from their gods. Janaki also gave a blessing to Hanuman, when she was pleased with him-

अष्टसिद्धि नौ निधि के दाता। अस बर दीन्हं जानकी माता।।

The Navnidhi's are- Padam, Mahapadam, Shankh, Makar, Kachchap, Mukund, Kund, Neel and Kharva. These are the nine treasures of Kuber. In Indian accountancy there is definite images of Kharva, Neel, Padam and Shankh.

There is another desire beyond these worldly things such as wealth prosperity comfort and magnificence and that is to improve oneself to go to the other world, to attain heaven, to be close to Brahma and to get freedom of coming and going. For this there are many paths of Sadhana, but the path of bhakti or devotion attracts more because of its simplicity. The devotee of bhakti wants to develop a relationship with that Almighty power in one way or another. Some become the servant of that Almighty ruler. Goswami Tulsidas is proud to be 'The slave of god' or 'The servant of god'. Kabir calls himself as the Bahariya of Ram. Meera does not even bother about the worldly shame or inhibitions, to get the Lord as her husband, although she has a husband in her life. Sufis consider god as their wife and to get her, they are ready to face four halts and seven climbs- **'चारि बसेरो से चढ़े सत ते उतरे पार'** The cowherds and gopis consider Krishna as their friend. They are not ready to accept Krishna superior to them in any way. They clearly say-

'जाति पाति तुमते कम नाहीं नहीं बसत तुम्हारी छैंया।'

The aim of all these devotees is a humble prayer before god. This bhakti is also of nine types-

श्रवणं कीर्तनं विष्णोः स्मरणं पादसेवनम्।
अर्चनं वन्दनं दास्यं सख्यमात्मनिवेदनम्।।

The listening and reading of religious books is the hearing or Shravan bhakti of god. To sing the praises of god miracles and his various qualities is second type of bhakti. To remember god's name and praise his miracles and qualities is the third type of bhakti. To meditate at his feet, to thing deeply about him and puja or worship is the bhakti of service at his feet, is the fourth type. In worship, the procedure of Shree Vigrah is performed with great faith. The highest bhakti and prayer is to bow before all living considering them to be the image of god. In Srimad Bhagvad says of bowing to all even dog, one at the cemetery, cow and donkey **'प्रणमेद दण्डवद् भूमौ अश्वचाण्डालगौखरान्।'** These are the six different means of bhakti (devotion). By following this or making it habitual devotion is emanated in oneself, after this rises the form or image of bhakti of Hanuman, Bharat, Lakshman, Nishad, Shabri etc. are of this type. To have friendship with god, is the friendly type of bhakti, this is the feeling of the bhakti of gop-gopis, Sudama and Draupadi. In the softer and sweet feeling for god, one can have relationship with him as a husband. To express one's pair and sorrow before god is a self-plea or prayer. Kabir, Tulsidas and Meera are these type of devotees. In bhakti one takes the help of mind, karma and speech. Self-expression, friendly feeling, slavery feeling or just the memory are the bhakti which is performed with the mind, whereas salutation, worship, listening, service at god's feet are all performed through the karma. Kirtan is a bhakti performed through speech. To achieve closeness with god is the final goal of Navadha bhakti. In today's scientific era also the devotees of Newadha bhakti are more than the others on the path of meditation. In Ramcharitmanas, Ram explains to Shabri about Navadha bhakti, in this way-

नवधा भगति कहऊँ तोही पाहीं। सावधान सुनु धरु मन माहीं।।
प्रथम भगति संतन्ह कर संगा। दूसरा रति मम कथा प्रसंगा।।
गुरुपद पंकज सेवा तीसरि भगति अमान।
चौथि भगति मम गुन गन करई कपट तजि गान।।
मन्त्र जाप मम दृढ विस्वासा। पंचम भजन सो बेद प्रकासा।।
छठ दम सील बिरति बहु करमा। निरत निरन्तर सज्जन धरमा।।
सातवँ सम मोहि मय जग देखा। मोतें संत अधिक करि लेखा।।
आठवाँ जथालाभ संतोषा। सपनेहुँ नहिं देखई परदोषा।।
नवम सरल सब सन छलहीना। मम भरोसा हियँ हरष न दीना।

In bhakti, where one does offering, prayer and worship with a desire to get something, also one prays to gods and goddesses for protection '**भय बिनु होय न प्रीति**' In this the love of god is not restricted to the worldly love. Love towards god is only bhakti. Goswami Tulsidas had written the 'Vinay Patrika' in Kaliyug due to mere fear. One reason for fear is the snake and its venom. The relation of snake and its venom is like that of qualifier and the quality. These two are also related to death. The wife of rishi Kashap, Kadru, is the mother of snakes, whose nine sons are named- Anant, Vasuki, Padam, Mahapadam, Karkotak, Shankh, Kambal, Kalik and aparajit. In some texts there is the mention of eight generation of snakes which have been described in chapter eight.

One more thing that is remarkable is that out of those eight six name are included in this list. There is the name of Takshak and Shesh and here there are three names Kambal, Kulik and Aparajit which are not there in that list. The moment a snake is mentioned venom immediately come to memory. The venom is also of nine types- Vastsanam, Haridrik, Saktuk, Pradipan, Saurashtrik, Shringak, Kalkut, Halahal and Brahmaputra. A common person is known only to Kalkut and Halahal. One who is afflicted by venom or poison has to go to a doctor's rescue and in Ayurveda there is special importance of Navang. In Navang, there are nine things- Dry ginger powder, Peepal, Chilli, Harad, Baheda, Amla, Tea, Chita and Vayvading.

With the number nine, we remember the nine Brahmins in Puranas who were born due to mental pledge. They emerged due to the Yoga of Lord Narayan. Brahmins who have been described in Puranas are- Marichi, Bhrigu, Angira, Pulastya, Pulaa, Krtu, Pracheta, Atri and Vashishtha. In some other texts nine Brahmins or rulers as- Marichi, Atri, Angira, Pulastya, Pulaha, Vishwamitra, Bharadwaj, Gautam, Jamdagni. The propagator of Vikram Samvat or era, Vikramaditya is very well known for his love of justice, at the same time he is famous for his nine gems or Navratna. In Vikramadityas cabinet were such well known members and luminaries as- Dhanvantari, Kshapnak, Amarsinh, Shanku, Vetal, Bhatt, Ghatakrapar, Kalidas, Varahmihir and Varruchi, who were extraordinary in the fields of knowledge of medicine, astrology, politics grammar and poetry. Although it is different that some great learned people think that it is mere imagination to connect these nine gems to the cabinet of Vikramaditya.

Indians have faith in varied views and religions. The Nath cult has also influenced a large part of society of this country. They are the followers of complete chastity or Brahmacharya. They keep away from Tamasik food like meat and wine, are submerged in Yoga sadhana, and being Hindus completely do not burn their bodies after death. The believers of 'Alakh' that is the path of Naths, there are nine of them, they are- Gorakhnath, Jwalendranath, Karinnath, Gohininath, Charpatnath, Revannath, Nagnath, Bhartrinath (Bhartrihari) and Gopichandranath. Its main seat of worship is in Gorakhpur in Uttar Pradesh. The disciples of

Gorakhnath are called 'Kanphata Yogi' Nepalis being the disciples of Gorakh call themselves as Gorkhas. They consider Gorakh as the incarnation of Lord Pashupatinath. The present chief minister of Uttar Pradesh Yodi Adityanath is the highest official of the Gorakhpur seat.

While discussing nine, nine imminent emotions are necessary to mention because these emotions are the permanent residents of all hearts-they are- Love, Laughter, Sorrow, Anger, Excitement, Fear, Curiosity, Surprise and Nirved, these take birth in the heart and stay dependent in heart's refuge, these get exposed when a spark of moment gets excited and later these are enjoyed by the senses and turn to the beautiful feeling or taste of that sense. So there are nine types Rasas- Love, Joy, Sad, Anger, Bravery, Horrible, Disgusting, Extra ordinary and Calm are called as Brahmananda. In these rasas, there are the godly poets, who have the pride that the creator of nature has made only six rasas and we have created nine rasas-

विधि ते कवि सब विधि बड़े यामै संशय नाहिं।
षटरस विधि की सृष्टि में, नवरस कविता माँहि॥

An understanding person should not oppose these nine things. When Marich did not co-operate with Ravana during the kidnapping of Sita and when Marich was threatened to be killed by Ravana, then Marich thinks in his mind-

तब मारीच हृदय अनुमाना। नवहिं बिरोधें नहिं कल्याना॥
सस्त्री मर्मी प्रभु सठ धनी। बैद बंदी कवि भानस गुनी॥

One does not know when a person with arms may attach you, our near and dear one's open up our secrets, when a master may give punishment, fools may commit some utter foolishness, when one gets the need of a wealthy person, enmity with a doctor can tell upon one's life. A poet and a folk singer can sing the songs of praises, but one doesn't know when they will read or write the story of shame and who knows when a cook can feed anything if he is a rival. Maharshi Dayanand Saraswati's death was due to his cook.

One who goes to the rescue of god is called Sharanagata. There are nine characteristics of this refuge-Helplessness, Purity,

Truth, Help to others, Complete surrender, Complete faith, To be admired by all, To forget oneself, and Ananyata. In Mahabharat, Duryodhana had called his nine valiant and brave soldiers as the strength of his army and on that basis he had divided his army into nine divisions. Those nine brave-hearts were-Bhishma, Drona, Kripacharya, Karna, Shalya, Kritverma, Shakuni, Ashwathama and Duryodhana himself. In the end, after the worship of nine planets, while worshipping the nine goddesses, while hoping for the welfare of this earth and accepting the Navadha bhakti, I conclude this chapter.

❐

10 (Ten)

The first among basic numbers 1, when meets and lines with symbol of the great zero, then the combined image is 10. During the number or numerical system during the Vedic era the basic number was ten. All are aware of the importance of the counting further than 10. The synonym of the Endless or Infinity is zero it becomes countable after only attaching to 1. Zero came after the number 1 and the numbers kept on increasing. The distances between earth and other planets and other solar system can be measured on the strength of only this couple number.

India is primarily a religious country. Here religion has a wide perspective. Religion does not mean procedures of worship or any specific cult. Religion has ten characteristics, be is religious, even if his worship rituals may be any or may have faith in any god. Manu Smriti is the first text on religion, so the ten characteristics according to it-

धृति क्षमा दमोऽस्तेयं शौचमिन्द्रियनिग्रहः।
धीर्विद्या सत्यक्रोधो दशकं धर्मलक्षणम्।।

– मनुस्मृति 6-92

They are-Stability, Forgiveness, Power, Cleanliness, Providence, Control on senses, Education, Truth and Sobraiety. Those secular leaders of a state or a country vouch for it, should be asked if they wish to keep the state away from these qualities? Does anyone smell? The quality of any cult or religion in these 10 characteristics. Religion is said to have 10 parts in Padma Puran. These 10 are-Chastity, Truth, Tapa, Charity rules, Forgiveness, Cleanliness, Non-Violence, Peace and Clean attitude. In Matsya Puran also a religion is shown to have 10 parts, they are- Non rebellion, Abstinence from greed, Control, Kindness, Chastity, Truth, Abstinence from anger, Forgiveness and Stability. So the meaning is that religion is not any synonym of worship rituals or any cult. Religion is solely related to the imminent values, which is believed, by all human-beings of this world.

Patience is when one moves on the path of his duty without losing self, not being excited, not diverting from the path and be able to have the strength to bear any pain or sorrow. Harishchandra, Prahlad, Dhruv and Pandavas had to face the test of their patience. Kalidas says- **'विकार हेतौ सति विक्रियन्ते येषां न चेतांसि त एवं धीराः।'** The test of patience is at the time of crisis Goswami Tulsidas writes-

धीरज धरम मित्र अरु नारी।
आपदकाल परखिए चारी॥

Forgiveness is to keep oneself in control and give a reply, by bearing even the guilt of others and still not have any feeling of revenge towards the other persons **'सत्यपि सामथ्येऽपकार सहनं क्षमा।'** With these feelings Vishnu had forgiven Bhrigu and Vashishth had forgiven Vishwamitra. Gandhiji says that forgiveness is the weapon of the powerful or strong, which is known by this statement since ages **'क्षमा वीरस्य भूषणम्'** National poet Ramdhari Singh Dinkar writes in his book, Kurukshetra, thus-

क्षमा शोभती उस भुजंग को, जिसके पास गरल है।
उसको क्या जो दंतहीन विष रहित विनीत सरल है॥

Control is to maintain oneself, control one's mind even if there are adverse or indifferent thoughts. To suppress the mind or control the mind is called Dam. **'मन एव मनुष्याणां कारणं बन्ध मोक्षयोः'** Because concentration of the mind, takes towards the work of various senses. After being united or in co-ordination with the mind, our senses start to do their work. So the mind should be engaged in Karaniya karma and should be kept away from irreligious works. Only after the mind is controlled **'मा गृधः कस्यस्विद्धनम्'** This feeling is then felt within oneself. Not to steal through one's mind, speech and karma is the feeling of Asteya. To abstain from the feeling of owning other's wealth, one is protected from many bad qualities. Along with internal and external cleanliness, the purity of food and drinks is also cleanliness but for mental and physical cleanliness, it is necessary to have economic cleanliness because **'सर्वेषामेव शौचानां अर्थशौचं विशिष्यते'** Control of the senses is to keep away the senses from objects and also their good and proper use. If these senses are engaged in their rightful religious work, then there will be no place for addiction, hatred and jealousy. Dhee is said to be the state of the mind which is flawless and free from the evil and which has the discreatory power of knowledge from good and bad that is called Dhee. Self-study and being open to lot of listening, other things are learned through education, so education is called the eye **'नास्ति विद्या समं चक्षुः'** By giving up untrue and unbeneficial speech, one can inculcate good speech on being well educated. If there is the co-operation of Dhee and Education, so because of Dhee one would get the close company of good people, and the person will sacrifice laziness and bad entertainment and also abstain from unedible foods and take the best foods and thus be the ruler of knowledge on being educated and concentrating the three faculties of the mind, speech and karma and gain the practical knowledge from the earth to god. The ultimate truth is to visualize the Truth form of god, in all things as they are and all persons as they are. One who worships truth will neither speak hard words nor will make any untrue lectures or speech. Due to truth many good qualities automatically come within you. The siblings of truth are-Sacrifice, Politeness, Purity, Generosity, Good character, Sweetness etc. to control one's anger even when one is angry is called Akrodh.

Being different from Manu, ancient religious text of Garud Puran has shown 11 characteristics.

सत्यं दमस्तपः शौचं सन्तोषश्च क्षमार्जवम्।
ज्ञानं शमो दया दानमेष धर्मः सनातनः॥

Just as the ten characteristics of religion, it also has ten wives- Laxmi, Dhruti, Medha, Pushti, Shraddha, Kriya, Kirti, Buddhi, Lajja and Mati, these ten daughters of rishi Daksha are the ten wives of religion. This is a combination, which means that by having these ten qualities one can attain religion or one who wants to get these 10 qualities, he has to follow the 10 religious characteristics described by Manu. They are also called the gates to religion that means one can enter into religious field or religious work through them.

In some texts, the 10 characteristics of religion are further divided into two parts five each on the basis of yam and niyam. They are- Non-violence, Truth, Control, Chastity, Abstinence, Cleanliness, Satisfaction, Tapa, Self-study and God as the Supreme. The first five are yam and the later five are called niyam.

According to Vyas there are 10 yam- Truth, Forgiveness, Simplicity, Deep thinking, Lack of Cruelty, Abstinence for Violence, Control of mind and senses, Always Joyful, Pleasant attitude or behavior and soft feeling towards all and 10 niyam are- Cleanliness, Bath, Tapa, Charity, Silence, Yagna, Self-study, Pledge, Fasting and Control of the Rising senses. For pledge also, there are 10 niyam or rules-

क्षमा सत्यं दया दानं-शौचमिन्द्रियनिग्रहः।
देवपूजाग्निहरणं सन्तोषोऽस्तेयमेव च।
सर्वव्रतेष्वयं धर्मः सामान्यो दशधा स्मृतः॥

In the ten forms of religion, ten persons are unknown such as- Drunkard, Reckless, Proud, Tired, Angry, Hungry, Hasty, Greedy, Fearful and Lustful, they remain in capable to follow their actions according to religion, due to their mental dependence-

दश धर्म न जानन्ति धृतराष्ट्र निबोध तान्।
मतः प्रमत्तः उन्मतः श्रान्तः क्रुद्धो बुभुक्षितः॥
त्वरभाणश्च लुब्धश्च भीतः कामी च ते दशः।
तस्मादेतेषु सर्वेषु न प्रसज्जेत् पण्डितः॥

-विदुरनीति 1-106-107

All that is done contrary to religion is called Adharma. One get piety from religion and sin from non-religion. Both dharma and adharma have their relation to mind, speech and body. The sins that are related to these three factors are also 10. Because of these sinful acts, a person move away from religion. To always think about getting the wealth of others, its continuous deep thought and effort, to have the desire in one's mind to do unwarranted. Karmas, to consider only one's body by not having any consideration for life, soul, god, heaven and hell, to utter harsh words, utter false or wrong speech, gossip of others, meaningless talks, to hurt somebody with one's mind, speech and karma, to take somebody's belongings without giving, to have physical relation with other men or women, come under the category of sin. A person who frees himself from these 10 sins and follows the 10 religious principles of Manu, he is a stark religious man even though he may not perform sandhya thrice a day or read the namaz five times a day or go to the church every Sunday or bear the five things with the word 'K'. These 10 characteristics of religion are not connected to any religion or special cult or any worship rituals but these are the principles of behavior for the entire human kind.

In Vedas, Rigved is the most important. It is stated to be one. Many of its mantras are found in other three Vedas also. Rigved has ten divisions, the thinkers of those mantras as in these various divisions are different rishis. The thinkers of 1st and 10th divisions of mantras are many rishis, but from 2nd to 9th divisions, each has only one rishi. They are for the 2nd division or mandal rishi Gritsamad, 3rd Vishwamitra, 4th Vamdev, 5th Atri, 6th Bharadwaj, 7th Vashishth, 8th Kanv and 9th Angira rishis. The thinkers of all these mantras are all rishis- **'ऋषयो मंत्रदृष्टारः'** In the process of creation, god created 10 sons who were his mind's sons and who are considered as the ten rulers. These ten Prajapatis or rulers of people are- Marichi, Atri, Angira, Pulastya, Pulaha, Krtu, Pracheta, Vashishth, Bhrigu and Narad. In the last chapter nine Brahmins have been mentioned. They are also among the Manas Putra or sons of the mind. Here only Narad is a new name. In the last chapter, while describing the nine rulers or Prajapati the names of Vishwamitra, Bharadwaj, Gautam and Jamadagni were also there. It seems that the later writers added the names of some famous rishis in their list and deleted some of the names. This is the reasons that the difference of names and 9 or 10 is seen. It is believed that from Lord Brahma's mind Marichi evolved, from eyes Atri, from mouth Angira, from ears Pulastya, from navel Pulaha, from hands Krtu, from skin Bhrigu, from breath Vashishth, from thumb Daksh and from lap Narad, all of them evolved. In this list the name of Daksh is also included among Brahma's sons.

There is the importance of external cleanliness to follow religion and for external cleanliness, it is necessary to bath. Bathing has ten benefits. If a person bathes with due care daily early in the morning he has-good looks, glow, strength, purity, age, health, ungreediness and intelligence and his bad dreams are destroyed. In some other texts these 10 benefits have been shown for a person who takes regular bath-strength, good looks, sweet voice, fair complexion, softness, fragrance, purity, beauty, handsomeness and beautiful women.

गुणा दश स्नानशीलं भजन्ते बलं रूपं स्वरवर्णप्रशुद्धिः।
स्पर्शश्च गन्धश्च विशुद्धता च श्रीः सौकुमार्य प्रवराश्च नार्यः॥

If both the lists are seen, it is easy to conclude that if one bath daily at an early morning hour, there are a many benefits. The religious kind of livelihood also has 10 means, by which one should survive. They are- Teaching, Handicrafts, Service as servant, Protection of cows and other animals, Business, Farming, to live life with collection of grains from the farms, to ask for food, and earn one's living from interest.

Teaching is considered first in the means of coming a livelihood. A teacher gives knowledge in charity, but it is necessary to bear in mind that there can be only 10 types of persons who have the right to have that education. So they are- son of a teacher one who renders service, one who exchanges knowledge, religious person, pure person, one who is capable to study and is powerful, one who gives money , a good friend etc. a close person or relative, or a family friend, these are the one's who can get education from the teacher. In a yagna performance 10 things are required to please the gods- oil, curd, milk, somlata, unhusked rice, or lapsi jow or sattu, cooked rice, ghee, raw rice, fruits and water.

There is restriction of having marriage relations with 10 descents or families-like, where there is no excellent work, there is no excellent person, there is no knowledgeable or learned person, has diseased body is a patient of anaemia, has the illness of tuberculosis, has the illness of epilepsy, has dysentery due to bad digestion, has white-skin disease, has leprosy, in these families a daughter should not be married, nor daughters to be taken in marriage from these families. It is believed by the Indian that god comes to this earth as incarnation for the protection of religion and to destroy the evil practices. The Mahabharat war was the reason for the incarnation of Krishna during that time, in which the armies of Kauravas and Pandavas, 11 and 7 gallantries were razed to death. In the first chapter of Gita, Sanjay or Krishna had counted the names of both parties Valliant's and warriors to Dhritarashtra, out of all of those names only ten were alive. On the Pandava side, the five brothers, Krishna and Satyaki and on the Kaurava side Kripacharya, Kritverma and Ashwathama. It is easy to get to the path to heaven, if one follows these 10- things-Truth, Looks, Study, Education, Aristocracy, Good behavior, Strength, Wealth, Bravery and One who talks sense, they have all the happiness of heaven on earth by these 10 good qualities. Among these qualities only good looks and aristrocracy is due to birth but the rest of the qualities a person has to inculcate or try to attain. Actually, all these qualities are appreciated and lauded when the person engages himself in the service the welfare of other. They are called the gates to heaven as good and religious feelings are attached to it-

सत्यं रूपं च विद्या च कौल्यं शीलं बलं धनम्।
शौर्यं च चित्राभाष्यं च दशेमे स्वर्गयोनयः॥

In addiction, sex or lust is counted as the first and foremost. One who is lustful is engulfed by 10 other addictions- Mrigaya (Hunting), to gamble or play dice, to sleep during the day, gossiping, have relations with women more often, to sing, play and dance, to have addiction to drugs or to go around like a vagabond, are all inspired by lust. Every Indian has respect and honorable feelings for the 10 gurus of the Sikhs. Nanak is the first guru, and Guru Govind Singh the last guru. After Guru Nanak was Angad (1539), Amardas (1552), Ramdas (1574), Arjun dev (1581), Hargovind (1606), Har Rai (1644), Har Krishnaray (1661), Teg Bahadur (1664), Govind Singh (1675) are famous and they have contributed a lot for the protection of Vedic dharma. After Guru Govind Singh, the tradition of guru ended. Now, Guru Granth Sahib has the status of guru. The sacrifices by Guru Arjun dev, Guru Teg Bahadur and Guru Govind Singh, their bravery, abstinence, love and concern for other's sorrows are such examples, which will be remembered by mankind always.

According to the belief of Vedic religion god being omnipresent and omni period, for the protection of religion and destruction of evil religion, comes to this earth at times, in incarnated form. This incarnation is called as the avatar of god. These incarnations of god as avatar and their number has been described differently in different texts. But in the Hindu society, the 10 avatars of Lord Vishnu has special importance, they are-Fish, Kurma, Varah, Narsinh, Waman, Parshuram, Ram, Krishna, Gautam Buddha and Kalki. Among them the first four Matsya, Kurma, Varah and Narsinh in Sat era, Waman, Parshuram and Ram in Treta era, Krishna in Dwapar era and Gautam Buddha in Kalyug or Kal era. The tenth incarnation of Kalki is awaited, who will be born in a city named Sambhal in the district of Moradabad in Uttar Pradesh. In Mahabharat, among the 10 incarnation, Buddha is not included, but Balram is included, so the fact is established that Mahabharat war and system were prior to the birth of Buddha. Rest of the other names are as they were.

Then necessity of an incarnation is the will of god. According to Gita, an incarnation is for the destruction of evil people and protection on saints and good people. Matya, the avatar of Lord Vishnu had killed the demon named Haygriv. During the churning of the ocean, for the good of gods, the avatar of Kurma had lifted the Mandrachal. The Varah avatar had killed Hiramyaksh and freed the earth from his clutches. The Lord took the avatar of Narsinh and killed Hiranyakashipu and saved the Vedic dharma. Parshuram had killed evil and terrorizing Kshatriyas twenty one times. Ram had killed the king of demons, Ravana. Krishna had killed the companions of Kauravas and unjust rulers, Buddha had given freedom from ritual worship forms, fake religion and Karma and. If Kaki take avatar, he will have to wage war against corruption and those that nurture corruption prevalent all over the country.

In the chapter of nine, the nine doors of the body has already been described. But above these nine doors, there is one 10th door. Sufi poet Jayasi has said thus-

नव पौरीपर दसम दुआरा। तूटि पर बाज राज घरियारा।।

Here there is always the super sound or Anhad Nad. Kabir calls this as inverted well **'आकासे मुख औंधा कुआं'**. In the words of Hath yogis, this is Brahmarandhra or the vibrations of Brahma. Best types of meditators, through the 10th door, take their breath out or die, and feel the joy of closeness to Brahma. 10 types of persons are fit to be punished according to their crime- Drunkard, Mad, Dacoit, Smuggler, Cheater, Vagabond, Gambler, Perjurer, Corrupt, they are non-beneficial for society. So they all must be punished. One commits sin through these three karmas. So they are called Tyajya karma (karma to be relinquished). They have been divided into three divisions. They are 3 physical karmas, 4 karmas of speech and 3 mental karmas. The three karmas that are physical sins are- to kill somebody, to steal and to have physical relations with other women. The four karmas that are the sins of speech are- to speak evil, to speak harsh, to gossip and to tell lie. The three karmas that are mental sins are-greed for other's wealth, hatred or envy with all living beings and not to have faith on the result of one's karmas.

In the context of nine Navdurga or Navkumaris have already been described. Where Durga has ten hands, she also has ten names due to her different appearances. She is worshipped as revered as Durga, Dasbhuja, Singhvahini, Mahishmardini, Jayadhatri, Kali, Muktakeshi, Tara, Chhinnamasta and Jagat gauri. The goddess with 10 hands. Mother Durga, taking on the appearance of Kali, on the vehicle of a lion, shows her disastrous image letting loose her long tresses and thus Mahishasur loses his life. The doer of all good to this world, Jagat gauri, sometimes becomes so aggressive and tormenting that she cuts off her own head and starts drinking her own blood, who can stay in position as stable before this Chhinnamata goddess.

After the 10 characteristics of dharma as the foundation of the varna or caste system, for the higher varnas, there has always been the expectation of the natural good qualities. According to this analysis for the Brahmins, 10 qualities should be shown in one's behavior, such as Suppression, Control, Penance, Purity, Satisfaction, Forgiveness, Simplicity, Devotion to god, Kindness and Truth.

शमो दमस्तपः शौचं संतोषः क्षान्तिरार्जवम्।
मद्भक्तिश्च दया सत्यं ब्रह्मप्रकृतयस्त्विमाः॥

–भागवत–11–17–16

Kshatriyas have been shown different qualities- Glow, Strength, Patience, Bravery, Tolerance, Generosity, Entrepreneurship, Stability,

Devotion towards Brahmins and Prosperity, one who is adept with these qualities is fit to be called as Kshatriya.

तेजो बलं धृतिः शौर्यं तितिक्षौदार्यमुद्यमाः।
स्थैर्यं ब्रह्मण्यतैश्वर्यं क्षत्रप्रकृतयस्त्विमाः॥

-भागवत 11-17-17

The fact of this division is that the caste system should not be ascertained by birth but with the related behavioral natural karma. A person should be considered in that varna on the basis of the dominance of qualities in a person. Parshuram the brave archerer and Dronacharya, the rishi were not accepted, although they were born in Brahmin families but are considered as the famous brave warriors. Vishwamitra is among the seven rishis though he is the child of Kshatriya parents.

Some of today's short time leaders who are despising the Indian tradition by calling it Manuvadi or Brahmanvadi on the same rich heritage and tradition, not only once but many a times there have been attacks of controversial thoughts and also dirty physical attacks. The followers of Gautam Buddha, and the so called followers who are antagonistic, may have forgotten that Gautam had blown his trumpets against this Vedic religion and by hearing one call from Shankaracharya the Buddhist religion was expelled from its birth place, India. On this pious land of India, no thought can ever bloom and nurture which does not have faith in god, veda and yagna. As soon as Shankaracharya comes to our memory, it is natural to remember his 10 Advaiti disciples. Revered Shankaracharya has four main disciples- Padyapad, Hastamalak, Sureshwar and Trotak. Among them Padmapad had two disciples Tirth and Ashram, Hastamalak had two disciples Van and Aranya, Trotak had three disciples Giri, Parvat and Sagar and Sureshwar has three disciples Puri, Bharati and Saraswati, these were the names of the Dasnami Sanyasis. From Sharda Math (Dwarka), the traditions of Tirth and Ashram are in practice. Puri, Bharati and Saraswati sanyasis are connected to Shringeri Math, Van and Aranya come under Govardhan Math of Pari. Giri, Parvat and Sagar come under Jyotir Math (Joshimath). These 10 sanyasis, went travelling all over India and removed Buddhist religion which did not believe in Vedas and god, and thus established the glory and importance of Vedic dharma. Even today, these sanyasis are always trying to save the Vedic dharma Indian culture and Indianness'.

Vedic dharma has many views and debates included in itself. This is the reason that people opposing the yagna tradition have accepted the same in the long run, which have been described in Vedic dharma. The followers of Gautam Buddha believe that he is filled with ten strengths. They are- Charity, Good character, Forgiveness, Bravery, Meditation, Deep thought, Strength, Solution, Pledge and Knowledge. Gautam Buddha has been included in Vedic dharma as one of the 10 incarnation or avatar or Vishnu because all these strengths are the natural qualities of a Brahmin and Kshatriya. Only the words are different. Gautam had given 10 advices to his followers to maintain pure attitude. These rules are called the 10 sheel- Not to have greed of other's wealth, To stay away from violence, No to tell a lie, To abstain from intoxicatin drungs and drinks, Non-Violence, Not to participate in music or dance, Not to use fragrant things, Not to eat at odd times, Not to have a soft bed and stay away from women. Among them the first five are for householder and 10 for bhikshu. There might be many differences between Vaishnav and Shakt, but the goddesses worshipped by them are only 10. The ten Durgas of the Vaishnavs is duly described in this chapter. With very few changes the Shakts also have 10 goddesses or idols of goddesses or 10 Mahavidyas. On both the sides, many names are as it is, like-Kali, Tara, Shodashi, Bhuvaneshwari, Bhairavi, Chhinnamasta, Dhumavata, Bagula, Matangi and Kamla.

The countries of this world may talk about four directions but Vedic tradition accepts ten (10) directions. Direction shows us the position of any place. With just four directions this work cannot be completed fully that is why 10 directions have been ascertained. They are the East, Aagneya (South-East), South, Nairitya (South-West), West, Vayavya (North-West), North, Ishan (North-East), Urdhva (Upper) and Adha (Lower), for these 10 directions 10 gods are believed to protect them as guardians, who are called as Dikpal. The 8 Dikpals for the 8 directions have been mentioned in the eighth chapter. For the Urdhva or Upper direction the guardian is Brahma and for Adha or Lower is Anant.

In the Vedic culture, rich with traditions and heritage, there is the principle of 16 traditions for the mankind. In this, 10 traditions are believed to be very important from the beginning of pregnancy to marriage. They are Garbhadhan, Pansvan, Simantommayan, Jatkarma, Namkaran, Nishkraman, Annaprashan, Chudakarma, Upanayan and Vivah, among these 10 traditions, most of them have even maintained their importance today. A woman's pregnancy is a joyous and happy moment in every family, because a woman's greatness is only in motherhood. To maintain the piety of this tradition, and to maintain the progress pattern of nature, the texts have cautioned and have expectations by their by their guidelines **'ऋतुकाले दाराभिगमनं कार्यम्'** When the signs of pregnancy show in the second or third month, one should perform with yagna the tradition of Punsvan, for a son. **'व्यक्ते गर्भे तृतीये तु मासे पुंसवनं भवेत्।'** At this time the pregnant woman is given nutritious food, have best attitude and behavior, this is advised Simantonnayan tradition is performed during the fourth month for the stability of the foetus, its safety and the health of the mother. During this time the pregnant woman is advised not to do more hard work or stay awake late at night. From this time the woman should read holy and religious books, should not sleep during the day and try to fulfill the wishes of the family members. Jatkarma is the tradition when before cutting the umbilical chord of the mother, the mother should be given honey and ghee in small proportion on a gold strip to be licked by her. Mantras are recited in the ears of the newborn child to be long lived and prosperous. After the 10th or 11th day or on any auspicious day the child is given a name. This tradition is celebrated with immense joy. According to the texts **'एकादशे अहनि पिता नाम कुर्यादिति'** But the decision of the day, is according to one's hereditary tradition or as per one's convenience. Nishkran is the tradition to take the child out of the house after 4th or 6th month. On his occasion after the worship of the gods, the father shows the sun and the moon to the child. The annaprasan tradition is to feed the child its first nutrious and digestible food on the 6th month. Till now the child lived on his mother's milk, now he also gets his teeth, so cereal food can be given to him. Chudakarma tradition is the shaving of the child's hair for the first time after birth at some holy place or pilgrimage, at 1st or 3rd year after birth, normally during the months of Chaitra or Paush. The Upanayan traditional ceremony is performed, when a child goes to a guru at gurukul for the first time. Now-a-days this ceremony is performed one day prior to marriage ceremony. When one enters as the householder. The tradition is called Vivah. Among all traditions this is the most important. This tradition is celebrated by every family with full joy and gaiety as per their means. Due to the logic of the modern scientific era and due to the busyness of life, now out of 16 traditions only three, birth, marriage and death are performed.

There are 10 faulty hindrances in the path of Yoga Sadhana- Lust, Anger, Fear, Dream, Love, More food, and unusual mental weakness, Disease, Laziness and Greed. These are in the category of nurture, they are- Mother, Father, Guru, Brother, Countrymen, Poor and destitute, Refugees, Guests, Sudden arriving persons and Fire. There has been the discussion of Ashtasiddhi in the eighth chapter. But by the special development of good qualities 10 more great achievements can be made, it is thus said in the texts. They are-Not to have too much craving for hunger and thirst, to have a foresight, to hear things that are far away, to reach a place with both mind and body, to take any form as per desire, to move into other's body, death as per one's wish, to see the plays between the gods and angels, the achievement of any pledge and obedience by all, these 10 achievements or successful ventures. Everyone is aware of the wishful death of Bhishma and Adya Shankaracharya's movement to the other body.

Charity has its own important and it also has many types, but some charities are considered Mahadaan or great charities whose number is 10. To donate gold, horse, sesame, elephant, slave woman, chariot, land, house, bridge and Kapila cow is called as Mahadaan. One ruler who has knowledge and information of 10 divisions of his own and enemies' strength. These ten strengths are-Minister, State, Fort, Treasury and Punishment, these 5 of his own and the same 5 of his enemies makes total 10 divisions. It is natural to mention the 10th rasa as the Vatsalya rasa love for a child apart from the nine rasas already mentioned. Its stable form is the feeling of Vatsal. In the Hindi literature Vatsalya rasa is well established but the experts of Sanskrit call this Vatsal and consider Vatsalya as the innate and permanent feeling. There is a feeling of

Vatsal in the hearts by the parents, elders for their children, disciples or some dear ones, the maturity of that feeling is Vatsalya rasa. Shringar and Vatsalya both have the union and separation and are so divided into two. In the separation of Virahini or the pining lover in Shringar rasa, 10 stages are mentioned. They are known by the names of-Desire, Worry, Memory, Praises, Excitement, Exchange of talks, Madness, Illness, Rootedness, or stillness and death. Ravana is called Dasshish or 10 heads or Dasmukh or 10 mouths. Actually the desire to enjoy through the 10 sensory organs is called Dasmukh. Like Dasrath is the one who had kept the 10 sensory organs under control. The 10 mouths of Ravana are the symbols of 10 bed qualities. The 10 heads of Ravana are Irrationalism, Lust, Anger, Greed, Attraction, Matsar, Violence, Harrasment to women, and Extortion of other's wealth. It is so said that Ravana not only extorted the state of Lanka and Pushpak Viman from Kuber but also raped his daughter-in-law. There are 10 stages of strike for are-

1. **Aadan** – To take out the arrow from quill
2. **Sandhan** – To put the arrow on the bow
3. **Mokshan** – To strike the arrow at the goal.
4. **Vinivartan** – After striking the arrow, knowing the status of the enemy as weak or armless, get the arrow back through the power of mantras
5. **Sthaan** – To keep the arrow on the bow
6. **Mashti** – Fingers which load the arrow to the bow
7. **Prayog** – With third and middle finger or middle finger and thumb locate the arrow
8. **Prayashchit** – The gloves worn on the hands to stop the injury from self or others by the strike of the arrows
9. **Mandal** – By striking the goal by going round on the chariot
10. **Rahasya** – With due words to strike one or many goals

Ten types of people are the gossipers-Ill, Poor, Mournful, Punished by State, Shath, Villain, One free from activity, Mad, Jealous and Lustful, Pandu's middle son Arjun has 10 names-

अर्जुनः फाल्गुनो जिष्णु किरीही श्वेतवाहनः।
वीभत्सुर्विजयः कृष्णः सव्यसाची धनंजय॥

- महा. विराटपर्व 44-9

1. The word Arjun has three meanings-glow or light, equality, white or pure. Explaining great son Uttar Arjun say, "All around me is light, I have equal feelings for all and perform pure work. So I am Arjun"
2. I am Phalgun because I was born in the Northern Phalgun star.
3. I am a victorious person, to catch me or neglect me is very difficult. So I am Jishnu.
4. After defeating the demons Indra had put Kirit on my head. So I am Kiriti.
5. My horses are of white color. So I am Shwetvahan.
6. White in war, I don't do shameful or disgusting karmas. So I am famous among the gods and mankind as Bibhatsu.
7. I don't return without victory from the war field. So my name is Vijay.
8. The meaning of the word Krishna is dark skinned and attractive the complexion of my skin is the mixture of dark and fair, and my father was very much attracted towards me. So I am Krishna.
9. I can pull the strings of the bow with both hands. So I am Savyasachi.
10. After being victorious, I take wealth and remain within the wealth. So I am Dhananjay.

During the days of victory all around Arjun had accumulated lot of wealth. So he got the name of Dhananjay. Folk poets have given 12 names to Arjun. I had listened to a well composed song by my late father in which there were those 12 names with their meaning and description. That was my childhood, so today only one line I remember from that song.

सुन बेटा बैराट भूप के तुझे बारह नाम गिनाऊँ।

Ten persons are of the category of reverence- 1. Teacher 2. Father 3. King 4. Mama 5. Father-in-law 6. Grandfather (father's father) 7. Grandfather (mother's father) 8. Uncles 9. Elder brother and 10. An elderly relative. These are all male relatives. Similarly the female relatives are also reverend.

Ten types of the karmas of sins should be removed from the mind, speech and karmas. They are-Violence, Stealing, Wrong karma, Gossiping, Cruel speech, To tell lies, Hot and Contradictory discussions, Misbehavior, Aethism, Wrong attitude.

हिंसास्तेयान्यथाकामपैशुन्यं परुषानृतम्।
सम्भिन्नालापव्यापादममिथ्यादृग्विपर्ययम्।
पापकर्मेति दशधा कायवाङ्मानसैस्त्यजेत्॥

-शुक्रनीति सार-3-6

For the house holders 10 things give happiness-Beautiful wife, good son, best education, Wealth earned with honesty and integrity, Best friend, Best servant, Good woman for service, Healthy body, Best home and Just king.

सुभार्या सुष्ठु चापत्यं सुविद्या सुधनं सुहृत्।
सुदासदास्यौ सद्देहः सद्वेश्म सुनृपः सदा।
गृहिणां हि सुखायालं दशैतानि न चान्यथा॥

-शुक्रनीतिसार 3-288

In the context of 10, there are such words which have stored a story in them. They are Vijayadashmi or Dashera, it is the word which campaign for defeating the 10 directions or dimensions. Being celebrated on the 10th day of moon light fortnight, in this festival after worshipping the victorious goddess, kings with the desire to extend their empire, cross into the limits of the other's state and consider this as their rightful Kshatriya duty. Today Dashera is celebrated as the day of victory of Ram on Ravana, but the truth is that on this day, after worshipping the victorious Lord Ram had started his campaign to wage a war against Ravana. These lines of some poet proves this fact

थी विजयादशमी यहीं जब राम ने दल साजकर।
गिरी प्रवर्षण से चढ़ाई की थी लंका राज्य पर॥

Goswami Tulsidas describes the pondering and worried Ram in the search of Sita after the season of rains and after the coming of autumn or Sharad season **'बरषा गत निर्मल रितु आई। सुधि न तात सीता कै पाई॥**

Ashwin and Kartik are the months of Sharad or Autumn. On the 10th day of Ashwin comes Vijayadashmi after 20 days of that comes the festival of Deepavali. So Dushera is the festival of the beginning of campaign for victory and Deepavali is the festival of victory. With number 10, one remembers the 10 Ashwamedh Ghat. It is believed that in the city of Kashi of Lord Bhootnath Shiva, on the banks of Ganga, Brahma had performed 10 Ashwamedh yagnas. Even today the religious persons believe that if one takes bath on this bank or ghat he gets the virtue of 10 Ashwamedh yagna. In the end remembering Ram, who defeated 10 faces and gave freedom from 10 mouths, I worship the god with 10 hands, taking 10 persons together, for 10 generations, with the desire 10 times that is 100, for everyone's welfare, I conclude this book.

❑❑❑